Zoey Gomez lives and writes in sunny Somerset. She saw *Romancing the Stone* at an impressionable age and has dreamed of being a romance writer ever since. She grew up near London, where she studied art and creative writing, and now she sells vintage books and writes novels. A good day is one where she speaks to no one but cats. You can follow @ZoeyGomezBooks on X and Instagram.

As a child, reading the Ladybird book *The Nurse* sowed the seeds for **Colette Cooper**'s future career. Using her experiences as a nurse to write medical romances with vibrant, interesting heroes and heroines to fall in love with is a dream come true. Colette lives in a beach house in Australia in her daydreams, but in reality she lives in the Heart of England—just about as far from the sea as it is possible to be in the UK, but very close to the home of Mr Fitzwilliam Darcy! As well as writing, she practises yoga, which she isn't bad at, and French, which needs much more practice!

Also by Zoey Gomez

The Single Dad's Secret

Also by Colette Cooper

Nurse's Twin Baby Surprise

Discover more at millsandboon.co.uk.

ONE-NIGHT REUNION WITH THE VET

ZOEY GOMEZ

WEDDING FLING TO FOREVER

COLETTE COOPER

MILLS & BOON

All rights reserved including the right of reproduction in whole or in part in any form. This edition is published by arrangement with Harlequin Enterprises ULC.

This is a work of fiction. Names, characters, places, locations and incidents are purely fictional and bear no relationship to any real life individuals, living or dead, or to any actual places, business establishments, locations, events or incidents. Any resemblance is entirely coincidental.

Without limiting the author's and publisher's exclusive rights, any unauthorized use of this publication to train generative artificial intelligence (AI) technologies is expressly prohibited. HarperCollins also exercise their rights under Article 4(3) of the Digital Single Market Directive 2019/790 and expressly reserve this publication from the text and data mining exception.

® and TM are trademarks owned and used by the trademark owner and/or its licensee. Trademarks marked with ® are registered with the United Kingdom Patent Office and/or the Office for Harmonisation in the Internal Market and in other countries.

First published in Great Britain 2025
by Mills & Boon, an imprint of HarperCollins*Publishers* Ltd,
1 London Bridge Street, London, SE1 9GF

www.harpercollins.co.uk

HarperCollins*Publishers* Macken House, 39/40 Mayor Street Upper, Dublin 1, D01 C9W8, Ireland

One-Night Reunion with the Vet © 2025 Zoey Gomez

Wedding Fling to Forever © 2025 Colette Cooper

ISBN: 978-0-263-32513-3

07/25

This book contains FSC™ certified paper
and other controlled sources to ensure responsible forest management.

For more information visit www.harpercollins.co.uk/green.

Printed and Bound in the UK using 100% Renewable Electricity
at CPI Group (UK) Ltd, Croydon, CR0 4YY

ONE-NIGHT REUNION WITH THE VET

ZOEY GOMEZ

MILLS & BOON

This book is dedicated to Cindy, Silver,
Charlie Brown, Snoopy, Mouse, Plip, Plop,
Coco & Garfield, and Scruffy Cat. To all the pets
I've had and all the vets who looked after them!

CHAPTER ONE

Molly radioed an update on her position to her destination, Killearn Veterinary Surgery, currently sitting a mile or so northeast of her plane. It was protocol to keep them informed of her progress.

The radio crackled to life. 'Dr Wilde! This is Jon. We spoke on the phone. Have you got eyes on the surgery's landing strip yet?'

Molly recognised Jon's voice and his soft Glaswegian accent. He was her new clinical director and had conducted her job interview via video call. Due to the clinic's remote location, there was no requirement to keep in touch with air-traffic control, so Jon had taken it upon himself to become her radio contact on the ground. Molly could monitor any other nearby aircraft easily from her cockpit's instrument panel, so radio contact on the ground wasn't necessary, but it would certainly be useful if there were any problems.

'Good morning. I don't have eyes on it yet, no.' Molly peered into the distance. All she could see spread out beneath her plane was a green-and-brown patchwork of fields, with the grey-blue sea bracketing the land to the west.

'You'll be its maiden landing. I mowed it myself.'

Molly smiled. 'Thank you. It's very much appreciated.'

Being the very first flying vet in Scotland meant that her new veterinary practice had elected to transform their unused meadow into a landing strip and their huge barn into a hangar in the months before she was due to start.

'You're very welcome. It won't be as smooth a landing as you'd get at an airport, but it should be just fine.'

It probably wouldn't be the roughest landing she'd ever made. Especially when compared with her time in Africa when she'd had to dodge the occasional rhino, or with the landing strip that covered the entire length of a Pacific island, which would have deposited her straight into the sea if she hadn't managed to come to a stop in time.

'I'll let you concentrate. See you when you land.'

'Roger.' Molly clicked off the radio and adjusted her headphones. The locals were certainly friendly. And there was the landing strip. A long green field with a marked smooth strip right down the middle, leading to a wide-open-fronted barn that appeared to be just the right size for her plane. She breathed a sigh of relief as she began her descent. Her beloved plane should be nice and safe in there. She'd had her plane for two years now, and had been flying for four. It had been her lifelong dream to be a flying vet, and the fact that she was finally doing it never failed to give her a thrill of pure happiness. Molly had designed and painted the exterior herself, named it after her favourite author and washed and waxed it faithfully once a month. Maybe she was a little attached. But she'd sleep easier knowing it had a safe place to call home.

The runway ran parallel with the sea, about five hundred metres to the west. Which meant there would always be a lot of wind interfering with take-offs and landings, but it should be manageable. She caught sight of a beautiful sandy beach and a few scattered surfers on the waves as she glided down to earth. They really had done a great job in making the strip smooth, and after a little bump and a momentary rise up, she brought the plane down easily and taxied up the strip towards the hangar.

As she crossed from the grass to the huge, flat expanse of tarmac in front of the hangar, she saw something she'd missed during the landing: two smiling people watching her. She turned off the engine, yanked off her headphones and gave them a quick wave as they beamed at her. They waved back enthusiastically and clapped as she undid her belt, the noise becoming louder as she popped open the door.

As they approached the plane, Molly quickly ran a hand through her hair, trying to straighten it out a little. She grabbed her bag then jumped down onto the tarmac and was immediately surrounded.

'Hi! That was so amazing! I'm Lara.' A long-limbed, beautiful young woman with an explosion of brown curls grabbed her hand and shook it with enthusiasm.

Molly smiled back, nonplussed. 'All I did was land a plane.'

'And it was epic.'

'Welcome, Molly. We spoke on the radio,' said a man a little older than Molly, with short hair and eyebrows so blond they were almost invisible.

'Lovely to meet you in person at last, Jon.' Jon shook Molly's hand warmly, then stepped back, smiling. 'Come on in. You can meet everyone properly after you've had a nice sit-down and a cup of tea.'

Molly's cheeks felt hot from all the attention, and she was grateful for a moment to gather herself as they all moved en masse towards a one-level brick building just behind the hangar.

'Thanks for everything you've done to get the place ready for my plane. It looks great.'

'It was a pleasure,' said Jon. 'As I've probably already told you, introducing a flying vet has been a pet project of mine for years. I'm just thrilled you're making it a reality.'

They climbed a small grassy incline up to the building, and Molly took her first look at the surgery she'd be working in from now on. It was a gorgeous old building, built with warm brown brick and covered in brightly flowered hanging baskets, with pots of marigolds lining the pathway. They entered through the back and walked past several consultation rooms before reaching the reception area, where big windows with yellow-painted frames threw light into a large, welcoming, high-ceilinged room. Two people sat on yellow plastic chairs, each with a pet basket sitting by their feet, and stared at Molly. She smiled and nodded at them as she passed, guessing it wasn't every day you saw a small plane land right outside your waiting room.

'How many people do you have working here in total?' Molly asked once they reached the staff room. She was fairly sure she already knew that from the interview stage, but she was feeling too overwhelmed to recall.

'You're number five,' said Jon. 'You've met me and Lara. Ellen's with a patient right now, and number four is around here somewhere. I guess he decided not to come out to greet you, but don't mind him. It's nothing personal.'

That sort of made it sound like it *was* something personal, and Molly couldn't help feeling intrigued. Had she done something already to annoy this guy? She'd only been here five minutes. Lara thrust a mug of tea at Molly, and she took it gratefully. Flying was thirsty work. She'd been in the air for about two hours, flying into Scotland from London. The day before that, she'd flown the plane into London from France, so she was understandably exhausted.

'Would you like a tour now?' asked Jon. 'Or would you prefer to find your digs and have a quick orientation tomorrow?'

She was due to start her first shift tomorrow morning. But her curiosity about the fourth mystery vet had given her a second wind. 'Let's have the tour now.' She smiled brightly at Jon. She had all afternoon and evening to find the small house she'd rented, unpack what little she'd been able to fit into the back of her plane and get some rest in.

But her curiosity would have to wait a moment, as Jon took her to the hangar first. He seemed very excited about it, which endeared him to Molly. Anyone who loved planes like she did was all right by her. He held the door open and Molly stepped inside. It was a cavernous space. One entire wall of sliding doors was already open to the view outside. And what a view. The hangar looked out over sandy beaches stretching off into the distance, and the ocean glittering in the morning sun.

Jon led her on a detailed tour through the consultation rooms, the storeroom, the overnight ward, the staff room and finally came to the door of the last room in the building. He knocked, then showed her in and introduced the man inside.

Molly wasn't sure what she had been expecting, but she certainly hadn't anticipated being slapped in the face by a visceral memory of one of the most humiliating moments of her life.

Jon knocked at the same time as he opened the door, which annoyed Ethan from the get-go. Why knock if you were just going to walk in anyway?

Jon had been especially upbeat over the past few weeks, ever since he'd found 'the perfect flying vet.' Providing care for all the animals that were currently out of their reach had been his dream for years. There were so many rural farms and pet owners in the surrounding countryside who couldn't get to a vet, and so many places the vets travelling by car couldn't reach in time to help with emergencies. Jon had originally set out to employ a new vet and a separate pilot to fly them around. However, the cost had stopped the plan in its tracks. But finding a vet with a pilot's licence? A gift sent from heaven if you believed Jon. It was sort of sweet how happy it had made him, but Ethan would rather eat his own arm than tell him that.

'Knock knock!' said Jon, and Ethan rolled his eyes before he turned around, pasting a welcoming smile on his face.

That smile wobbled as he saw the woman at Jon's side.

He took a breath and stepped back to lean on the counter behind him. The messy blond curls were heart-stoppingly familiar.

Seeing her sent a thousand different emotions thundering through him. But underneath all of them, seeing her face reminded Ethan that she was the one person whom he'd been with on the very worst day of his life.

Surely, this woman couldn't be her. Last he heard she was off in Africa somewhere, never to return again to the dull shores of the UK. He shook himself figuratively. Clearly, the fact that he thought of her so often had tricked his mind into seeing her in front of him. This woman couldn't be Molly. She was too tanned, for a start. Molly had always been so pale, like porcelain, and she never had so many freckles. *And* she never looked at him like she'd seen a ghost. Ethan's heart stopped. All the sounds of the room flooded back in, and he realised he'd been staring at her, open-mouthed like a guppy for a good few seconds.

'Here he is!' said Jon. 'Molly, meet Ethan James.'

Maybe this woman also happened to be called Molly. Maybe it was just a coincidence. Ethan forced himself to reach out a hand and shake hers. Her hand felt warm and small in his. A jolt of electricity travelled up his arm as he shook it and nodded hello.

Her look of shock transformed into curiosity. 'We know each other, don't we?' she asked.

'No,' Ethan said firmly. 'That's not possible.'

She raised an eyebrow and for a moment, he was sure he detected a brief flash of hurt before she schooled her features back to a polite smile. 'Well then, it's lovely to meet you.'

'Likewise.'

His heart raced as memories from his university days with a girl called Molly flashed before his eyes. Her hands in his hair, her breath on his neck. How peaceful she'd looked, fast asleep, wrapped up in bed sheets the last time he saw her. The more he looked at the stunning woman in front of him, the more he saw things he recognised. The way her eyes flashed green in the autumn sunlight streaming through the window. The distracted way she tucked her hair behind her ears with both hands at once as she spoke to Jon. The way she stood, weight on the balls of her feet, ready for anything, always poised and ready to go at any moment. Her comfortable, confident, easy manner, like she'd never felt self-conscious a moment in her life—that was just the same as it always had been. He smiled at all the little things he'd forgotten about. They hadn't interacted a lot, until that one night. But he'd always noticed her; he hadn't been able to take his eyes off her. Ethan had to accept it. This really was his Molly. A jolt of shame over what he'd done to her hit him so hard he almost had to sit down. He had never stopped feeling guilty for not keeping in touch.

Suddenly, they both turned and looked expectantly at him, but he had no idea what they might have just asked him.

'You can really fly a plane?' Ethan blurted out without thinking. He tried too late to keep the incredulous tone out of his words, and judging from her expression, he evidently didn't do a very good job of it.

She tilted her head and stared at him. 'Yeah, they let women do that now.'

'My apologies. That's not how that was meant to come out.'

'Please try not to upset my new star vet before she's even finished her first cup of tea,' said Jon. For once, Ethan was grateful for Jon trying to lighten the mood.

'So how long have you been flying?' asked Jon.

'I learned to fly in Australia, just after lockdown.'

'What?' asked Ethan.

'Yeah, I got bored.'

'Right, me, too,' Ethan replied. 'I made banana bread.'

Jon laughed and tried to cover it up with a cough. 'We're lucky to have you, Molly,' said Jon. 'I'm sure you'll find our little Scottish village a bit of a change from the last few years of your career, but I hope you'll enjoy working here. We're a close-knit community, and if you need help with anything at all, just ask any of us and we'll be glad to help.'

'Thanks, I'm definitely ready for a change of pace.'

'That it will be.' Jon tried to pull Ethan into the discussion, and Ethan realised he hadn't spoken for a little too long. 'Did you hear where she's spent the last few years?'

'I didn't.'

'Molly's been all over the globe doing wonderful things, working for Veterinarians Without Borders. Let me see if I can remember what you told me in your interview, Molly. You spent some time saving baby rhinos in Africa. Then you moved to rescuing chimpanzees in Mozambique. And your most recent project was…' Jon hesitated. 'I want to say vaccinating livestock in Vietnam?'

'In Laos. But nice recall! You know more about my career than I do.'

Jon laughed, while Ethan reeled at how much she'd achieved since he last saw her. Yeah, this was his Molly. Now he thought about it, solo piloting a plane was exactly the sort of thing he would have expected her to end up doing when they were back at university. She'd always been a little bit different. He wondered whether Molly would be happy, living in such an isolated place as this. Working here was about as far as possible from the exciting, adventurous life she'd been used to. Judging from her previous work, she must have chosen to specialise in exotic animals after they'd parted ways. So how had she ended up in Scotland? He couldn't believe she'd stick around for long.

Jon clapped his hands. 'So, now you've met all of us, even Ethan. The one and only. The oxymoron. The only vet in the world who hates pets.'

'I do not hate pets,' said Ethan wearily. He'd been through this argument a hundred times already.

'You have to admit you're not a fan of anything small, cute or fluffy.'

'They're just not my area of expertise. I trained with large animals.'

Jon turned to Molly conspiratorially. 'He hates cats and dogs.'

'For goodness' sake, I do not.'

'Well, that's handy, because Mrs Bandersway has brought in her Maine Coons to get their claws trimmed, so you can take her now in room three.'

Ethan squared his jaw, exhaled through his nose, glared at Jon and grabbed his thick protective gloves. 'You're doing them next time.'

Jon laughed delightedly. Then seemed to remember Molly was there. 'Oh, perhaps you'd like to shadow Ethan for this appointment. Get the lay of the land in preparation for your first morning tomorrow.'

'No problem.' Molly smiled and followed Ethan closely all the way to room three.

Why had he said, so confidently, that they didn't know each other? Yes, he hadn't been sure at first. But deep inside he'd known. And now he was stuck working with her in close quarters. This was going to be a nightmare.

CHAPTER TWO

MOLLY STOOD AND watched as Ethan worked his way through five of the most enormous Maine Coon cats she'd ever seen. Ethan's certainty that they didn't know each other had left her confused and a little hurt. At the time, she had schooled her face to hide the dozen emotions rushing through her. She hadn't wanted to make a fool of herself by contradicting Ethan and getting into an argument in front of her new boss. Maybe Ethan had similar reasons, not wanting to discuss personal matters in front of his boss. Or maybe he just didn't remember her. But she remembered him. Who could forget those beautiful dark eyes, or that gorgeous husky voice and Stirling accent?

The cats had come in for a nail trim, and Ethan blinked warily in response to their fierce growls. The cat he was holding writhed in his grasp, but Ethan looked determined to come out on top. The cat hissed at him and unsheathed huge claws that wouldn't have been out of place on a big cat in Africa, and Molly stepped in, thinking Ethan might appreciate some help.

He flashed her a look of annoyance. 'I don't need your expertise in exotic animals to handle a domestic cat.'

Molly ignored his grumpiness and stroked the cat he

was currently gripping, tickling it under the chin and cooing over its beautiful long fur to distract it.

She couldn't pretend it wasn't satisfying seeing Ethan out of his comfort zone. She remembered the rather relaxed, confident stride he'd had about him as a veterinary student, and couldn't help but wonder if it was as much *her* as the cat who was putting him off. At least that would explain why he hadn't come out to greet her with the others. Perhaps he'd known somehow that she was coming and decided to hide in his consultation room instead? It wouldn't have been hard for him to hear the name of the new vet before she arrived. And there couldn't be all that many veterinary-trained Molly Wildes in the world. Would have been nice to have had some sort of warning herself before she walked in and saw his stupid face right in front of her again.

It had to have been at least nine years since she'd last seen him, when they were both in their third year of a six-year veterinary degree at Cambridge. Ethan had filled out a little since then. He had always been beautiful, but back at uni his brown eyes and long, dark eyelashes had still given him the look of a baby deer. Now that he'd grown up, his face had transformed into a more lived-in, rugged jawline, one now covered attractively in short facial hair. He was wider and more muscular in all the right places. Broader shoulders, thick upper arms and a wide chest that she'd tried hard not to stare at. His hair was the only thing that hadn't changed, still thick and dark, the exact same colour as his deep brown eyes. And still silky-soft-looking, like it was asking for you to run your hands through it.

He'd done quite the number on her self-esteem. He was one of the very first people she'd ever slept with, after two years of crushing on him from afar. They'd shared a staircase in the halls of residence, but they'd never really been in the same circle of friends. When Molly hadn't been studying she'd hung out with the performing arts society, while he'd spent most of his time with the sporty lot. But after they'd slept together, he'd disappeared before she'd even woken up the next morning. And not just disappeared from her bed; he'd literally dropped out of university. He dropped out, moved away, took everything with him and was never heard from again.

But now he was here, and clearly a qualified vet, so he must have transferred to a different university and finished his training at some point. What on earth could have caused him to give up his spot at Cambridge? And whatever it was, why couldn't he have told her? Molly smoothly helped the newly trimmed cat back into its pet carrier and shut the door, then returned to the table to help Ethan with the others. The cats were purring now, completely the opposite from how they'd started the appointment, hissing and swiping at Ethan's hand.

Ethan looked up to find Molly watching him, and he smiled. All of a sudden she felt nineteen again.

'Thanks for distracting them,' he whispered.

She took a step closer, almost unconsciously, into Ethan's orbit.

'They seem calmer now,' he continued. 'Would you mind taking care of the next one for me? I can talk you through it if you need help.'

Molly tried not to be offended. She was pretty sure she

could handle trimming some claws all by herself, but she guessed she was the new girl.

'Here, take these trimmers,' said Ethan. 'I have an old pair somewhere I can use.' Ethan passed Molly the small scissor trimmers, and their hands touched softly as she took them. She felt herself flush at the contact and was relieved she could turn away to pick up a cat and hide her reaction. After Ethan had rifled through a drawer, he pulled out an old pair that looked awkward to hold and even harder to use. Molly had to admit it was sweet of him not to hog the good pair.

Once the cat was relaxed it was a very quick job, and Molly scooped up all the trimmings and popped them into the bin that Ethan held out to her.

'Just in case you thought being a rural vet was all glamour,' Ethan murmured.

'Although it might not sound like it, I'm very used to run-of-the-mill cases, as well as the more exotic ones.'

'Well, that's lucky, because I'm not sure you'll find many rhinos in the local area,' Ethan said drily. 'I fear you might find us lacking in the kind of excitement you're used to.'

Molly glared at him, the effects of his smile forgotten, now that he was making fun of her. She couldn't let her guard down for a second without getting hurt again.

Of course, this guy couldn't wait to get away from her nine years ago, just like all her other relationships since, so she probably didn't have anything to worry about.

His voice was deeper now, but those eyes were exactly the same as the last time she'd seen him, all those years ago. Back then she couldn't help but wonder if she'd been so bad in bed that the mere prospect of having to see her again had sent him running for the hills. She'd been mortified. But she'd told herself she was better off at the time. She concentrated on forgetting that boy, graduating from Cambridge, landing a job straight out of training and travelling the world, living her dream.

So it was incredibly annoying that that very boy was now apparently a drop-dead gorgeous man who hadn't lost any of his infuriating charm, and was pretending not to remember her at all. Well, that was fine by her. She'd accepted this job in the smallest of small-town Scotland so she could avoid any possibility of romance altogether. She'd had quite enough of romantic partners. Especially Lucy the livestock specialist on the Laos project, who had dumped her three months ago and was already engaged to someone new. They'd been together longer than she'd ever been with anyone. She'd even thought marriage might be in the cards, and then Lucy had dumped her with absolutely no warning. Lucy must have been planning to end things for a while, but Molly hadn't sensed anything wrong at all. It was enough to make her give up on relationships altogether. What was the point when she couldn't trust her instincts or sense that she was having problems? How could Molly ever relax in a relationship again, when even the people she trusted the most could leave at any moment with no warning? Molly took a deep breath and willed herself to think about something else. Yes, she'd been badly burnt, yet again, but this was her new start. One where she wouldn't be letting any gorgeous man or beautiful woman turn her head. Running into her first love could have put a spoke in the wheel of that plan. But if he was going to pretend he didn't even recognise her then that problem was solved.

Unless he wasn't pretending and he really didn't remember her at all. Unless the boy she'd never quite been able to get out of her head had lived the past nine years in blissful ignorance of her very existence. Maybe she was just that forgettable. She looked herself up and down in the reflection of the window. She hadn't changed *that* much.

There was a sudden commotion from outside the reception, and while Ethan finished off the last Maine Coon cat, Molly rushed out to see if she could help.

A man and a woman wearing jeans and gilets stood in the reception room, both wild-eyed and frantic, the man holding a large black Labrador in his arms.

'Please help her. She's impaled herself on a stick.'

Sure enough, as soon as Molly reached them she saw a thick piece of wood the size of a chair leg jutting out of the poor dog's belly. She reached out to help him bear the weight of the dog. 'Which exam room is free?' she asked Ethan, who had rushed out to join them.

'Room four?' Ethan asked the receptionist. After her quick nod, Ethan rushed down the wide corridor and held room four's door open for Molly and the couple. The dog safely on the table, Molly pulled a pair of gloves on. 'What's her name?'

'Hazel.'

'Hi, Hazel.' Molly stroked the Lab's head gently, checking her eyes and vitals.

'What happened to her?' Ethan asked the couple.

Still panting from exertion, and probably adrenaline,

the man who'd carried her in spoke haltingly. 'She was running through the forest off-lead on our walk. She jumped over something and we heard a yelp. We found her just impaled on this branch.' He stroked the dog's leg and held her paw in his hand. 'Please help her. I'm sure she's insured for everything, but we'll pay whatever it costs. She's a member of the family. I sawed the branch off using my Swiss Army knife. Hope I did the right thing.'

'You did,' said Molly. 'That was quick thinking. If you hadn't, she might not have made it. She needs an ultrasound scan before we can remove the stick. Please make yourselves comfortable in the waiting room and we'll let you know the second we know what we're dealing with.'

Molly noticed Ethan raise his eyebrows and minutely shake his head at the floor. Was he annoyed because she'd taken the lead before officially starting her first shift? Well, tough. She had no time for office politics. The couple quickly gave Hazel a careful kiss and a pat, before reluctantly heading out to the waiting room. Ethan injected Hazel with a sedative, which took almost immediate effect, then he and Molly carefully hoisted Hazel onto a stretcher and wheeled her straight through a swing door that led to the ultrasound room.

After conducting the ultrasound, Ethan studied the image on the screen. They both stared at what was very obviously the pointed end of the stick lodged firmly in Hazel's liver.

'I'll go out and tell them Hazel needs immediate surgery,' said Molly.

Ethan nodded. 'Thanks. I'll get her ready.'

Once Molly rejoined Ethan, Hazel had already been manipulated onto her back. Her face lay to the side, and she remained completely unconscious. The stick jutted horribly up from her belly, and Ethan was just finishing up as he shaved off a large patch of fur around the wound. Hazel's poor belly showed up pale through her shaved black fur.

They both dressed in gowns and pulled on blue latex gloves, standing either side of Hazel, and got down to it. After twenty minutes of surgery, Molly could finally pull out the stick with a pair of pincers. She gently started to remove it, marvelling at how it just kept coming. Finally, it was all out, and she dropped it onto the waiting tray with a thump. Ethan checked inside the wound to make sure no splinters remained, then all that was left was to repair Hazel's damaged liver and torn diaphragm.

Molly assisted while Ethan operated. She watched his deft fingers working quickly and efficiently to repair the wound in the liver. It was impressive work, and as Molly watched Ethan work on Hazel she resisted the temptation to confront him. How dare he not remember her? Or for that matter, lie and pretend not to. She wasn't sure which was worse. Was it better to be lied to or forgotten? If only she'd challenged Ethan immediately; perhaps if they'd been alone she would have. But this wasn't the time for confrontation. They had to concentrate on the patient. Molly used the suction pipe to remove blood from the area, to help Ethan see more clearly what he was doing.

'Excuse me.' Ethan reached past her to grab an instrument from the trolley, and Molly didn't lean out of the way in time. Thus, for five unbearable, exquisite seconds she was in close contact to Ethan's warm, firm body as he quickly picked up and dropped the scalpels until he found the one he wanted. She could feel his breath on her cheek and smell his aftershave. Something woodsy and delicious.

Hazel's blood pressure monitor alarm went off, making Molly jump. They both ran numerous checks, Molly's tension rising with every second, but when Ethan adjusted the intravenous fluids, Hazel's blood pressure level and heart rate finally returned to normal. Before Molly knew it, two hours had passed by in a flash. Ethan sewed his last stitch in the three-inch wound. Molly cleaned the area one last time with a sterile swab, and they were done. Molly blinked at Ethan, only now realising how close their heads had been this whole time—she'd been so focused on treating Hazel. Ethan wiped the sweat off his brow with his sleeve, and as he pulled off his gown and gloves and threw them in the bin, his hair was a tousled mess and his eyes looked bright and excited.

'That was amazing. Nice work.'

'You, too,' Molly managed to say, breathless all of a sudden.

'Do you think they'll want the stick?'

Molly laughed. 'Now we can be pretty sure Hazel will recover, yeah, it'll probably make a collectable talking point.'

Ethan looked at it. 'Jesus, it's huge. Let's measure it.' He grabbed a ruler from a shelf by the window and laid it next to the stick, then snapped a photo with his phone.

'They're not the only ones who keep weird collectables,' Molly mumbled, more to herself. The piece of stick measured twenty-one centimetres. Fifteen centimetres of which were still lightly stained red from poor Hazel's blood. Molly felt her cheeks flush as she remembered something. She'd kept her own memento of the night she and Ethan had spent together. Ethan had left his T-shirt behind, and even in the aftermath she hadn't been able to bring herself to throw it out. In the end she'd kept it, telling herself it would serve as a reminder to never be that vulnerable again.

While Hazel was taken for post-op care, Molly happily told the owners they were confident she'd eventually make a full recovery, and they would be closely monitoring Hazel for any signs of complications, such as infection. She went on to explain the aftercare instructions, medication details and follow-up visits. They were so relieved. Molly couldn't remember the last time she'd felt so fulfilled. She had spent the past few years in locations all over the world treating wild animals who had no owners. She'd loved it, but it did lack something. She'd known she wanted to get away from her usual life and find something completely different, but she hadn't known quite what she was looking for. Maybe this was part of it. Maybe the human interaction made more of a difference than she'd realised. She hadn't just saved a beautiful creature…she'd saved a beloved pet who was part of a family.

After they finished up with the black Labrador, Jon convinced Molly it was time to go home. Her first day was supposed to have been tomorrow, but she'd already done practically a half day's work. Jon promised she'd get paid for it, but regardless, she'd thoroughly enjoyed herself, especially after having helped Hazel and her owners. The new colleagues she'd met were so nice, they almost made up for Ethan. However gorgeous he may have become, she had to remember he was still an idiot. And a duplicitous, lying, grumpy idiot, at that.

Jon had offered her a quick lift home, and when he reminded her she had a small plane full of her belongings to transport, she gratefully accepted. As Molly waited for Jon outside, the reality of having to work with Ethan started to dawn on her. She'd been so excited to start her new job and her new life. But how could she do that when memories of her old life kept holding her back? She didn't like the memories of rejection that bubbled up when she was around Ethan, and she was going to have to be around him every day. Seeing him had thrown her right back to being twenty-one. All her friends had known about her long-time crush on Ethan. She'd tried to get his attention more than once, but he was always with some other girl. The blank look on his face when they'd been introduced today just brought back all the memories of when she'd felt utterly invisible to him at university. Which in turn brought back childhood memories of being ignored at home by her parents.

Molly had always had to fight to be noticed at home. She'd been a surprise baby, an only child to older, workaholic parents, and was left to her own devices a lot growing up. She'd always been invisible to someone, and she hated it. She'd been a quiet kid, and it was at university that she'd tried for the first time to break out of that mould. She'd tried to become more outgoing, more noticeable.

Tried to be comfortable taking up more space. And she'd gotten pretty good at it! She was way more confident and outgoing now than she'd ever dreamed of being as a kid. At least on the outside.

So when Ethan had finally noticed her, and they'd had that one perfect night together, she thought it was the start of something real and genuine. When he vanished the next day without a word of explanation it had let her down badly, reinforcing all the old hurts from her childhood. She'd never had such a strong emotional connection with a person, combined with such sizzling chemistry, and she'd never been able to find it again. Ethan had been the first person she cared about to reject her, but he hadn't been the last. And she'd tried to avoid falling too hard for people ever since.

The thing was none of the people she dated, male or female, had caught feelings for her, either. And they'd all left her in the end. This felt like proof that she was nothing special. So why bother looking for someone special? She preferred to reject people before they rejected her. She hid her insecurities with bluster and overconfidence. She'd had to accept she just wasn't loveable. And that was okay. Not everyone could be. Some people were the type to get proposed to umpteen times, and getting married was just a matter of choosing which prince to say yes to. Molly's best friend Julie was one of those people. She'd had proposals from four different boyfriends before she settled down. But not everyone was like Julie. Some people just weren't meant to find the one.

Molly's last partner had dumped her and gotten engaged to someone new within weeks. And two of her other exes were engaged now. She was never anyone's 'the one'. She was just the practice girlfriend, the 'she'll do for now' girlfriend. Not the girl anyone wanted to be with forever. Everyone she knew had started settling down, and sometimes she felt like a misfit. She'd never wanted kids, a mortgage, or a regular nine-to-five job. Her parents had been slaves to their large mortgage and busy jobs. They'd supplied her with plenty of money and possessions, but hadn't given her any of their time or affection.

That left her feeling ill equipped to be a parent herself, and unwilling to get caught in such a life of responsibilities and drudgery. She'd always vowed that was not for her.

But she'd never been very good at picking people who shared her ideals. They always seemed to end up wanting more from her than she was able to give. Anyway, it was obvious she wasn't what anyone was looking for. And so what? She'd never needed anyone. She'd always been better off alone.

She could feel herself getting angrier and angrier with Ethan. Not only had he abandoned her at university, now his infuriating presence was also causing her to obsess over whether he was pretending not to remember her or if he really didn't. But she was going to put a stop to it now. Molly made a vow to herself. She absolutely could not fall for this man again. She didn't have to talk to him. She would only see him at work, where she would be civil, do her job and avoid him as much as humanly possible. Outside work she could forget he existed and concentrate on how lucky she was to be living in this beautiful place.

Molly took a deep breath. She couldn't let Ethan ruin her new beginning. She would focus on the job. She came here to be the best pilot and vet she could be, and to avoid getting hurt again by steering clear of romance. She thought she'd have an easier job of it, since she'd taken a position in the most remote place she could find. But she could still do this. At least she'd be away from Ethan when she was in the sky. She could deal with anything as long as she had the freedom she felt when she was in her plane, the one thing she could always rely on to be there for her.

'Ethan! A word.'

Late that afternoon, Ethan had almost made it out the door. He stepped back into reception, where he and Jon were now alone.

'I'd like you to partner with Molly for tomorrow.'

'Sorry?'

Jon paused. 'Clearly, judging from your work today on the black Lab, you work well together, so I'd like you to go with Molly tomorrow on her first job.'

'With her?' Ethan felt ambushed. 'In the plane?'

'How else do you plan on getting there?' asked Jon.

Ethan couldn't have been less keen to set foot on any kind of flying tin deathtrap. But since there were animals to treat, he guessed he didn't have much of a choice.

He'd been right before. This really was turning into a nightmare. Just when life was exactly how he wanted it—predictable, safe and uneventful—she had to burst back in.

He admired how smoothly she'd taken charge as soon as Hazel had come in, but he hadn't been able to stop himself from shaking his head in disbelief. Most people might need a few days to settle in to a new job and feel comfortable, but not Molly. Part of him almost felt a thrill at the thought of spending more time with her. She'd always seemed like the sort of person people gravitated towards. He'd felt so lucky the night they'd finally spoken. He already felt that familiar need creeping back in. The urge to be near her, to bask in her sunlight.

But the guilt he'd felt over the years whenever he thought of how he left things with her was a thousand times worse in her presence. She'd been so unlike anyone he'd ever been with before. So utterly free and unselfconscious. He remembered every moment they'd spent together. Her hair had smelled like vanilla and her mouth tasted like the hot chocolate they'd shared. He'd had a reason for walking away from the best night of his life, but it wasn't one he'd had the time to discuss with her. He was sure she'd soon forget him anyway. Was he really going to continue to pretend he didn't remember her? How could he possibly keep that up? It would come out eventually. The whole situation was mortifying.

As Ethan strode up his garden path and ran up the steps to his front door, he could already hear voices inside his house. He pushed open the door and the racket became louder.

'Can you keep it down? I could hear you halfway down the street,' Ethan said. A little exaggeration never hurt anybody.

'Kai took my shirt without asking and now it's all stretched out because of his stupid yeti shoulders.' Harry brandished a blue T-shirt in his fist and waved it at Ethan angrily from the top of the stairs.

Harry and Kai were fraternal twins, with the same light brown eyes and the same shaggy brown hair. But Kai had shot up six inches in height and his shoulders had considerably broadened some time last year. And Harry was still indignant about it, however many times Ethan told him they were only fourteen and he had plenty of time to catch up.

'Kai, stop stealing Harry's clothes. Harry, I'll buy you a new T-shirt,' Ethan said firmly, hoping Harry would hear the finality in his voice and let it go. They were only ever home from school for a few minutes before Ethan got in from work, but they always, without fail, managed to get themselves into some kind of argument. He was lucky Jon was understanding about him working school hours, so he could be there for his siblings once they came home. 'Where is Maisie?' Ethan asked, changing the subject.

'Here.' Ethan saw an arm rise from the sofa, which faced away from him in the open-plan ground floor of Ethan's house. The large hallway was open to the kitchen to his left, a wide staircase in front of him and the living room to his right. They had two large sofas facing a fireplace, with a TV above it. Ethan smiled. He was never quite so happy or contented as when he knew all three kids were safely at home and accounted for.

Ethan clapped his hands together. 'All my favourite people in one place. Who's hungry?'

The twins both shouted in the affirmative.

'Can we get a puppy?' Maisie called from the sofa.

'Nope,' Ethan answered and headed for the kitchen. Maisie asked that question at least once a day. He wasn't sure if she somehow thought he might answer differently if she caught him off guard, or whether she thought she might wear him down if she asked enough times. But she was sorely mistaken either way. The animals stayed at work. If he ever gave in and started bringing them home, he knew it would never end. There was always a new animal at work that needed a home, whether it was a kitten, a dog, a hamster, or a calf. It was hard enough keeping on top of a full-time job and running a house with three kids in it—a house, by the way, that would probably need a new roof in the next few years, and probably wasn't big enough for all four of them in the first place, now that the kids all needed separate rooms and couldn't sleep in bunkbeds like they used to. He just couldn't face the stress of moving. Ethan knew his limits. If he added an animal menagerie to that roster, his house would be a complete pigsty within days, and he would never claw it back. The kids, as sweet as they were, would never keep up with feeding, cleaning and exercising a pet. It would all be down to him. And that didn't even touch the issue that he didn't want them to get emotionally attached to yet another thing that would just end up inevitably dying and hurting them. They'd already had enough loss to cope with for a lifetime. The wisest move was to just keep saying no, as much as twelve-year-old Maisie's sad eyes broke his heart.

Later, after he fed the kids, he cajoled them into helping him load the dishwasher. They then retreated to their rooms to finish their homework—which was mostly code, he knew, for playing video games and messaging their friends. Ethan felt he could finally relax. He filled a mug with scorching hot coffee and took it out to the front porch, his favourite part of the house. A raised wooden deck, level with the front door, ran across the entire front of the house, with wooden supports holding up a small slanted roof. He could sit outside with a hot drink, even when it was raining softly, and watch the world go by. It wasn't raining tonight—in fact, it was unseasonably warm. The streetlights had flickered on, despite the sky still bearing the soft yellow light of sunset. He sank onto the swing seat Maisie had begged him to get, leant back into the cushions and held his mug on his knee, waving away a moth with his free hand.

His mind still raced from having spent the day with Molly. He'd handled that badly. He should have just said yes when she asked if they knew each other. But after he'd said he didn't know her it was too late to admit he did, without sounding like an idiot. Ethan had to wonder: Had he just looked vaguely familiar to her? Or did she remember exactly who he was? And if so, why hadn't she challenged him? Perhaps she didn't want to rake over the past. Perhaps she didn't care at all.

Just as he shouldn't. Why was he wasting his evening second-guessing what she meant? He swallowed as he remembered the flash of hurt in her beautiful eyes when he'd denied knowing her. Her eyes weren't the only thing that was beautiful about her. He always thought his memories must have painted her as more perfect than she really was. No one could be that beautiful. But she was even more gorgeous now, if that was possible.

Speaking of Molly or, more precisely, Ethan's apparent new job role he didn't ask for, he fished his phone out of his pocket then typed 'how many people die in small plane crashes per year' into the search engine. He didn't particularly like flying in a jet, let alone the prospect of flying inside a tiny propeller plane.

Apparently, the global number of civil aviation deaths last year was only in the hundreds. Hmm...not as bad as he'd expected. He sipped his coffee and kept reading. According to one study, the odds of dying in a plane crash were one in eleven million, which was much lower than the odds of dying in a car. Still, he thought, it only took one. Ever since he'd lost his mother in a car accident, he'd found himself a lot more aware of the dangers around him. He was now more careful, responsible and risk-averse than he could ever have imagined he would be. He had the twins and Maisie to think about. The person he'd been at Cambridge would have hardly recognised him now. He'd never exactly been Casanova, but he'd probably dated more girls in one month at uni than he had in the past several years. He'd been a little more like Molly then. Up for anything, thrill seeking, open to adventure. But now he couldn't think of anything worse. Ever since he became guardian for the kids, life had been a whirlwind of responsibilities and hard work. With help from his extended family, and especially Aunty Anne, he'd managed to finish his vet training at Glasgow, just over an hour's drive away. It was years of early mornings and late nights, but he'd finally qualified.

He was about to search for information on how many people survived small plane crashes and tips on how best to do so, when he noticed a movement across the road. There was something moving outside the small, green-painted cottage opposite his house. He peered into the gloom curiously. The house had been empty and up for rent for at least a year and he'd wondered if it would ever find a tenant. It was a nice little house with a huge back garden and a couple of yellow blossom trees he'd always been quite envious of.

'Oh, you have got to be kidding me,' he whispered to himself as he realised whom he was looking at. Molly was walking back and forth between a car he now recognised as belonging to Jon, and the cottage's open front door. Her arms were full of boxes and bags. And there was Jon, carrying a suitcase from the car. Ethan was about to reluctantly stand up and go over to help when Molly slammed the boot of the car closed. Apparently, that was all she had. She must have flown some of her belongings over in the plane, and Jon was dropping them off here. To her new house. Right opposite Ethan's. Ethan let his back fall hard against the seat cushion, and he looked up at the now indigo sky. This was going to be awkward.

He wasn't trying to eavesdrop, but in the still evening air, he could hear every word of their conversation. He heard Jon ask if she needed any help indoors, and heard her thank him and tell him to get home. Then he watched as Jon pointed across the road at Ethan's house and waved at him enthusiastically. Ethan inwardly died, then saluted Jon and nodded at Molly, who just stared back at him. This was probably the first she'd heard that she'd be living opposite one of her colleagues.

Ethan knew he should go over there and welcome her

to the street, but he couldn't seem to get his legs to work. Molly hesitated for what felt like a full minute, then appeared to come to some decision, rummaged inside one of the bin bags piled by her front door, then crossed the empty road, heading right towards Ethan. As she got closer, Ethan could see the expression on her face. It was not friendly. Ethan winced. He wasn't surprised after he'd declined to admit he knew her.

She came to a stop at the bottom of the wide steps leading up to his porch. Her hands were placed firmly on her hips. She stared up at him and snapped, 'Ethan James, do you remember me or not?' Her eyes flashed angrily, and two spots of colour flared on her cheeks. She was remarkable. He blinked. 'Of course I remember you,' he breathed.

That seemed to ruffle her determined facade and for a moment, she just looked confused.

'Well, good, because here's your T-shirt back.' Molly threw a crumpled wad of material into his lap, and he opened it up to find something weirdly familiar.

'I think I used to have one like this,' Ethan said slowly.

'Yes, you idiot. It's yours.'

It finally dawned on him what she meant. This was the Joan Jett T-shirt he'd been wearing that night, nearly a decade ago. He'd never realised what had happened to it. But he must have left it behind. Had Molly really kept it all these years? She'd been travelling the world but had still somehow kept hold of his T-shirt? Surely, this must mean something. Surely, he must mean something to her. He felt another painful wave of guilt. Was it possible that she'd thought of him all this time, just as he had her?

Molly glared at Ethan, waiting for a response. Ethan wondered if he also detected a flash of hurt. 'So, what happened? Was I so bad in bed that you had to disappear from public life? Did I insult you in my sleep? Did I give you groin strain?' Ethan nearly spat out his coffee. 'What possible reason could you have had to disappear like that?'

'You did not strain my… Look, why don't you come up here and sit down. We can talk. Would you like a drink?' It was time she knew everything, past time, really. Ethan would finally have to explain what had happened to him. It was almost a relief after all this time. He'd wondered about her over the years. Where she was, how she was, whether she was with anyone.

She sighed and climbed the steps. 'Fine. You have a very lovely house.' She sounded almost reluctant, but Ethan would take a somewhat reconciliatory compliment when he could get it.

'Thank you very much. Coffee?'

'No, I'm good. I'm planning on sleeping tonight, not staring at the ceiling, plotting Jon's demise for making us fly together.'

Jon must have told her he wanted Ethan to accompany her on the plane.

'I wouldn't say no to a whisky or something, though,' Molly added.

Ethan raised his eyebrows. 'You never used to drink whisky.'

'No, I was twenty, going on twenty-one last time we spoke. I was a half a shandy or a pink Bacardi Breezer kind of girl. Things change.'

She had a point. Once Molly was settled on the opposite end of his swing seat, Ethan dashed inside and grabbed a bottle of whisky and two small glasses from the drinks cupboard. He was grateful that the kids were still upstairs. He had a feeling Molly was going to ask him some questions he didn't need an audience for.

But just as he opened the door to join Molly, he heard three sets of feet thundering down the stairs. He let the door fall shut behind him, hoped they would stay indoors and poured Molly a drink.

She took the offered glass and peered over her shoulder, through the window into his house. She frowned. 'Ethan, I hate to tell you this, but there are three teenagers in your living room.'

Ethan looked across automatically, just in time to see Maisie throw a very well-aimed cushion at Kai's face. He turned back as he heard Harry shout with laughter and Kai groan in mock pain. Maisie shrieked in hysterical laughter and Ethan winced.

'Who are they? Do you look after kids in your spare time or something?'

'No, I don't.'

'An outreach group for troubled teens?'

'No. No, they live with me. Full-time.'

Her mouth was a perfect O. 'When did you have kids?' She screwed up her nose and her forehead crinkled. 'Wait. How old are they?'

'Maisie's twelve and the twins are fourteen.'

Molly tilted her head, and Ethan could see her quickly doing the maths in her head. He decided not to help her out and just waited for her next question.

'Whose kids are they?'

'It's a long story.'

'Well, let's go back to the start. Let's pretend we only just reconnected.' Molly settled back into her seat and took a delicate sip of whisky. 'So, what have you done since I last saw you, nine years ago, running away from me and disappearing into a tiny dot on the horizon?'

Ethan smiled. But he knew now he had no choice but to have the conversation. The one that made people give him the sympathetic face and pitying pat on the knee, before an awkward change of subject matter. He took a deep breath and jumped right in. 'Do you remember I got a phone call that night?'

'That night?' She used her fingers to make air quotes. Ethan nodded, trying not to smile.

'I think I do remember. You woke me up with your talking before you left the room. I thought it was a fake phone call to get away from me, because you regretted us sleeping together. Anyway, I fell back to sleep because you were gone for so long.'

'No, it was a real phone call.' He paused. 'That's how I found out that my mother had died.'

'What?'

'My mother and stepdad were killed in a car accident. I went back to my room, packed up my stuff and got the train home that night.'

'Jesus, Ethan. I'm so sorry. I had no idea at all.'

Ethan shrugged. 'You couldn't have known. I didn't tell anyone.'

'Still. God.'

'It's a long time ago now.'

'Why didn't you tell anyone?'

'I'm not sure. I guess because there was so much to do back home. It felt like home and school were two entirely different worlds. I didn't know how to combine them. I didn't stay in touch with any of the friends I made there.'

'I'm so sorry. I feel terrible. That must have been so difficult.'

Ethan thought he saw a flash of guilt in her eyes for just a second, and he wondered what she was thinking. Ethan shrugged sheepishly. 'You didn't really think I dropped out of Cambridge just because I slept with you?'

'It may have fleetingly crossed my mind. But no, my ego isn't that big! I did always wonder what made you leave, though.'

Ethan smiled. 'Well, it wasn't you. You weren't that bad.'

Molly gasped and slapped his biceps. Ethan laughed and dodged her. 'I'm kidding! Listen, I can't say I remember every little thing about that night,' Ethan lied. 'But from what I do remember, I had a wonderful time.'

'I'm sure you did.'

'How about you?' Ethan asked.

'It was acceptable.'

Ethan laughed softly and sipped his drink.

'So, the kids…?'

'Well, my real dad died when I was a kid, and the accident killed my mother and stepdad, so I had to come home because I didn't have a choice. I was needed here. Those kids are my little brothers and sister.'

'Oh, Ethan. You were suddenly all orphaned?' Molly looked stricken.

Ethan nodded and finished the last of his now-cold coffee. Then set it down next to his empty whisky glass.

'I didn't even know you had siblings. I guess we really didn't know each other all that well. So, it's just been you and them since you left uni?'

'I've had a lot of help along the way from extended family, especially while I finished my training, but yes.' Ethan paused. 'Have I actually apologised yet? If not, I'm sorry.'

'Oh, don't. I'm mortified that I made such a big deal of it.'

'Don't be. I should never have just left you wondering. Would it make you feel better to know that I've felt guilty this whole time? I never forgot you.'

Molly smiled teasingly. 'Never forgot me, huh?'

'Yeah, you're the kind of person that sticks in the mind.' Ethan smiled. 'I vaguely remember you standing on a table in the college bar declaring that you were very much against the idea of the patriarchy keeping you trapped in the cage of being dependent, barefoot and pregnant.'

Molly laughed delightedly. 'I was insufferable, wasn't I?'

'I think it's almost obligatory to be a little bit insufferable at twenty-one. I know I was.' Ethan paused. 'So do you still think that?'

'I've certainly grown out of thinking every woman with kids is somehow a victim of the patriarchy. But giving birth is definitely not on my to-do list.'

Ethan nodded.

'I mean, no offence to them.' Molly gestured inside Ethan's house. 'I'm sure they're lovely.'

'You clearly haven't met them. You want to?'

Her horrified face said it all. 'Oh, I have zero experience with children. They probably wouldn't like me.'

He nodded. 'Fair enough.'

He was pretty sure that Molly was wrong about that. When the boys found out he'd been talking to an actual pilot, their heads would explode. But it reminded him of what he did know about Molly. He remembered their one night together in vivid detail, and he still remembered some of the things she'd said on the rare occasions they'd shared space. They hadn't been friends, but they'd hung out in a group sometimes. He'd had a crush on her, but couldn't be sure if she felt the same way, until that one amazing night when they'd bumped into each other alone, without all their friends around them, and finally managed to make a connection. But even at that age she'd been the sort of person who knew exactly what she wanted out of life. Adventure, excitement and definitely no responsibilities. That was what he'd loved about her. He couldn't predict what she might say or do next, and it looked like she hadn't changed at all. Which he admired in a way. To know yourself so well at such a young age was impressive. Ethan hadn't felt like he knew himself until well after university. Maybe not even now.

One thing was still the same, though—his level of attraction to Molly was still through the roof; he still felt that same irresistible pull. But he had to resist it, because she was all wrong for him. Her risk-taking, fearless nature that had been so appealing in college was now the opposite of what he needed in his life.

Even if he was the luckiest man on earth, and this attraction were to go anywhere, she wasn't someone he could encourage the kids to get attached to. She'd spent her whole career moving from place to place looking for ever more exciting roles. He still suspected she'd get bored of their tiny village in Scotland soon enough. She wouldn't stay. And she'd made it pretty clear she wasn't into having kids. He couldn't do that to the twins and Maisie again. Love was not in the cards for Ethan. No one could want him when he had three ready-made kids in tow. He'd learned that first-hand when he let himself and his family get close to his ex, Carrie. They'd met when she brought in her mother's sick poodle. They'd shared a spark immediately and dated for months. Long enough that he'd felt safe introducing her to the kids, since he'd believed she'd be a permanent presence in their lives. But that was his mistake. She hadn't understood the reality of having three kids in the house. She'd grown up as an only child, and somehow seemed to be under the illusion that the kids would do as they were told, complete their homework quietly and then be tucked up in bed by eight, and that she and Ethan would have acres of privacy and time to themselves. Once she'd realised how things really worked, a frosty awkward distance set in between them before she finally left him, snapping that she didn't want to be landed with three older kids that weren't even hers. It had broken his little sister's heart and hardened Ethan's. He'd vowed never to put them through that again. His siblings had lost enough people. As irresistible as he might find wild-child Molly, he had to provide a stable life for his sister and brothers. They'd had it tough; now they needed security and predictability. He would just have to keep his distance from Molly.

He felt melancholy and just wanted this strange day to be over. But first, he had to make sure things were straight between them. They'd be working together for a while at least. 'I'm sorry I acted so strangely earlier today.'

'You mean when you pretended not to know who I was?'

'Yes. But to be fair, you didn't exactly challenge me on it. When you didn't say anything else, I wondered if perhaps you didn't want Jon to know how we knew each other. I was just following your lead. Besides, I almost didn't believe it could really be you.'

'When did you know?'

Ethan laughed once. 'When you casually said you learned to fly a plane in Australia after lockdown. I thought yep, that's my Molly.'

Molly raised an eyebrow, and Ethan flushed as he realised what he'd said. 'Not my, I mean, that's…'

Molly smiled wryly. 'I know what you meant. Listen, thanks for the drink. I'd better get back.'

'Lots to unpack.'

'You said it.'

Molly headed back over the road to her new place, her head spinning. She hadn't even had a decent look around her new home yet, but she didn't care, because all she could think about was Ethan. He'd been just twenty-one years old when he'd found out his parents had suddenly passed away. He'd had to make the decision to drop out of university, forget all his plans, at least temporarily, and head home to raise a three-year-old and two five-year-olds by himself. She couldn't even imagine it. He must have been terrified that his siblings might get taken into the system if he didn't step up.

She was drenched with guilt that she'd spent the past nine years resenting him for disappearing. In fact, she felt a little like disappearing herself right now. Her cheeks flushed hotly as she remembered shouting something about groin strain at him not twenty minutes previously. Mortifying. How was she going to face him tomorrow at work? Part of her was sad that Ethan hadn't felt he could share such a terrible thing with her at the time, that he hadn't felt they'd had a strong enough connection. It was heartbreaking that he hadn't had more help when he'd so badly needed it.

He was so sensible and responsible now. Back at uni he hadn't seemed like that at all. He was the star of the rowing squad. Everyone had thought he was by far the most gorgeous, desirable man at their college, and he'd never been without plenty of attention. Well, he still had those beautiful brown eyes, his kind manner and the strong jaw. She shook her head. That wasn't the point. She'd had a point a moment ago; what was it?

She carried her boxes and bags into the living room of her new home and stared at the rather pathetic collection of belongings. She was almost thirty and this was all she had to show for herself. It wasn't like she'd ever wanted kids, but Ethan's home, from what she could briefly see through the window, had looked so cosy and welcoming. She'd been living out of a suitcase for the past few years. Her whole adult life actually, now she came to think of it. She'd moved from her childhood home into university, then lived on the move ever since. Her ultra-conventional parents hated her unpredictable lifestyle and abhorred the fact that she refused to settle down. And she couldn't pretend that hadn't been at least a tiny part of the appeal. What they couldn't see was that she was terrified of turning into them. But she was shocked to find herself envious of Ethan's life. That wasn't what she wanted at all—all that responsibility and a boring scheduled life, each day always the same, always looking after other people, probably never having time to yourself. Never being able to just go somewhere on the spur of the moment, always having to plan everything down to the last detail. She'd never wanted that. For the past six years, the only responsibility Molly had had was to her job. She was free to go and do anything she wanted, whenever she wanted. But how often did she actually do that? She'd been drawn to the remoteness of this job. Drawn back to the UK, away from living abroad and working on temporary projects, and month-long stays in wherever had a free bed. She was also drawn towards places where she'd have the time and space to heal from her latest rejection. So this was an experiment, and it might go wrong. But maybe staying in one place for a while and having her own house might be nice. She looked around at the empty room and stared at the squares of slightly darker carpet where the last tenant's furniture had been. Getting a sofa would be a start. She suddenly had a thought and ran up the stairs. She found the main bedroom and pushed the door open, relieved beyond belief that Jon had been right and the house came with a bed. A pretty nice one, too. A king-size, with a simple oak four-poster frame. She threw herself onto the mattress, bouncing up and down a few times from the momentum, and giggled to herself. The bedroom curtains were drawn back, and when she got up to close them and switch some lights on, she realised she could see across the street right into Ethan's house.

His porch was empty now. Ethan was inside the living room with the kids, watching TV and chatting, one of the boys gesticulating wildly. Her gaze slid up the house. Across from her, on his first floor, she could see right into a bedroom, lit dimly by the light from his hallway streaming in through the open bedroom door. Maybe it was Ethan's bedroom? Molly yanked her curtains closed. The location of Ethan's bedroom was neither here nor there.

Get it together, Molly.

She hadn't come here for another temporary fling. Especially with Ethan, who was far too tempting for his own good, and who had three very good reasons of his own why he wouldn't be interested in starting up anything temporary with her. And temporary seemed to be all she was good for. Not to mention that she had never been great at connecting with children. She'd always been brought up with the idea that children were just a nuisance; at least that was what her parents had led her to believe.

CHAPTER THREE

THE NEXT MORNING Ethan met Molly outside the hangar with two steaming cups of coffee in his hands and his medical kit, full to bursting, in a messenger bag strapped across his chest.

She ran up, dropped her bags and unlocked the door to the hangar. 'Are you really thirsty or is one of them for me?'

Ethan held the second cup out and she took it gratefully.

'I didn't know how you liked it, so I had to guess,' said Ethan.

'As long as it's hot, I'm not fussed.'

Once inside, Molly pressed a button and the entire front wall of the hangar began to slide open horizontally, until all four leaves slid away to the far side.

Ethan had never paid much attention to the big barn at the back of the surgery's property, but now he was there he saw the fruits of Jon's labour. Jon had talked extensively about all his plans, so much so that Ethan had tuned him out after a while. But it was clear that Jon had made a lot of changes to transform the place into Molly's hangar. He'd had it insulated, redone the floor to take the weight of a plane and widened the doors on the front of the building. Plus, he'd cleared the whole place out so there was plenty of room for maintenance and repairs. As Ethan followed Molly inside, he admired the new security camera system that Jon had installed. Although he was pretty sure no one local would even know what to do with a plane if they did steal it.

Suddenly, Molly darted over to the edge of the open wall and reached out for something.

'What is it?' Ethan asked.

'There's a butterfly caught in a cobweb.'

Ethan stepped closer and saw it, its red-and-black wings fluttering uselessly as it tangled itself farther in the sticky web.

Molly gently pulled the web away from its wings and after a few moments, the butterfly was free. It fluttered around Molly's head then danced off and away into the trees. Ethan smiled. Molly might be tough on the outside, but she clearly had a soft heart and compassion for fragile, vulnerable creatures. He looked away and cleared his throat. She might be adorable, but he was not going to let that affect his determination to keep her at arm's length.

'You ready for your first flight?' Molly asked.

'Ready as I'll ever be.' Ethan ignored his lifelong dislike of flying and the drop in his stomach as he contemplated going up in the tiny plane. Ever since he'd become his siblings' guardian, he'd often felt like he wasn't doing a good enough job, that he could never be as wonderful a parent as his mother was. He was never going to be a person who would do something risky or irresponsible like bungee jumping or skydiving, nothing that could risk his life and take someone else from the kids. So getting in this plane seemed like a bad idea.

'She's the most reliable small plane there is. Can fly through almost any weather at all. Gale-force wind, lightning storms, you name it!'

He'd prefer not to, thank you very much.

'Jon just filled me in on our first job,' Molly continued. 'And it's not a particularly happy one.'

Ethan's heart sank a little. 'Where are we going?'

'We're seeing a woman named Winnie. Apparently, she has a big piece of land up the coast.'

Ethan nodded. 'I know her. But only by reputation.'

'She has an elderly horse who's been getting worse by the day. It's thirty-seven years old and lost a lot of weight over the last month. She thinks it might be time to give the horse a dignified end. I've got all the details on where we're going. Apparently, Jon will be near the radio all day.' Molly frowned. 'He said he wants constant updates.'

Ethan smiled at Molly's perturbed expression. 'He's pretty excited about the whole thing. I'm sure he'll calm down after the first day.'

Molly grabbed a clipboard from the wall and started walking around her small plane, checking items and ticking things off the chart. Ethan took his first close-up look at the plane he'd soon be ten thousand feet up in the sky in. He blew out a breath. The drama of the day before had successfully knocked out of his brain the fact he was going to have to fly today. He'd barely flown anywhere in the past decade, certainly not in something this small. It looked like it could be blown over by a small breeze.

'It's safe, Ethan.'

'I know.' Ethan tried to wipe whatever doubtful or suspicious expression must be apparent on his face as he looked at her plane.

It was a beautiful aircraft—a spotless and shining white paint job, the wheels painted in a glossy burgundy, which matched the propeller. He tried not to imagine how easy it would be for a goose or even a pigeon to bash into that propeller midflight and cause them to crash to the ground.

Molly started pushing the plane out of the hangar and on to the tarmac, which led to the runway. Ethan paused for a second, shocked that the plane could be moved so easily by one person, then managed to collect himself enough to run after the plane and help, by pushing it from the other side. Even though it was clear Molly didn't need any help, he stopped pushing when Molly did. The plane's call sign was painted in numbers and letters on its side, but also the name *Verne* in script.

'Planes have names? Like boats?'

'They can.'

'What does Verne mean? If that's not too much of a personal question.'

'I probably wouldn't paint it on the side of my pride and joy for all to see if it was private, Ethan.'

Fair point.

'It's the name of the author who wrote my favourite book. Do you read?'

Ethan shook his head.

'Well, maybe you should crack open a book sometime.'

'Oh, I'm sorry. I've been a bit busy the past few years, not gallivanting around the world on an extended gap year.' He winced as soon as he said it. But from Molly's hard stare it wasn't clear whether she had taken it as the, admittedly terrible, joke it was intended to be, or as a serious jab.

'Sorry, that was...'

'Hop in.' Molly didn't let him finish. She pulled open a squeaky door and jumped in easily. Ethan scratched the back of his head nervously and took a deep breath, before climbing up into the cockpit. With difficulty, he folded his six-foot frame into the passenger's seat. They slammed their doors shut in unison, he apparently a little too hard, judging from the look Molly gave him.

'Please treat my plane like the lady she is.'

Ethan rolled his eyes. 'My utmost apologies.'

Molly pulled on a headset, then passed Ethan one. 'I need one, too?' he asked, and she nodded. 'That's how we speak to each other.'

He was dismayed to find that there was a control yoke on his side as well as hers. The control panel was an impenetrable jumble of buttons and dials with a large square screen in the centre. How could anyone know what all of these did? He could never learn if he had a million years.

'Okay, ready for your passenger briefing?' When Ethan nodded, Molly quickly explained exit procedures and emergency equipment and how to operate the safety belts. The speech was probably designed to be comforting but only made Ethan more nervous. 'Clear?'

'As crystal.'

Molly nodded. 'I just have to do some more checks before we take off.'

'By all means.' Ethan was happy to wait while she did

all the checks she needed, to reduce the possibility of anything going wrong. The cockpit was comfy but cramped, and his shoulder touched Molly's—no matter how much he tried to lean away and give her room. She typed something on the touchscreen and a map appeared. She then tapped through several screens, one showing weather, another showing numbers, and clicked back to return to the map. The land showed up as bright green, separated by the familiar line of the coast, the ocean in bright blue.

Ethan was somewhat surprised to find that Molly started the plane with a simple ignition key. He didn't know what else he'd been expecting, but this whole process was a mystery to him. The engine hummed smoothly, and she let it run for a few minutes before heading onto the runway. She pulled the yoke forward and the one in front of Ethan came with it. He parted his knees to make room and realised his knee was now pressed into Molly's. He tried to ignore the tingle that ran through him at the contact and shook his head at his reaction. Why did she still make him feel like a teenager?

Molly released the brake and pushed in the throttle. Ethan gulped as he felt the plane gather speed as they bumped softly onto the grass runway and continued along its track. He grabbed tightly onto the arms of his seat. He resisted the urge to squeeze his eyes shut and breathed evenly. It would be fine. Molly was a qualified pilot with lots of experience. Flying was safer than driving. They would land safely at the other end, do what they had to do and return without issue. His brothers and sister would not lose another loved one, he would not lose his breakfast and everything would be fine.

'You doing okay there, champ?'

Ethan nodded.

'We'll be okay. I hardly ever crash.'

Ethan whipped around to face her, and she laughed delightedly. 'I'm sorry, I'm just kidding. I promise we'll be fine. You might even enjoy it. Try to relax.'

She gently pulled the steering column towards her, and seconds later they left the ground.

Ethan only had the headspace to acknowledge two feelings. The power of the adrenaline that rushed through him as they swooped into the huge blue sky, and how incredibly sexy Molly was at the controls of the plane.

Ethan's nausea faded away as they soared higher and higher, and he got distracted by how beautiful everything looked. He'd lived here all his life, aside from those years at university, and he knew every inch of the place inside out, but he'd certainly never seen it from this angle.

As they flew, Molly started pointing to various levers, dials and buttons and telling him what they did and how to use them.

'What are you telling me for?'

'What if I drop dead midflight?'

'Is that likely?'

'Anything could happen. You just need to remember the basics so you can help me in an emergency.'

Ethan shook his head in despair and tried to take in some of what Molly was explaining. He was never quite sure if she was serious or messing with him, but at least she was never boring.

They flew for a while in silence, Ethan marvelling at how far across the ocean he could see from up here.

Soon, he started to sense the plane getting lower. 'Where are we going to land?'

'There's a long piece of flat farmland to the south of her farmhouse. I've been assured that it's smooth and unobstructed.'

'You're going to land in a field?'

'Of course. You think Winnie randomly has her own landing strip?'

He hadn't really had time to think about it. 'Without offending you at all, you are totally trained in landing, right?'

'Nah, this is my first time.'

He smiled tensely. Knowing she was joking, but also knowing this was going to be a difficult landing either way. He gripped the edge of his seat and stared out at the rapidly approaching ground.

'Hey,' she said quietly. 'I've flown planes for four years. I'm a professional pilot. I'm very good at what I do. We'll be just fine.'

Ethan nodded, and finally felt able to relax back into his seat.

'This is it, I think,' said Molly.

The farm was stunning, even from above. A huge, long stretch that looked like three fields joined together was obviously the improvised airstrip. A large L-shaped house and what looked like a converted barn formed the living area, and several ramshackle barns and stables surrounded it, with paddocks dotted around, marked out with white wooden fencing. Various cows, pigs, sheep and horses munched on grass and hay and ignored the plane above them. There were thick woods on three sides, and a large pond, or maybe a small lake sat at the bottom of a grassy hill in front of the house.

'Wow, it's beautiful,' said Ethan, in disbelief.

But Molly was all business. 'It looks smooth enough. That's good. Believe me, losing a wheel to a pothole, or having a propeller hit the ground on landing is no joke.'

Ethan stared over at Molly. 'Thanks for those images.'

She shrugged. 'I've had worse happen and I survived. It'll be fine.'

Ethan took in her relaxed stance at the controls and once again found her casual confidence and sheer competency hugely sexy. The landing was extremely bumpy, but a huge relief. Ethan had been somewhat distracted from the landing by the X-rated thoughts rushing through his mind about the pilot, but he was ecstatic to be back on the ground. Molly taxied to the end of the landing strip, then turned the plane around, ready for the journey back. The plane came to a complete stop, and Molly turned off the engine.

'So, you know this woman by reputation?'

'I've heard about her farm, but we've never met. She sometimes takes in the odd injured animal, or aged-out breeders who might otherwise be put down by the farmer, and keeps them comfortable. Gives them a happy life. I've seen Jon set things up between her and farmers locally when he hears about an animal she might take. She's pretty elderly herself, so she's never come all the way into the practice. Jon's driven out here a few times, though. Think he delivered a couple of Gloucester old spot pigs to her last year in person.'

'She doesn't run the place all by herself?'

'I think she might.'

'Oh, wow. I like her already.'

'That must be her now.' A woman approached the plane, smiling widely and holding a hand up in greeting.

She looked like one of those very capable, no-nonsense women who could just as easily skin a rabbit as bake a cake and not produce a sweat over either. Ethan wasn't in the habit of guessing how old women were, but he wouldn't be surprised if she was retirement age, despite how sprightly she seemed.

They jumped down from the plane and she greeted them both with warm handshakes.

'I'm Winnie. Thank you so much for coming out to see me. I'm ever so grateful.'

'No problem at all. It's our job. It's lovely to finally meet you. You're pretty famous back at the practice,' said Ethan.

Winnie laughed. 'I'd offer you tea, but if you don't mind I'd like you both to look at Heather first. Then I'll make you all the tea you want. Might even throw you in a biscuit.'

She joked, but Ethan could see the sadness in her eyes. 'We're here to do whatever you need us to.'

Winnie nodded despondently. 'I'll take you to meet Heather.'

They walked towards the stables that were situated right by the farmhouse.

'She's the best horse you could ever hope for. The sweetest temperament. Never got sick. We've had thirty-seven long years together. She wasn't a rescue. I had her since she was a foal.'

'I bet she's had an amazing life,' said Molly. 'I would love to have lived here for thirty-seven years.'

Heather was in her stall, by a full bag of hay, but not eating it. She looked very thin, tired and just about done with life. Her eyes lit up a little when Winnie got close and opened up the stable door.

'She hasn't eaten anything of note for several days, and she's lost a lot of weight. I think it's time.'

Ethan and Molly gave the horse an examination. Ethan wanted to make sure there wasn't something else going on first. The patient could be suffering from mouth ulcers or a problem with her teeth that made eating too painful. But unfortunately, they were soon satisfied that it was simply old age and there was nothing more they could do. Ethan's eyes filled with compassion as he turned and spoke to Winnie. 'I think you're right. It's her time. We'll give her a very gentle send-off.'

'I've got everything ready over by the trees.' She nodded towards the edge of the forest. 'I feel so guilty.'

'You mustn't,' said Ethan. 'She's had a long, wonderful life thanks to you. It's the kindest thing to do now. You don't want her to suffer.'

Winnie led Heather out of her stable. The horse was quite wobbly and hesitant in her gait, and it was clear, even without their assistance, she probably wouldn't last much longer. Euthanasia really was the only good option at this point.

'Here it is.' Winnie stopped at the edge of the trees next to a huge hole in the ground with a sloped end leading down into it. It always felt a little morbid but when it came to euthanising a big animal like a horse or a cow, it was only logical to perform the procedure at the place where they would be buried. Some animals were simply too big and heavy to move afterwards.

'You dug this by yourself?' Ethan asked.

'It's the least I could do for my best friend. Took me three days, mind.'

'I'm not surprised. You've done a spectacular job. And what a peaceful place to be laid to rest.'

The sun dappled the grass through the trees, and bees buzzed lazily between the wildflowers. Ethan would honestly have been happy to spend the rest of eternity here himself, if he wouldn't miss his kid brothers and sister too much.

Ethan sedated the horse to keep her calm. And Winnie said her last goodbyes while Molly and Ethan stepped back to get the catheter ready. When Winnie looked up, wiped her face with the end of her scarf and nodded to them, Molly stepped forward and patted Heather's neck softly, before carefully inserting the catheter into a neck vein.

'I'll be essentially giving her an overdose of anaesthetic, so she won't feel a thing,' Molly said quietly.

Winnie led Heather down the slope into the hole, and once there, Molly got the needle ready. 'Once I press this, it'll be fast. I'll take her rope as soon as I've done it, and you'll need to step away, because she'll go right down.' Winnie nodded, gave Heather one last long kiss on the nose and stroked her head as she watched Molly administer the lethal injection. Then she passed Molly the rope and walked back up the slope she'd dug. Winnie turned away as Heather sat back on her hindquarters and lay down, and Ethan put his arm around her shoulders, patting her arm. 'She's okay. She's going now,' he murmured. It was a pretty graceful fall, and Ethan was relieved. An awkward fall could be an upsetting thing for an animal's owner to see, especially as the last image they would be left with.

Winnie wiped her nose with a tissue and turned back, and all three stood in silence for a moment as Heather went to sleep. Ethan checked that there was no heartbeat with his stethoscope and confirmed Heather's death. Molly wordlessly removed the rope and halter and handed them both to Winnie.

'Thank you so much.' She took a few deep breaths, then seemed to make a decision to let Heather go. 'How about we head inside for a cup of tea before you go.'

'We'd love to,' said Ethan. He caught an approving look on Molly's face, and he smiled briefly, relieved that she supported him on this. They hadn't agreed on much so far.

They all ended up having coffee in Winnie's large, cosy kitchen. Molly chose coffee to keep her alert for the flight back, and Winnie also decided she needed a little extra vim to get through the day after a terrible morning.

'Your farm is beautiful. And huge. Are you living here alone?'

'I am. I have a farmhand who comes in every day to do some of the tougher work. And my sister lives nearby. She visits a couple of times a week for a natter. But I live here alone. I always said I'd work the farm until my last days on Earth. But, to be honest, it's getting a bit much for me now.'

'Do you have any children?' Ethan asked. He caught Molly frowning at him, and he added quickly as an afterthought, 'If that's not too personal a question.'

'Two boys. Neither of them are interested in the farm. They both left for city jobs. They don't get the chance to come back very often.'

'Well, they're missing out on some truly excellent coffee,' said Ethan. 'And one of the most beautiful places I've ever been. I can't imagine what they're getting in the city that they couldn't get here.'

'Oh, nightlife and strip clubs, I'd reckon,' Winnie joked wryly, and Molly laughed in shock. Even Ethan cracked a smile.

Winnie excused herself for a moment, and Ethan wondered if it was possible for them to pop out and see Winnie more often. He downed his coffee and got Molly's attention. 'You feel like doing some digging?'

It only took a second for Molly to realise what he was suggesting, and she smiled and nodded. They jogged back to the grave together. Ethan grabbed the shovel from where he'd spotted it leaning against the fence and handed it to Molly, then went to the tool shed standing open nearby and searched for another one for himself. They quickly worked together to fill in the grave as much as possible. He couldn't bear to think of Winnie doing it all by herself.

He thought Winnie was going to start crying all over again when she eventually came to find them after about half an hour. 'Thank you so much, Doctors. I'm going to plant grass seed and more wildflowers over her to make a grave marker. She loved eating dandelions, so soon she's going to help some grow.'

Back at the plane, Ethan threw his medical bag in the back and hoped the heater would be quick to warm up his cold hands. Molly was strangely quiet. 'You okay?' Ethan asked.

'Of course.'

'That was pretty intense for your first day. Have you done a lot of things like that before?'

'It was pretty intense.' She paused and looked over at Ethan. 'You should try it with an elephant.'

Ethan laughed once, but wondered if Molly was always like this, showing no emotion after a rough job. She clearly had a big heart; maybe it was just how she needed to be to get through work. Rather than letting her brush him off, Ethan decided to try to gently coax more out of her. 'It was pretty sad today. Thirty-seven years is a long relationship. Longer than any of mine, now I come to think of it.' He hadn't even had the opportunity to know his own mother that long. It was strange to think Winnie and her horse had known each other longer.

'It was sad.' Molly hesitated and brushed something off the wing of the plane. 'I suppose I'm just not used to dealing with people that are so personally invested in their animals.'

Ethan almost held his breath. Molly was opening up and sharing her emotions with him for what felt like the first time, and he didn't want to do anything to stop her.

'I mean, everyone cared deeply about the projects I've

worked on, but the animals weren't part of the family, and I guess I just don't know how to—'

'Hey!'

Ethan swung around, frustrated at the interruption, to find a man hailing them from the farmhouse next door to Winnie's property. They stopped and waited as the man ran over, the moment gone.

'You the vets?'

Molly nodded.

'Sorry to bother you. You wouldn't have a minute to take a quick look at one of my sheep?'

'Of course,' said Ethan. He introduced himself and grabbed his medical kit again as Molly and the man shook their hands. 'The name's Jack. Sad to hear about old Heather.'

Ethan wiped his hands on his trousers, still grimy from the dirt he'd just spent half an hour replacing. 'She's not in pain anymore.'

Jack nodded. And as they rounded the corner onto Jack's field, he gestured over to the paddock at a lone sheep with curved horns.

'Here's Bertha. She bashed her head on the fence a few weeks ago, trying to get her head through to eat the grass on the other side. And since then her right horn seems to be growing back into the side of her head.'

Bertha was already standing, trapped inside a tiny pen in the corner of the paddock. And she was not happy to see Ethan. Her eyes wide, she tucked herself against the far side of the pen as he approached. He spoke to her gently, trying to calm her down. 'Hello, Bertha. Are you going to let me take a look at you?' Ethan slowly climbed over the fence into the pen with Bertha. 'I'm probably freaking her out because I smell unfamiliar,' he said to the farmer.

'I'll give you a hand.' Molly leaned over the fence and wrapped her arms around the sheep's body, holding her still so Ethan could take a look. Ethan firmly held Bertha's head, looking closely at the horn, stroking her nose with one hand. 'I think we're going to have to take the horn off. But it's a pretty simple operation. I can do it right now.'

Ethan looped a rope around Bertha's neck and nose to keep her head still, while Molly snipped off the longer fur around her horn with a tiny pair of scissors.

Ethan emptied a syringe of anaesthetic into Bertha's head, then used a wire tool, similar to a cheese wire, to remove the horn. It didn't take long, and the friction generated enough heat that blood loss was minimal and cauterising was unnecessary.

Molly then sprayed the area with a blue antiseptic spray, and they let the sheep free, Bertha bounding away happily.

Ethan presented the curved horn he'd removed to the farmer.

'I'll give that to my grandson. He'll love that.'

'Enjoy!'

As they walked back to the plane, Molly murmured, 'Anyone would think you agreed to help that sheep just to put off getting back in my plane.'

Ethan laughed. Once they were seated, Ethan finally got to warm his hands by the heater. 'You've officially saved your first Scottish animal. How do you feel?' he asked Molly.

'She wasn't my first. I saved a butterfly from a web.'

Ethan smiled. He'd forgotten all about that. He looked at his watch. It had been three hours since they'd left the hangar, and Ethan already felt like he'd done a twelve-hour shift. He stretched and yawned, his back clicking. 'How has sitting in a plane made me so exhausted?'

'I think that might be more a result of burying an adult horse.'

Molly had a point. It wasn't every day you had to do that. But it was better than the thought of poor Winnie having to do it by herself. Ethan was so glad they'd been able to come over and help her. Maybe the whole flying vet thing wasn't such a bad idea after all. Ethan still felt frustrated that Molly hadn't fully opened up. They'd just been starting to get somewhere when Jack had turned up and interrupted them. But after that, she seemed to shut down again. He could only assume that Molly had seen and dealt with some very emotional things in Africa and her other travels, and this was just how she had learned to cope with things.

CHAPTER FOUR

THERE WERE NO more long-distance emergencies or visits on the schedule, so they headed back to base, where it was Molly's allocated afternoon to tackle the paperwork. But all she did was get frustrated with herself when her mind kept drifting back to Ethan. He was obviously trying to get to know her better. She'd tried so hard to remain professional at Winnie's, but perhaps she'd done too good a job and come across as uncaring. She'd seen the clear compassion in Ethan's eyes; he was so good at expressing sympathy and care. But she knew if she'd put herself fully in Winnie's shoes, she might have started crying and not stopped for a good, long time after losing such an old, devoted friend as Heather. She just couldn't seem to get the balance right.

'Molly? Ethan needs you in exam room two.'

Molly abandoned her paperwork and followed Jon out, rushing into room two immediately, ready to glove up.

Ethan, halfway through an operation on a rabbit, glanced over as she entered the room. 'I'm not going to be finished to get home in time for the kids,' he said.

Molly nodded sympathetically and eyed the rabbit laid out on the operating table. 'And you want me to finish up here?' She pushed her sleeves up in anticipation.

'That's okay, Molly. The owner specifically requested that I do the surgery, otherwise I'd swap with you, but thank you for offering. Actually, I was hoping that maybe you could…'

Molly frowned at him, wondering what on earth he was getting at. And why he looked nervous to actually put it into words. Until suddenly it hit her. He wanted her to go and check on his kids. Well, his siblings. She wasn't going to help him ask her; he could do it himself.

'Could I possibly ask you a huge favour?' he finally managed to force out.

'Maybe.'

'Could you just drop by and look in on my brothers and sister, since you're walking right past my house anyway when you head home? I'll speak to Jon about it, too, in case you're worried he'll say anything about you leaving a little earlier than usual.'

'I guess.'

'And then could you maybe stay there for an hour or two until I get back?'

'What? What am I supposed to do with them?'

'All you have to do is be there. Make sure they don't set the house on fire.'

'Is that likely to happen?'

'It hasn't so far. But maybe that's because there's usually an adult in the house.'

'Can't someone else do it? I don't know how to talk to kids.'

'You talk to them like you would anyone else. I promise, it's not rocket science. I'm sure you're perfectly capable. They'll love you. Please, Molly, there's no one else I can ask. Everyone else is at work or away.'

Molly sighed.

'You won't turn into a pumpkin at the sight of a child, you know. And you don't have to change any nappies. They grew out of that at least a couple of months back.'

Even Ethan himself had never had to change a nappy. They'd been three and five when he took responsibility for them.

'God, fine. I'll do it just to stop you nagging.'

His face split into a smile that felt like the sun coming out.

'If it helps, think of yourself as more in a bouncer role than a babysitter.'

That did sound slightly less intimidating.

'I owe you one.'

'Yes, you do. A big one.'

His eyes narrowed as if he was worried about this coming back to bite him. But he was too relieved to complain.

Just as Molly was about to leave, Ethan spoke again. 'I'll make you dinner tonight, if you want to stay and eat with us. What's your favourite kind of pizza?'

'Pineapple,' Molly said, smiling at the disgusted face Ethan made. Molly paused. 'Are you asking me out on a dinner date?'

Ethan held her gaze. 'It's whatever you want it to be.'

Molly's face flushed pink. She was flustered at how easily he'd turned the tables on her.

'Okay, but that doesn't count as the favour you owe me.' She swung out of the room, trying to regain some of her dignity. 'Don't be too long! After all, there's no one watching me to make sure I don't burn the house down.'

Molly was already having second thoughts as she left work and checked on her plane one last time, before she headed home. The evenings were really starting to get chilly, so she pulled on her gloves and rubbed her hands together to warm them up.

She wasn't joking; she really didn't have much experience around kids. But she'd faced plenty of challenges before, and she wasn't going to let this one stop her.

She used the key Ethan had directed her to take from his bag at the office, and let herself into his house. It looked like the kids had only just gotten home.

'Oh, hi, what're you doing here?' The taller twin dropped his school bag on the hall floor and stared at her. She was pretty sure this one was Kai.

'Is Ethan okay?' asked Maisie, starting to look worried.

'Your brother's fine. He's still at work. There's a rabbit with abdominal problems who desperately needs his help. He sent me to tell you he's going to be late.'

'Oh, okay.' Maisie shrugged.

They all headed into the kitchen, and Molly decided she might as well follow them.

'Will the rabbit be okay?' asked Maisie.

'I'm sure she'll be fine,' Molly answered. She certainly hoped so anyway. 'Is it okay if I hang out with you for a bit?' She thought they might not take too kindly to being babysat, and she should couch it in a less annoying way.

Suddenly, and for no apparent reason, she really wanted them to like her.

'What was your name again?' Harry asked.

'Molly. I work with your brother at the clinic.'

'Oh, you're the one who flies a plane!'

'That's me.'

'That's so cool!'

Molly tried not to preen but there was something about kids saying you were cool that just really hit the ego spot. 'It is pretty fun.'

'Dangerous, though.' Maisie pulled a packet of sweets from her coat pocket and offered Molly one.

She accepted with a smile. 'Not if you're a good pilot.'

'I guess. How do you fit, like, a cow in the plane?'

Maisie's brother laughed at her. 'They don't put the animals in the plane, dummy.'

Maisie threw a sweet wrapper at her brother, and Molly jumped in to defend her. 'Actually, I plan to rework some space in the body of the plane so that in future we could, if necessary, transport smaller animals back to the surgery in case they urgently need to be treated with equipment we can't fit in the plane.'

Maisie made an 'I told you so' face at her brother and he laughed.

Maisie apparently had a lot more questions.

'What's it like being a pilot? Do you have a boyfriend?' She paused for a second. 'Or a girlfriend?'

Molly grinned. This kid was adorable. 'It's great. And no, I don't.'

'Ethan doesn't have a girlfriend.'

Molly nodded and wondered where Maisie was going with this.

'He hasn't had one for a long time.'

Molly knew she should change the subject. This was none of her business. But she couldn't help but be curious. And Maisie's description of Ethan sounded so different from the boy she remembered at university. He was so popular, and he always had a girl or two hanging around him, desperate to be his girlfriend. And from what Molly could remember, he seemed to date plenty of them. 'So what music do you like?'

Maisie thoroughly ignored Molly's attempt to change the subject. 'Carrie was the last one. She was nice for a while, but apparently we scared her off.'

'Maisie. Ethan doesn't like us saying that,' warned Kai.

Undeterred, Maisie continued. 'Ethan pretended that she left because of him. But I heard what she said. She didn't want to be stuck with us.'

Molly winced. 'That's awful. I'm sorry.'

'We really liked Carrie, when she left I felt bad.'

Poor kids. This Carrie person probably shouldn't have gotten involved with Ethan in the first place, if she wasn't happy to take on his kid siblings. This was exactly why Molly always made it clear from the start of any relationship what her boundaries were, so nobody got hurt. Although of course, despite her efforts, inevitably the person who seemed to get hurt the most was Molly.

'Do you play video games?' Harry asked.

'Sometimes.'

At that, Harry pulled gently on her sleeve and headed

towards the living room. 'Do you want to play a racing game?'

'I happen to be amazing at racing games.'

'Excellent.'

Molly threw herself on the surprisingly squishy sofa and bounced a little, before Harry dropped a controller into her lap.

After playing three rounds of games driving around Paris at breakneck speed, Maisie somehow tricked Molly into explaining the rules of poker with a deck of cards. An hour had passed before Molly even thought to check her watch, and she was shocked to find she'd been there so long. It was surprising how easy she found it to connect to these kids. Maybe she was just seeing them as an extension of Ethan; maybe she would have liked them whatever happened. No, that didn't sound right. Maybe she was interested in them because they were interested in her? Whatever it was, it was unexpectedly rewarding.

Maisie had just whipped out a deck of cards, when the front door opened. And in poured what seemed like ten lively, chatting strangers, but was only four once Molly counted.

'Hi, all!'

'Aunty Anne!'

'Don't mind us. We're just here to drop off some supplies for the weekend and see if Ethan's made his lasagne yet.'

Maisie jumped up and ran to check inside the double fridge. 'No, it's not in here. He must have forgot.'

Molly floated at the edge of the crowd now in the kitchen. They were all obviously very used to spending time there and all were bustling about busily, taking off coats, pulling out stools and fussing over the kids.

'Hi.' Molly raised her hand in a wave. 'I'm Molly, from Ethan's work.'

The woman who seemed to be in charge of the group of visitors threw her a warm smile. 'Hello, dear. Call me Aunty Anne. Is Ethan here?'

There was no way Molly was calling a complete stranger Aunty anything. 'No, he's at work, but he's due back at any minute.'

Anne stopped bustling and sat down on a kitchen stool and looked at Molly properly. 'You're the girl who's moved in across the road. The one Ethan knew at university?'

Molly nodded, and Anne gripped her hands warmly. 'It's lovely to meet you. I've heard wonderful things.'

Molly doubted she'd heard anything at all, but it was nice of her to say. She felt a warm glow in her chest.

'He didn't mention a lasagne to you, did he?'

'He did not.'

'We're having a street party this weekend. You're invited of course. And that was going to be his contribution. Never mind. I can whip one up to freeze and cook on the day. You don't have to bring anything of course. You'll still be busy settling in. Probably haven't even got your kitchen set up yet, I bet! Is there anything we can help you with? Any furniture you need moving?'

Molly's head was spinning from all the questions and information Anne had been able to squeeze into one breath. She still hadn't built her sofa or kitchen table yet; the instructions said it was going to be a two-person job, but she'd been putting it off, telling herself she'd manage it somehow.

'I can tell there's something you need! Uncle Dan here can help. He's all muscle. And the boys.' She nodded towards the twins. 'What do you need?' she asked kindly.

'Well, I ordered this huge new sofa and a table. And I haven't been able to put them together yet. They're too big, really. I just got overexcited. I've never really had a whole house to myself before.' Molly forced herself to stop talking. This was unlike her; she never shared her problems with a stranger, but these people just seemed so kind and genuine.

Anne clapped her hands together. 'Wonderful. Let's do it now.'

'Shouldn't we wait for Ethan to get back?'

'Oh, you're right. He'll wonder where everyone is. Okay. We'll get started on the lasagne, then after dinner we'll get your furniture made up.' She turned a concerned look at Molly. 'How many days have you spent here without a sofa or a table?'

'Oh, not many. I honestly just got here. It's not a big deal.'

'Ethan said you're an adventurer.'

Molly bet he had. That dig Ethan had made about her being on a perpetual gap year flashed through her mind. She hated that he thought of her as some frivolous fun-seeker. She wasn't flaky, or irresponsible. She just valued her freedom.

Anne patted her arm. 'Even the most adventurous of us need a comfy sofa to come home to.'

***

When Ethan finally returned home, he looked surprised to see everybody there with Molly. Surprised and perhaps a little pleased as well, at the very least that she hadn't let them burn the house down, and, she hoped, perhaps even happy that she'd done a good job looking after his siblings.

'Where did you all spring from?' Ethan asked, pulling his coat off and greeting everyone.

Ethan deftly pulled Molly to the side for a moment away from the others. 'I'm so sorry you got inundated by everyone. You didn't have to stay after they got here. They could have watched the kids if you needed to get home.'

'Oh,' said Molly, suddenly deflated but not sure why. Suddenly, she was irritated with herself. She wasn't doing a very good job of keeping her distance from Ethan. She had to work harder to remember that she could never give him what he needed: a joint caregiver for the kids.

'But I'm glad you stayed. I promised you a meal, after all.' He smiled and lifted his bag aloft. 'I got pineapple for your pizza.'

Molly soon got wrapped up in eating pizza with his family, helping them make lasagne to freeze for the party, and then trekking them all over to her house, where they managed to make all her furniture in no time. With everyone there, chatting and laughing, her house felt like a home for the first time. Suddenly, being included as part of a large, welcoming family made her feel strangely happy, not suffocated or trapped at all. Maybe there were positives to being a part of something bigger? Maybe it depended on the people and the family in question. She hadn't exactly been blessed with a responsive, inclusive family in the past. Maybe being part of a family could be a good thing.

Ethan looked at her quizzically across the room, probably trying to work out what on earth she was doing, gazing into space and thinking so hard.

Back at Ethan's house, after his family had gone home and the kids had gone up to bed, Ethan suggested Molly stay for one last drink. And to his delight, she warily accepted. She'd looked a little spooked when he first came home but Ethan was glad to see her relax a little. Molly was so fascinating to him. She seemed so confident on the outside but showed intriguing, brief signs of vulnerability underneath. He wished he could learn more about what made her tick. Ethan grabbed a bottle of beer from the fridge and poured Molly a glass of wine, and they ended up on the sofa, cosy and warm by the fireplace.

'So, what did you get up to without me?' Ethan asked. 'The family spill all my secrets?'

Ethan was only joking—he didn't really have any secrets left to spill. But when Molly laughed and took a sip from her drink, Ethan could tell from her face that someone had said something to her, something that she didn't want to mention.

'Was there anything?'

'Well, Maisie did happen to mention something about an ex of yours.'

'Ah, the infamous Carrie.'

Molly nodded.

'What did Maisie say? Was she upset?'

Molly frowned. 'Oh, no. Not exactly. She did seem to think that she and the twins scared her off, though.'

Ethan sighed and took a long sip of his drink. He'd hoped that he'd convinced Maisie it was all his fault Carrie had left. But she was a smart kid; she could see right through him.

'I don't mean to speak out of turn,' said Molly. 'But honestly, this Carrie woman doesn't sound so great.'

'That's an understatement.'

'Yeah, I was holding back out of politeness.'

A flash of something crossed her face, an emotion Ethan wasn't quite sure he was interpreting correctly. Jealousy maybe? Could Molly be jealous of his past relationship with Carrie? The thought made him feel breathless and hopeful. Ethan laughed briefly. 'She wasn't all bad. She just wasn't ready for all the responsibilities I come with. I can't really blame her.' Ethan picked at the label on his beer.

'I can.'

Ethan looked up at Molly.

'You four come as a package. She had to know that from the start.'

Ethan smiled. He was touched that Molly could see it from his side, especially as he would have expected her to side with Carrie, about kids at least. Molly just kept on surprising him. She was such a mystery. Ethan suddenly wondered if he'd been asking the wrong question. Molly had made it clear that she didn't want to have kids of her own. But that was a whole different issue from whether she could see herself being with someone who already had kids.

Theoretically, someone who felt like that would in fact be the exact opposite of Carrie, who had wanted her own kids and not someone else's. Ethan didn't particularly have any plans to make babies. He had quite enough on his plate with the three kids he had. A woman who might one day learn to love his family, too—that was the sort of woman who would be perfect for him.

'You think you have it bad?' Molly asked with a wry smile. 'How many of your exes got engaged soon after they dumped you?'

Ethan pulled himself out of his own head and thought about it. 'Well, I don't know about Carrie. She could be by now. That's got to hurt, though. That's happened to you?'

'Three times.'

'Three?'

'Yep. I don't know why I'm telling you this. It doesn't make me look good.'

'Makes them look like idiots, to be honest.'

Molly smiled. 'To our idiot exes.' She held out her wine glass for a toast, and he shifted closer to her on the sofa so he could clink her glass gently with his beer.

'Without them we wouldn't be here now,' said Ethan.

'That's true,' she murmured, looking at Ethan's lips.

Ethan felt his heart rate rise. All it would take was one tiny movement, one lean closer, and he could finally kiss her. Finally feel Molly's soft lips against his own again, after all these years of memories. He remembered that sweet, hot-chocolate kiss. The one he'd relived a thousand times over the years. The one where she'd climbed on top of him and held him down. The first slow, deep kiss after all their quick and desperate ones. The one that felt like it meant something.

He leaned closer and her eyes drifted shut. He felt her warm breath across his lips and breathed in her scent. He should kiss her now. He should do it. But then she'd regret it. Then she'd remember that he had guardianship of three kids, and that there were rhinos in Indonesia that needed her help. And he'd be left alone again. He backed away swiftly. 'I'd better check on the kids.'

'Yes. It's time I got home, too.' Molly stood quickly and looked for a place to put her glass. She looked almost as flustered as Ethan felt. He'd never felt so sexually frustrated in his life, but he knew he'd done the right thing. But he was so close to disregarding all sense and logic and just kissing her anyway. Before he could make a move again, Molly abruptly left the house and shut the door behind her.

CHAPTER FIVE

THE NEXT MORNING Ethan glanced out his window to find the unexpected sight of the woman he'd dreamed about sharing a bed with all night leading a donkey up her front path and into her garden. He'd woken up even more sexually frustrated than he'd been the night before. She was slowly and quietly driving him up the wall.

The kids were still asleep, so he quickly got dressed and jogged over the road to investigate. He followed their route up the side of her house and found Molly tying the donkey's rope to a fencepost in the back garden. He'd hoped he might be able to act normally around her, but as soon as he saw her, all he wanted to do was pull her into his arms and kiss her. Nevertheless, the way last night had ended filled him with awkwardness. He was better off pretending it hadn't happened.

'Okay, how did you manage to acquire a donkey before eight o'clock in the morning?'

Molly looked up, flushing pink at the sight of him, and appearing somewhat guilty at being caught. 'Jon mentioned a farmer with a donkey yesterday. He'd been asking about putting it to sleep. But she's healthy enough. Just old, and the farm didn't really have a use for her anymore.'

'Is she from the Taylors' farm over by the church?' Ethan recognised her. He'd treated her a few times for abscesses. He suspected part of the reason Taylor wanted to offload the donkey might be because he was getting sick of paying for treatments.

Molly nodded. 'I stopped by, and Taylor said he originally got her to protect the llamas.' She stroked a hand over the donkey's back. 'But they don't have the herd anymore.'

Farmers often kept a donkey to protect other livestock, like llamas, sheep and goats. They were territorial creatures and could be quite fierce when they wanted to be. 'Did they sell the herd? I'm surprised they didn't sell the donkey along with them.'

'Yeah, the new owner wasn't interested.'

'Poor old girl.' Ethan stroked her ears and she tossed her head happily.

'You know she suffers from regular abscesses?'

Molly shrugged. 'I do now. She's a handsome beast, isn't she?'

Ethan glanced around her garden. 'Where are you going to keep her?'

'Jon agreed to let me keep her at the clinic in the stables out back until I find her a new home. I'm going to walk her over there today.'

'Well, after you're done with that, are you busy this morning?'

'Not really, why?'

'It might not be your sort of thing, but I wondered if you might want to come with us to collect the pumpkins for the Halloween street party.'

Molly frowned, adorably confused. 'Pumpkins?'

'Yeah, it's mainly an Aunty Anne thing, but everyone joins in. They decorate the whole street with pumpkins. Arrange them on the steps, line the paths, light them up. They string up lots of lights, too. It actually looks pretty good.'

'You don't have to convince me, I'm totally in.'

Ethan laughed, relieved she still wanted to spend time with him after the previous evening's aborted almost-kiss.

Molly hadn't been sure at first. She didn't want to intrude on what sounded like a family tradition, and after their moment last night, when she'd been so sure he was about to kiss her, she felt a little awkward. But Ethan had seemed so keen for her to say yes that she'd agreed. And she was glad she had. The genuine smile she got from Ethan felt like a warm hug. A hug she kept feeling all day, from simply being included in their day. She hadn't realised how much she'd missed out on, not having a big family around her.

During all the years she'd worked abroad, she'd only spent the occasional weekend dropping by to visit her family between jobs. She was an only child, so her close family only consisted of her mum and dad. She'd always been envious of people who weren't only children, and had wondered wistfully what it would be like to have a big raucous, loud, busy family. For the first time in her life, she'd found a family just like that, and was feeling the urge to be a part of it. But her instincts were telling her it was too dangerous to make that leap. It might be fun at first, but she suspected she would soon feel overwhelmed. She just wouldn't know how to navigate it. She was much better off sticking to her job and dedicating her life to animals, seeing as love let her down so often, as well as her parents. She was scared of getting hurt again, and that part of her wanted to keep away from Ethan's family to protect herself. Unfortunately, that part of her was also sometimes too weak to say no.

There was a pumpkin field on the edge of town. All throughout October, the farmer let people come and buy pumpkins, and apparently kept a whole small field at one end for the James family street party pumpkins. They could purchase them for a great discount, but they had to go pick them and bring all of them back to the street themselves. So somewhere along the way, they'd turned it into a big fun event.

They all got dressed up warmly in scarves, hats and gloves, and drove to the pumpkin field in two or three cars. Sometimes they could fit in two, but with Molly plus the gaggle of friends the kids had brought this year, they needed another. Ethan offered to drive his Jeep, and Maisie and her friends climbed in the back. 'Come with us, Molly,' called Maisie from inside the car. Ethan made eye contact with Molly and pulled open the passenger-side door. He stared at her for a moment, then winked. And although Molly laughed it off, it made her stomach flip.

One of Ethan's cousins drove an all-terrain vehicle with a large trailer attached to the back for all the pumpkins to be piled into.

'How many pumpkins can we possibly need?' Molly asked.

'You would be surprised,' said Ethan.

The field was covered in clusters of pumpkins large and small, tiny and enormous, in orange, yellow, green, white, blue and every combination. Some with stripes, some with spots and lumps. Everyone set off, wandering around the field in twos and threes, collecting pumpkins in the wheelbarrows that were lined up by the entrance.

Molly and Ethan somehow ended up alone with a wheelbarrow. Molly could feel Ethan's gaze on her at times, when she was sure he thought she wasn't aware. They collected pumpkins as they worked their way around the field. Molly fell in love at first sight with a tiny blue pumpkin. She wasn't sure whether to pick it now or leave it to grow a bit bigger, so she left it where it was, and they continued up the hill towards the others. Their wheelbarrow had a loudly squeaking wheel, and it reminded Molly that she needed to remember to get some WD-40 on the door of her plane.

Molly watched Ethan's cousin as he jumped on the all-terrain vehicle and started the engine. He drove it up the hill to bring the trailer closer to the pile of pumpkins they'd all amassed, then parked it at the top of the hill and jumped out.

Everyone started piling up the pumpkins carefully in the trailer, filling it with what Molly was convinced would be too many pumpkins for anyone to ever use. It looked like there were at least a hundred in there. Molly piled her wheelbarrowful into the back corner of the trailer, filling the only gap left. Now the trailer was full, everyone wandered away to return their wheelbarrows. Molly suddenly remembered the tiny blue pumpkin. She decided she couldn't leave it behind after all, and she ran down the hill alone to grab it.

Once she'd found it, Molly noticed something move out of the corner of her eye. Then she turned and watched, frozen in horror, as the trailer started moving slowly backwards. Ethan's cousin must not have pulled the handbrake properly when he parked it. It was so heavy with all the hundreds of pounds of weight it now carried, that it started to gather speed as it headed alarmingly down the trail. Molly immediately shouted out in warning, but she'd gone so far down the hill that no one heard. The trailer was destined to collide with the hedge at the bottom of the hill, but not before it mowed down the person standing, blissfully unaware, in the road. As the rest slowly turned their heads, Molly realised it was Maisie. She spotted Molly, and smiled and waved, not realising what was coming straight at her from behind. Without thinking, Molly dropped the pumpkin and sprinted towards Maisie. The girl's expression turned to shock as Molly collided with her and pushed her out of the way, seconds before the trailer raced past them. Molly tried to roll underneath her so that Maisie would have a softer landing. She thought about how it had almost hit Maisie squarely in the back. And only once they came to a stop on the muddy grass did Molly realise the trailer must have clipped her, as her leg hurt like hell.

'Maisie, are you okay?'

The others ran towards them, shouting, and Molly sat up just in time to see Ethan rather heroically jump on to the vehicle and slam on the brakes. The trailer stopped just before the hedge, and not even one pumpkin rolled out of the trailer.

Ethan was at their sides immediately and after helping Maisie up, who thankfully seemed fine, he knelt down beside Molly.

'Where are you hurt?'

'My lower right leg.'

He gently took her leg in his hands and moved his fingers up and down her jeans. 'There's no blood.' Luckily, they weren't tight jeans, and he easily pushed up the denim to her knee to take a look. 'No broken skin.' There was a huge red mark over one side of her leg. He touched one finger to it lightly as she wiggled her toes experimentally. 'That's going to be a killer bruise.'

'It doesn't seem to be swelling. Do you want to try to stand on it?'

Molly nodded, and he took her cold hands in his big warm ones, and gently, slowly, pulled her up. He kept his hands around her waist and encouraged her to put a little weight on her foot. It was sore, but it clearly wasn't broken. 'Oh, thank God. I think it's all right.'

He pulled her into a hug. Molly felt tingles everywhere their bodies touched. Almost in shock, she wrapped her arms around his wide shoulders and pulled him closer, his body warm against hers.

'Thank you so much,' Ethan whispered into Molly's ear, his words hot on her neck.

He pulled back slightly to look her in the eye. 'You saved Maisie. None of us even realised what was happening until it was too late.'

'Is she all right?' Molly asked. 'I took her down pretty hard.'

Ethan stopped hugging her so they could turn towards Maisie, and Molly almost wished she hadn't asked. She was cold without Ethan's strong arms around her. But she was relieved to find Maisie all in one piece and smiling.

'You saved my life!'

Molly shook her head. 'Let's not go that far.'

Ethan took Molly's shoulders and spoke quietly, while everyone fussed over Maisie. 'I know I go over the top sometimes about keeping them safe. But that was real. She could have been knocked down and crushed underneath the trailer's wheels.' He shut his eyes for a second as if to block out the image. 'She would have been seriously injured. We'd be calling out an ambulance or a damn rescue helicopter right now. Thank you, Molly. I mean it. I felt like time stood still when I saw that trailer about to hit her. I'd be devastated to lose Maisie. I've lost enough already.' Ethan pulled back and stared into Molly's eyes, brushing a strand of hair softly out of her face and tucking it behind her ear. 'That was the most terrifying moment of my life. Thank you so much. I don't know how I'm ever going to repay you.'

And then Molly got another one of those delicious, bone-crushing hugs, and all she could do was mumble, 'No problem,' into Ethan's chest.

It hadn't really been all that dramatic, had it? She only did what anyone else would have done. She just happened to be the only one who looked over and saw it coming. She didn't even get hurt too badly. Sure, she was limping a little, but nothing serious.

Even if she'd broken her leg, it would probably have been worth it to see Maisie safe. Both her legs. Maybe even more. That idea stopped her in her tracks. She ran the thought through her head for a moment. This must be what it felt like to have siblings, instinctively putting their safety before your own. Had she ever thought that about anyone like this before? She ran through a list of her exes. She wouldn't even risk breaking a nail for any of that sorry crew now. But at the time she was with them? No, maybe not even then. It came as a shock to Molly that in such a short time of being around Ethan again, and knowing his family, that she had developed such an attachment to them all.

She loved the way Ethan interacted with his family. He was their rock and the one person they all revolved around, the centre of their world. And it was making *her* long to be at the centre of Ethan's world. She felt like she didn't even know herself anymore. In fact, it was terrifying, and it made her want to run for the hills.

But she was soon invited out for dinner that night. Molly was toasted at least ten times by various members of the family, and she had a wonderful time. Cosy, safe and appreciated inside the bubble of the James family. Despite that, there was a thread of unease pulling at her all night. Telling her that she wasn't really part of this family, that she'd never really felt part of any family, even her own. That she had been independent for so long that she was probably just enjoying the novelty.

Near the end of the night, it all got a bit too much for her. She excused herself and went out the back door for a breath of fresh air. She was only out there a moment, admiring the clouds her breath made in the cold air, before Ethan joined her.

'I just wanted to say thank you again.'

Molly sighed quietly. She appreciated it, but she'd had enough thank-yous to last a lifetime. 'I'd have done it for anyone.'

The hurt look she detected on Ethan's face before she followed him back inside made her regret her wording, but not her sentiment. She had to regain some distance.

Just after Molly got home, her phone rang and she glanced at the caller ID, expecting to see an unknown number that she would assume was an insurance scam and decline. There were only two people she answered calls from—her mother and her best friend. Molly laughed out loud when she saw Julie's name and the picture of her from first year that she still used for Julie's contact photo. She answered immediately. 'You haven't called me for ages, you miscreant.'

'Lovely to speak to you, too,' said Julie.

'I actually have missed you,' said Molly as an unfamiliar rush of homesickness ran through her at the sound of her oldest friend's voice. She sat down on the end of her bed, relieved to take the weight off her sore leg.

'Aw, likewise. And where in the world might you be today?' Julie teased.

'You know perfectly well I'm in Scotland. You liked my Instagram pictures of the new house. And the donkey.'

Julie snorted a laugh. 'I did. She's adorable. How's Scotland?'

'Cold. And beautiful. I actually feel really good here.'

'Oh, really? You think you might actually stick around, then?'

Julie sounded shocked, and Molly couldn't really blame her. She hadn't spent longer than six months in one place since she'd graduated.

'It's far too soon to tell. But you never know.'

'That's amazing, Molly.'

'And you will never believe who I ran into.' Molly's heart rate sped up as she realised Julie was the one person who would actually understand the magnitude. 'Well, I say ran into… I'm literally working with him every day.'

'Who?'

'Ethan James.'

There was a short silence on the other end of the line. 'The boy that slept with you and then pulled a total Mary Celeste on you?'

Molly had forgotten that was how Julie would remember him. 'Well, yes. But now he's explained why, and believe me it's totally understandable.'

'I'll have to take your word for that.'

'Honestly. It wouldn't feel right telling you the personal details, but I promise you wouldn't blame him, either.'

'Okay, I believe you.' Julie paused. 'So now we know why you're so open to staying!' Molly could hear the smile in her friend's voice.

The evening had turned a little darker while she'd been talking on the phone, and all the windows were lit up in Ethan's house. She really needed to teach him to draw his curtains.

'So what's he like now? Still a ladies' man?' Julie asked.

'Oh, my God, no. He's completely different from how

he was at uni. Well, from how he seemed at uni. I mean, we never really knew him, did we? I'm not so sure he ever really was a ladies' man. I think we just believed the gossip.'

'I suppose so. But he had enough of a reputation that it seemed like we knew every last bloody thing about him, whether we wanted to or not.'

Julie was right. Everyone at uni knew Ethan James. The most handsome eligible man in school. The golden boy, with the pretty face and the come-to-bed eyes. He was rumoured to have slept with half the girls on campus, but Molly never knew if that was true or spread by jealous fellow students.

The night they'd spent together nine years ago had begun sometime after midnight at the tail end of a May Week ball. Somehow, Ethan had lost track of all his friends, and on her way home after a couple of drinks, Molly had discovered him sitting alone on the wet grass under a tree, looking dejected. She'd planned to walk past in elegant silence and say nothing, but she'd tripped on the edge of the path. He'd laughed, then tried to cover it up with a cough, and asked if she was okay.

She'd pointed at the grass next to him and asked, 'Is that seat taken?'

He'd laughed again and looked up at her with those dark, pretty eyes and said, 'Be my guest.'

They'd talked for hours. There was something about the fact that they were both sitting in the dark, and were finally alone together instead of being surrounded by their very disparate friend groups, which allowed them to finally click. He gave her one of his purple woollen gloves to help keep her hands warm, and they ended up going to her room to make some hot chocolate. She'd sobered up by the time she asked him to stay the night, but she was still running on adrenaline when he said yes. The night they spent together had been wonderful. Perfect, in fact. The odd previous fling had been nothing to write home about, awkward, stilted and utterly forgettable. But for some reason, with Ethan, it was everything she'd ever fantasised about from a romantic encounter. He'd even wanted to cuddle afterwards. Another first. And it was just as she was falling asleep, warm and safe in his arms, wondering what aftershave he wore because he smelled delicious, she'd heard him get a phone call. He'd whispered something, then shoved on his boots, left his Joan Jett T-shirt. And she'd never seen him again.

'You never forgot about him, did you?' asked Julie.

Molly almost denied it, but decided at the last minute she was sick of pretending. 'Not for want of trying.'

'Are you sure you didn't know he would be there?'

'Yes, it was a total shock. Apparently, this is the village he was born in, and I guess he's never really wanted to leave.'

'Hmm.' Julie hummed thoughtfully. 'You did sleep with him. And don't think I didn't know about the years-long crush you had on him from afar before that. Maybe you knew where he was from, and you were subconsciously drawn there, even though you consciously forgot.'

'I've missed you using your psychology degree on me.'

'I've got plenty more where that came from.'

'Spare me. I only ever knew he was Scottish. Don't forget. I'd never talked to him properly until that one night when I suddenly had a burst of confidence, and we can blame the white wine spritzers at the ball for that. I certainly never got to know him well enough to find out where his home town was or hear his life story. And after he left, I never exactly got the chance.' Back then, Molly hadn't known Ethan's real reason for leaving. All she could surmise was that the connection she'd thought was there clearly wasn't. Something must have happened for him to leave, and he hadn't even bothered to confide in her what it was, so what they'd shared must have meant nothing to him. She'd always struggled to make connections with people, especially after growing up ignored by her parents, so his rejection stung particularly hard, after having liked him from afar for so long. Their perfect night together had raised her hopes only to have them dashed when he left without a word.

So after Ethan, all through university and even into adulthood, all she pursued were fun relationships with fun people, never going too deep, never allowing herself to catch real feelings. Keeping it shallow and safe. Molly wasn't sure Julie had figured that part out yet. So much for her psychology degree.

'Is he still good-looking?'

'It's not about looks,' said Molly. Ethan's beautiful brown eyes and dark lashes flashed through her mind. His broad shoulders and tanned arms and strong hands and long, elegant fingers.

Julie tutted. 'It can be a bit about looks.'

Molly gave in. 'Let me tell you he has aged like a fine wine.'

Julie laughed delightedly. 'So he's a vet, too? Does he live in the village?'

'Yes. Don't hate me but I can see inside his house right now.'

'Molly! Oh, my God, stop spying on that poor man. Are you in the street?'

'No!' Molly burst out laughing. 'I'm in my bedroom. His house is right opposite mine.'

'Oh, that's handy. Can you see into his bedroom?'

After they both stopped giggling, Molly sighed. 'I can, actually. But I promise I've not looked. That would be wrong.'

'Yes, it would. So, is he single?'

'Yes. And he has three kids.'

'Wow, three?'

'Yeah. They're great. They're his little brothers and sister. He's their primary caregiver. It's complicated.'

'Oh. That's a pretty amazing thing to do.'

'Yeah, it is.'

'And they must be pretty amazing, too. I don't think I've ever heard you describe any kid as great before.'

'I'm a changed woman,' Molly joked.

'Sounds it.'

'Just kidding. I'm still the same old weirdo you know and love.'

'I do love you, and you're not a weirdo,' Julie said softly. 'I know you struggle with the thought of turning into your parents. But you know you're nothing like them. You never could be.'

'I guess.'

'I bet you're wonderful with those kids. You've grown and changed for the better, despite how your parents treated you. It would be a shame if you let your whole future be dictated by their views on children and family.'

'Thanks,' Molly whispered back. 'You know, you and Nick should come up and visit me sometime. I have a spare room now.'

'You really are a new woman.'

'I know! I'll even make sure it has a bed and sheets and everything before you come.'

'Maybe after Christmas?'

'Yes, or over New Year's!'

'Oh, that would be fantastic. I've always wanted to spend New Year's Eve in Scotland.'

'Best place for it.'

'Marvellous, I'll tell Nick in a minute.'

'Love that. Not asking him what he thinks, just telling him where he's spending New Year's.'

'Naturally! He doesn't mind where he is as long as there's a cosy pub and plenty of Guinness.'

When Molly eventually ended the call, she felt lighter and happier than she had in months. She felt something like hope unfurling in her chest. Maybe Julie was right. Maybe she was better than her parents. Maybe she could do this.

CHAPTER SIX

WHEN MOLLY NEXT saw Maisie she was lying on her living room sofa, Kai plumping up a cushion behind her back and Ethan tucking a blanket around her. Molly placed a large bowl of potato salad on the kitchen table, one of the only dishes she knew how to make, as the boys left to prepare for the street party outside. She went back to the living room to see Maisie and perched on the edge of the coffee table to check on her.

'Look at you all comfy. Almost makes me wish I had brothers.' Molly had spent a long childhood wondering what it would be like to have lively brothers she could play games with, or sweet sisters she could share clothes with. Anyone to keep her company, whom she could love and be loved by in return.

'They're not usually like this.'

'I bet.'

'Thank you again, by the way,' said Maisie.

'My pleasure.'

'You literally saved my life.'

'I don't know about that. I'm just glad I was there.'

'Me, too. So is Ethan. He says you're a marvel.'

'He does, does he?' Molly's chest fluttered.

Maisie nodded. 'I think he likes you.'

'Glad to hear it.'

'I mean *likes* you.'

Molly pretended not to know what Maisie meant. 'How are you feeling now? Any pain?'

'They keep saying I've had a shock and I need to rest.' Maisie pulled herself up by grabbing the back of the sofa, and glanced at the door to check none of her brothers were returning. 'Can I tell you a secret?'

'Of course.'

'I'm fine,' she whispered. 'But they keep bringing me snacks and drinks, even without me asking for them. And Harry let me be in charge of the remote.'

'You've never had it so good, huh?'

'Never. I should leap in the path of runaway vehicles more often.'

Molly laughed. 'You'd better be joking.'

'I am. How's your leg, Molly?'

'It doesn't hurt anymore,' she said quietly. 'But do you want to see a really disgusting bruise?'

'Yes!'

Molly showed her the large bright purple bruise spanning her calf, and Maisie seemed appropriately impressed, while also somewhat jealous that she hadn't bruised at all.

Ethan came across and handed Maisie a drink. As Maisie took it, she made a face at Molly as if to say *See?* and Molly tried not to laugh.

'Have you thanked Molly for saving you?'

'Yes, Ethan,' Maisie said, glaring at him.

Molly nodded solemnly. 'She has.'

Ethan left them alone then, but not before he rested his large hands on Molly's shoulders and leaned down to whisper in her ear. 'Thanks for coming to visit her.' He squeezed the back of Molly's neck affectionately as he left, causing shivers to run up and down her spine at his touch.

Molly planned to sit with Maisie for as long as she could, but soon it was time to go home and get changed for the party. Molly was really starting to see how badly her parents had influenced her views on children. She couldn't believe she'd spent so many years dismissing them as something of a nuisance, a presence that would get in the way of a meaningful life, rather than enriching it. Julie had been right; she needed to focus on not letting her parents shape her own views about family.

Suddenly, Ethan's front door slammed open. 'Ethan!' Kai yelled, 'come here, quick.'

Molly jumped up and ran with Ethan to meet Kai, who was closely followed by Harry, holding a cat in his arms.

'We found it lying by the road round the corner by the fields,' Harry said, breathing hard. 'I picked him up really carefully. I didn't hurt him even more, did I?'

Ethan grabbed a towel from the kitchen and reached out to carefully transfer the cat into his own arms. 'Don't worry, Harry.'

'Is it dead?' Maisie cried.

'No, look, it's still breathing,' said Molly. The cat's ribcage was clearly moving steadily in and out, which was a positive sign.

Maisie threw herself at Molly, wrapping her little arms around her waist. Molly rubbed her shoulders and crouched down to get level with her. She pulled her sleeve over her hand and gently wiped Maisie's face, drying away all her tears. 'We'll look after the cat, sweetheart.'

'Is he going to die?'

'We'll do everything we can,' said Ethan. 'We're going to run to the surgery. You three wait here for Aunty Anne.'

Ethan drove them swiftly to the clinic in minutes, throwing his phone to Molly so she could send Anne a quick text explaining what had happened. They rushed into the exam room, where Ethan unwrapped the cat from the towel. 'How's it looking?' asked Molly.

Ethan carried out an initial assessment. 'I think we might be lucky. I'd guess we have one broken leg. He's clearly been hit by a vehicle, but it seems to have been a glancing blow. I don't recognise the cat. He might be a stray.'

There was nothing Molly hated more than people who could hit an animal with their car and then leave them there with no assistance. They gave the cat some pain relief and intravenous fluids.

'There could be bruising to the lungs. We'll have to keep him in, of course,' said Ethan. 'I'll give him blood tests and an X-ray, but hopefully it's just the one fracture in his back leg. Can I have my phone? I want to call the kids, make sure they're okay.'

Molly handed him his phone. He was just as caring and sweet with the animals as he was with the kids. It was very attractive. Molly stroked the sleeping cat while she waited for Ethan to finish his phone call.

The cat had no collar, so she quickly scanned him for a microchip, but found there wasn't one.

'What are you up to?' asked Ethan.

'There's no chip. As soon as he's out of danger I'll look after him at home. If no one claims him I'm happy to keep him. He's a sweet little thing.'

Ethan rolled his eyes. 'You really are trying to rescue every animal on the planet, aren't you?'

Molly shrugged. 'Maybe.'

By the time they made it home from the clinic, Ethan didn't have long until the party would be starting. He reassured Maisie that the cat was going to recover and that Molly was planning to adopt him, and she was back to normal in minutes. 'Can I take flying lessons?' Maisie asked as Ethan placed frozen sausage rolls on a tray and threw them in the oven for the party.

'What do you think?' Ethan answered drily.

'Yes?'

'Absolutely no way.'

'What? Why not?'

'You're too young,' said Ethan. 'And even more importantly, it's literally the most dangerous thing you could possibly have come up with. I don't even like the idea of you learning to drive a car in five years, let alone a plane.'

'Molly does it.'

'Yes, she does. And is Molly my little sister?'

'No.'

'Well, you are. And I will do everything I can to keep you safe.'

'You go in Molly's plane practically every day. Why can't I?'

'It's part of my job. I would never set foot in it if I didn't have to.'

'You like it now, though. I've heard you talking about it.'

That made Ethan pause. Did he like it? He'd been so set on hating it that he hadn't even considered the possibility of feeling anything else. But now he thought about it, he had to admit it had a certain exhilarating effect. Take-off and landing were still a little tense, but being up there, seeing the ocean and fields below him, was pretty wonderful. Even a little thrilling. But that didn't mean he wanted Maisie up there.

'Come here,' he said softly.

Maisie folded her arms and glared at him, refusing to move.

'Please, Maisie.' He held his arms open, and after a minute she must have felt sorry for him because she rolled her eyes and stepped reluctantly into his embrace.

'Once you're a grown-up you can do anything you want to do, and I'm sure you'll do it brilliantly. I won't be able to stop you because you'll be your own person and your own responsibility. And although that scares me to death, I trust you to make good decisions. But until you're a grown-up, it's my responsibility to look after you and make the bigger decisions for you. Does that make sense?'

'I suppose.' She paused and thought before asking, 'When am I a grown-up? What age?'

'Twenty-one?' Ethan took a stab in the dark.

She sighed. 'Great. I'll be an old woman before I get to do anything fun with my life.'

She looked so sad that Ethan couldn't help what came

out of his mouth. 'If you really want to go up in a plane then maybe I can ask, just ask, Molly if she thinks it would be a good idea for us to take you up in her plane one day.'

The screech of joy was directed into his left ear, and he felt equal parts pain and happiness. He laughed as she jumped up and down on the sofa. 'Just *one* trip.'

'Yes, yes, yes!' She continued to bounce joyfully.

Part of him wondered what the hell he was doing letting her try something so dangerous. A while ago he would have scoffed at the very idea of it. But he trusted Molly, and now he'd been up there himself, it just didn't feel as dangerous as it once had. But while he trusted Molly in the sky, he still couldn't trust her with his heart, or Maisie's. Ethan was still convinced she would leave when she felt the pull of the next exciting venture abroad. He remembered again their almost-kiss, and felt an equal mixture of frustration and relief that the kiss hadn't happened. His body might want her more than anything, but his brain was insisting on caution.

'So, am I back in your good books?'

'Yes.' Maisie grinned. Then added, 'For now.'

Ten minutes later, Maisie was back in the kitchen. 'Molly's so cool.'

Ethan nodded, trying to read a magazine article about feline hydration, while the sausage rolls cooked in the oven. It was almost time to take them out.

'She's really pretty too, isn't she?' Maisie said.

Ethan looked up from his article. 'Yes?' Ethan answered hesitantly, getting the feeling Maisie was going somewhere with this that he wasn't going to like.

'Do you like her?'

'Yes, we're friends. Do you like her?' Maybe he could change the subject by turning it back to Maisie.

'Obviously. She's the coolest person I've ever met.'

'Yeah, I think you mentioned that.' She'd only found a way to say it every single day since she'd met the woman.

'I think you should ask her out.'

'I'm not really looking for a partner, Maisie, remember?'

'Why?'

He didn't really want to explicitly remind Maisie about his ex-girlfriend; she was definitely a sore spot for the whole family. 'Well, I'm too busy, for one thing.' He didn't want to mention the fact that even if he was looking, Molly likely wouldn't want a guy with three kids in the house.

'Too busy to go on one date? It only takes an hour to eat a meal.'

'I just... I'm not really looking for romance.'

'Why not?'

'I'm happy just concentrating on spending time with you three and doing my job. That's all I need to be happy.'

'I don't think you are happy.'

'You don't?' Ethan straightened up and put down the magazine. He shifted closer to her. 'I promise you I am. You make me happy.' He bopped her nose and she giggled softly.

'I think you aren't as happy as you could be.'

'I guess if I won the lottery I'd be a little bit happier.'

The doorbell rang and Ethan smiled in relief. Saved by the imminent flood of street party guests.

Various aunts, uncles, neighbours and cousins streamed in over the next hour, leaving bowls and trays of food on Ethan's kitchen counter, and stuffing his fridge full of drinks and meat to grill on the barbecue outside. Molly arrived arm in arm with Aunty Anne herself, giggling about something Ethan didn't even want to ask about. He smiled at the sight of them, heads close, whispering secretively. Sometimes Molly already seemed like one of the family. She fitted right in. Even the kids all liked her, and they rarely agreed on anything. But he still got the sense that she felt skittish at times. As though she still had one foot outside the door. The twins thundered through the house chasing their cousin's white fluffball of a Samoyed into the back garden, shouting hello to Molly as they passed.

A couple of hours later, after Ethan had manned the first shift at the barbecue, and eaten more than his fill of burgers, he headed upstairs to change out of his shirt, which smelled smoky and was covered in grease spatters, then pulled a clean one over his head and joined the others in his living room. There were a few spots free, but he sank into the space next to Molly.

Molly wasn't sure where Ethan had disappeared to, but it was embarrassing that she had even noticed. He'd only been gone five minutes then reappeared in a different shirt. The light blue colour really accentuated his tanned skin and brown eyes. She couldn't help feeling all tingly when he picked the spot right next to her. He lowered his tall frame onto the sofa, and she could feel the warmth radiating off his body, only inches away from hers.

'Maisie said you have something to ask me?' Molly said.

Ethan looked stricken for a moment, but then seemed to remember something and he made a face and shook his head. 'I do. She's got it into her head that she wants to go up in your plane. And somehow, I ended up agreeing to ask you if we could take her up for a quick flight sometime.' He frowned down at his hands. 'Although saying it out loud is making me start to have doubts.'

'No, no, that's a great idea. I'm really proud of you.'

Ethan looked up. 'You are?'

'Yes. You didn't even want to go up yourself on our first flight. Now you're comfortable enough to let Maisie up there with us.'

He shrugged grumpily. 'It's not as bad up there as I thought.'

Molly smiled. He was like a reluctant growling bear. But she found his grouchy protectiveness over Maisie adorable.

'I'll let you tell her the good news next time you see her. I'm surprised she let you out of her sight, to be honest.' Ethan looked around for Maisie.

'She's outside playing with that gorgeous Samoyed dog.'

Ethan nodded and relaxed back into the sofa cushions, his shoulder now touching Molly's. She let herself lean into him a tiny bit, and was pleased to find that he didn't move away.

'Have you had any more thoughts about the D-O-G situation?' asked Aunty Anne.

Ethan groaned and pulled one of the sofa cushions over his face, sinking down into the seat. 'Please don't start bringing that up again.'

'I said it quietly, so none of the kids heard!'

'Very kind of you,' Ethan said drily.

'What's this?' Molly asked, smiling at Ethan's reaction.

'Well,' Anne began, sitting primly on the edge of the armchair. 'I don't know if you heard the terrible news a couple of weeks back, I mean it happened before you moved here, Molly, so maybe you didn't, but sadly a policeman two towns over died in the line of duty.'

'What happened?' Molly was surprised. A police death seemed unusual for such a sleepy place in the Scottish countryside. 'Was he shot?'

'No, it happened on the road. A stolen vehicle crashed into his police car and pushed it off into a valley.'

'Oh, my God, how awful.'

'Terrible. He died immediately.' Anne paused and took a sip from her enormous glass of punch. 'The amazing thing is his police dog was in the car with him.'

'Oh, no.' Molly wasn't sure she wanted to hear the rest of this story.

'No, it has a happy ending. The dog survived with no injuries.'

'Thank goodness.' Molly leaned back in her chair and breathed for what felt like the first time in a full minute.

'And the reason I'm telling you all this is that they've

retired the dog from the force, and they can't find anyone to take him on. I know someone who works there. He's a chocolate Labrador, an ex-drug-detection dog, and has the sweetest little face you can imagine.' She sipped more punch. 'Apparently, when he was a puppy, his foster family noticed that he had above-average intelligence and they put him forward for police training. The trainer agreed and he passed his training in three months flat. He was always a bit too friendly for the force, but he was paired up with a police officer and he served them impeccably for ten years. Then the poor thing's owner died in that crash.'

'Aunty Anne, don't you think I've got enough to juggle here without adding a dog to the list?'

'She wants you to take him on?' Molly asked, barely able to hold her smile of disbelief in.

Ethan looked at her quizzically. 'Yes, what's so weird about that?'

Molly shrugged. 'I don't know. It's just hard to imagine a pet-hating vet adopting a dog.'

'Aha!' Anne held up her finger victoriously. 'That's why this dog would be perfect. He's police trained, so he wouldn't be as boisterous as your average dog. Plus, he's getting older now, so he'll be calmer. And the kids have been begging you for a dog for the last nine years.'

'I know.' He sighed. 'And it's not as if I don't feel guilty about it. Especially back when I first got them. Of course they wanted something soft and comforting to cuddle, after everything that they'd just been through. But all I could think about was what if something happened?

They'd already lost their parents…what if I got them a pet and then it got sick, or ran away? I couldn't risk it.'

Anne reached over and patted his knee. 'I never realised that was the reason, sweetheart. That makes sense.'

'And I always let them come in and visit the animals at work,' Ethan said defensively, although he seemed to be losing steam and sounding a little doubtful about his decision. 'They're around animals all the time. It's not like I'm refusing them the joy of being around animals.'

'It's not the same as having a family pet of their own, though,' said Aunty Anne. 'Anyway, it's your decision. Just wanted you to know all the information.'

Anne left the room to get more punch. And Ethan scratched his nose and looked over at Molly to find her watching him. 'What?'

'Sometimes it's healthier to take the risk than not take it.'

'Risks? You're one to talk.'

'What does that mean?'

'Nothing. Just that you're clearly not prepared to take a risk yourself by letting kids into your life. And to be honest, I'm not quite sure why you have an issue with that in the first place.'

Molly frowned. How dare he say something like that? He didn't know anything about her life, or her past. 'The risk of taking on an older dog is not the same as committing to a life with children.'

Ethan flinched and pulled away from her. They glared at each other for a long moment, then both seemed to remember at the same time that they were in the middle of a house full of people who could rejoin them at any moment. Some of the tension between them lessened, but it didn't disappear.

Ethan narrowed his eyes. 'Are you going to walk the risk for me when all three kids get bored of it?'

Molly smiled coolly. 'Maybe it can join me and my donkey.'

Ethan shook his head and covered his eyes with the cushion again.

'Seriously though, if you don't want him, and no one else has any plans to, I'll take him.'

'Molly, you can't take in every single waif and stray. You'll have your own zoo soon. You can't rescue everything. Sometimes you just have to be realistic.'

'Forget realistic,' said Molly. 'Why can't I rescue everything? Who makes these rules? It's like when you watch a nature documentary, there's this accepted fact that they mustn't intervene. If a baby rabbit they've been following for a month is about to get eaten by a fox, they have to just document it and let it happen. Well, if I was there, that fox is getting chased off and that baby's getting saved.'

'But then what is Mummy Fox going to feed Baby Fox?' asked Ethan.

Molly snorted a reluctant laugh. 'I know. I get what you're saying. Maybe I'd drop off some nice steaks at the foxes' den. But it's the principle that annoys me. *You can't save everything...you have to let things suffer.* No. You really don't. If you can help, you should help.'

'That's very admirable,' Ethan said. 'Although, what would happen to the animals you take in when you—?'

Molly frowned. 'What? Crash my plane and die in a huge fireball?'

'What? No, I didn't mean that.'

'Then what did you mean?'

'You know. When you decide to…move on.'

'Who says I'm moving on?'

'No one,' Ethan said. But that was clearly how he thought of her. She was just here for now. Just *temporary*. Ethan frowned and looked away, clearly unwilling to carry on the conversation since it wasn't going anywhere. Molly was left with a sinking heart. He was only telling her what she already knew—that she didn't have a good track record of sticking around. Her good feeling after the conversation with Julie trickled away as she lost the confidence she'd found in herself that had told her maybe she could do this if she really wanted to. Did she even want to? When would she know?

As it got darker, they'd moved the party outside to enjoy the decorations. There were fairy lights in all the trees, and the pumpkins had been arranged to line the edge of the road and decorate every front path on the street. Any that were left over were arranged on peoples' front steps or dotted along the tops of garden walls. Somehow, it looked even more beautiful this year than it usually did.

Things were still tense between them since their argument. They needed space away from each other so Ethan retained his distance, but he kept an eye on Molly as his family swarmed around her, offering her food and asking her questions. He knew they could be a bit much. He was back in place at the barbecue before long, and it was time to give the meat one last turn. It would be ready in a couple of minutes. He tried not to stare at Molly, but listened while Kai and Harry peppered her with questions.

'Could you land a plane on the sea?'

'I was briefly trained to use a seaplane, yes. But I've never had the opportunity to try it since. And I couldn't land my usual plane in the sea, unless it was an emergency landing. We would probably sink. Quickly.'

'Can you loop the loop?'

'I can.'

Ethan found that weirdly sexy. Although it would be the opposite of sexy if she ever did it with him in the plane. In fact, she'd better have a good supply of airsickness bags in the plane.

'The Australian guy who first taught me used his plane to herd cattle. You had to do some pretty acrobatic stuff to get them to go where you wanted.'

'Wow. Can we come up in your plane?'

'You'll have to ask Ethan.'

'Could you land on a road?'

'Yes, as long as there were no bridges or power lines.'

'Or traffic.'

'Yep, good call. Cars don't like it when you land on them.'

'Have you ever crashed?'

'Not really. Had a few rough landings. One time I narrowly avoided colliding with a rhino.'

'You're lying!' Kai shouted gleefully.

'I am not!'

'Boys, please, give her a break,' Ethan called out.

***

Ethan had connected his laptop to a set of speakers in the living room and put them over by the open window facing out. He'd set a playlist of music to play while people hung out in the front garden and over the street, but it was just loud enough to be background noise. He spotted Maisie fiddling with something over by his laptop, and sure enough a few minutes later the volume went up and Taylor Swift blared out.

Maisie jumped up and down in delight, and started dancing immediately in that carefree way kids could still master. Then she headed straight over to Molly. When Ethan saw her grab Molly's hands and try to pull her up from her garden chair, he got up. Molly looked like she needed saving. But before he could reach them, Molly hopped up and let Maisie pull her to a free space, then started dancing happily to the music with Maisie.

Ethan stayed put. Clearly, she didn't need his help after all. He came to a stop by the food table and grabbed a skewer of chicken and sweet potato. As he ate, he couldn't help but watch Molly as she spun around with his little sister, Molly's blond curls swinging around her shoulders. He couldn't bear to think how Maisie was going to feel if, or when, Molly left. He could slowly feel the ground opening up beneath his feet all over again.

Molly danced so easily. If Ethan tried that he'd have someone's eye out, never mind the fact that he'd cause everyone in the area to die from embarrassment. But on her, dancing just looked so natural and cool. People were even joining in. He snorted with disbelief as even Harry and Kai grabbed some of the younger kids and added themselves to the fray.

'She's a special one,' his great-uncle said, nudging a cold beer into Ethan's free hand. 'You literally couldn't wipe that soppy smile off your face if you tried, could you?'

Ethan snorted. 'Very funny.' He hadn't even noticed that he was smiling, but it was true; his cheeks actually ached a bit from it. How long had it been since he'd been made to feel this happy? And just by watching someone dancing for goodness' sake. Seeing her happy, and his siblings happy, made his heart feel like it had grown three sizes. He wasn't supposed to be like this. He was supposed to be concentrating on work and kids. That was it.

The last time he'd felt anything like this was with his ex, Carrie. And everyone knew how that ended. But had he felt as happy as this with her? No, if he was honest with himself—it didn't even compare. Carrie had gotten on well with the twins and especially Maisie, who had taken their break-up harder than Ethan had himself. She'd been sad and quiet for months after Carrie had left. But Ethan was sure Carrie had never quite felt like one of the family, like Molly did. Did that mean that things with Molly could be different? Or did it simply mean that he would fall that much harder when this all went south and she inevitably left? He was terrified at the thought of history repeating itself, with his heart bruised yet again and the kids upset. Should he pull his family back, out of Molly's orbit, to protect them? Or should he have some kind of conversation with Molly about the importance of not letting his kids down? He had absolutely no idea where to go from here. Should he risk everything and just kiss Molly like he longed to, or leave well enough alone?

Dancing with Maisie and the kids had wiped Molly out. Maybe she wasn't quite as fit as she used to be. Or the painkillers she'd taken for her leg had worn off. She sat down in the kitchen, where most of Ethan's family was, to get her breath back.

Aunty Anne and her husband knocked her for six when they joined her and invited her in advance for Christmas dinner. Molly looked to Ethan to see if he looked horrified at the idea. But he smiled and nodded. 'It's a whole big event. There'll be dozens of people there. But plenty of room for you to join.'

Molly's own parents liked a quiet Christmas; they were quite elderly now. They'd never made a huge deal of it, even when she was a kid. It was more about going to church than presents and Santa Claus. She hadn't been able to get home for three out of the past five, and honestly, they hadn't seemed to mind too much. Her parents always went out for a quiet Christmas dinner at the local pub and spent the day with their friends. They wouldn't miss her, and she could always visit in between Christmas and New Year's if they did.

Molly smiled. 'If you're really sure, I'd love to.'

Aunty Anne handed out yet more punch from her seemingly never-ending supply.

'Harry wants to be a vet when he's older, don't you?'

'I want to be an emu farmer now,' Harry said.

'That's unusual,' said Molly. 'I like it.'

'Why did you go off the idea of following in Ethan's footsteps?' asked Aunty Anne.

'I don't want to put animals down. Ethan hates doing it.'

So did Molly. You never got used to it. 'You know, there are other important jobs you can do at a surgery that aren't being a vet,' said Molly.

'Like what?'

'We need someone to come in and help with the overnight stays.'

'What are they?' asked Harry.

'The pets who need to stay overnight so we can keep an eye on them, or for operations and treatment. Studies have shown that animals heal better and faster if they're read to.'

'Read to?'

'Yep, how would you like to come and read to some cats and dogs and rabbits?'

'What would I read?'

'Anything. Your favourite book, a newspaper. They just like the company and the sound of your voice.'

Harry agreed shyly, and Ethan ruffled his hair, looking pleased. Molly was glad she hadn't overstepped the mark inviting Ethan's brother to work. Sometimes she spoke before she thought, but they both looked pretty happy about her idea.

Molly couldn't help but compare Ethan's family to her own. Her childhood had been pretty lonely, and she'd always dreamed of having a brother or sister. This was what she had always imagined having a big family would be like. Always someone to chat to, lots of noise and action and laughter. Everyone stopping by each other's houses with no warning. Everyone on the street was friendly and outgoing. Like *The Waltons* meets *Gilmore Girls*. She never thought she'd live in a place like this. To be honest, she'd never wanted to. She had always valued her privacy. She never really liked to mix social groups together; she would never have spent time with her friends and her family in the same room. She'd always liked to keep things compartmentalised. Maybe because she always felt like she was a different Molly with different people. Fun-loving Molly with her friends, studious, successful Molly with her parents. Who would she be if those people were all together?

But here, with these people, she was just Molly. And honestly, she'd never felt so comfortable or accepted, or more like herself. But there was something big missing. Ethan. After their argument earlier in the evening, she was still feeling a sense of disquiet. She longed to talk to Ethan privately to try to sort it out, make him understand what she was thinking and feeling, although that might be a little difficult when she wasn't entirely sure herself. She was starting to get the sense that she might have been viewing family through the prism of a difficult childhood, but now, through Ethan, she'd seen what being part of a large family could be like. And it was making her rethink everything.

Back at her house alone after the party had dispersed, she lit some candles and gazed out at the street. There were still a few stragglers out there sitting on garden chairs, listening to music at a low volume. She could faintly hear people talking and laughing. The fairy lights still lit everything in a soft glow, coloured light dancing off the dozens of orange and multicoloured pumpkins lining people's garden paths and porches.

Out of the stragglers came a shape, a man walking over the road and up her drive. A decidedly Ethan-shaped man.

'I brought you a peace offering,' said Ethan gruffly, brandishing an armful of boxes at her front door.

'Not more punch?'

He laughed once. 'No. I think Aunty Anne finally finished that off.' He handed Molly three Tupperware tubs in various sizes and shapes.

'Thank you, this is great. You didn't have to do this.'

'It wasn't just that… We didn't really get to say goodbye properly.'

'You came all the way over here just to say goodbye?'

He shrugged his broad shoulders again. 'And goodnight.'

Molly put the boxes down on a side table and put her hands in her pockets.

Ethan took a step closer and then hesitated. 'Molly…' he murmured.

Molly closed her eyes against the wave of arousal that hit her when she heard him say her name in that deep voice with a hint of frustration.

Ethan reached out and gently tugged her hands from her pockets, then held them in his, stroking his thumbs lightly over the backs of her hands. She watched as he swallowed, a flicker of indecision in his eyes as he weighed up the pros and cons, before his resolve settled, his desire flared and he smoothly pulled her into his arms. He leaned down and captured her lips in a hungry kiss. Molly moaned into his mouth as he pressed against her. Her hands found their way into his hair, and Ethan's hands seemed to grab anything they could. He gripped her waist, then ran his hands desperately all the way up her back until he cupped the back of her head. He delicately kissed the sensitive skin on her neck and it sent shivers down her spine.

She could happily stay right here and do this for the rest of her life. Suddenly, that thought sent a flash of panic surging through her. She was being too vulnerable. This would turn out to be a mistake; it always did. She couldn't let him do this to her again. She couldn't handle being left by Ethan twice, even if he did have a good reason the first time. She'd been rejected by her parents and then everyone else she'd ever tried, and failed, to connect with. Her panic started to spiral.

It was safer for them to be friends. It made more sense. They had to work together, fly together. He had three kids, for goodness' sake. What did she know about bringing up children? Nothing! She only knew what it was like to fail, with her parents as an example. She couldn't get involved with that. It was too much.

Or was it? Maybe she was wrong.

But it was too late. Ethan had sensed her retraction and he was already pulling away.

'I'm sorry, was that too much?' Ethan asked.

'Maybe. I don't know. I don't know if this is a good idea...'

He looked absolutely mortified. 'I'm sorry, I misunderstood. I won't touch you again.' He took a step away from her, then turned back meeting Molly's eyes. He stared for a moment as if confused by what he saw in them. 'Unless you ask me to,' he said softly. Then strode away, down her path and across the road back to his house.

CHAPTER SEVEN

ON MONDAY MORNING Molly couldn't bear the thought of running into Ethan, so she did the mature thing. She hid.

Molly hid in everyone's favourite room in a veterinarian surgery—the overnight ward. Everyone that was except infamous pet-hating vet Ethan. Of all the places at work, Molly concluded this was the place she was least likely to run into him.

There were two sibling domestic shorthair kittens in the same cage. One ginger-and-white-striped, and one white all over. They started mewing madly as soon as she entered the room. She grinned. 'Hi, babies, you wanna play?'

She had ten minutes before her shift started, and she'd already done all her checks on the plane, which was sitting prepped and ready in the hangar. She unlocked the cage and carefully placed a hand under each tiny warm belly, lifting both the kittens out. She sank down onto the linoleum floor and let them play with the woolly strands on the end of her scarf. She cooed over their tiny ferocious white teeth and little pink noses as they play-attacked each other, then the scarf, then her hand.

Then the door clicked open, and the one person she'd been trying to avoid walked right in.

'What are you doing here?'

She hadn't meant to sound so accusatory, and he frowned, looking grumpy, and reminding her of the Ethan she met when she first arrived. Then he hid his hand behind his back. 'Nothing.'

'What are you holding?'

'Nothing,' he repeated.

'Why are you being so secretive?'

He rolled his eyes and reluctantly brought his hand forward and opened his fist. He revealed a pink cat on a string. 'I got them a new toy.'

He was so sweet. Molly sighed, dismayed that she'd lost that connection with Ethan that had been tentatively growing.

Things were slightly less awkward between them for the rest of the day. But there was still a tension lingering. A wall had gone back up, and Molly wasn't sure how to knock it down. He was being distant and withdrawn, giving her space. Never standing too close, taking care not to touch her. Which was what she thought she wanted. She'd gotten herself into this mess by doubting their kiss. Now she missed the Ethan she was getting to know all over again. She was just trying her best to protect her own heart from getting hurt once more.

The next morning, Molly forced herself to wake up as she loaded her coffee machine and squinted at the buttons. She'd already showered and dressed on autopilot, but she still felt half-asleep. She tapped her radio to switch on the local station and hoped their usual mix of country and pop music would finally break through the fog in her brain, even if it did result in bad music-induced rage. But what she heard woke her up in one second flat. They weren't playing music at all. They were reporting a warning for a big storm headed for the west coast of Scotland. It was coming straight from Bermuda, where it had originated as a hurricane and had already killed hundreds of people.

Molly forwent her coffee altogether as she pulled on her coat and ran across the road to Ethan's house. The grey clouds only sent down a blanket of drizzle for now, but as she squinted into the sky, the tops of the trees were already swaying in a significantly strong wind. Molly flew up Ethan's steps and rapped on his front door.

He answered it whilst talking on the phone, and after a moment of staring, held up a finger to Molly, mouthing, 'One second.'

Molly nodded and stepped inside, focusing her attention on the wall in the hallway, covered in kids' drawings, to at least give the impression that she wasn't listening to his conversation. But she couldn't help hearing every word, since he was standing right next to her and had made no move to step away. She couldn't help but relive their kiss in her head. The taste of his lips and the feel of his hands in her hair.

She tried to take her mind off it. She concentrated on his phone call. She could almost hear the voice at the other end. Not enough to make out words, but enough to recognise it as Jon.

'Yeah, it's heading in fast,' Ethan said into the phone, then paused to let Jon answer.

'I heard ninety-mile-an-hour coastal winds, with hundred-mile-an-hour gusts.'

Ethan waited then replied again. 'Worst storm we've had in years, decades maybe. Hopefully, the house will be okay, our street is so protected, but I want to board up the windows at the surgery, at least the big ones that face the ocean, since it's coming in from the west.'

He nodded at Jon's response. 'Okay, I'll be over there soon.'

He hung up the phone. 'You heard about the storm?' Ethan was still a little distant, but Molly could see that he was trying to focus on the matter at hand. She realised with a pang that she might have done too much damage for them to ever recover a good working relationship again.

'I thought I'd left extreme weather behind me.'

'No, it can get pretty bad up here. The schools are closing for the day, so I've dropped the kids off at Aunty Anne's. I don't want them home alone. So now we need to head to the surgery and, well, I'm sure you heard the rest.'

Molly attempted to smile. 'You caught me.' Her smile wasn't reciprocated, so she switched to being practical and professional, ignoring her bruised heart. 'Does this happen a lot?'

'We've only resorted to boarding up windows once before. That had to be five…six years ago now? But they reckon this storm will be worse.'

By the time they arrived at the surgery, Jon was already outside with a stack of plywood boards and a tool kit by his feet. The wind was a lot sharper and colder now they were near the ocean.

'Maybe we should close for the day, except to emergencies. What do you think?' asked Molly.

'Yeah, good idea,' said Ethan. 'I'll get Lara to postpone any nonemergency appointments, then I'll send her home.' Molly started helping Jon while Ethan rushed inside to do just that.

'Watch out for splinters,' Jon said as they each grabbed one end of a sheet of plywood and propped it up on the sill below the first window.

'I should have brought my gloves.' As Molly eyed the ancient hammer Jon fished out of his old toolbox, she wished she'd brought her tools as well. Her dad, as distant as he was, had always taught her to get the best quality equipment she could realistically afford, whether that was a stethoscope, a spanner or a casserole dish. Either way, she just hoped Jon's hammer would last till they got this place boarded up.

Ethan reappeared. 'Lara's a star. I told her she could go home, but she wants to stay with the pets. Keep them company, make sure they don't get scared.'

'Have I ever said how much I love her?' asked Molly.

Ethan laughed a little, despite himself. 'She's one of the best.'

Molly held the board in place, pressing the edge down as firmly as she could, and gazed at Ethan as he concentrated on the job at hand. Hope began to spark inside her that maybe Ethan could forgive her for hurting him and giving him mixed messages. He made quite the picture as he hammered nails in, hair whipping against his face. He squinted against the freezing rain, holding the next nail between his teeth, and heaved the next board into place, hammering the last few nails in carefully to secure it.

'That'll have to be good enough.'

Ethan burst into the staff room where Molly was making coffees and trying to warm up next to the radiator. 'We got an emergency call from Winnie. But Jon couldn't understand what she was saying. All he got was that maybe a wall has come down, and some animals might be injured or trapped.'

Molly dropped her spoon onto the counter. 'Let's get going.'

'We have to let the storm blow over first. There's nothing we can do now.'

'Of course there is. We can get to her and help the animals now.'

'We can't fly in this, Molly.'

'I've flown in much higher winds than this.' Molly wasn't sure that was precisely true, but she'd certainly flown in winds equally as strong. Yes, it had been a little treacherous, but she was a good pilot; she'd landed the plane. And she could do it again.

Ethan stared out at the storm clouds and the trees bending in the wind. 'We can't.'

'I can.' Molly grabbed her keys and pulled her jacket on, then rushed out the door, only to be stopped by a large, firm hand on her arm. He immediately pulled it away as if she'd burned him. Molly rolled her eyes. Was he seriously keeping that stupid vow of not touching her, even now?

'Molly.'

She pulled her hair out from underneath the collar of her jacket and stayed close to him, so he could hear her shout over the noise of the wind and rain. 'I understand that you can't risk it. You have kids to look after. It makes sense for you to stay here. But I don't. I can't leave Winnie on her own. She'll be outside in this trying to save the animals herself. You know she will.'

Molly left Ethan standing in the rain and strode towards her plane. Her mind was already racing with the route and what she would do to make sure she landed safely.

A moment after she slammed the plane door shut and grabbed her headphones, the passenger door opened and Ethan jumped in, along with a shower of rain and wind.

'Obviously, I'm coming with you.' He grumpily grabbed his shoulder harness and clicked it into place.

Molly wiped the rain from her face and stared at him. The swell of relief she felt that he was joining her shocked her, but she didn't know what to say when things were still so strange between them. So she fell back into the bickering they'd recently gotten used to. It was much easier to understand. 'Don't do me any favours.'

He avoided her gaze and glared through the windscreen. 'Let's just get going.'

She studied her GPS nav/com screen. 'The storm is travelling west to east. From Winnie's farm towards us. It's already hit her and left. I'm going to try to fly around the worst of it, then approach Winnie's farm from behind the storm. We should be fine.'

As confused as Molly still was over what had happened between them, for a moment she had to fight to keep a smile off her face. Not just because she wanted him with her, but Ethan joining her meant that maybe he was losing some of that fear of taking risks he'd built up over the years they'd been apart. Which gave her double the reason to make absolutely sure nothing happened to him. She was going to precision fly this plane and give him a textbook landing if it was the last thing she did. And despite that unfortunate turn of phrase, she tucked away her feelings, turned the ignition and started taxiing out onto the runway.

'You might want to close your eyes. This is going to be bumpy.'

CHAPTER EIGHT

ETHAN HAD JUST started to get used to flying, was maybe even beginning to enjoy it. So it was a terrible time to experience a storm. All the ease and confidence he'd built up inside Molly's plane went right out the window as they climbed closer to the ferocious charcoal clouds.

In any case, his worries about the storm took second place to his preoccupation over what had happened with Molly. He was still mortified about the kiss, and hurt that she'd rejected him. He hoped the whole mess hadn't hastened her desire to leave. He was almost grateful to the storm for providing a distraction so they wouldn't have to talk about it.

He hadn't realised how much they touched day to day, how close they had gotten in such a short space of time. Trying to avoid that touch was a full-time job in itself. Making sure to take one step away from her every time they were in the same room. Being careful not to touch hands when he passed her something at work. And most difficult of all, avoiding bumping shoulders or thighs when they were trapped in the plane together. But he had to continue to try. He wanted her to know that they could work together even if she wasn't interested in him. He couldn't risk chasing her away. He didn't want to be the reason she left even earlier than she was probably going to. Her pulling away had only cemented that feeling. The other reason was less important but all encompassing. He knew that one touch would drive him crazy, and if she was the one to pull away it would put a crack in his already bruised heart. He sighed and reminded himself that he'd recovered from romantic disappointment once, with Carrie, and he could do it again if he had to. Even though, deep down, if he was honest with himself, he knew he was in far more trouble with Molly than he'd ever been with Carrie. And that was probably a sign that he should have held Molly at an even greater distance right from the get-go.

They flew around the storm without too much turbulence. Ethan saw flashes of lightning in the distance, far enough away that it didn't worry him too much. And when they reached the now familiar runway by Winnie's farm, they both looked down to see what damage had occurred. At least five trees had come down, and everything looked like it had been thoroughly thrown around. But at least from their viewpoint, the house and major outbuildings still seemed to be standing.

They landed bumpily, Molly making sure to avoid the stray branches that lay all over the field, having been torn off the trees by the gales. They came to a stop, jumped out of the plane and rushed towards the farm.

Molly was right; the worst of the storm seemed to have passed. But freezing-cold rain still lashed down unrelentingly, and the wind was constant, with gusts that almost made Ethan lose his footing.

They tried Winnie's house first. Ethan rapped his

knuckles on her front door with no response, then knocked on the kitchen window. Molly pressed her face against the glass, cupping her hands around her eyes to block out the reflections. 'She's not in there.'

'You head that way, I'll go this way and we'll meet around the other side,' instructed Ethan. He and Molly split up, and he ran through the courtyard towards the hay barns and the outbuildings. The place was a mess. Hay bales had blown down and were scattered all over the place, distressed cows were wandering freely and chickens huddled in corners together, trying to keep warm. A trailer had blown over and was lying on its side. There were several roof tiles missing, and the top of the chimney was missing entirely, but at least the rest of the house looked undamaged. But where the hell was Winnie? Ethan's chest tightened.

Ethan shouted Winnie's name, but his voice was whipped away by the wind. Then he rounded the corner. First, he saw Molly, then he followed her shocked gaze. What had once been the front wall of Winnie's stables was now a huge pile of brick-red rubble. And there was Winnie, right on top of it.

Molly was right, as usual, and Winnie had taken it upon herself to save her animals singlehandedly. She had climbed up onto a pile of bricks and was tugging them up and throwing them onto the yard behind her. She stopped momentarily to push her wet hair behind her ears and happened to catch sight of them. He thought he saw a flicker of relief on her face before she admonished them. 'You flew here? In this weather? Are you crazy?'

'It's smoother up there than it looks,' Molly shouted over the sound of the wind.

Ethan held his tongue, but you could have fooled him. If the pilot had been anyone other than Molly, he'd never have set foot in that plane. He jumped up and joined Winnie in grabbing bricks and tossing them out of the way. 'Who are we looking for?'

'Twenty head of sheep and my two Gloucester Old Spot pigs. I moved them inside the stables for safety. Then the wall fell in, blocking the doors. If they die, it's all my fault.'

'They won't die,' said Molly, climbing up to help.

'You can't promise that, Molly,' warned Ethan.

They all fell silent and concentrated on tackling the rubble. For a few minutes, aside from grunts of exertion, all Ethan heard was the wind and rain, the lowing of confused cattle and the occasional bleat from the sheep inside. At least they knew some were still alive in there, if not uninjured.

Ethan pulled some more wet bricks out, and finally made a hole through to the stable. He crouched down to peer through. 'Looks like they're all huddled together on the undamaged side. If we make this hole bigger, I can drop through and take a closer look.'

'We don't want you getting injured as well,' said Winnie.

'I'll be fine.' Ethan untucked his T-shirt and used the dry end to wipe his soaking wet face. It would help if he could see properly.

'Just don't fall on one of the sheep, for God's sake,' muttered Molly quietly.

She scraped her hair back, now dark brown it was so

wet, and somehow twisted it into itself and tied it into a knot on the back of her head in one practiced move.

'Oh, I was planning to aim for one for a soft landing,' Ethan said drily and equally quietly. She grinned at him. He smiled back, pleased that at least they were managing to put aside their own conflicts and work well together in the face of this disaster. His heart lifted for a moment before he sternly reminded himself that Molly had already given him a very clear indication that anything more than a professional relationship between them was off the table. And he had to respect that.

They slowly made the hole bigger, until Ethan could climb down and drop the few feet to the ground. It felt marginally warmer down there, thanks to the straw-covered floor. He smiled at Winnie's two pigs, both fast asleep. One sheep bleated at him inquisitively, and he worked his way through the flock, checking each one as best he could. Twelve sheep and seven lambs, seemingly safe and well. That meant one was missing.

'You said twenty sheep?' he called in the direction of the hole.

'Yes,' answered Winnie. 'How many do you see?'

'Nineteen. Just hold on a second.'

One of the sheep he'd already counted was standing away from the others, sniffing and pushing at the fallen bricks with her nose. Ethan rushed over and carefully moved the bricks, trying not to cause a Jenga-like collapse. Underneath, he found a bucket of feed and the twentieth sheep. A young lamb had managed to end up in a pocket of space between the bucket and the fallen bricks. Ethan thought he was unharmed, but as he got up, he bleated and limped towards his mother, favouring his front right leg. Ethan cursed softly and picked him up before he made it worse by walking on it.

'I've got an injured lamb,' he called up. 'But everyone else seems fine.'

Molly and Winnie had widened the hole farther and Ethan passed the lamb gently up to Molly. 'Winnie, how about you take him indoors and keep him warm, and we'll get the others out. Watch his leg.'

One by one, Ethan passed up each sheep and lamb to Molly and she set them free into the courtyard. The pigs were a little more difficult, and Ethan ended up making a sling out of his sweater. With a lot of manoeuvring, everyone got out safe. Ethan scrambled out last.

Winnie had managed to herd all the sheep into the barn where they could stay and keep warm for a while. She poured some food into the trough inside, then insisted Molly and Ethan come in the house for a hot drink.

Ethan could use one. He was soaking wet and cold, and the adrenaline from helping twenty-two animals through a hole in the roof was starting to wear off.

The wind howled around them as they rushed indoors to the safety of Winnie's kitchen. It was a relief to close the door behind them and shut out the weather outside.

Ethan joined Molly at the kitchen table where he could feel the warmth from the fireplace crackling in the corner. It was a huge kitchen, but the yellow walls and warm oak furniture gave it a comforting, cosy feel.

Ethan noticed the lights were on. 'You didn't lose power, then?'

'I lost it when the storm started, but it came back on not long ago. I've always got the generator if it goes off again.'

'Do you have plenty of food? Do you need anything?'

'Trust me. I'm set for an apocalypse.'

The injured lamb sat on a blanket on one end of the huge wooden kitchen table. It bleated at Ethan mournfully. 'I know, little man. Let's get you fixed up.'

He gave the lamb as thorough an examination as he could. 'I suspect his metacarpal bone could be fractured.'

'Do you want to take him back to the surgery with us?' asked Molly.

'Can we take him in the plane?'

'Sure. I'm planning to make the plane more accommodating to take emergency cases to and from surgery at some point. But this time he'll have to travel on your lap. Can you handle that?'

'I think I'll manage. In the meantime, let's make him a splint for the journey.' Ethan helped the lamb sit back down on his blanket, where he seemed fairly happy to stay. 'Winnie, do you have a spare cardboard tube from a roll of kitchen paper?'

Winnie nodded. 'I'll get you one.'

While Ethan gave the lamb an injection of painkiller, Molly pulled out some cotton wool and a roll of pink vet wrap bandage from her bag and passed them both to Ethan. He wrapped the lamb's leg carefully in cotton wool, then cut down the edge of the cardboard tube, fitted it around the leg to keep it straight, then wrapped it well with the vet wrap. The bandage was designed to only stick to itself so he didn't need to fasten it with anything. 'There. That should do until we get him back to the surgery.'

'Your roof is going to need some work, and the chimney,' said Ethan.

Winnie sighed. 'I saw. God knows where I'll get the money for that.'

'I know my way around a roof, and I know a few people who'll want to join me,' said Ethan, thinking of his surgery coworkers plus a few practically minded neighbours whom he knew wouldn't want to leave a local in need without help. Since Molly and her plane had come along, distance meant less. Winnie felt like as much of a neighbour to him as the people next door on his own street. Their circle of familiarity had widened. Ethan wondered what would happen to this newfound sense of community if Molly left. He would definitely make sure to talk to Jon and encourage him to find a new pilot if that were to arise, because even if it wasn't Molly, it was clearly a service their vet practice needed to provide. But it felt terrible to think about it not being Molly.

'I helped build a surgery from scratch in Zambia,' Molly piped up. 'I'm pretty good with a drill and a handsaw.'

'You're both very sweet,' said Winnie. 'But I'm not sure if this might be a sign.'

'A sign of what?'

'That it's time I retired.'

Ethan and Molly shared a look as Winnie placed a steaming mug of coffee in front of each of them.

'What would you do instead?'

Winnie sighed. 'I always wanted to pass the farm down

to one of my boys. But as I mentioned before, neither of them are interested. I used to hope they'd carry on after me and run the place, or have children who'd want to, but no. I swore I'd never sell a stitch of land to a developer, but there has been one sniffing around, and now I'm wondering if it might be best.'

'I know what it's like being stuck with a house that needs work.'

Molly looked quizzically at him. 'But your house is lovely?'

'It's a little small for us now, plus I'm pretty sure the whole roof needs doing. It's not urgent, but it's always hanging over my head, knowing I'll have to get it done sometime. There's just always something else that needs doing first.'

'With three kids, I'm not surprised.'

Ethan and Molly spent the time it took to drink their coffees trying to help Winnie brainstorm different solutions to her problem. But really all it came down to was finding someone to buy the place and take it on as it was, warts and all, or letting a developer have it. It broke Ethan's heart to think of the whole beautiful property being flattened and turned into a huge house estate or a golf course.

After washing his and Molly's mugs in the sink, Ethan told Winnie it was time they got the lamb back to the surgery.

'Thanks for all your help,' Winnie said. 'I couldn't have done it without you.'

'It's what we're here for.'

'Wait. I'll get you some milk for the lamb.' Winnie quickly prepared Ethan a bottle of milk with a teat.

'Thanks. We'll get him back to you as soon as we can.'

Ethan scooped up the lamb and tucked it inside his coat, before stepping outside where they were soaked to the skin within seconds.

'It feels like it's gotten worse again.'

'It's just a squall,' said Molly.

'Are you sure you don't want to fly back with us and wait out the storm there?' Ethan asked Winnie.

'No offence, but there's no way I'm getting inside that thing. Besides, I don't want to leave the animals. I'll be fine. I've been out here for far worse storms.'

Ethan could believe it. She'd been living out here for decades. He felt bad leaving her, but she insisted that was what she wanted, and to be honest, despite trusting Molly implicitly, he wasn't entirely convinced Winnie wouldn't be safer at the farm than in a plane in this weather.

'Maybe we should stay, too.'

Molly, to give her credit, didn't disagree immediately. She looked up at the sky for a long minute, searching for what, Ethan didn't know. But after taking in the clouds and the wind, and doing some kind of calculations or pilot magic in her brain, she shook her head. 'No, I think I can fly underneath it.'

'Underneath it?'

'The lightning's stopped. I think the safest route is beneath the storm.'

Ethan shrugged, ready to put his life in her hands yet again and just be done with this day. 'Okay.'

They sprinted to the plane, and Ethan supported the

lamb snugly in one large hand as he used the other to grab the door frame and pull himself into the aircraft. Once in his seat, he grabbed the seat belt then settled back. 'You cold, little man?' He pulled the lamb more firmly against his chest and wrapped his scarf around it, tucking it in gently. He could feel its little heartbeat thrumming against his chest.

And soon, Ethan's was doing the same. When Molly had said she'd fly under the storm, she wasn't joking. After take-off, she'd hardly climbed at all. It was certainly exhilarating but at one point Ethan swore she had to pull up to avoid an electricity pylon, and that was when he realised he was holding the lamb a little too tightly. He relaxed his hand and stroked the lamb's head in apology with one finger.

The storm clouds were dark, and lightning was still visible in the distance. Rain lashed the windscreen, and wind buffeted the plane from side to side. They hit what Ethan had to assume was some particularly strong turbulence, and the plane wobbled violently. The lamb bleated, then he heard a small pop from the direction of the engine.

'What was that? Is the plane all right?'

Molly tapped one of the dials on the control panel and flipped a couple of switches. 'Okay, don't panic.'

Ethan's stomach dropped. 'What's happened?'

Molly didn't answer, but clicked on the radio and stated her call sign. 'Oban Traffic, Skyhawk six-two Delta.' There was no answer, only a steady crackle on the line. She quickly barked, 'I think I've lost the engine.'

A bolt of lightning lit up everything and revealed to

Ethan the sickening realisation that the propeller was completely still. Only then did he notice that the engine noise had stopped altogether. An eerie silence filled the plane. Ethan's blood ran cold, but after a moment of pure panic, an inexplicable wave of calm hit him. He took a deep breath. 'Can I help?'

Suddenly, the engine made a loud cracking noise that even Ethan knew it wasn't meant to make, and he could smell the unmistakeable scent of smoke and oil.

'Damn.' Molly got back on the radio. 'I don't know if anyone can hear me, but my engine's gone. We've lost power and there's smoke in the cockpit. I'm going to have to find somewhere to set down immediately.' She gave the position of the aircraft and turned to Ethan.

'We're not going to suddenly fall out of the air or anything. I'm just going to glide us down slowly.'

Ethan scanned the ground beneath them. 'Down to where?'

Molly checked her dials and screen constantly as she spoke. 'There are no airports close enough, and I can't see a straight piece of road. I'm going to head to this patch of flat ground here—' she tapped the screen swiftly '—and set us down.'

There was another flash of lightning and Ethan couldn't help but think of Kai, Harry and Maisie. Who would look after them if he died? He knew Aunty Anne would probably step in. She was so maternal, and she'd offered to take on the kids right back at the beginning, but Ethan had refused. The kids would be with him and no one else. He'd accepted her help while he finished his degree and been grateful for it. But if they lost him, too, he was pretty sure the kids wouldn't come back from it. He should never have gotten in the plane with Molly, or allowed her to come out here in the first place in this storm.

'Don't be scared. You know I wouldn't let anything happen to you.'

'Or your plane, I know.' It was very sweet of her to try to comfort him even mid-emergency landing, so he tried to make a joke and flashed her a smile, which probably came off more as a grimace. He carefully tucked the lamb farther inside his jacket, then zipped it up around him. He supported the lamb with one hand and gripped the armrest with the other. 'Is there a brace position for a small plane?'

'Your shoulder harness will keep you from hitting your head on the panel. Cross your arms in front of you, and keep hold of our passenger,' Molly said tightly.

Ethan nodded.

They descended quickly, and in the lightning flashes it was clear that they were surrounded by fields, no buildings to hit, or roads to crash into. Hopefully, no one else could get hurt, whatever happened.

'Brace,' Molly said firmly.

Ethan pushed himself back in his seat and crossed his arms over his chest, keeping the lamb in place and making sure not to crush him between his chest and arms. He held his breath. They hit the ground hard and bounced twice before setting down. They seemed to be travelling too fast and for too long, so Ethan glanced over at Molly.

'We're okay. Hold on.'

They finally came to a stop, nose almost in contact with the hedge at the far end of the field. She'd landed perfectly and Ethan had never felt such a strong combination of relief, exhilaration and to be quite honest, attraction. Molly was a goddess. A goddess who was currently ripping off her harness and jumping out of the plane into the storm. Ethan unclenched every muscle in his body by force and checked on the lamb. The ridiculous thing was fast asleep.

Ethan grabbed his bag and jumped out after her. She was by the engine, which was still slightly smoking and covered in a black patch in one corner. The smoke stopped as they stared at it.

'Damn it.' Molly hit the side of the plane with her palm flat, then looked like she regretted being so mean to her beloved plane.

Why was she angry? She'd just delivered the most miraculous emergency landing Ethan could ever imagine witnessing. She'd saved all their lives with her talent and expertise.

'Are you okay?' asked Ethan, shouting over the sound of the rain.

'Yes,' she snapped.

'Am I okay?'

Molly glared over at him, her eyes flashing, but he caught a moment of intense relief on her face as she ran her gaze down over his body, checking for injuries. 'You look fine. And your friend. We have to get out of here and find shelter. There's no point in me taking the casing off and looking at the engine until after this storm.'

'Was it the storm? Were we struck by lightning?'

'I don't think so. I won't know till I can take a good look. Maybe rainwater got into the fuel tank and blew it.'

It was getting dark, but due to the terrifying flashes of landscape Ethan had seen on the way down, he was pretty sure he knew exactly where they were. The ocean was on their left, and he was sure he'd spotted the tiny shape of Otter Island just off the coast. That meant they were near a place he knew well. A moor that he'd spent a lot of summers hiking on.

'I know where we can go. Follow me!' he shouted.

CHAPTER NINE

ETHAN FOLLOWED THE line of a river he recognised. It was usually a peaceful brook, but tonight it had turned into a cascade of rushing water. They struggled through whistling wind and rain that pelted them in the face for half an hour, then Ethan stopped and grinned in victory as he spotted the small stone structure exactly where he'd expected it to be.

A one-storey stone building sat nestled between the trees. An ancient bothy, one of many that were scattered throughout the Scottish countryside. The bothies lay empty and were a haven for any walkers who were beset by bad weather or needed a place to stay the night. He'd stayed in this one before, but just for an hour or two until the rain stopped, never overnight. He was impressed that he'd remembered the location so well. It had been a while since he'd found the time to get out and hike, especially once the kids weren't interested anymore.

He unlatched the door, slipping clumsily with wet hands, and held it open for Molly. Once inside, he dropped his medical bag and pushed the door shut against the wind, locking it closed, and leaning against it, suddenly exhausted.

The bothy was old but remarkably well built. The noise

of the storm was quieter now, and no wind seemed to be getting in through any cracks in the doors or windows. There were dark stone walls and a wooden floor, and if they didn't find a way to light the two fat half-melted candles on the table, it would soon be too dark to do anything.

'Give me the lamb.' Molly held out her hands and he gratefully passed him over.

Molly started to get together a bed for the little thing, and Ethan had a quick look around. There were two rooms in the bothy, the main room and a very basic bathroom off to the side. Most bothies didn't even have that, so they were lucky. The main room had an old wooden table and three chairs, and a fireplace at the other end, with a pile of dry wood stacked neatly next to it, all ready for burning.

'The last person to use the bothy left fuel in here, thank God. I thought I'd have to go searching for dry wood somewhere.'

And next to the fireplace sat one solitary double bed. Two mismatching pillows and a small pile of blankets sat on top neatly folded. He turned resolutely away from that discovery and pulled open his bag. 'Please let me have a lighter in here,' he mumbled.

Molly carefully placed the sleeping lamb inside its makeshift bed on the table and cleared her throat, then threw him a lighter as if from nowhere.

He piled some of the logs in the fireplace and ignited the lighter. They soon had a crackling fire, giving off much needed warmth and casting a cosy orange glow over the whole room.

Ethan tried his phone, but as he'd suspected there was no signal. Molly's was the same, and as she put her phone back in her bag, Ethan noticed something.

'Molly, you're bleeding.'

She looked down as if surprised to see the small patch of blood soaking through her sleeve. Then she shrugged. 'It's just my arm.'

'Well, you only have two of them. Come here.'

She shrugged off her soaking wet coat and draped it over a chair then let him softly tug her close. It was the first time they'd really touched since their kiss, but Ethan was more worried about her arm than keeping strictly to his promise.

He rotated her arm gently and found the source of the blood. A graze on her elbow.

'You must have knocked it when we landed.'

'I didn't even notice.'

'Must be the adrenaline.'

He wouldn't need much of his medical kit. First, he cleaned the cut with iodine-soaked cotton wool. He dabbed as gently as he could, but Molly still let out a small hiss. He covered the graze with a square antiseptic pad, then wrapped a bandage around her arm several times and fastened it securely.

All done, he finally looked up and found her face closer than he expected. When he eventually dragged his gaze away from her full mouth and looked into her eyes, he found he couldn't look away. 'You've really been getting into trouble lately, haven't you?' Ethan whispered.

She tilted her head in that adorable way that meant she was confused.

'Your leg, now your arm,' Ethan continued.

'Lucky I've got you on hand to patch me up every time.'

'Always.' Ethan smiled. He took a deep, fortifying breath, reminding himself that Molly didn't want him, and forced himself to leave her side. 'Stay put. I'm going to make you some food and a hot drink.'

'Where are you getting food from?'

'I always have food. I look after three kids.'

'Fair point.'

Ethan was pleased to spot a box of teabags someone had left behind on the shelf above the table. He looked closer and found they'd also left some instant soup mix that was still in date. Probably a better choice than the child-friendly snacks and granola bars he had in his bag. He boiled the kettle over the fire and made them two mugs of soup, which they both devoured hungrily.

'Now, I know how this sounds, but we've really got to get out of these wet clothes.'

Molly snorted.

Ethan rooted through his bag and tried to control his body's physical reaction to her by sheer force of will. He pulled out a hoodie and a woollen hat. 'These are all the spare clothes I have on me.' He threw the hoodie towards Molly's good arm, and she caught it. 'Take off your wet things and put on that and some of the blankets. We'll hang up our clothes by the fire and they'll be dry before we know it.' Ethan turned and grabbed a blanket for himself.

'Where are you going?' asked Molly.

'I'm going to change in the bathroom.'

Molly rolled her eyes. 'You don't have to run away. You won't turn to rock if you see me naked.'

It was Ethan's turn to snort.

'Oh, very mature,' said Molly.

Ethan shrugged. 'I'll stay here if that's what you prefer.'

Ethan turned away from Molly. She was damn well going to get some privacy whether she cared about it or not. He was a gentleman. He swore under his breath as his new position gave him an accidental view of Molly changing in the reflection of the window. He averted his eyes and concentrated on not falling flat on his face as he pushed off his boots and tugged down his wet jeans. Mercifully, his boxers were dry, so he left them on and peeled his soaking sweater and T-shirt off over his head.

Molly tied a scratchy blanket around her waist like a sarong, and sent up a debt of gratitude to any gods who might be listening that she had thought to shave her legs earlier. Not that she should care, since nothing was going to happen between them. In fact, it would be far better if they looked like a forest, then she might not be so tempted to throw herself into his arms.

She pulled on Ethan's hoodie and was pleased to find that it smelled like him. She took in a deep breath; it was soft and warm, just like Ethan. She had to admit it was sweet of him to give it to her, especially when all he had left for himself was a woolly hat. Trying to get comfortable on the bed, Molly pushed a pillow against the wall and leaned back into it, the fire still keeping her feet warm.

Which fortunately, or unfortunately, gave her a front-row seat to Ethan stripping off all his clothes. Fortunately, because he was absolutely beautiful and somehow already had his jeans off. Unfortunately, because it was not doing her attempts to keep away from him any favours at all.

She stared up at the ceiling for a moment.

Stay strong, Molly, she told herself. *If you can help an injured elephant give birth without so much as a stethoscope, and scare off a pair of chimpanzee poachers using a mobile phone in your pocket as a fake weapon, you can resist one perfect, beautiful man in a cosy, cramped bothy where there is only one bed.*

She watched his slim waist broaden into wide shoulders and muscular upper arms as he pulled his clothes off. She watched the muscles flex under the honey-coloured skin of his back as he pulled the shirt and sweater apart and leaned over to drape them both over the chairs near the fire. She remembered every detail about his body last time she'd seen it, in microscopic detail. His twenty-one-year-old body had been gorgeous, but it wasn't a patch on his fully grown mature one. It almost took her breath away how much he had changed in the past nine years.

He turned as he slung a large blanket over his shoulders and pulled it around himself, and Molly swallowed hard as she briefly saw the muscular planes of his chest and hard stomach. She knew he didn't have a spare minute of time to work out in a gym, so that body was simply an accidental side effect of the hard work of being a vet, spending time outside and lifting heavy animals all day long. And a naturally fit body had always been her particular weakness. Why was she trying so hard not to do something she really wanted to do? She suddenly couldn't remember.

Ethan joined her on the far end of the bed and carefully laid back, but since the bed was small and the only spare pillow was right next to her leg, she suddenly found herself with half a lapful of Ethan's head. He smiled up at her. And she tried to calm her racing heartbeat.

'Comfy?' she asked drily, trying hard to disguise her inner feelings. She really needed to snap out of it. He was off-limits. And that was down to her and her own reservations. She'd chosen to pull away and she needed to stick to it. If she took that step, if she gave in and made love to him again, she might not ever be able to leave him.

'Very much, thank you,' said Ethan. 'Is this okay?' He gestured at himself and the bed in general.

She rolled her eyes. 'Of course it is.'

She couldn't bring herself to move away and create a couple of inches of space between them. She needed the extra warmth, she told herself.

The pillow hid Molly's leg so as he wriggled into place, getting comfy, he unknowingly moved his head farther onto Molly. 'I hope the kids are all right.'

'Didn't Anne say she'd watch them?' asked Molly.

'Yes. But Kai hates storms. He's never normally one for displays of affection, but storms are the only time he comes to me for a cuddle.'

Molly slapped her hand to her heart. 'That's so adorable.'

'Yeah, he's not as tough as he likes to pretend.' Ethan glanced up. 'Don't hate me, but part of me secretly loves it when I hear thunder. I don't want him to be scared, but at least I get to hug him.'

This family was going to be the end of her.

She gazed down, admiring Ethan's deep brown eyes. His long black lashes cast shadows over his cheeks in the flickering light from the fire. A lock of his hair fell out of place across his forehead, and she couldn't help pushing it back into place. 'Do you want your hat?' she asked softly.

He shook his head, and her fingers caught in his hair. The little details about the reality of having three growing kids were endlessly surprising to her. She was impressed all over again at how Ethan had managed to overcome all the odds and provide a stable home for his siblings, despite being so young himself. It was admirable. She wondered how she would have coped under the same circumstances when she found it so hard to stay in one place for any length of time. But seeing the bonds that Ethan and his siblings shared, it was starting to dawn on her that some sacrifices were well worth making. She knew he wouldn't change his situation even if he could.

His skin felt warm under her cold fingers, and she found herself carding her hand through his soft, thick hair, still damp from the rain but warm in her hands. It gave her something to do, and distracted her from thinking about the storm and how her plane was doing out there.

Ethan's eyes drifted shut as she stroked through his hair softly. 'Will your plane be all right outside?' he asked as if reading her mind.

Her heart melted further at him still caring about her plane's well-being.

'I won't know what happened to the engine until the morning, but she should be okay,' Molly answered. 'I'll check on her at first light.'

'Are all planes shes?'

'They can be whatever you want them to be.'

Ethan looked up at her again. 'She's very beautiful.'

As Ethan gazed into her eyes, she wondered if he was still just talking about the plane.

'If you're trying to get on my good side by complimenting her…it's working.'

Ethan laughed. He sighed softly as Molly's hand stroked through his hair. 'That feels good.' He closed his eyes. 'You really are an amazing pilot, you know.'

Warmth spread through her chest at the compliment. 'I'm not bad.'

'Not bad? You saved my life. We could have died.'

Molly wasn't so sure about the first part. But she didn't want to tell him how right he was about the second. Landing with no power, in such low light, on an unpredictable, rough surface, any number of things could have gone wrong. Catastrophically wrong. They could have hit power lines, a hedge, a tree, or even a herd of cattle. They'd been very lucky. She felt terrible. 'Ethan, I'm sorry for insisting we come out in such a bad storm.'

'No.' Ethan touched her wrist and made eye contact. 'It was worth it to make sure that Winnie was okay.'

Molly nodded.

'Did you always want to be a pilot?' Ethan asked.

'Not from the beginning. I always dreamed of running a sanctuary. But then I realised I couldn't do that and travel at the same time. Then while I was in Australia, that farmer taught me to fly his plane, and I suddenly had a new dream.'

'You really love travelling, don't you?'

'I like discovering new places. I never would have seen a stampede of zebras migrating across the Serengeti or been in a Jeep attacked by two hippos if I'd stayed in England, I guess.' She had loved travelling. It used to be all she thought about. Where hadn't she been yet? Where would she like to go next? But Molly wasn't sure if she might have had enough of new places. She was starting to wonder if she might have finally found the place she'd been searching all over the world for.

'You must miss all that adventure,' Ethan murmured.

'Sometimes,' she answered, noncommittally. 'What made you decide to be a vet?' Molly asked as she suddenly realised she had no idea.

'When I was a kid my uncle's cattle farm came down with bovine tuberculosis. Hundreds of animals killed just like that,' he said, snapping his fingers. 'It was awful. It was the first time I'd seen my uncle cry. Or any man in my family, I guess. That's when I knew what I wanted to be.'

'Wow. Sorry, Ethan.'

Ethan shrugged, then smiled. 'I know why you wanted to be a vet.'

Molly raised a doubtful eyebrow. 'Go on, then. Enlighten me.'

'You want to save everything. You never met a living being you didn't want to save. Butterflies, ants, birds, donkeys.'

Molly laughed, but didn't disagree.

'So what would this dream sanctuary be like, then? Did you plan it out?' asked Ethan.

Molly settled back into her pillow. 'I'd buy a really big plot of land. And I'd take in all the abandoned animals that have nowhere to go. Farm stock that was no longer viable, or no good for breeding. Injured animals. Anything anyone no longer wanted. And I'd give them all a safe, happy home for the rest of their lives. However long or short that might be.'

Ethan's smile grew. 'Yeah, I can see you doing that. If I die and come back as a donkey, I'd happily live at your sanctuary.' He stared up at the ceiling, avoiding Molly's gaze. 'I felt like me and the kids could have used somewhere like that, back when everything happened.'

Molly's heart broke a little. It didn't seem like it at the time, but when she looked back at them in college, they hadn't been adults. Ethan had still been practically a kid himself. She was reminded again about what Ethan had been through, dealing with losing his mother and figuring out how to take responsibility and provide for three young kids.

'Obviously, we weren't abandoned on purpose,' Ethan added. 'But that doesn't make much difference when you're feeling alone and scared. I always try to protect them from feeling like that again. Which can make things tough sometimes. You know, relationships end. The kids feel unwanted again. Anyway, it was a pretty rough time.'

'Of course it was. You say I saved your life, but you

saved theirs. All three of them. That's way more heroic than knowing how to land a plane.'

'I guess we're both a couple of heroes.'

Molly laughed. 'I guess so.' She glanced over to the table to check on the lamb, who was still blissfully fast asleep. Suddenly, Ethan shot up from her lap and scrambled to sit farther away. Molly's heart leaped out of her chest. 'What? What is it?'

'Nothing. Sorry. I just realised I was on your lap.'

Molly rolled her eyes. 'Oh, for goodness' sake, Ethan.' He was serious. He really was never going to touch her again unless she asked. Molly regretted ever having let him say something so stupid. And to be quite honest she was getting sick of the whole thing.

Ethan reclined opposite her at the other end of the bed. His apparent cool exterior annoyed her. Especially with all the inner turmoil she was currently experiencing. All because of him. The gorgeous idiot. He leaned back on one elbow and let his legs stretch out on the bed. He was trying to fit politely around her body, but the bed was so small that his long limbs couldn't find anywhere to go. She could feel the heat from his body as he tried to get comfortable. He was one of those people who always looked at home in his own skin. So even here on this threadbare bed in an old stone cottage, his hair all mussed up, wearing a blanket, for goodness' sake, he managed to look like a model in a fashion magazine.

He was frustrating, and tempting and so beautiful she suddenly wanted to cry. He'd been so vulnerable with her, and now she felt almost closer to him than she could bear.

She wanted Ethan to touch her. She couldn't think of

anything in the world she wanted more. To feel his hands on her face, for him to press his hot honey skin against hers, to taste his beautiful mouth on hers. But he'd made it very clear that she was going to have to use her words and damn well ask him. And that might just be the most terrifying challenge she'd ever faced.

'We'd better get some sleep,' said Ethan.

She would definitely ask him. Just not right now.

'The sooner we sleep, the sooner morning comes and the sooner you can check on your plane. I know that's all you're thinking about.'

Yeah, that and wanting your tongue in my mouth.

Her eyes widened as that thought jumped into her head unbidden. And she shook her head to get rid of it.

'Do you want to top and tail or...?' Ethan asked.

'No! We're not twelve. Just lie down here.'

'Okay, okay.'

They climbed under the covers, Ethan taking the side of the bed next to the wall and making sure Molly had at least her fair share of all the blankets.

'You warm enough?' Ethan asked.

Molly nodded and they both settled down side by side, lying on their backs. She couldn't help but be reminded of the last time they'd shared a bed. It felt like a lifetime ago, when they'd both been two very different people. The fire cast the room in shifting orange light, and the only sound was the wind and rain outside. Molly had never been more aware of her body, and how close it was to Ethan's. She catalogued every millimetre of her skin that was in contact with his. Their shoulders were just touching, and she could feel his arm grazing her hip as he breathed in and out. This was torture. She closed her eyes and listened to him breathing softly. The sound was comforting, and eventually it soothed the squally mess in her head.

She somehow drifted off to sleep, only to wake sometime later, in the pitch-black. She could no longer hear the crackle of the fire, and her feet were freezing. But her body was cosy and warm, and she slowly realised why. They had somehow both shifted position in their sleep and now they were facing each other. Her head was comfortably cushioned on Ethan's biceps and his other arm was draped protectively over her waist. She felt safe, cocooned snugly by his warm embrace, and there was nowhere she would rather be. He moved his arm minutely, and tingles ran up and down her spine.

She looked up at his face in the moonlight and gasped. Ethan's eyes were open. He blinked sleepily.

'Hi,' he whispered.

She felt like she'd been waiting a whole decade to be this close to him again. There was something about the darkness, the intimacy of the moment, that made her say something she might never have said in the light of day. 'I never stopped thinking about you,' Molly whispered.

'Neither did I.'

She reached out a hand and laid it gently over his cheek. He leaned into her touch like a cat, and she rubbed her thumb over the soft skin under his eye and pulled him close. Close enough to feel his breath on her lips.

'For the love of God,' she whispered. 'Please touch me.'

Their lips crashed together as Ethan surged forward. He wrapped his arm around Molly's shoulder and pulled her close, until she could almost feel his heart beating through her chest.

Molly sank into the kiss and ran her hand through his hair, the silky strands slipping easily through her fingers. His free hand found hers between their bodies, and he slid his fingers in between hers, gripping her tight. When they paused for breath, Ethan ran his hand softly up her arm leaving goose bumps in its wake. Then she pressed her head back into the pillow as he kissed her jaw, his hot mouth moving slowly down her neck, pressing kisses all the way down her throat to her collarbone.

It was even better than the last time they were together. He had a man's body now. All firm muscle and smooth planes, and strong arms holding her to him, and large, practiced hands that knew exactly what they were doing. Touching her just right, pulling her in, gripping her tight.

'Are you sure you want this?'

'I want this. I want you,' she breathed.

'Then I'm not leaving this bed until I've tasted every inch of you.'

CHAPTER TEN

ETHAN WAS WOKEN at dawn by a soft bleat. Everything that had happened last night came back to him in a rush, and he realised Molly was still in his arms. Which was probably the only reason they hadn't expired from the cold. The fire must have gone out hours ago. He couldn't help but wonder what would happen when Molly woke up. Maybe she would emotionally withdraw from him again, put her barriers back up. He hoped not, but he knew the happy bubble they were in couldn't last forever. Maybe nothing had changed. Maybe she was still just as likely to leave as she ever had been. But there was a tiny spark inside him now that was allowing him to hope. Rather than jump up and get the fire started again, he snuggled down under the blankets and pressed closer to Molly, partly to steal some of her body heat, but mostly to follow his instincts and get as close to her as humanly possible. She grunted adorably, still fast asleep, and unconsciously wrapped her hand around his wrist.

After enjoying their closeness for as long as possible, Ethan knew he had to check on the lamb. He slowly extricated himself from Molly's grip and tested their clothes. They were finally dry. He quickly pulled his jeans and sweater on, then checked on the lamb. His blanket had kept him warm, and his splint was still in place. Ethan fed him the spare bottle of milk that Winnie had provided and gave him a quick cuddle.

'You two are so cute,' Molly mumbled from her pillow.

'It's about time you joined the land of the living,' Ethan said.

Molly yawned and stretched, thrilled to hear her clothes were dry. Ethan noticed that she kept his hoodie and pulled it on again over her clothes.

They both tried their phones again, but there was still no signal.

'I hope the kids won't be too worried about you,' said Molly.

'If I know Aunty Anne, she will have covered for me. They won't know anything's wrong yet. I'm sure she will suspect we simply stayed at Winnie's until after the storm. I really need to get somewhere with a signal, though.'

'I guess we probably should have stayed at Winnie's,' Molly said contemplatively.

Ethan shrugged. If they'd stayed at Winnie's, none of what happened last night would have happened. And he was not mad about it. He made Molly some tea, thrilled to be stuck alone in a bothy with the most beautiful woman in the world. But he had to be careful. Until she was prepared to have a conversation about their future, he couldn't assume anything.

As they ventured outside into the early-morning light, they saw for the first time what the storm had done to their surroundings. Fallen trees and scattered broken branches as far as they could see. They left the bothy as they'd found it, minus a couple of packs of instant soup, and plus a few granola bars.

Once they found the plane, they discovered the trail of destruction behind it. Carnage from where they'd touched down all the way to where they finally came to a stop. They'd busted through three small bushes and left two very visible, deep lines through the crops and grass. The nose of the plane was inches from an old oak tree growing from the middle of the hedge that Ethan hadn't even noticed last night. 'Glad I didn't hit it.' Molly ran her hand over the trunk.

Molly walked around her plane a couple of times inspecting the damage. She magicked a screwdriver from her bag and unscrewed the casing on the engine. She poked around while Ethan stepped back and kept quiet, stroking the lamb's head.

'Well, the engine's done for. I think water got into the fuel during the rainstorm.'

Ethan winced. 'Sorry.'

'I can replace it. Plus, she's got a lot of scratches and scrapes from the landing, but I think everything's repairable.'

'Can she fly home?'

Molly shook her head. 'Definitely not. I'll have to come back out here with a mechanic and fix her later. Or, if not, hire some transport that can tow her home.'

'Talking of home, how are we going to get back?'

'How do you feel about hitching a lift?' Molly asked.

'Fine, as long as you promise to fight off any serial killers.'

'It's a deal.' They shook hands, and Ethan took the opportunity to pull her in for a soft kiss.

'I'm glad your plane survived.'

'Me, too,' she said and hugged him tightly around his waist. He buried his face in her soft blond hair. The intimate moment was only interrupted by a mournful bleat coming from inside Ethan's jacket.

They hopped up on top of a farmer's gate on the grass verge at the side of the road and sat next to each other, waiting for a vehicle to pass their way. It felt like now might be a good time to attempt to draw Molly into having some sort of serious conversation about their relationship. Ethan took a deep breath and prepared himself for Molly's walls to go back up; he knew he had to approach this carefully.

At this point, the main thing was to get them both home safely. Pushing her for a commitment when they were stranded and she couldn't escape from the conversation would be unfair of him, and might be too much for her.

'I really enjoyed last night.'

He was relieved when Molly smiled shyly. 'Me, too.'

A goofy smile spread itself over Ethan's face whether he wanted it to or not. 'I won't lie. I've been wishing that could happen again for the last nine years.'

Molly smiled, then gazed into his eyes. 'There's something else you want to say, isn't there?'

Was he that obvious? 'There is something I wanted to talk about, yes.' She waited patiently for him to continue. 'It's about the kids. I know you know this, but they've had a pretty rough childhood up to now. I can't really put them in a position where they are likely to get hurt again.'

'Hurt how?'

'By people they've grown attached to leaving them.' Ethan maintained eye contact, waiting for her to understand.

'Oh. You mean me.'

Ethan nodded.

'They're attached to me?'

Ethan smiled. 'Of course they are. My whole family loves you.' *And so do I*, he found himself thinking. The sudden realisation made him feel unsteady on the gate, and he tightened his grip on the railing.

Molly stared into the distance, her forehead wrinkling with concentration. 'I would never want to hurt them, Ethan. My own childhood, well, it wasn't great.' She paused for a moment. 'I was a mistake. My parents never planned to have me. My mother thought she was too old to fall pregnant. They weren't great parents, and they didn't really know what to do with me. All they cared about was working hard and making money. So they treated me like a burden. I grew up thinking that's what children were.'

Ethan put one arm around her and squeezed her shoulder, encouraging her to continue.

'I've always been a bit lonely, you know? I only really came into myself for the first time at university. I got that first taste of freedom and never wanted to let it go. That's why I became a pilot, I think. So any time I want I can get away from everything and fly free.'

Ethan pulled her closer to him. 'That makes a lot of sense.'

Molly put a hand on Ethan's knee. 'So, I guess that's

why I've always thought I'd be bad with kids. I didn't want to become my parents.'

Ethan put his hand on top of Molly's. 'I think you're looking at this all wrong. I think your experiences can help you be amazing with kids. You know exactly what not to do. You know exactly how not to treat them.'

'Maybe.'

Ethan carefully jumped down off the gate, making sure not to shake it, and turned to Molly. He stepped closer and wrapped his arms warmly around her shoulders, pulling her close and holding her tight. 'Thank you for opening up to me, Molly.'

She pulled him closer. 'I feel better having told you,' she said.

Ethan smiled and pressed a kiss into her hair. Maybe this was finally a sign that she might be ready to move forward with him, or that she might consider it at least. His tiny spark of hope glowed a little bit brighter.

After a long day, which started with finding their way home with a lovely farmhand named Michael, and ended with booking a plane mechanic, reuniting Ethan with the kids, who as he suspected hadn't known anything was even amiss, and getting the lamb treated properly and settled in the overnight ward, Molly hadn't had much time to think about what had happened between her and Ethan. She almost never talked about her childhood. After all, who wanted to tell people they were a mistake? But she'd felt strangely lighter after sharing it with Ethan. Maybe now he would understand that she might never be able to give him what he needed from her. He'd sent her home early to get some proper rest, but now she was alone, the doubts were beginning to creep back in.

Her phone interrupted her emotional spiral, and she was excited to see who it was.

'Julie!'

'How's tricks? Anything to share?'

'Well, actually...'

'Oh, my God, what's happened?'

Molly suddenly felt nervous. She wasn't entirely sure how Julie would react. She nervously fiddled with a pen and doodled a heart on a page in her notebook. 'I may have spent the night with Ethan.'

'Wow.'

'Yes. And this time I am relieved to report that he did not run for the hills.'

'Ah, well, that's a relief. But I never had any doubt.'

'You didn't?'

'Who would want to run away from you?'

Molly made a face. Try everyone? 'Anyway, I doubt you called just to talk about my love life.'

'Regrettably not. I'm reluctantly calling you to tell you something.'

'Oh, no, don't tell me you can't come for New Year's anymore?'

'It's nothing to do with that. I'm reluctant because I don't think I should tell you this, but I promised I'd tell you if anything came up.'

'Can we start again? I don't think I've had enough coffee yet for this conversation.'

'Nick's setting up a new project, and there's a position for you if you want it.'

'Oh, wow. Where?'

'Romania. They're setting up a lynx rescue. Building it from the ground up. It's at least a six-month project, maybe longer.'

'That sounds…interesting.' It did. Any time in the last decade she would have been all over it. Would have jumped at the chance to drop everything and go and start a new adventure. She'd always wanted to see Romania, and lynx were beautiful. One of her favourite wild breeds. But…

'You didn't want to tell me?'

Julie seemed to pause carefully. 'I think you're happy where you are.'

Molly wrote the offer down on her notebook. Writing things out on paper always helped her think them through.

Job offer. Romania. Lynx rescue. Six months or longer.

'Don't be in a hurry to decide,' said Julie. 'Nick says there's no rush.'

For the first time in her life, Molly didn't know what she was supposed to do. She was a free spirit. She wasn't meant to stay in one place. When she was growing up, lonely and ignored, she'd promised herself that she would always fly free. Talking to Ethan had brought back all her doubts. If she wanted to be true to the real her, she should go. Right? Ethan appeared to be giving her the right signs, the feeling that he wanted more with her, but how could she be sure when she'd made so many mistakes in the past? And this time there were three vulnerable children in the mix. What would happen if he got tired of her, if he found her lacking, or went off her like all her other partners had? After having opened up to him, she was suddenly feeling exposed to him in a way she hadn't been with anyone else. She felt the almost irresistible urge to do what she usually did and move on, but something inside her was telling her to stay and fight.

But should she really listen to that inner voice when it had steered her wrong so many times before?

'I'm just not sure whether there's anything keeping me here, Julie.'

'I think there is.'

A little while after Molly hung up, her doubts crept back.

Would anything have happened if she and Ethan weren't stranded together, sharing a bed? Was he really interested in her, or was she just in the right place at the right time? Was she just kidding herself that they'd always had something special? Maybe he'd sent her home because he was sick of the sight of her and didn't know how to let her down gently.

Across the street, Ethan sat on his porch, gazing out through the pools of orange light from the streetlamps. His phone rang, and after looking at the caller he picked it up.

'Do you need us again?' asked Ethan.

'No, no,' said Winnie. 'Stand down, soldier. Just calling for a chat.'

Ethan settled back into the swing seat and put his feet up on the coffee table. 'How are the animals doing?'

'All good. How's my lamb?'

'He's doing great. He's staying overnight at the surgery, but rest assured he's getting a lot of attention from everyone.'

'Glad to hear it. You can't keep him, you know.'

'Tell Molly, not me. She loves him. Your electricity is still okay?'

'Yes, everything's fine.'

'I spoke to Jon about your roof. We're getting some people together. We're hoping to drive out at the weekend and get it all fixed up in one day. Would that work for you?'

'I'm hardly a social butterfly. I'll be here whenever you can come. I'll be stuffing you all full of food and drink and treats, I hope you know.'

'That's why I'm coming.'

Winnie laughed. 'Now, listen. I called for a reason.'

Ethan had suspected as much.

'I've been thinking more about the farm. I decided I do want to give it up. But not to developers. I want it to go to a family.'

Ethan was relieved. 'That sounds perfect. It should be a home, not a golf course.'

'I quite agree.'

Ethan still wasn't sure why Winnie was calling him in particular about this. 'Did you want some numbers for estate agents? I can look some up for you.'

'No, I don't need them. I have another idea.'

Ethan suddenly realised he might have figured out why she'd called him. 'Wait, just so you know, I cannot afford to buy your farm. I couldn't afford it, Winnie. As much as I'd love to. And I would love to. You know I think it's beautiful out there.'

'That's not quite what I have in mind. I don't exactly want to sell it at all.'

CHAPTER ELEVEN

MOLLY WAS ON the phone when Ethan knocked on her front door. She stared at him for a moment, then beckoned him inside.

'Take your time,' Ethan whispered. 'I can wait here.'

She nodded, held a finger up to him to denote she'd only be a minute and scampered upstairs, still holding the phone to her ear.

Ethan waited in Molly's living room, buzzing with anticipation. As soon as he'd finished his conversation with Winnie, he knew what he had to do. And he suddenly couldn't wait to do it. It was time for him to trust Molly with his heart and take the biggest risk of his life. Yesterday, after they'd spent that remarkable night together, being so open with their bodies and their feelings, Molly had finally opened up to him about her past. Everything that had stood between them made sense to him now. And he knew they could overcome all of it. If only they both wanted it. And now, he was sure she did.

He'd seen Molly interacting with his siblings. She clearly cared for Maisie and the twins, and now he knew more about her past, he was sure he could support her growing confidence with them.

He could faintly hear Molly's voice from upstairs over

the noise from the street outside. Someone's car alarm had been going off down the road for the past few minutes, and he tried to tune out the annoying noise.

Ethan's phone vibrated in his pocket and he took it out to find a message from Maisie. He was needed at home. Kai had set off the fire alarm trying to cook. That was what that noise was. He crossed to the window and pulled Molly's blinds up. There was no smoke visibly billowing from his house, at least. He'd have to run over and check on them. But it would be quicker to leave a note for Molly rather than wait for her to finish her phone call. He looked in her kitchen and saw a notebook lying on the counter next to the fridge.

But as he read what was written on the first page, he felt his lungs seize.

Job offer. Romania. Lynx rescue. Six months or longer.

His heart pounded so hard he felt sick. He knew it. She was leaving him. He felt the disappointment crushing him.

He was such an idiot. He'd known this would happen; he'd told himself time and time again not to get attached, not to let the kids get attached, because he knew she would do this.

There was a tiny heart drawn in biro underneath the note. Clearly, she was excited to go. And he could hardly blame her. Of course Romania and lynx were more exciting than being in the middle of nowhere in Scotland. With him. Of course Molly didn't love him like he loved her. He knew now for sure that he was truly and passionately in love with her. It wouldn't feel this crushing if he wasn't. It had always been her, ever since university. He'd never forgotten her, never been able to get her out of his head no matter how much time passed.

He couldn't deal with this right now; he had to check on the kids. The idea of leaving Molly a note forgotten, he headed for the door.

'Where are you going?' Molly's voice rang out, an audible smile in her voice. Ethan's hand was already on the front door handle. He froze, not turning around.

'Nowhere. Just home. That noise you can hear right now is my kitchen fire alarm going off.'

'Oh, I thought it was just a car alarm.'

Ethan turned the door handle and pulled it open. 'I have to get going.'

'Are you okay?'

Ethan swallowed. He knew it was strange that he hadn't looked at her yet, and that she could tell something was up, but if he turned and looked into her eyes, he wasn't sure he would be able to pretend he didn't know about the job offer. He couldn't act like he hadn't just found out something that had made his entire world fall from beneath him.

The fire alarm fell silent in the stillness between them.

'I guess they figured it out without you,' said Molly carefully.

Even the kids didn't need him. Ethan breathed in once, then let it out. 'When are you leaving?' he asked quietly.

Ethan heard Molly step closer to him and he gripped the door handle tighter.

'What are you talking about?'

'Don't pretend with me, Molly. Please?' Ethan finally turned. 'I saw the note.' He gestured in the direction of the notebook, still sitting on the counter. But she didn't look. She obviously knew what he was talking about now.

Her gaze dropped to the floor. 'I haven't decided if I'm going yet.'

Ethan nodded, not sure what to say.

'I knew you would do this,' Ethan said, more to himself than to Molly. 'It's not even your fault. You can't help it. It's just what you do.'

Molly's eyes snapped up to his. 'What do I do?'

'You move on. You never stay in one place. And I knew that from the start. I can't compete with years of conditioning from your parents, convincing you that you have to keep seeking out excitement wherever you can because you can't find fulfilment inside yourself. You don't recognise when you have something of true value right in front of you that's worth more than a brief shot of adrenaline.'

'Oh, really? And why do you even care?'

'I just thought maybe you'd changed, finally grown up, perhaps.'

'Is there something wrong with how I was?'

'No! I just thought maybe you were ready to—'

'Settle down? Is that what you were going to say? Not everyone wants to settle down. Not everyone wants to have a mortgage and two point four children.'

'Believe me, I know that,' Ethan said.

Suddenly, he felt transported back to when Carrie had left him. But this was so, so much worse. He felt infinitely more for Molly than he had ever felt for Carrie. He hadn't meant to, but he'd let himself imagine Molly becoming a permanent member of his family. He shut his eyes for a moment to process the pain. He'd always feared this would happen. No woman could ever want him as he was, with the commitments he had to his family. And he'd never, ever swap them for any woman, not even Molly, as much as he felt for her. Her words stung so much he could no longer bear to ask her to stay; he needed that decision to come from her. At least Maisie hadn't been around to hear it this time. He couldn't bear to think about how he was going to explain to her that this had happened again.

Molly looked stricken, like she knew precisely what he was thinking.

'What exactly would I be staying here for? You know me so well, you tell me?'

Ethan thought desperately. 'You love your job. You're helping people. You get to fly. You love flying.'

'What else?'

'You have a house, a home of your own. You never had that before.'

'And?'

Me, he wanted to say, you have me. But he couldn't bring himself to say it and get rejected by the only woman he'd ever really wanted. He couldn't let down that last, final barrier and expose all his vulnerability to her. He felt stupid now for having thought she would or could change. 'Listen, I get it. I get why you want to go on an adventure to a new place, to build something new. I guess I just hoped...'

'Hoped what?'

'That building something new with me might be enough,' he answered quietly. He couldn't look at her while she rejected him; he couldn't even listen to the words she was about to say, so he quickly carried on talking. 'I'm sorry for what I said to you about your parents. I'm only angry with myself, not you.'

'I should hope not. I haven't done anything. What would you even be angry with me for? Living my life? Putting myself first? I don't have anyone else to think about. I never have. No one's ever been interested.'

Ethan frowned. He had to accept that she'd never actually promised him anything. It was all just hope that he'd built for himself. It was time to do some damage control for his pride's sake. He took a deep breath.

'I think you should go. I think it's the right decision.' He met her eyes. 'I was wrong to ask you to consider staying. We don't need you here. I'm sure you'll be happier in Romania.'

She suddenly looked like she'd been slapped. Her face closed down, and her emotions shut off as Ethan turned away.

Ethan had finally stepped through the door he'd been glued to and walked away. And she'd let him.

All she'd wanted was for him to ask her to stay. But she'd been left disappointed. *We don't need you*, he'd said. He couldn't make it any clearer than that. He hadn't asked her to stay. Even Ethan couldn't love her. All her past failed relationships rattled through her head. She wasn't enough for any of them.

She'd thought Ethan might be different, but he was just another person who could see that she was unlovable and inadequate as a life partner. He probably knew she'd be useless as a joint caregiver to his siblings. She was going to miss them so much.

She knew he'd be fine without her. This was what she did; she was the person people dated before they found the one. Judging from her history, the next woman Ethan dated would be the one he married. She shuddered; the thought of Ethan with another woman felt like being stabbed in the heart, so she scrubbed the idea from her mind.

In the morning, Molly called Julie to tell her she was accepting the job. But halfway through the conversation, something made her ask Julie a question.

'When you called me, you said you thought there was something keeping me here. You meant Ethan, right?'

'No, I didn't.'

'What, then?'

'I meant you. You are keeping you there. I think you've finally found what you've been travelling the world looking for.'

'What?'

'Yourself. Your new self. For the last few years you loved going to new places, doing new things, moving on. And some people might spend their lives happily doing that forever. But not you. I think you're done. I think you're ready for your next adventure. And that's staying put. Finding out all the amazing things you can experience in one place.'

'He didn't ask me to stay,' Molly said quietly.

Julie paused for a moment. 'Did you really give him a chance to?'

Maybe she hadn't given Ethan a chance. Maybe she'd pushed him away to protect herself.

'And to be honest, is that really the most important thing?' Julie continued.

'What?'

'You should stay for you, not just for him. Do you want to stay?'

That was the question. Maybe she could finally open her animal sanctuary in Romania. Or maybe after this one last job she could start again somewhere new. Every country in the world had unwanted animals she could save. The world was her oyster.

But the thought of starting her sanctuary without Ethan by her side left her cold.

Suddenly, she noticed the boxes of food Ethan had brought her that night, still stacked on the table by the door. She'd forgotten to put them in the fridge. As she got closer, she noticed something sitting on top of them. A purple woollen glove. She recognised it immediately. The night they'd spent together at uni, he'd left behind his T-shirt, but he'd also left behind the glove he lent her to keep her warm that night he'd split the pair, one glove each. She'd lost track of hers over the years; this must be his. She picked it up and held it against her hand. He'd kept a memento of her, too. All these years.

CHAPTER TWELVE

ETHAN SAT ON his porch, watching over Maisie as she played in the garden, digging up weeds from the flower beds with her bright pink trowel.

He spent most of his time gazing furiously at Molly's house, telling himself it was better to feel cross than admit his heart was breaking. He wondered if she was in there packing. He tortured himself with how depressing it would be to look over there in a few days when she was gone. Or in a few weeks when someone else lived there. What the hell was he going to do without her? He could feel the hole she would leave in his life already and she hadn't even left yet. He knew it was time to warn Maisie about what was happening. He beckoned her over, and she joined him on the swing seat, jumping on his lap.

'I don't want you to feel too sad, but I wanted to tell you that Molly got a job offer in another country.'

'She's going?'

'I think so, yes. I'm sorry. We'll all miss her, but like I told her, she needs to follow her dreams. We all do.'

'You told Molly to go? Are you an idiot?'

'Maisie!' The kid had never reminded him more of Molly. 'It was for her own good. She'll be happy there.'

'She was happy here.'

'Yes, I think she was.' Ethan sat back and wrapped his arms around Maisie. 'I guess that means you might not get your trip in her plane. I'm sorry, sweetie.'

'That's okay.'

'It is?'

'Are you okay?' Maisie twisted around and looked up at him, full of concern. And he realised how grown-up Maisie had gotten lately. She wasn't crying or shouting about Molly leaving. She even seemed more worried about him than about losing out on her plane trip. He hugged her close. Maybe the kids weren't as delicate as he thought.

His thoughts returned to Molly again. He wanted Molly in his life. Carrie's leaving didn't define his worth, or control his ability to be loved again. And Molly was nothing like Carrie. Even the kids knew that. He thought of the look on Molly's face when he told her to go. Hope suddenly sparked as he realised he hadn't given her the chance to have her say. Maybe if he'd worded things differently she might have opened up to him, too. Maybe he jumped the gun? He'd jumped to old conclusions about her, about himself. It was time those preconceptions changed, for both of them.

Molly opened the door of the clinic and Ethan held out a bunch of wildflowers. She stared at them, frowning.

'They're from my garden. Maisie helped me pick them.'

'They're very beautiful.'

'Maisie said you can feed them to the donkey if you want. I made sure they're all edible.'

Molly snorted a short laugh. 'I might just do that.'

'I was wondering if I could talk to you for a minute. If you're not busy.'

She gazed at him for a moment. Ethan wanted to pull her close and never let go, but everything felt delicate, like he could say the wrong thing and lose his mooring at any moment. 'You can come with me to feed the donkey,' she said.

Molly led the way through the clinic and out the back door. She made her way through the yard and out to the stable behind the building. The donkey ambled out to meet them, and Molly held the flowers over the fence and let her munch on them.

Ethan smiled and rubbed the donkey's head. 'I was wondering if you'd mind flying somewhere with me today.'

'Do we have a job?'

'No, it's not a job.'

'We can't just fly off, Ethan. We have work.'

'No, we don't. Jon gave us the morning off.'

'What on earth for?'

'If you come with me, you might find out.'

'Why are you being so mysterious?'

'Come on.' Ethan smiled. He gave the donkey one last pat and held out his hand to Molly. She stared at him, the corner of her mouth twitching and threatening to turn into a smile. She rolled her eyes, left the rest of the flowers behind for the donkey and followed Ethan all the way to the hangar.

The plane looked good after its recent adventures, if a little rough around the edges. Jon already had an aircraft mechanic on standby to help keep the plane in working order for their patients. Which meant that he'd been able to get her picked up and her engine replaced quickly.

'Doesn't she look great?' Molly asked, running her hand gently over the fuselage.

'She does.'

'There are still some nicks and scrapes that need repairing before she's back to perfect condition. But I want to tackle those myself.'

'She's okay to fly?' Ethan checked. His plan would be pretty useless if she wasn't.

'Yes! It'll be her new engine's maiden flight.' Once they were both strapped in, Molly looked over at Ethan. 'Where are we headed? You're going to have to tell me something, unless you want to try flying this thing.'

Ethan laughed. 'Not a chance. Just fly north.'

'Ethan!'

'Okay, okay. Head to Winnie's farm.'

'Why?'

'Only one way to find out.'

She shook her head and started to get the plane ready. Ethan grinned. It was time to be brave for both of them and take a risk. Only this risk didn't even feel scary anymore.

The farm looked completely different from the last time they'd been there. Its lush green fields stretched out under the cold blue sky. She was so happy to be spending time in such a beautiful place. She'd travelled all over the world, but she could honestly say the rugged Scottish landscape was her favourite. She'd be lucky if she could spend the rest of her days flying over it.

They landed smoothly, and Molly wasted no time ripping off her headset and jumping out of the plane.

'So what are we doing here? No more stalling.'

Ethan took her hand, and they started walking slowly towards the farm. 'If you are going to Romania, I want you to know that I fully support that. But I was thinking that maybe in six months, when you've saved all the lynx, you might want to come back home...to me.' He looked at her, and she blinked back, nonplussed. 'Only thing is,' he continued, 'home might look a little bit different then.'

Molly frowned. 'What do you mean?'

'You see, Winnie had an idea. It's a little off the wall, but I talked to the kids and they jumped at it. She wants to house-swap.'

'House-swap?'

'Yeah. We get the farm...she gets a manageable house in a beautiful street with wonderful neighbours.'

Molly couldn't help but laugh. The idea was so ridiculous that it almost made sense. 'Are you serious? This is what she wants?'

'It was all her idea. Obviously, there are things to sort out. I'd have to get my roof looked at before handing it over to her. We'd have to figure out the kids' schools. But that's all doable.'

Molly gazed into Ethan's eyes. 'This is what you want to do?'

'Yes.'

'It's a pretty big risk.'

Ethan nodded and brushed a hand through her hair, tucking her curls behind one ear. 'You're worth it.'

Chills ran through her body from where he touched her. 'Why do I love this idea?' asked Molly.

Ethan's smile lit up his face. 'You think you might want to join us?' he asked shyly. 'After Romania?'

'Who needs Romania?' She'd been zigzagging the globe for the past six years. She knew now that it wasn't the travelling part of her life that filled her with passion; it was the part where she got to help people and animals. And she could do that here. She'd finally found somewhere she wanted to settle and people she wanted to settle with.

'Seriously?' asked Ethan.

'Seriously. I'm done searching for adventure. You guys give me plenty of excitement right here.' Molly suddenly thought of something. 'Won't you miss living so close to all your aunts and uncles?'

'Aunty Anne's already informed me that if we move, they're all coming to stay for Christmas, birthdays and any other holiday you can think of. And this place is so big we won't even be on top of each other.'

'But what about work?'

'We can fly in.'

'You trust me, after the storm?'

'Even more after the storm.'

Molly flung her arms around Ethan's neck, holding him as close as she could. He wrapped his arms tightly around her back and pressed her to him. She gasped when she realised something. 'I could start my animal sanctuary here!'

'Exactly. It's perfect.'

'You're perfect.'

He shrugged. 'I'm not bad.' Ethan pulled away and cupped her face with both hands. He stroked her cheek gently with his thumb. 'I'm so glad you found your way back to me. I think I've always loved you, and I know I always will. You're perfect with Maisie and the twins, and my whole family loves you as much as I do.'

Molly smiled happily. 'You're the family I've always dreamed of having. And the man I never thought I'd get. I certainly took the long way round, but I got here in the end.'

EPILOGUE

MOLLY SHUT THE door of her farmhouse and walked past the redbrick stables. She patted the heads of her donkeys as she passed and let the horses sniff her hands. She wandered onto the grass and eventually found Ethan, sitting under a tree near the marker for Heather's grave.

All wrapped up in a soft wool sweater and a cosy scarf, she held her mug with both hands and sipped her steaming coffee. It was late summer and today was the first day Molly had felt that autumn chill in the air. It was warm in the sun, but chilly as she passed under the shade of each tree.

'Is this seat taken?' she asked and joined him on the grass when he laughed.

The infamous pet-hating vet was currently scratching the head of a chocolate Labrador ex-police dog, and unable to get up because two of their three barn cats were snuggled up on his legs.

Molly smiled to herself and passed him her coffee. Aunty Anne was still smug about finding them the police dog, and when Molly had finally met him she'd burst out laughing because he looked exactly like Ethan. Long, dark eyelashes and deep brown eyes. It was meant to be. He was a good-natured dream of a dog. He let the cats walk all over him—literally—and they were often found sleeping together in a warm pile on the kitchen tiles by the fireplace.

Kai, Harry and Maisie were all in the far horse paddock. They'd all decided to learn to ride since they'd made the move out here to the farm, and Kai had picked it up immediately. Now he was helping teach the other two. Harry was still an inch shorter than Kai, but he was getting there slowly. The twins sat on the fence and watched Maisie, still learning to mount a horse. They shouted encouragement at her, and she finally made it up onto the saddle. Molly and Ethan could hear her laughing all the way from their vantage point.

They'd been taking in injured and unwanted animals for a few months now, and Winnie's old farm was getting fuller every week. Retired service dogs, misfit cows and donkeys from farms that would otherwise be put down. They'd even found a lame emu for Harry, but they hadn't gotten him yet. He was going to be part of Harry and Kai's birthday surprise.

They'd fixed the roof tiles and the chimney right after the storm, rebuilt the stables. Then fixed the roof in Ethan's old house for Winnie. She fitted right in with the old crowd on Ethan's street, and made the best barbecue chicken Ethan had ever tasted for the street parties. Winnie had even let them keep the lamb. They'd called him Joan Jett, never feeling the need to explain when people asked them why he had a girl's name.

Molly had liked her little green house, but she'd never really fallen in love with it. Not like this place. Here she already felt protective of every brick, every flower bed and every tree on the site. And her favourite people from the street, she'd brought with her. And the others, all the collected aunts, uncles and cousins, had visited them numerous times already. There was no shortage of company. The extended family was planning to spend the whole summer there, followed by Christmas, and Molly couldn't be happier.

Molly watched their third barn cat jump off the fence onto their still rather overweight British Saddleback pig. She walked in circles on its back before lying down for a snooze. The pig completely ignored her and carried on snuffling the ground and eating the grass.

Ethan took her hand and squeezed it. 'I'm so glad we found our way back to each other.'

Molly smiled and met his eyes, honey-brown in the sunlight. 'I'm glad I finally found what I never knew I was looking for.'

'I'll have to think about that one, but I'm sure it was a compliment.'

Molly laughed and kissed him.

Ethan wasn't risk-averse anymore. He loved that Molly was a daredevil—after all, if she hadn't been willing to risk her life she might not have saved his sister. Some things were worth a risk. He saw now that Molly's adventurousness, far from being a negative, was actually a positive. He loved every piece of her.

Ethan was finally happy. Molly filled in all the gaps in his life.

And Molly finally had incontrovertible proof that she

was loveable—a whole family's worth of it. Ethan made her feel special every day.

Surrounded by family and animals, neither of them would ever get the chance to feel lonely again.

*****

*If you enjoyed this story,
check out this other great read
from Zoey Gomez*

The Single Dad's Secret

Available now!

WEDDING FLING TO FOREVER

COLETTE COOPER

MILLS & BOON

For my dad,
who instilled in me a love of books and storytelling.

CHAPTER ONE

'Helicopter inbound. ETA five minutes. Thirty-two-year-old male patient. Car versus bicycle. Multiple injuries including head, chest and pelvis. Peri arrest.'

Though calm and measured, Sister Tilly Clover's voice immediately had everyone's attention, and the team in the vicinity of the red trauma-phone in London's Trafalgar Hospital's resus room turned to look at her and await instructions.

The patient heading towards them was going to require every single member of the team to give the best they had—he was peri arrest, on the verge of his heart stopping altogether, which was as bad as it got. She knew full well that what she said next could affect the outcome for the patient they were expecting and having the shrewd, dark eyes of consultant Dexter Stevens surveying her as she spoke did nothing to quell the sudden banging of her heart against her ribs.

'Mark and Hannah, come with me to Resus, please. Ally, can you bleep the ortho and neuro registrars? Anika, run a unit through the blood warmer at four. I'll bleep the radiographer.'

How many times she'd done a similar call to arms, she couldn't begin to remember, but every time the thought that someone's life had just changed, might even end, sent a shot of unwelcome yet rousing adrenaline surging through her veins. This was why she loved her job so much. Dealing with situations like this was second nature, and knowing she could make a difference to someone's life was so incredibly rewarding.

The fact that she'd come so close to death herself just a few short years ago was a constant reminder of the vital role that highly trained, caring professionals had in people's lives—but also of the fact that life could be taken away so easily and so randomly.

'I'll take this.'

Dexter Stevens' commanding tone told her he didn't expect her to challenge him, and she wasn't about to surprise him by doing so. The lead A&E consultant, with his smouldering eyes, hard-edged cheekbones and ability to look disarmingly dashing even in hospital scrubs, was the best option the patient being air-lifted towards them as they spoke was going to get. The problem was, he knew it.

'He'll be in four,' said Tilly.

'I heard,' he replied. 'And?'

Tilly knew what he meant. Dexter Stevens was a man of few words and those he did speak were precise, to the point and always brusque. 'Witnesses say the cyclist was hit from behind at around forty miles per hour. He has multiple injuries including head, chest and pelvis; possible spinal injuries; immediate loss of consciousness, and was peri-arrest after being scooped by the heli medics. He's already intubated and on a portable ventilator.'

'Impossible to tell from that whether his biggest problem is brain injury or blood loss,' he replied, slipping the 'Team Leader' tabard on over his scrubs.

How could he make that sound as though it was her fault?

'Quite,' she replied, flicking the switch to turn on the monitor, its coloured lines flashing to life on the screen. 'I suppose it's our job to find out.'

'It's that of the CT scanners, to be precise.' He checked his watch.

Tilly rolled her eyes. He was so literal. 'And there's me thinking we had a useful role to play.' She grinned at him, but the tiniest twitch of his dark eyebrows drawing inwards and the slight confusion in his intense blue eyes told her that her quip had flown completely over his dark, stormy head.

Those eyes, a piercing cobalt blue, seemed to bore into her soul and see her innermost secrets and thoughts. Hopefully not—for, if they could, they'd see that she wanted to gaze into them, melt into his strong arms and kiss lips that, though they were rarely seen to smile, were nevertheless entirely kissable.

She swallowed hard, unsure whether it was the incident they were about to have to deal with or Dexter Stevens' dark gaze that was the cause of the adrenaline suddenly coursing through her veins. What she did know was that she was grateful that the consultant striding away from her with such purposeful, feral grace was here right now and would give this desperately ill patient the very best chance he had of surviving the extreme trauma he'd suffered.

The doors to Resus crashed open as the helicopter medics rushed in with their patient. The calm before the storm was over.

'Okay, team,' said Dexter, looking suddenly more at home. 'This is a category one trauma—a proper cat one. Let's go. Airway?' He stood at the patient's side, addressing the helicopter medic, taking control, calm, assured, poised and dominating the scene.

'Intubated and patent,' replied the heli medic.

Dexter fired orders, which everyone immediately and swiftly obeyed. 'Ally, put in an arterial line and take bloods, including a cross-match for ten units. Mark, obs. Hannah, direct pressure to the left thigh wound. Anika, run the O-neg through stat and have the next ready. Tilly, check pelvis for stability. Questions, anyone?'

'BP eighty over forty,' called Mark, one of the nurse practitioners. 'Heart rate, one twenty and temperature is thirty-five.'

'Instigate the MHP,' said Dexter. 'We need to stabilise him as much as possible; get him into the CT scanner and see fully what we're dealing with here. I suspect he has massive internal bleeding from the pelvis and possibly intra-abdominally too.'

The MHP, or massive haemorrhage protocol, was only instigated for life-threatening blood loss to carefully manage the need for rapid transfusion support. Dexter had recognised the need immediately and was swiftly coordinating the actions of the team to maximise this patient's chances. Literally every second counted. The man lying battered, bruised, broken and bleeding on the trolley before them had a limited chance of getting through this, but he was being given the best chance possible because Dexter Stevens had decided to take control.

Inspecting the pelvic binder that had been applied by the paramedics, Tilly knew Dexter's eyes were on her. She could feel the power they exerted, burning into her, scrutinising her every move, assessing, judging. This patient was a category one trauma—the worst there was—and Dexter was in his element. He was completely at home, ensuring that every single member of the team pulled their weight to give the patient every chance there was to survive this. Somehow, he had the ability to bring out the best in the team when it really mattered...and Tilly hadn't yet quite worked out exactly how he did it.

'How's he doing at the head end?' asked Dexter. The trauma team-leader had overall control of the situation without being bogged down in performing any of the individual tasks the rest of the team carried out and, as far as Tilly was concerned, Dexter was one of the best she'd ever seen. It was an extraordinarily stressful position, but he was able to perform in the most difficult circumstances with the utmost competence and calm professionalism. He also managed to do it with an undisputable and impressive authority that, much to her increasing despair, Tilly found achingly attractive.

'Oxygen sats ninety-six; good air entry,' replied Trent, the heli-medic.

'Pelvis?' said Dexter, turning his attention to Tilly.

'Pelvis unstable; belt in situ,' she replied. 'Abdomen distended and firm, indicating bleeding.'

'Check if CT are ready. We'll need a full body scan to find out what's going on in there.'

'Sure,' she replied, stepping away and lifting the phone to call CT.

Why did the way he'd looked at her make her heart bang even harder in her chest?

It had happened the very first time he'd locked his eyes on hers four months ago, when she'd started her job at Trafalgar Hospital, and every time since. But Dexter Stevens was the last man on earth she should get involved with. If she was going to get involved with anyone ever again, she wanted someone steady, reliable and sensible. Someone who wouldn't flee like a scalded cat when he found out about her leukaemia. Someone who'd genuinely care about her, who would be there if things got tough again and would stick around even if she wasn't always the life and soul of the party. In short, someone who wasn't in the least like her ex, Lachlan.

Her jaw clenched. She was over him…way over him. But he had left a mark. She should be grateful to him, really. He'd taught her a lesson: steer well clear of men who were only interested in having a good time; hold out for someone who genuinely cared about her, who would be reliable through good times and bad; and definitely don't be so easily seduced by handsome good looks.

No. Safe, steady and reliable were the absolute prerequisites for giving her heart away again.

And Dexter was none of those things. Darkly luscious, always composed, he had a brooding charisma, which meant that, although everyone in the department held him in the highest esteem, no one really seemed to know anything about him. He didn't socialise with the team, nor did he have any friendships within the department.

He was a lone wolf, neither welcoming nor seeking friendship from anyone. He never went for a coffee or drink after work, and never entered into any conversations about anything other than what he needed to about patients. He was Head of Department but was the one person everyone knew the least about. Which meant he was the last person she should spend so much time thinking about.

She returned to the cubicle. 'CT scanner is ready whenever we are.'

'Excellent.' This time he didn't floor her with his penetrating gaze but glanced at Mark. 'Obs?'

'BP ninety-five over fifty; heart-rate ninety.'

'Better,' replied Dexter. 'GCS is still nine. Let's get him into CT. Trent, stay at the head; Tilly, you come along too.'

Tilly loaded all the portable monitoring equipment onto the bed alongside their patient. It turned out he was a thirty-two-year-old teacher called Martin Cookson who had simply been out for a leisurely bike ride along the country lanes near his home when a car had ploughed into the back of him, throwing him into the air and causing him to land heavily on the road. Luckily, the friend who'd been riding with him was a junior doctor who'd recognised the need for an air ambulance and had been able to give first aid.

The control room in the scanner suite was necessarily darkened. The only light came from the bank of monitors that glowed with images of scanned slices through Martin's body which Dexter was examining silently. The small room hadn't been designed to provide much in the way of appropriate personal space, and somehow she'd ended up with him on her left and the wall on her right. She leant against the cool wall, pressing herself into it just to try to create a little space between them. The thought of accidentally brushing against him sent a delicious shudder through her spine but she knew that, if she did brush his skin with her own, he would once again be the last thing she thought about before she fell asleep that night. It was already happening all too often lately.

'Subdural bleed in the left occipital region in keeping with the abrasion on the head,' remarked Dexter, his focus on the CT scanner screen, which was whirring and beeping its way methodically down Martin's battered body. 'Cervical spine intact; left-sided haemothorax as expected.'

He stood, hands casually in the pockets of his navy scrubs, legs apart, dark head bent slightly as he gazed at the mesmerising, ever-changing images on the screen. He could have been a movie star, he was so damn handsome.

Was that why she was so drawn to him? Because of his perfect good looks, toned body and smouldering, 'come to bed' eyes?

Hell, no. Someone that good-looking was surely not to be trusted. Was it because she admired his incomparable ability as an A&E doctor? There was no doubt she did admire that, but she'd worked with plenty of excellent medical staff before and not found herself drifting off to sleep at night thinking about them.

'Vital signs holding,' she advised.

Dexter continued his running commentary.

'Thoracic spine clear.' But then his eyes narrowed. 'There's one culprit. He has a splenic tear—grade five.'

Tilly's heart sank. Grade five was the most severe and suddenly Martin's life was in even greater and more imminent danger.

'Hi, what have we got?' Robert Luscombe, general surgeon, strode in.

'Cyclist versus car,' replied Dexter, still studying the screen. 'Forty miles an hour; minor subdural bleed; treated haemothorax; grade five splenic injury and…there we go. A fractured pelvis with significant bleeding. This is going to take some sorting out.'

His expression was impassive. He was just stating a fact—a cold, hard fact. Tilly's heart went out to the young man who'd simply been enjoying the fresh air on a summer's day and now lay with his life held in that fragile place between life and death, completely in the hands of the medical team around him. But Dexter Stevens, once again, was emotionless. In the four months she'd worked at this prestigious major trauma centre in the heart of London, she'd never seen a shred of emotion from him—not under any circumstances. Nothing ever touched him.

'Have the orthos answered yet?' Dexter asked, moving away from the screen, having apparently seen everything he needed to.

'On their way,' replied Tilly.

'We'll have to work with the orthos on him at the same time,' said Robert, grimacing. 'He's in a bad way, poor guy. I'll get into Theatre now, so send him straight from here if you like.'

'Will do,' said Dexter, opening the door. 'Let's go.'

Tilly glanced at him, her stomach doing a silly somersault as she briefly caught his eye, before slipping back into the scanner room to ready the patient for transfer.

Why on earth did she find him so fascinating?

It made no sense. Instinctively she knew she shouldn't go within a million miles of him, but something about him drew her in. It was more than unnerving. Dexter Stevens was an untouchable, cool operator with a heart of ice, and every fibre of her being told her to stay well away from him. The problem was, although her head logically told her that, it only seemed to make him all the more interesting.

His exceptionally quick, analytical thinking was highly impressive and had served him well in stabilising their seriously ill patient, diagnosing his injuries and instigating treatment. But if he cared about poor Martin Cookson, he didn't let it show. Not one bit. And that should be a red flag—a big red flag—waving in the breeze as a warning to stop wondering what it would be like to be held in his strong, toned arms. But, for some unfathomable reason, the red flag didn't shout a warning to Tilly, it beckoned her, tempting her, luring her towards him. For, if there was one thing her brush with her own mortality had taught her, it was that she wanted to live.

Tilly Clover bothered him…much more than he cared to admit. He glanced at her sideways as he wrote in his patient's notes. She'd scooped up a crying toddler with bloody knees and a bleeding head wound, said something in his ear and made him stop crying in seconds. The child was now safely ensconced on an examination couch and Tilly was playing some game with a teddy bear, making the now calm and happy toddler chuckle with delight.

Was she a child whisperer or something? Why couldn't he do that?

'Dr Stevens?'

He swung round, startled, hoping he hadn't been clocked looking at Tilly. It was Pearl, one of the junior doctors, and she was smiling.

'I've just had a call from ITU—Martin Cookson, the cyclist from this morning, is out of Theatre. It's good news—they managed to do an open reduction and internal fixation on the pelvis, and the splenectomy was successful.'

He nodded. 'Can you see the patient in Majors, bed five, please, Dr Giles?' he replied, aware her eyebrows had drawn together very slightly at his response.

'I just thought you'd want to know.' She turned and left, heading towards Majors.

It was good news that their earlier patient was now much more stable, but there were currently scores of other people in the department who needed to be seen, and his policy had always been that once a patient left A&E he tried not to think further about them. That was how he rolled. Caring too much about everyone who came through the doors would be a sure-fire way to burn out faster than a cheetah could chase down a tortoise. Remaining detached was far preferable and had served him well all his professional life—most of his life, full stop. Living with a grieving, angry, alcoholic father had taught him many things, one of which was that emotions and caring about people only got him hurt...in more ways than one.

'Dexter, can you have a look at a three-year-old in seven, please?'

Tilly. Sister Tilly Clover. He'd know that sunshine voice of hers anywhere, even with his eyes shut. Whoever had recruited her into his department four months ago hadn't realised just how much of an effect her presence would bring—both to A&E and, disconcertingly, to himself. It wouldn't be an exaggeration to say that, although she'd brought with her first-class nursing skills, she'd also brought what he could only describe as the brightest and most annoying sparkle he'd ever seen. She hummed everywhere she went, and when she wasn't humming she was singing. Everyone had immediately taken to her as though she'd sprinkled magic fairy-dust on them...

Everyone except him. According to everyone else, she was one of the wonders of the world and had breathed fresh air, light and energy into the department. But, as far as he was concerned, the department had been fine as it was. Tilly Clover was an excellent nurse, there was no question of that. But she hadn't arrived quietly and apprehensively, as new members of staff usually did; she'd arrived with a flourish, a penchant for fun and a quick wit, which she far too regularly directed at him. And he didn't know how to respond.

'What's the problem?'

'James: three years old; bright as a button yesterday but this morning was difficult to rouse from sleep. Temp thirty-nine point five; resps forty-five; fretful but drowsy. I've checked him for a rash and there's nothing, but his hands and feet are pretty cold. I'm concerned it could be meningitis. Would you take a look at him, please?'

If Tilly was concerned about a patient, then so was he. She

wasn't one to worry for no reason. 'Any other symptoms? Aversion to light? Vomiting?'

'No. It could just be a simple viral infection, but the cold extremities are a bit of a red flag, and I want you to cast your eyes over him. Better safe than sorry.' She pulled back the curtain to the cubicle and addressed James's mum, Emma Carpenter, who was cradling him. 'This is Dr Stevens.'

'Sister Clover has asked me to take a look at your son.'

'Of course, Doctor. On the couch?'

'He's fine there,' said Dexter. The boy was white as a sheet and clearly febrile. He barely registered as Dexter examined him, carefully checking every inch of his skin, gently turning him to look at his back and finding a small but telling rash. Tilly had been right to be concerned. He needed to get a lumbar puncture done and a specimen sent to the lab asap.

'Sister, can you set up for an LP and ask one of the staff to draw up the antibiotics IV? I'll get a line in and take bloods.'

'What's an LP?' asked James's mum, her gaze darting from her son to Dexter.

'A lumbar puncture,' he replied. And the pressure to get it done was immense.

'That rash has appeared in the last few minutes,' said Tilly, her startlingly unusual amethyst eyes full of concern. 'I did check.'

'The trolley, please,' replied Dexter. Time was of the essence. There was no time to reassure Tilly that he was sure she'd checked or to remind her of what she likely already knew—that a meningitis rash could be absent one minute and present the next.

'Is he going to be all right, Doctor?' Emma Carpenter's eyes were wide.

'We need to do the tests to be sure, Mrs Carpenter,' he replied. 'Can you place James on the couch, please, on his side?'

'Try not to worry, Emma,' said Tilly, touching the woman's arm lightly. 'You did the right thing, bringing James in, which means we can do the tests and start treatment nice and early. Mother's intuition is a wonderful thing.'

She smiled, drawing the curtains aside, calling to one of the other staff to get the antibiotic. She'd registered the seriousness of the situation; he'd seen it in her eyes when he'd uncovered the rash. Those extraordinary eyes...always sparkling with joy, fun and laughter. He'd learned very quickly that they only lost their sparkle when she was truly worried. And right now, quite rightly, they were full of concern.

'Just going to insert a cannula, Mrs Carpenter.'

'What's that for?' she asked, still looking terrified. As ever, difficult as it was, Dexter tried not to look into her eyes, at least not for longer than he had to. Getting involved emotionally with patients was never a good thing. Remaining detached, keeping a cool head, was far better for everyone involved.

'I need to take some bloods, and we'll use it to give fluids and any drugs too.'

'Do you want me to run saline through that?' asked Tilly, reappearing with the silver trolley.

'Yes,' he replied, thankful she hadn't taken long. This little boy was in a bad way. Every minute they delayed could be the difference between him living to recover completely, being left with a lifelong disability or not making it at all. His mum planted a tender kiss on the top of his head, still cradling him, and for a moment Dexter watched the way she looked at her son, her eyes full of both love and fear for the little boy.

Tilly had been correct; Emma Carpenter had been right to bring her son into hospital as quickly as she had. He never underestimated a mother's intuition when it came to knowing her child. Would his own mother have been the same with him...if she'd lived? He'd never know but, growing up, he'd always liked to think that she would have loved him, as this mother clearly loved little James.

'I'll gown up,' he said, dismissing the thought. It was no

good thinking like that—that wasn't going to help James or his mum.

He snapped on the sterile gloves as Tilly tied the back of the gown behind him. Blue sterile drapes in place, Dexter carefully located the exact point of entry for the spinal needle, inserting it swiftly and aspirating the clear spinal fluid that would tell them if, as suspected, James had bacterial meningitis. The effect of the adrenaline surging through his veins was difficult to ignore. This procedure was intricate and carried grave risks.

It would be easy to acknowledge the way his heart rate had ratchetted up and put it down to the fact that he cared. But caring alone wasn't going to help James and his family, was it? What they needed right now was someone who was competent, could think clearly and get this diagnosis and treatment right. Caring didn't come into it. Caring was best left to people like Tilly—people who seemed to know what to do with feelings like that.

'Ready for the dressing?' asked Tilly.

He moved his hand in answer to her question and she reached in, brushing his arm as she smoothed the dressing down and leant in to whisper in James's ear.

'All done, James. You did really well. Stay lying down there and Mummy will read you a story.'

She smiled at his mum, her eyes full of sparkle, again and his stomach clenched. And, not for the first time in the last four months, Dexter Stevens was worried. Finding a woman physically attractive was one thing but, with those exquisite amethyst eyes, glossy dark hair highlighted with subtle wisps of the same colour and vivacious ability to make everyone smile when she entered the room, Tilly Clover was something else.

He drew in a breath. *Stop it.* He admired her abilities as a first-class nurse—end of. That was all.

'What happens now?' asked James's mum, stroking her son's blond head but with her gaze still firmly fixed on Dexter.

'We give the antibiotics,' he replied, 'and wait for the LP results.' He pulled the gown, tearing the paper ties and scrunching it into a ball before placing it into a bin. He wished he could say more, wished he could tell her that little James was going to be fine, but no one knew that yet, and he wasn't going to give false hope. Being disappointed over something that meant everything was devastating. He'd learned that lesson many times over.

'But he's going to be okay, isn't he? Doctor…?' Emma Carpenter's gaze flicked from him to Tilly and back again. 'Please tell me he's going to be okay.'

Her eyes were wide and glossy with quickly forming tears. His stomach sank. His training and experience meant that he knew exactly what to do for a sick child—piece together the puzzle of diagnosis by assessing the signs and symptoms, quickly formulate and instigate the correct treatment plan then rapidly and expertly perform the required procedures. What he was less able to do was provide Emma Carpenter with the cast-iron reassurance she wanted, because that would mean letting go of the strict rules he lived by.

'I'm popping the antibiotics in now,' said Tilly, throwing him a quizzical look as she attached an IV line to the cannula in James's arm. 'Which means they'll get working to fight the infection straight away. He's in the best place, Emma, and you did well to bring him in so quickly. It's a matter of keeping everything crossed now—and, more importantly, for you to read that book to James.' She smiled. It was a warm, genuine smile and Emma Carpenter managed a smile back before picking up the story book and turning her attention back to her son.

How did Tilly do that? How did she know exactly the right thing to say? And why didn't he? It was because the strict rules Dexter lived by didn't include giving the sort of things that Tilly could provide. In order to provide the high level of expertise he strived to achieve, he needed to remain professional at all times. And that meant becoming emotionally involved with patients and their lives wasn't advisable. Emotions muddied the waters, muddled clear thinking and confused logic. He was a better doctor for being able to see and think clearly without the distraction of sentiment.

'All done,' whispered Tilly, smiling at Emma, who smiled back, continuing to read out loud to James. 'See you in a bit.' Emma nodded as Tilly pulled the curtain to one side.

'I'll give the lab an hour,' said Dexter as they left the cubicle. 'And if we haven't heard anything I'll give them a call for the results.'

'Do you think he'll be okay?' asked Tilly, tapping on a tablet to sign for the antibiotics.

'Hopefully,' replied Dexter. 'It looks as though it's been caught early. The rash appeared practically before our eyes and we got the antibiotics in quickly.'

'Perhaps it would help Emma if you told her that.' She glanced up at him, her lips pressed together and one dark eyebrow raised.

'I don't want to give her false hope. I'll give her more information when I have it.'

Tilly drew in a breath. 'It's not really *false* hope, though, is it? It's *actual* hope. I think sometimes, it's good to give that—patients need hope. Try it some time.' She picked up a phone at the nurse's station and dialled a number.

Dexter blinked. *Had she just had a go at him?* He sat down and logged into a computer. He'd just done a damn good job. He'd made a diagnosis and initiated the correct treatment efficiently and effectively. He'd done what he'd trained hard to do but Tilly Clover seemed to think that his medical expertise wasn't complete because he hadn't offered empty promises to a concerned mum.

He opened James notes and updated them with the facts, and not with false platitudes. He was good at his job, and no one was going to tell him differently.

One of the reasons he'd wanted to become a doctor so badly,

despite the obstacles which had lain in his path, was to give something back. One of the few times he'd ever felt he mattered to anyone had been as a young child, when he'd been admitted to A&E himself with appendicitis. He'd seen how flawlessly professional the doctors and nurses had been—how swiftly they'd acted, how calmly they'd performed what they'd needed to and how grateful he'd been that they'd taken over from the chaos that had been his drunken father.

He'd been so determined to study medicine that even his father telling him that the idea was preposterous, and that he should get over himself with his grand ideas, hadn't deterred him. Neither had the fact that he didn't exactly come from the sort of background that medical students usually came from. He hadn't been able to afford extra tuition to pass the entrance exams or the books to study from. Even earning enough money to scrape together enough for the train fare to go to university open days and for interviews had required him to work long hours in the evenings and weekends in a supermarket warehouse. And he'd done it. He'd passed the exams to be awarded a scholarship to study medicine at Oxford and graduated with first class honours.

But he'd never rested on his laurels—he wanted to be the best A&E consultant. He wanted to be able to give other people the same level of care he'd received as a frightened child when his father had been escorted down to the café to sober up and the staff left around him had, for the first time in his life, made him feel that he mattered. Their professionalism, their attention to detail and their expertise was what had saved his life. He'd never admired anyone until that point. But suddenly he'd found his purpose, and he couldn't thank them enough for providing it.

He'd achieved what he'd set out to achieve. He was a consultant in one of the most prestigious emergency departments in the country. Every day, he made good decisions; every day, he made a difference to people's lives—and he didn't need Tilly Clover pointing out that doing all that wasn't quite good enough.

He didn't need that because he already knew. He was a good doctor but he had rules. Rules that Tilly Clover wouldn't understand: Keep a professional distance.

Don't let emotions get in the way of logical decision making.

Dexter Stevens didn't do feelings—in fact, he'd spent almost his whole life avoiding them with patients and everyone else. It had worked for him…mostly.

Helena had been the exception. He'd allowed feelings in then. Or thought he had. Apparently, he hadn't let them in enough and she'd found someone else. He'd tried to erase the words she'd shouted at him when he'd seen her new lover leave through the back door of her house as he'd come in the front.

Someone who doesn't have a heart of unbreakable steel… Someone who can tell me he loves me…

He'd thought he had shown her he loved her. He'd never told her, though. And it hadn't been enough.

His heart wasn't made of unbreakable steel. It had shattered. And he was never going to risk it shattering again.

Which meant sticking to his rules. Emotions and feelings were Tilly's forte, not his. He had no need of them. He could function better without them. Emotions only complicated life, and were to be avoided at all costs, because he'd known for a long time that feeling something would end the world as he knew it.

CHAPTER TWO

ANIKA, ONE OF the nurses, sank down into a chair at the nurse's station beside Tilly with an exhausted sigh.

'You okay?' said Tilly, looking up. 'Anything I can help with?'

'Dexter dealt with it,' replied Anika. 'In his usual affable way. I'd put a couple of sutures in this patient's eyebrow... disagreement in the pub as per...and he started kicking off about his wait time. Anyway, Dexter must have heard, came in and read him the riot act in that cool-as-a-cucumber way he has that somehow shuts people up in a second.'

'Go and get a coffee,' said Tilly. 'I'm almost finished here, so I can crack on with the next patient. You deserve a quick break.' The job was challenging enough without having to take abuse, and staff needed to support each other when that happened.

'You sure?'

'Absolutely. Go, go!' Tilly smiled and waved her away like a mother hen, just as Dexter came round the corner and walked towards them.

'Ah, Anika,' he said. 'Have you finished in cubicle twelve? I need it for a patient.'

Anika brought her palm to her forehead. 'Oh, sorry—I haven't cleared away, have I?'

'I'll do it,' said Tilly, 'if you can run that errand for me... please?'

'Oh...the errand...yes. Thanks, Tilly.' Anika gave Dexter a weak smile and left.

'She's thanking you for getting her to run an *errand*?' said Dexter, a dark eyebrow raised above the bluest eyes. Tilly's stomach flipped.

'She's very polite,' replied Tilly, turning back to the computer, reluctant to look away from him but hoping that by doing so her heart rate might return to normal. It didn't. 'I hear you just booted a lively patient out of the department.'

He sat down and logged onto the computer, his nearness making her breathing deepen as always. 'Not booted, no. I merely explained that I was giving him the opportunity to leave quietly. He very wisely took the advice.'

'I don't know how you do it, Dexter—you have the knack of being able to persuade people like that guy to behave. Security love it—you do their job for them.' She logged out of her own machine and swivelled her chair to get up.

'Good to know I have your approval on that at least, Sister,' he replied. 'Anyway, there's no need for heavy handedness.'

'It's the only language some people understand, though, isn't it?' He was referring to her remark earlier about reassuring James's mum. Dexter wasn't completely beyond reproach, especially when it came to his communication skills.

'There's nothing that can't be solved with the right words,' he replied.

'And yet, you're a man of so few.' She smiled at him, slotted her pen back into her pocket and headed for cubicle twelve. In her first four months at Trafalgar Hospital, Tilly had got the lowdown on every single member of staff, from cleaners to consultants. She knew their names, their partners' and children's names and, most importantly, how they liked their tea. But Dexter Stevens was a closed book. No, not just closed… He was like one of those secret diaries she'd had as a teen, with a great big padlock and key hidden away where no one could find it.

And that was what pulled her towards him. That and those piercing blue eyes, not to mention the ripped body and glossy raven hair that flopped casually over one eye when he dipped his head at a certain angle.

'Cubicle twelve,' he called after her.

She didn't turn round but raised her hand in acknowledgement as she continued to walk away from him. Dexter Stevens might well be in possession of a body that could only be described as perfection, and eyes she could lose herself in for days, but although the pull of him was powerful she was determined to resist. Dexter Stevens was a delicious temptation but the dark, mysterious air he pulled around himself like a cloak was a warning to stay back.

She cleared the cubicle quickly.

'Ready?' Dexter peered round the curtain.

'All done,' she replied. He'd given her all of one and a half minutes.

'I'll get the next patient.'

'Oh, before you go...did you get James's results?'

'As expected,' he replied. 'Bacterial meningitis.'

'Have you spoken to his mum?'

'Not yet.'

'I'll come with you, after this.'

'I'm quite capable of—' he began.

'I know,' butted in Tilly. 'But she was super-worried and she'll probably be upset.'

Dexter looked back at her, a slight frown creasing his brow.

'She'll need an explanation and a bit of support,' clarified Tilly.

His frown deepened.

'And we all know that's not where your particular strengths lie, Dr Stevens.'

His eyebrows nearly reached his hairline. Tilly held up her hands. 'I'm just saying,' she continued, 'that your strengths lie more in your practical skills rather than in...you know... being nice to people.'

'That's not true.'

She pursed her lips, folding her arms. 'Let's just say, there's room for improvement.'

'Knock, knock,' came a female voice from the other side of the curtain.

'Come in,' said Tilly.

The curtain inched open. It was Geetha Iyengar, the hospital's chief executive.

'Ah, here you are, Dexter—tracked you down at last.'

'Can I help?' he replied.

'I don't want to bother you if you're busy; have you got a moment?'

Dexter looked pointedly behind the CEO to the overflowing waiting area, saying nothing. He didn't need to. Geetha turned to look, took a moment and returned her gaze to meet Dexter's cool, questioning stare.

'I think I'm still missing your RSVP,' she said, her hands clasped in front of her.

'Think?' he replied.

'I *am* missing it,' she clarified. 'Unless you've posted it in the last couple of days?'

'I haven't.'

She sighed. 'Then can you, please? The hotel needs numbers and it's only two weeks away now.'

'I bet you can't wait,' said Tilly. 'Two weeks until your wedding. It sounds amazing. I'm looking forward to the banana-leaf meal.'

'I'm so glad you're coming, Tilly, and thanks for your RSVP. It's just you, isn't it? No plus one?'

'Just me,' she replied with a smile.

Dexter once again looked pointedly behind Geetha to the full waiting room. 'We should probably get on.'

Tilly couldn't help but roll her eyes at Geetha, whose gaze darted back to Dexter, who was checking his watch.

'If a verbal RSVP is adequate, I accept your invitation,' said Dexter. 'Now, we really should see some patients.'

Tilly blinked slowly. *Had he really just spoken to lovely Geetha as though she were the hospital cat? And had he actually meant it to sound as though, by accepting her kind wedding invitation, he'd done her a favour?*

'Thank you, Dexter—will there be a plus one?'

'No,' he replied.

'I'll leave you to get on, then. I have a meeting with Finance this afternoon to discuss the possibility of purchasing the new ENT equipment you requested. I'll let you know how it goes at some point…when you have time.'

Tilly smiled gleefully at the CEO's punchy parting shot, Dexter's scowl as he watched Geetha leave only widening her smile further. Well, he shouldn't have been so rude.

'See?' said Tilly, nodding towards the curtain. 'Room for improvement.'

'No one's suggested that before, but thank you for your advice.'

'You're welcome.' She beamed.

'I'm going to get the next patient,' he said, arching an eyebrow.

She gave a mock salute, making his eyebrow rise further. He walked past her, his earthy, warm, masculine scent filling her nostrils as he breezed out. She took a deep breath, breathing in more of him, aware her heart was beating a little harder and faster, as it did every time her attraction towards him reached her awareness…as it did far too often. She threw the wipes into the bin and pulled down a fresh sheet of paper roll to cover the couch, glancing round the cubicle and making sure everything was in order.

It was—much more in order than her head, which currently seemed to be controlled by two conflicting creatures: a sensible fairy godmother who reminded her that Dexter Stevens, with his surly manner and sarcastic quips, was the absolute opposite of the kind, caring, thoughtful man she wanted; and an annoying, prodding imp who made her wonder what the contours of the muscles beneath his navy scrubs would feel like under her fingers. When he wasn't near, the voice of the fairy godmother was louder, but in his presence the imp shouted loudest and was becoming impossible to ignore.

She wanted adventure, didn't she? Throughout the years of chemo, dreaming of the adventures she might have one day was what had kept her going, kept her fighting. Becoming a nurse, leaving home, going to work in London were all things she'd dreamt of when life itself had been hanging in the balance. Leukaemia had almost claimed her life, but it had also given her dreams, and now she was determined to live them. That was what going to work in Australia was all about—finding the biggest challenge, the greatest test, the ultimate dream.

Not knowing how long she had left to live had focussed her mind. And Tilly's mind had focussed over and over again on the same thing: an adventure that had started as a tiny nugget of an idea one night when she hadn't been able to sleep because of the exquisitely painful mouth ulcers she'd developed during the second round of chemo. A nurse had done a session of guided imagery with her and she'd tried to imagine herself on a wide, sandy beach, soaking up the warm rays of the sun, picking up a handful of warm sand and letting it run through her fingers as she listened to the waves lapping softly a few feet away.

She'd imagined the beach was in Australia and the rest was history. A plan had taken shape, online research had been done and an adventure had emerged bit by bit that she'd clung onto through every subsequent round of chemo. It had been the best therapy. It had sustained her through two years of active treatment and through the draining tiredness, the unrelenting nausea, the weight loss and the infections.

And the smothering love from her family. She could only imagine the hell her family had gone through when she'd been diagnosed aged thirteen and when she'd gone through the rounds of gruelling chemo. Naturally, they'd wanted to protect her—she understood that—but being wrapped in cotton wool so tightly had become stifling. As her friends had planned their careers and trips abroad, got boyfriends and planned their futures, she hadn't even known if she would have a future. Everyone around her, well-meaning as they absolutely were, had only confirmed that in the way they'd protected her so fervently. She'd longed to be free from the constraints her well-meaning family had placed around her; maybe even take a risk or two. The gilded cage they'd constructed around her had become more and more restricting, making its presence felt more than ever when her consultant had told her she was in remission.

Suddenly, she'd had the green light to live the life she'd dreamt about. But she'd been so fiercely guarded that the longed-for freedom to live had felt too new, too unfamiliar and way too daunting. She'd missed out on the years in which self-confidence and independence should have been built and it had left her desperate to make her dreams come true but unable to believe she had it in her to do so. Her parents hadn't wanted her to become a nurse, but her need to give something back had given her the strength to push through their objections and her own insecurities about her abilities and do her training.

When she'd been offered the job in London a few months ago, her parents had begged her not to leave home, and she'd had to battle with them as well as her own fears about leaving her small home counties town to go and live in the city. But it had been a step towards the bigger goal—if she could move to London and be okay, maybe she could make Australia happen too. Small steps towards the big dream. Eventually, her family had finally understood and given her their blessing. Telling them about Australia had been a whole different story...

Dexter walked back into the cubicle, followed by a patient who most definitely had the 'appendicitis walk'. The young man was bending forward and clutching his right lower-abdomen.

'Hello,' she said, taking the man's arm and guiding him towards the couch. 'I'm Tilly, one of the nurses. What's your name?'

'Sam,' he replied, grimacing.

'Okay, Sam, let's get you on the couch so the doctor can have a look at you. Keep holding your side and I'll swing your legs up.'

Dexter went to wash his hands at the sink. He was the opposite of fun-seeking, immature, unreliable Lachlan, but Dexter Stevens wasn't the sort of man who would tick the boxes that Lachlan had inadvertently taught her she needed ticking. He wasn't fun-seeking, responsibility-shirking Lachlan, but he also wasn't the warm-hearted, considerate, emotionally open, solid man she needed either. He was something entirely different.

She glanced at him as she placed a pillow under Sam's head. Dexter Stevens was an adventure waiting to happen. The pull of him was powerful. If she was honest with herself, it wasn't just the fact that she admired him as a clinician; it wasn't just that he was the very definition of achingly handsome... No, the reason he made her heart bang against her ribs and her breathing deepen was because there was something darkly exciting about him—something forbidden, something risky.

She'd battled her illness and fears. She was over responsibility-shirking Lachlan. And now, despite her head screaming at her to play safe, she really wanted to take a risk.

'Any chance of some painkillers?' groaned Sam as Tilly lowered the back of the couch down to allow Dexter to examine him.

'I need to examine you first,' said Dexter. 'How long have you had the pain?' He placed his hands on the obviously tense abdomen.

'Just this morning. It's got worse.' He winced. 'Ow!'

'Relax,' said Dexter, frowning in concentration as his hands methodically palpated, moving towards the right iliac fossa where the pain appeared to be centred.

'I can't; I'm in agony.'

'We'll give you something for the pain in a moment,' said Tilly, smiling down at him.

'Can't you give me something before there's any more prodding?'

'Palpating,' said Dexter. Why did patients insist on using that word? It made the skilled process of assessing abdominal pain sound so crude.

'Pal...what?' replied Sam.

'The technical word for "prodding" is "palpating",' explained Tilly, smiling and giving Sam's arm a light squeeze. 'Some doctors like to be a bit technical; they think it makes them sound clever. Nearly done, though...hang on a moment longer.'

Dexter caught her look as he glanced at her—her eyes sparkling with mischief and her lips not quite suppressing a grin. He got it. It wasn't the first time she'd teased him like that. She'd called him 'a stickler' on her first day in the department, 'a nit-picker' on the third and she'd given a variety of other names to describe what she clearly thought best suited what he saw as his vigilant, perhaps slightly perfectionist, personality at various times since. He was no longer taken aback at what she clearly saw as amusing leg-pulling, and he refused to rise to the bait as she evidently desperately wanted him to. But it was getting increasingly difficult not to respond to the infectious sparkle in her eyes, and he'd had to turn away from her more than once to hide a smile that threatened his own lips.

'Let me know if this hurts,' said Dexter. He pressed onto the abdomen directly above where the appendix lay then released his hand from the area.

'Argh!'

Rebound tenderness—appendicitis. He'd been correct.

'Ten milligrams of morphine titrated to response,' he said, glancing at Tilly. 'I'll get a line in and bleep the surgeons.'

'Surgeons?' said Sam, looking startled.

'You have appendicitis,' replied Dexter, rewashing his hands and reaching for a cannula. 'You'll need an operation to remove the appendix.'

'Won't that morphine take the pain away?'

'It will,' said Dexter, pulling a tourniquet around Sam's arm firmly, 'But not for long, and it won't cure the underlying problem. Sharp scratch…'

'Would you like me to give the explanation about appendicitis?' said Tilly. 'Or would you prefer to?'

He glanced up at her and had the distinct feeling that she wanted *him* to explain. Fine—he could do that.

'Appendicitis is the most common cause of an acute abdomen, and is initiated usually by the obstruction of the lumen of the intestine, leading to inflammation and possibly peritonitis—'

'Perhaps in English?' interrupted Tilly.

He looked up at her again and frowned.

Tilly turned to Sam. 'Sometimes doctors have their own language and forget that everyone else speaks plain English.'

Sam managed a grimacing grin.

'The appendix is a tiny part of the bowel, just here.' She indicated to her own right lower-abdomen. 'It can become inflamed just like anything else can—your tonsils, for example—and once it's inflamed it has to be removed. It's a very simple procedure these days, though. It can be done with keyhole surgery so it won't spoil your six-pack.' She smiled at him and then at Dexter. 'I'll nip out and get your painkiller. Back in a tick. You're doing really well.'

Dexter didn't look up but he could hear her humming to herself as she made her way to the clinical room. Tilly Clover was an excellent nurse but this was another of those times when he had to clench his teeth. She could drive a sane person crazy. What was with the 'doctors have their own language' comment? His explanation, as far as it had gone before she'd interrupted him, was textbook. He could have been a lot more technical if he'd wanted to.

Sliding a cannula into place in Sam's arm, he drew off a set of bloods. And, if she hummed that particular song once more today, he was going to have to tell her to pipe down, or at least hum something different.

'Here we go,' said Tilly, coming back in. 'How are you doing Sam?'

'I'm in agony,' Sam replied, lying on his side, his legs now curled up.

'You'll feel better very quickly when this goes in,' said Tilly.

'Knock, knock.' The cubicle curtain moved slightly.

'Come in,' said Tilly.

'I hear you've got a customer for me?' It was Robert Luscombe. Dexter handed over.

'Twenty-four-year-old, usually fit and well. RIF pain since this morning, steadily getting worse. Tender, guarding, rebound tenderness. Pyrexial at thirty-eight; tachy at one ten. FBC, U&Es and clotting done. Morphine going in as we speak.'

'Any chance of that in English?' said Sam, his face now less contorted with pain.

'Doctor speak again,' said Tilly, rolling her eyes at Sam. 'What he means is that you have all the signs and symptoms of appendicitis, that he's taken a blood sample for tests and that we're giving you some painkiller.' She lowered her voice conspiratorially but kept it just loud enough that Dexter could still hear. 'I should start charging for interpreter services.'

Dexter looked at her and blinked. He'd handed the patient over concisely, providing all the information the surgical reg needed. There was nothing wrong with that, was there?

'Well, it certainly sounds as though you have appendicitis,' said Robert, smiling. 'How's your pain now?'

'Getting better,' said Sam, beginning to relax as Tilly slowly continued to administer the morphine, watching carefully for his response.

'It's good stuff,' said Tilly, removing the syringe and holding it up for Dexter to see. 'Seven mils.'

He nodded. 'Noted.'

'We'll get you up to the ward, Sam,' said Robert, 'and get your operation done this afternoon, so nothing to eat or drink from now; sorry about that.'

Sam nodded, now much more relaxed.

'Have you got any questions?' asked the surgeon.

'How long will I need to stay in hospital?'

'Probably only overnight,' he replied, smiling. 'We don't want you getting too used to the luxurious hospitality here.'

Tilly nudged Sam with her elbow. 'So don't worry about having to learn the language.'

'I'll see you up on the ward, Sam,' said Robert, raising his hand and beaming as he left. 'We'll look after you, don't worry.'

Sam nodded, managing a smile before he closed his eyes.

'Robert's lovely, isn't he?' whispered Tilly, looking at a lightly sleeping Sam.

Dexter had never considered whether Robert Luscombe was lovely or not and wasn't sure how to answer her question. The surgeon had turned up, confirmed the diagnosis and agreed to take the patient to Theatre—that was all he could ask for. Whether he was lovely or not wasn't relevant.

'He's so pleasant and cheerful and friendly,' she continued, her head to one side, as though thinking hard. 'And warm and sociable and…' She brought a finger to her lips and glanced at him, her eyes sparkling with humour. Ah; she was making a point.

'And I'm not?'

Damn it, he'd taken the bait.

She straightened up, pretending to look shocked.

'Oh, I didn't say that,' she protested.

But that was exactly what she'd been saying—and she was right.

She held out her hand towards him. 'If you pass me those bloods, I'll get them sent off.'

'So you're going to the wedding of the year, then?' said Dexter, handing her the bag. The revelation she was going to the wedding without a plus one had been oddly pleasing. Odd, because it didn't make sense—on any level.

'Of course,' she replied. 'A two day south-Indian wedding, held in a castle on the Northumbrian coast, who wouldn't jump at the chance of that?' She tucked a stray wisp of amethyst-highlighted hair behind her ear and cocked her head to one side, as though thinking again. 'Except you, by the sounds of it.'

He shifted his stance uncomfortably. He'd put off replying to the invitation from the CEO and knew exactly why. He hated parties, and he hated wedding-related ones even more. Being a page boy at his auntie's wedding when his father had ruined the reception by slowly getting more and more drunk, increasingly raucous and progressively louder was the first time he'd felt such shame. He'd gone outside after his father had knocked the top tier of the wedding cake to the floor and his auntie's new husband had found him in his hiding place in the branches of a tree.

'I forgot.'

Tilly snorted. 'Forgot? You don't forget anything—you have a brain like a computer.'

'Human brains are far more complex than computers.' He tapped his notes onto his tablet.

'Even more reason not to forget,' said Tilly. 'Well, I'm glad you're going. You don't want to end up with a reputation as being antisocial.'

He glanced up from his tablet, his eyes narrowed.

Was she baiting him again? He knew his reputation. He kept himself to himself and didn't engage in idle chatter about people's home or personal lives outside of work. People thought he was cool and standoffish. But that was how he liked it. Keeping people at arm's length was far more sensible than opening his arms wide and drawing people in towards him, as Tilly did. To do that would leave him vulnerable, an open target at which others could hurl whatever they felt like hurling. Best to keep a distance, not get involved and stay below the parapet. He was no Robert Luscombe, and he didn't walk into a room and light it up like Tilly, either.

'Right, I'll get these sent off and arrange for Sleepy Head to go up to the ward,' said Tilly.

'That would be helpful.'

'That's me,' she replied brightly. 'Always helpful. And talking of helpful…' She lowered her voice, even though Sam was now snoring gently. 'I think it would be really helpful to patients if your explanations could be a little less…medical.'

He frowned.

'You think I should give patients less medical explanations of their medical conditions?'

She nodded. 'Ones that are easier to understand.'

'Everyone knows what appendicitis is and anyway there was nothing wrong—'

'Sam didn't seem to,' she interrupted, staring at him, her hands on her hips.

'Wrong with…' he continued, ignoring the challenge in her stunning eyes, 'My explanation—as far as you allowed me to get with it.'

'Just try toning it down a little,' she suggested. 'You could try cracking a smile sometimes, too…like the lovely Robert Luscombe.'

He scowled. 'I'm here to provide medical care to patients, not to be an advert for teeth whitening.'

'I think it's good to make them feel welcome and to provide a friendly face.'

'Patients come to A&E because they need urgent, expert medical care.' He darted a glance at Sam, who was still sleeping. 'Are you telling me I don't provide that?'

Tilly straightened up, tilting her chin defiantly. 'Not for one second am I doubting that. But you could do all that with a smile occasionally, that's all I'm saying. Try it; it really doesn't hurt.' She jiggled the bag of blood samples. 'I'd better get these sent off.'

She spun on her heel, pulled back the curtain and left the cubicle. In a second, the humming began once again and he drew in a breath. How did she do it? How did she manage to make him want to gaze into her stunning eyes one minute and need to leave the room the next? How could he be so drawn towards her infectious sparkle and undeniable warmth yet find her deeply maddening at the same time?

And exactly why had he felt suddenly compelled to accept Geetha's wedding invitation when he usually avoided parties as a Grinch avoids Christmas?

Because Tilly was going…without a plus one.

And an enticing but puzzling thought had slipped, uninvited into his mind. The wedding was an opportunity to see Tilly somewhere other than work. But he wasn't interested in people's lives outside of work. And, as beautifully hypnotic as her eyes were, and as much as her ever-present sparkle somehow had him on a reel being inexorably drawn towards her, there was no way he wanted anything other than an entirely professional relationship with her.

So why had his heart lifted when she'd said there was no plus one? He drew in a deep breath, letting it out slowly, controlling it and regaining the power over his errant thoughts.

He wouldn't go to the wedding. But, damn it, he'd told Geetha he would. He ran his fingers through his hair. He'd held off replying to her invitation for weeks, hoping she'd forget she'd invited him, and on a whim he'd stupidly told her he was going.

And Tilly Clover, with her sunshine smile, irrepressible sense of fun and deeply annoying habit of getting under his skin, was the reason.

CHAPTER THREE

RESTING HER HEAD back on the soft towel she'd placed on the lip of the deep bath, Tilly closed her eyes, allowing the warmth of the water to seep into her muscles and inhaling the sweet scent of the jasmine bubbles she'd poured generously into the tub. The suite had a huge bed, a small sitting area with a sofa, a gorgeous view out over the rugged Northumbrian coastline and a large *en suite,* which she'd decided to make the most of before the Mehndi party that evening.

Dexter had clearly not been keen on coming to the wedding, but understanding why was confounding. The CEO had invited all heads of department. Yes, there was a little bit of pressure to attend, but Geetha was an excellent manager and completely lovely; besides which, this was going to be a spectacular event. It had been the talk of the hospital for months.

If Dexter did turn up, he'd probably skulk about in his usual dark, unsmiling manner wishing he were back at work, whereas she fully intended to enjoy the experience to the full and couldn't wait to share Geetha's joy and have a two-day party, whether he came or not. So why was she thinking about him?

Because she wanted him to come. And that thought hit her smack in the centre of her chest.

'You appear to be in the wrong room.'

Tilly's eyes flew open and she sat up, sending a wave

of water slopping back and forth violently as she drew in a sharp breath.

'Dexter!' Glad of the thick layer of jasmine bubbles, which came up to her neck, she nevertheless instinctively drew her knees in towards her, hugging them to her chest. Deep blue eyes bored into her, his expression unreadable—calm, assured and impassive, as usual giving nothing away, as though standing there while she was naked in the bath before him was the most natural thing in the world. 'What the hell are you doing here?' She glanced at the shocking pink bra and knickers she'd left strewn on the floor inches from his feet and willed him not to notice them.

'I could ask you the same question.'

'This is *my* room.'

'This is room five.'

'Is it?' She couldn't think straight. If questioned right there and then, she wasn't sure she'd be able to remember her own name.

'You'll have to relocate.' His eyes didn't leave hers for the longest moment but she couldn't read them. Dexter Stevens was master of mask-wearing. *How could he just stand there, impassive, with her shocking pink underwear at his feet and her naked in the bath?*

But his lips parted just slightly, and for a second his gaze strayed from her eyes to her mouth, and he drew in a breath. Perhaps he couldn't mask everything he felt. Emboldened, she lifted her chin. It was he who'd walked in on her, after all. She shouldn't be the one who was embarrassed in all this.

'Do you think you could perhaps wait in the bedroom while I get out of the bath and we can sort this out?'

'I'll unpack while you do that.' He lowered his head as he turned to leave and hesitated a moment, the toe of one of his expensive-looking shoes brushing her abandoned bright pink knickers. She cringed.

'Hang on a second,' she replied, having realised what he'd said. 'Unpack?'

'Take my things out of my bag,' he said, lifting his gaze and walking away.

'What if *you're* in the wrong room?'

He turned and stood in the doorway, his eyes sweeping the room and alighting on her—dark blue, powerful eyes making her pulse quicken and her breathing deepen.

'Well, although you seem to have made yourself very much at home, I was assured that my room was number five—the suite with the family crest of the Tynedales on the door.'

'That's what they told me.'

'Well, there must have been a mistake.'

'You don't say.'

'I'll go back down and tell them to sort it out.'

'You do that.' She watched him leave, waiting for the door to close before exhaling deeply, briefly closing her eyes and trying to slow her heart rate. But, when she opened her eyes, the shocking pink underwear was the first thing she saw, disturbed slightly where Dexter's shoe had inadvertently shifted it.

He'd carefully masked his expression but she knew him well enough to know that the way he'd looked at her was far different from how he'd ever looked at her before. He hadn't quite been able to hide the flame in his deep blue eyes when his gaze had lingered on her lips. The fire that had shot through her had been caused because she'd recognised something in them that hadn't matched the coolness of the words he spoke.

Perhaps spending time with him at the wedding wasn't something she should have looked forward to. She wanted to resist the pull of him, didn't she? He didn't tick the boxes—not even close. There were plenty of people to get to know at this wedding and Dexter Stevens wasn't one of them.

She relaxed back onto the towel, resting her arms on the sides of the roll-topped bathtub and looking around the steamy, luxuriously appointed room with its gold taps, beautiful tiling and large, ornate, gilt-edged mirror that stood propped against the wall in the corner.

She inhaled deeply. She hadn't had a break from work in far too long and she was going to enjoy these few days away. Much as she loved her job at the hospital, doing all the extra shifts was probably more than her consultant would advise. Her leukaemia had been in remission for eight years but Dr Banerjee, her lovely haematologist whom she now only had to see once a year, would likely have told her to slow down just a little. Moving out to Australia wasn't going to come cheaply, though, and seeing the money from the extra shifts building up in her account each month only spurred her on to do more.

Besides, the department was rarely fully staffed and shifts needed to be filled. As one of the senior nurses in A&E, the responsibility to ensure patient safety fell to her and she was *never* going to compromise that.

The water had cooled. Picking up her phone from the stand by the bath, she glanced at the time. There was an hour before the Mehndi party. Leaning forward, she opened the hot tap. Ten more minutes to relax would be fine. Closing her eyes and leaning back, the water quickly warming again, her thoughts wandered back to Dexter.

What if there hadn't been an error with the room? What if they had come here together, as a couple, for the long weekend in this beautiful castle *intentionally...*?

A delicious warmth spread through her and it wasn't solely due to the hot water running from the tap. She let her imagination fly... They'd spend most of the weekend in that huge bed in the next room, having food delivered when they wanted it, leaving the *do not disturb* sign on the door in between times, perhaps sharing this bath, soaping each other's bodies...

'You're going to flood the bathroom!'

She gasped and her eyes flew open to see Dexter striding across the room towards her looking horrified, reaching for the tap, turning it off, reaching down into the water yanking out the plug.

'What have you done that for?' Her heart thumped against her ribs at his sudden, unexpected and violent arrival.

'You were about to flood the place.' The sleeve of his shirt was dripping and covered in bath foam and he shook his arm, flinging foam in all directions. 'Had you fallen asleep?'

'No,' she replied indignantly, frowning and once more crossing her arms over her chest.

Had she? Had she, once again, been dreaming about him?

'I was just relaxed.'

'Too relaxed; I'm soaked.' He began to unbutton his shirt and her heart rate climbed further, but not with shock this time. Pulling the shirt from his back, he took hold of the sleeve and squeezed it over the water, then shook it out, turned and draped it over a towel rail. A perfect six-pack was revealed all too briefly before he turned, but she now had a view of his broad back—the powerful, wide shoulders tapering to his waist and carved muscles that moved beautifully beneath smooth, bronzed skin.

He turned to face her, hands curving over the waistband of his dark jeans. Her breathing deepened and she swallowed, wanting but unable to look away.

He was perfect.

She was naked.

She was right. There *had been* a heavenly body hiding away beneath those navy scrubs.

'It turns out there has been a mistake with the room after all,' he said.

Somehow, she found her voice. 'Oh, well, I hope they've put you in a room as nice as this one. Thanks for letting me know.'

'It's not quite as straightforward as that.'

Her heart sank. They'd put *her* in the wrong room. And he was clearly expecting her to be the one to move. 'I've hung all my things up now. You haven't unpacked yet. Couldn't *you* have the other room?'

'There is no other room.'

She shivered just as the bath let out a gurgle as the last of the water drained away, leaving her naked apart from the abundance of bubbles that still covered her.

'Do you think you could perhaps turn around if you're staying to debate this further?' She held up her arm, swirling her hand to indicate to him to look the other way. 'What do you mean, no other room?'

'They're fully booked,' he replied, reaching for a white towel from a neatly folded pile on a dressing table and passing it to her. 'Here.'

She took the towel from him, wrapping it around herself but remaining seated in the bath. He stepped back and turned round, his hands on his hips. Her gaze travelled the length of him, from his dark head to broad shoulders. Angular muscles slid over each other as he adjusted his stance, putting more weight on one leg, his hips tilting, drawing her gaze to his firm ass and down his long legs.

She closed her eyes briefly. 'Have they suggested another hotel?'

'We're in a tiny village that's hosting a huge wedding. Every room is booked. The nearest hotel with a vacancy is sixty miles away, back in town.'

'You're kidding me.'

'Does it look as though I'm kidding you?'

It looked as though he'd walked straight out of the pages of a celebrity special feature in a high-end glossy magazine. And he wasn't the sort of man who would 'kid'.

'So what have they suggested?' She pulled the towel tighter.

'I didn't hang around to find out. They've messed up and there's not much anyone can do about it.'

'This is because you didn't RSVP to Geetha on time.' This was his fault.

'The fact that the hotel has double-booked this room has nothing to do with the very slight delay in my RSVP and everything to do with their incompetence. I'll just go home. I didn't want to come anyway.'

'No, no, no, you're not getting away that easily. Is there honestly no other room?'

Dexter spun round. 'Why would I lie about it?'

Tilly swirled her hand at him again and he turned back round. 'Because it would be a perfect excuse not to stay for the wedding. You clearly didn't want to come, for some weird reason, and this would be a good get-out. Well, you have to stay, you're committed now.'

'And where am I supposed to sleep—in the dungeon?'

'It might be the best place for you if you're going to be so grumpy. No, you can sleep here. It's a huge room and it's only for two nights.'

He turned round again, his eyes wide.

'And where are you going to sleep?'

'Will you stop turning back around? I'm naked beneath these bubbles, thank you very much.'

He carefully held her gaze, as though if he let his concentration slip even for a second it would travel down her body. 'Sorry.' He closed his eyes and turned away.

'In answer to your question,' she continued, 'I'll sleep here too. It's a double room, after all.'

'There's only one bed.'

'Sherlock Holmes had better watch out.'

'Very funny.'

'Well, we just have to make the best of it, don't we? You've told Geetha you'll be here, and she'll be hurt if you're not.'

'I'm sure she'd understand.'

'She won't because we're not telling her. This is her wedding weekend and I'm not having her stressed because of some silly room booking error. She need never know.'

'And what about everyone else? The other people here—other staff from the hospital?'

'They don't need to know either.'

Her phone alarm went off, making her jump. She silenced it.

'I need to get ready for the Mehndi party. So, are we agreed?'

She watched his torso expand as he drew in a breath. 'I suppose there's no option, is there?'

'No. You go and unpack and get changed, then, while I dry off. We've got exactly twenty minutes to get ready.'

He walked out of the bathroom.

'Close the door on the way out,' she called after him.

He reached behind him without turning round, grabbed the door and pulled it closed.

They were going to have to share this room. For the next two nights.

She climbed out of the bath and stood on the rug, clutching the towel around her. She shivered. But whether the shiver was due to her body temperature dropping from getting out of the warmth of the bath, or from the thought of spending the next two nights in a fairy-tale castle with Dexter Stevens, owner of that flawless torso, she wasn't at all sure.

CHAPTER FOUR

DEXTER BRACED HIS hands on the stone windowsill and screwed his eyes shut, before opening them again and staring out onto the courtyard below without seeing the view at all.

Why hadn't he knocked before barging in?

He'd been so annoyed with the room booking fiasco—and himself for causing it—that propriety had eluded him completely. And suddenly he'd been standing in the bathroom with Tilly's dignity being shielded only by bath bubbles. Once he'd dealt with the threat of the bathroom being flooded, his horror at having walked in on her had all but paralysed him. He'd dealt with it the only way he knew how—by ignoring the way his heart had thudded in his chest and discounting the searing heat that had flooded his veins. He'd done what he always did—carefully masked his expression and turned his back on feeling anything.

Feelings were dangerous—they got a person hurt. How many times had he trusted the side of his father that had given him hope that things might change? How often had he longed for more of those brief moments when his father had been sober, smiled at him, told him a silly joke or taken him to the corner shop to buy him a bag of sweets? Those moments had never lasted long but he'd still cherished them. He'd always waited for the next time, always believed that one day his father would stop drinking and be like the other dads.

But that had never happened. His father had never changed.

And eventually Dexter had given up hoping. Trying to love someone who didn't love him back…enduring disappointment after disappointment, one rejection after another…was exhausting. It hurt. Having feelings for someone made a person vulnerable to all those things. It had made him vulnerable when Helena, the only woman he'd ever lost his heart to, had thrown his love for her back in his face. He *had* loved her despite the fact that, according to her, her reason for cheating on him was that he hadn't. But he had loved her; hell, he'd even wondered if they might have a future together.

He hadn't been enough for her, though, had he? And she'd been very clear about why that was—she'd wanted someone who would make her feel loved and cherished. Obviously, taking her to great restaurants, splashing out on luxurious holidays and buying her just about anything she wanted hadn't hit the mark. As it had turned out, she'd wanted the whole hearts and flowers, mushy, sentimental nonsense that he had no idea how to deliver. She'd wanted to get inside his head, have long talks about his past and about feelings. He wasn't that sort of man.

And he didn't want to feel any more. He'd rather be numb. Numbness had a beautiful, safe simplicity, and emotions ruined it.

His father's final rejection of him, some four years ago when he'd been in the last stages of liver failure on the palliative care ward, had come the same week as Helena's scathing appraisal of his shortcomings. He'd known his father's days were numbered. The liver cirrhosis had been in its final stages and Dexter had thought that his father might be a little more forgiving, given that he was coming to the end of his life.

His father had always enjoyed reading the sports pages in the newspaper, so he'd taken a paper to read to him on the ward—his father had been too weak by then to read it himself. But, instead of his father being pleased he'd tried to do something thoughtful, he'd snarled, scornfully telling him if he hadn't brought him a hip flask of whisky he might as well go home.

So Dexter had left, hoping to find some understanding from Helena. But he'd opened the front door to her house and seen a man hurriedly leaving by the back door, with Helena standing there in a bathrobe.

Which was exactly why he was never going to feel anything for anyone ever again. He was never going to be at the mercy of anyone else. Rejection hurt and took way too long to get over. His father was gone and Dexter had been released from continually trying and failing to be accepted by him. Helena was ancient history. The only women he occasionally hooked up with now always knew the score. He only did short term—very short term—and it was only ever physical. No one would ever get into his head again, including Tilly, despite her oddly captivating vivacity and enchanting eyes, and whether they had to share a room together or not.

He sighed heavily, still staring into space. He was still annoyed with himself. Tilly had been right—this was his fault. He'd delayed replying to the CEO's invitation because, stupidly, he'd hoped that by some miracle Geetha might not have noticed he'd not replied and he could get away with not going.

He hated parties. He loathed weddings. And this was an intolerable two-day mix of them both.

Turning away from the window, he caught his reflection in the long mirror that stood beside the wardrobe. Opening his suitcase, he drew out the shirt he'd brought to wear that evening, slipping it on. He didn't need a psychologist to work out why he felt the way he did about events like this and why he was much more comfortable being in the controlled, well-ordered world of A&E, where policies, protocols and procedures drove what people did and how they reacted to situations. Parties required easy conversation skills, the ability to schmooze, the obligatory consumption of large amounts of alcohol, singing and dancing…

He closed his eyes. He'd seen enough raucous parties to last him a lifetime. He didn't know whether his father had always been dependent on alcohol or if his drinking had only started after his mother had died giving birth to Dexter. What he did know was that he'd rarely seen his father sober. Although he'd drink when he was alone, he'd often go to the pub, bringing a few mates back home afterwards. Trying to go to sleep with a thin pillow wrapped around his head to block out the noise and then going to school the next day so tired he could barely keep his eyes open had been commonplace for Dexter.

So, no, he didn't need a psychologist to tell him that he hated parties because they reminded him of a childhood dominated by his father's drinking and terrifying volcanic rages, in which he'd never had the presence of a mum who might have cared he existed.

'Would you mind just fastening this necklace for me, please?'

He turned round. Tilly stood just outside the bathroom door in an ankle-length, softly flowing dress of rich, peacock colours, holding a gold chain around her neck ready to be fastened. He'd never seen her in anything other than her blue uniform scrubs and the difference was startling. Her glossy, dark hair was loose around her shoulders, the subtle amethyst highlights catching the light, matching her exquisite eyes. She was beautiful.

Standing behind her and moving her hair to one side, he took the ends of the chain from her fingers, their warmth infusing his own. He moved her hair back into place, his fingers lingering a moment longer than they needed to, savouring the softness of her hair and inhaling the light, floral scent of her.

'Thank you.' Her sing-song voice had returned, in contrast to the unfamiliar accusatory tone she'd used earlier. 'Are you ready to go down? Love the shirt…very vibrant.'

He looked down at the shirt he'd bought to comply with the dress code of 'bright colours'.

'I guess,' he replied. *Let's get this thing over with.*

'Ever been to one of these before?' asked Tilly, slipping on her sandals and picking up her bag.

'No.' He picked up the room key and slipped it into his pocket. 'Have you?'

'No. I've asked around about them, though. Traditionally the Mehndi party was for women only—a bit like a hen party—but more commonly these days men attend them too, so it's more of a pre-wedding party. You obviously read the memo about brightly coloured clothes.'

'I did.'

'I'm looking forward to getting some henna.'

'Henna?'

'Having your henna done is mandatory at a Mehndi. It's all about the bride having hers done, really, but all the guests have at least a little tattoo.'

'Seriously?'

'Oh, yes.' Tilly looked at him earnestly...almost too earnestly. He narrowed his eyes, unsure whether to believe her. He was getting used to her mischievous teasing.

'It's mandatory?'

'Absolutely. Come on.' She pulled open the door.

Great. They descended the spiral stone staircase in single file, Dexter squeezing and stretching his fists as they walked. The guests at this wedding weren't going to be the drunken, out-of-control losers his father had brought to their home.

Relax, Stevens. None of them are your father, either. There couldn't be many people on this earth—if any—who could match *his* violent temper.

He swallowed. Except maybe himself. The fear he'd lived with all his life crept from the dark recesses in his brain where he tried so hard to keep it buried. A demon that lurked so deeply but, no matter how hard he tried to not acknowledge it, refused to be ignored or silenced.

What if he was like his father? What if, under the right

circumstances—after a drink or in difficult emotional situations—he too had the propensity to be engulfed in the red mist, to let it cloud his judgement so he became enraged, violent and dangerous?

He'd inherited his father's temper—that had been made clear very early on in his life.

He'd lashed out at Harvey Larkin at school that time when he'd been ribbed about his uniform being too small and his trainers being a supermarket brand. The red mist had clouded his judgement then, just for a moment, and he'd struck the boy. He'd been given detention and his father had beaten him when he'd arrived home late.

'If—you're—going to—beat someone—up,' he'd shouted in between striking Dexter with the leather belt he kept by his chair in the living room, 'do it where—no one—can—see you.'

He didn't want to have inherited that vile, destructive temper—he didn't want to repeat the cycle. But he was his father's son; he'd grown up surrounded by violence, so it must still be within him to be unable to control it, but Dexter would let hell freeze over before allowing that to happen. The only way to ensure that it didn't happen was to control every emotion before it controlled him.

They exited the dimly lit stairwell out into the early evening summer sunshine of the grassy courtyard. A white marquee decked with bunting stood in the centre and a huge archway of brilliantly coloured flowers surrounded its entrance. There were food stations dotted around and tables and chairs set out, again bedecked with flowers. People were mingling, chatting, smiling and laughing, and they were all dressed in clothes far brighter than his own. Tilly took two glasses of champagne from a tray offered by a waiter and handed one to him.

He took the glass—it was expected—but he wasn't going to drink it. He'd only ever touched alcohol once, aged fifteen. His father's so-called friends had been around and they'd offered him a can of beer—more than offered, really, as they'd jeered him when he'd refused at first. And then it had occurred to him: if he joined them, his father might like him as much as he liked them. He never shouted at his drinking buddies; he never lashed out at them. Maybe he could become like them—have more of his father's better side, earn the respect he showed for his friends and be accepted. So he'd had the can...and then another...and then a proffered whisky.

He remembered throwing up. He remembered them laughing. He remembered vowing never to be in that position again. But he never stopped wanting his father's approval; never stopped trying to earn his acceptance.

That was what feelings did to people.

'Look at all this—it's fabulous,' said Tilly, turning to him, a thrilled, excited, beautiful smile lighting her face with joy that somehow, inexplicably, made him want to smile back. She tugged at his arm, leading the way. 'Come on; I can see Geetha over there.'

'Dexter, Tilly...so glad you made it. Come and meet Vijesh.' Geetha indicated towards a tall, distinguished looking man wearing a traditional South Indian kurta tunic of royal blue with batik patterns and bronze-coloured trousers. 'Are your rooms okay?'

Dexter opened his mouth to speak as they followed her across the grass towards the groom.

'Gorgeous,' replied Tilly, shooting him a look that told him in no uncertain terms to shut up. 'So, what's the order of events for this evening?'

'Oh, it's very relaxed,' Geetha replied. 'No formalities this evening; it's just a big pre-wedding party. Lots of food and dancing. Are you going to have some henna?'

'Absolutely. Dexter's going to have one too.'

'Excellent,' said Geetha. 'This is Vijesh. Vijesh, this is Tilly, a sister in A&E; and this is Dexter, lead consultant.'

'Pleased to meet you,' said Vijesh, shaking each of their hands. 'Thank you for coming. Can I get you a drink?'

And so it began. Tilly followed the very friendly and clearly very happy groom to one of the drinks stations, where she chose the fruit punch, which came with a ridiculously large paper umbrella and pink plastic straw. Dexter asked for orange juice, removing the accompanying straw and umbrella, leaving them on the bar. Tilly lifted her glass, chinking it against the one Vijesh held, and then against his.

'Happy Mehndi!'

Vijesh smiled then turned as Geetha called his name, summoning him to go and mingle with some other guests.

'You should have had the umbrella,' said Tilly as they made their way over to check out the various food stations dotted about the courtyard. 'It would have completed your outfit.'

'At least I feel slightly less overdressed, now I'm here,' he replied. 'But this...' he tugged at his shirt '...is going to the charity shop as soon as I get home.'

'Don't be such a sour puss.' She plucked the pink straw from her glass and plonked it into his orange juice with a grin. 'Here...lean into the vibe, not away from it. Let's get some food.'

He didn't want to lean into the vibe. He hated parties and didn't believe in happy-ever-afters. The only reason he was here at all was because of a professional obligation.

But that wasn't entirely accurate, was it? He was here because Tilly was here...without a plus one. Because the thought of spending time with her had been too tempting to turn down. He'd wanted to see more of that light that shone from her eyes and came from deep within her soul, the intrinsic joy which radiated from her and the almost infectious ability to delight in just about everything. Where did that come from? And why did it compel him to want to be around her?

He ladled some food into a bowl, watching her as she picked

up some bread and a spoon and wandered over to the nearest table, at which sat an older couple. He followed her.

'Hello, I'm Tilly and this is Dexter. Do you mind if we join you?'

'Please, sit down,' said the woman, smiling at Tilly.

'Isn't this beautiful?' said Tilly, pulling out a chair and looking around, her face full of wonder. 'It's like a fairy tale.'

The woman smiled. 'It is. I can't believe my granddaughter is getting married in a castle.'

'Geetha is your granddaughter?' asked Tilly.

And the three of them began chatting away, as though they'd known each other all their lives.

How did she do that so easily—just wander up to strangers and start a conversation? *He* could wander up to strangers but only if they were patients in his department. Chatting away to someone randomly, especially about something non-medical, was a very alien concept and not one he ever indulged in. He knew where his comfort zone lay—and it wasn't in places like this.

Suddenly Geetha's grandfather, sitting opposite, coughed. Dexter looked up sharply. The man coughed again and struggled to draw in a breath. He was choking. Dexter got to his feet, strode round to the other side of the table and slapped him sharply on the back between his shoulder blades, five times. But the elderly man clutched at his throat, staring up at Dexter with wide, terrified eyes.

In a second, Tilly was by his side, speaking to the man who was bending forward, desperately struggling for air.

'You're going to be fine.' Her calm voice was soothing, reassuring. 'Dexter is an A&E consultant and he's going to give you a sharp hug from behind to dislodge what you swallowed.'

The back blows weren't working. The breaths the poor man was trying to take were noisy and rasping. He had to try abdominal thrusts. He was aware that Geetha's grandmother had risen from her seat and that a few of the other guests had done the same and made their way towards the rapidly unfolding scene.

Grasping him firmly from behind, Dexter wrapped his arms around the quickly tiring man, one fist clasping the other just below the xiphisternum, thrusting upwards. He glanced at Tilly but the tiniest shake of her head told him it hadn't worked.

'And again,' said Tilly, addressing the man. 'You're doing really well.'

But the man was beginning to tire. Dexter braced himself again and gave a second thrust, once more glancing at Tilly, who was on her phone, dialling for an ambulance. But an ambulance wasn't going to get there before it was too late. This was on him. The old man had become a little heavier, taking less of his own weight. He had seconds before the man collapsed completely. More people had made their way towards them to see what was going on. He braced again; thrust once more.

Tilly...?

She shook her head, her eyes meeting his, their sparkle gone, saying more than words ever could.

The man slumped. Dexter took his weight, easing him to the ground and lying him on his back. He wasn't breathing. His airway was completely blocked.

'Grandpa!' Geetha ran towards them but Tilly caught her and held her gently back, giving Dexter room to do what he needed to.

An emergency tracheotomy. On a field, in a castle courtyard. Without any equipment.

He reached up onto the table where he remembered seeing a knife. Extending the old man's neck, he located the thyroid cartilage and, moving his fingers downwards, found the cricoid. Placing the knife, he sliced into the cricothyroid membrane and into the trachea, rotating it to widen the opening he'd made.

He looked up at Tilly. 'Straw.'

Thankfully, she realised what he was doing and grabbed the pink plastic straw discarded from his drink and handing it to him, still holding onto Geetha's hand. Inserting the straw into the opening he'd made, he blew two breaths into it, watching for the chest expanding as his own breath filled the old man's lungs.

It worked. Dexter watched him, willing him.

Come on, breathe.

A gasp from the old man. A collective release of breath from the gathered crowd.

Instantly, Tilly knelt down on the grass beside them, tugging Geetha down with her, taking the old man's hand.

'Hello, there. Try not to speak. Some food went down the wrong way but you're doing fine now. You're okay. Geetha's here.'

Dexter watched them, his fingers still holding the plastic straw in place as he drew his phone from his pocket and called the emergency services, to change Tilly's request for an ambulance to one for a helicopter. Geetha's grandpa was alive but he wasn't out of the woods yet.

Tilly had her arm around Geetha's shoulders and was reassuring both of them. Geetha's grandma joined them, looking relieved, her hand to her chest. Tilly took her hands in her own and spoke to her, and the old lady smiled back at her, opening her arms to embrace her as a spontaneous round of applause broke out. Dexter finished speaking to ambulance control and slipped his phone back into his pocket, looking up and realising that everyone was looking at him. Tilly was clapping too and beaming at him.

'Thank you, Dexter.' It was Geetha. She opened her arms wide. 'You saved his life.' And suddenly he was in her arms, being squeezed, one hand still holding onto the straw, the other like a rod at his side.

'They're sending an air ambulance,' said Dexter.

Geetha released him but her arms were immediately replaced by those of her grandma, who gave him an enormous squeeze before letting him go. Others came forward to shake his hand and grasp him by a shoulder, thanking him. He didn't need to be thanked for what he'd done. He'd just been doing his job.

'Well done,' said Tilly, giving him a smile that could have launched the proverbial thousand ships but which made him glance away quickly.

Tilly Clover smiled almost all the time…at everyone. But when she directed that smile at him, happiness shining out of her eyes, he found more and more that, beautiful as it was, it challenged him…in ways he didn't want to be challenged. The more he saw of her smile, the more he wanted to make her smile— be the cause of it; look into her amethyst eyes, into her beautiful soul, and stay there. Because somehow he imagined that doing that would make him feel as a ship's crew felt finally docking in a safe harbour after battling though a maelstrom…or like coming in from a snowstorm to a warm fire. It was enticing, inviting and becoming increasingly difficult to ignore.

Tilly Clover was different. He was drawn to her in a way he'd never been drawn to a woman…ever. This was more than physical…much more.

Tilly Clover—with her sometimes annoying in the extreme sing-song voice, captivating, twinkling eyes, tempting smile and irrepressible zest for life was more than a woman he simply wanted to take to bed. He wanted to look at her, listen to her, be with her…absorb her, somehow. Since Helena, he hadn't had a relationship that had lasted longer than a couple of nights and he'd made very sure that any woman he was with knew the score from the outset.

No promises.

No commitment.

No emotion involved.

And no way on earth could he ever be hurt, humiliated or

rejected. That was how Dexter Stevens did relationships now. But Tilly presented him with a problem. She tempted him to want more.

But he wasn't that sort of man. Helena had rammed that fact home with relish the night his father had died and she'd been in bed with another man—a man who'd been able to provide everything he apparently couldn't.

She'd been right though, hadn't she? He wasn't capable of being the sort of man who deserved a happy-ever-after. At least he knew his limitations. He wasn't capable of feeling love. That normal, human ability had been beaten out of him a long time ago by a father with two sides. Sober, his father had seemed to care—he'd spend time with his son, joke or laugh, kick a ball about in the garden. But, after a drink, the accusations, sarcasm and anger would build quickly and, eventually, Dexter had learned that it was never safe to try to be close to him. Love wasn't to be trusted—a shadow of fear always hovered underneath it.

'Good job I didn't turn my nose up at the straw, like you did.'

He glanced at her. Her generous lips were pressed together as she attempted to suppress a smile, which was clearly proving impossible, and her eyes sparkled with mischief. His stomach clenched and it took more effort than he could ever have thought possible to drag his gaze away from her.

He had to stop this. He had to put distance between them; stay away from the temptation of her. How that was going to be possible, when for weeks he'd been drawn towards her more and more, was impossible to imagine. But, if he didn't stop thinking about her in the way he had been doing, the danger of wanting her would only grow.

He'd keep his distance. She was just a colleague and would remain so. He could manage that.

And then he remembered the sleeping arrangements...

CHAPTER FIVE

'I MIGHT GO back to the room,' said Dexter, glancing round. The helicopter medics had taken Geetha's grandpa to hospital and everyone had dispersed, resuming the festivities.

'No,' said Tilly. 'There are cocktails to try and dancing to be done yet.'

'Not really my thing,' said Dexter.

'It's *everyone's* thing.'

'Except for me.'

'One cocktail…and a dance.'

'I don't drink.'

Tilly blinked at him, looking surprised.

'And I don't dance.'

'Of course you do.'

'I really don't.'

'But it's a wedding.'

'And I've shown my face—done what's expected of me—and now I'm going to my room.'

'Our room,' she corrected.

'Quite,' he replied, dropping his gaze. He'd afforded himself the luxury of not thinking about the night ahead and every possible ramification that might ensue…until now. 'You get a drink and dance if you want to. I'm leaving.'

'Okay,' she replied, 'you've done pretty well this evening.'

'I was just doing my job,' he replied.

She frowned for a moment and then smiled. 'Not the trachy…

I meant turning up. The completely non-Dexter bright shirt... not too shabby for a party pooper. You'll have to do better tomorrow, though, for the wedding.'

His heart sank like a lead weight to the very bottom of his stomach. She was letting him off the hook with the Mehndi party but tomorrow was a whole new day, and a whole new fresh hell of pretending that he was happy to be there.

He made his way back towards the castle. A man, clearly sight-impaired, walked past with a beautiful chocolate Labrador guide dog, making Dexter smile. He loved dogs. They were so much less complicated than humans—they asked for little, loved unconditionally and were devoid of the painful, complex baggage just about every human being carried around with them.

Murphy, his childhood dog, had been his port in the storm that was his father. Coming home from school had been like rolling dice. If his father was in the house and had been drinking all day, it never took much to set him off: a tear in his uniform; muddy shoes; growing too tall for his trousers and asking for new ones... But Murphy had always been there, welcoming him home, treating him as though it didn't matter that he was only Dexter, a frightened schoolboy with grubby shoes and too short trousers. To Murphy, he was superman.

Making his way up the spiral stone staircase, he opened the huge wooden door to the room and kicked off his shoes. He walked over to the mullioned window and looked at the grass courtyard below. The party was in full swing. Flashing coloured lights swirled away beneath the white canvas of the huge marquee, and the distant pulsing of the music could be heard even though the room was three floors up. No doubt Tilly was in there, dancing, having a great time, being the life and soul of the party. He smiled. Well, good for her. She was clearly a work hard, play hard kind of woman—not a *party pooper* like him. No doubt she'd be at least a couple of hours yet. He'd take a shower and crack on with the audit paper he needed to finish.

Minutes later soothing, hot water cascaded over him and he lifted his face, closing his eyes, an image of Tilly in her peacock-coloured dress slipping unwanted into his mind. He hadn't wanted to leave her—leave the party, yes, but not leave Tilly. He snapped open his eyes. He didn't want her popping into his head; he didn't want to wish he was still with her. How had she managed to take up so much of his head space?

It was because, somehow, he'd become fascinated by her. By her ability to be everything to everyone: a technically skilled and knowledgeable practitioner; a strong advocate for her team of staff; an empathic support for patients; someone people immediately warmed to... A strikingly beautiful woman he wanted to spend more time with.

Stop.

She was way out of his league. Tilly would want someone just like her—someone fun, sociable and outgoing. She needed someone who was as in touch with their feelings as she was; someone who was as warm and demonstrative as herself. Not someone who'd rather pull out his own fingernails than feel emotion. There was nothing about him that would interest someone like Tilly. Anyway, he didn't want to get involved with anyone. Relationships came with expectations, and he fell well short of being able to meet any expectations in that field...obviously.

Turning off the shower, he reached for a towel and wrapped it round his waist before stepping out from behind the screen.

'Touché.'

His eyes flew open. Tilly stood on the threshold between the bathroom and the bedroom beyond, arms folded, leaning against the door frame and grinning.

'Touché?' he managed, wiping water from his eyes.

'As in, you walked in on me and now I've walked in on you. At least you have a towel, though; I only had bubbles.'

Heat rose within him. 'I didn't expect you back this early.'

'Clearly,' said Tilly, looking him up and down. His stomach clenched at having her eyes on him. She was openly appraising him; a perfect, dark eyebrow rose as her eyes swept over him. His breathing deepened. She smiled slowly, a finger coming to her full lips, as though contemplating something. She reached up behind the door, grabbed a white towelling bath robe and tossed it to him. He caught it but the action caused the towel around his waist to slip and fall to the floor. Just in time, he drew the robe closer.

'To hide your blushes…' Her gaze seared his, and for the briefest moment her amethyst eyes darkened, making his stomach tighten. Her fingers played with the necklace at her throat.

He lifted his arm, twirling his hand as she'd done earlier. 'Perhaps you should turn around.'

A smile played at the corners of her lips and she shook her head slowly, her eyes not leaving his. It was the most seductive smile he'd ever seen.

'Not the same situation at all, Dexter. I came to see if I could drag you to the party—the band are excellent.'

'I told you—I don't do dancing.'

'No, you said, but why not? You've come all this way; why not enjoy it?'

'I can't think of anything worse.'

She stood up straight and scowled at him. 'What a grumpy-boots you are, Dexter Stevens. If it's just the dancing you don't like, we could have a drink instead.'

'I told you, I don't drink either.'

'Come with me and just enjoy the atmosphere, then. It's a lovely warm, summer evening and the marquee and the courtyard look amazing with the flowers and the lights.'

'I have work to do.'

'Instead of being at a party?' She stared at him as though he'd just arrived from another planet.

'Much more preferable,' he confirmed. 'And it's getting a

little chilly, standing here, so do you mind...?' He nodded towards the bedroom, not keen to let go of the robe he held in front of him.

But it didn't seem to bother Tilly. He drew in a breath, steadying his heart rate. She'd locked eyes with him just then with an assured confidence that was sexy in the extreme.

'I don't mind at all.' She grinned and lifted an eyebrow seductively. She'd never looked at him like that at work. But this wasn't the hospital, was it? They were in a fairy-tale castle on the wild Northumbrian coast, far away from reality.

And it was a wedding. People got all sorts of ideas at weddings. Damn the stupid hotel for getting the room booking wrong and putting him in this position.

He nodded again towards the door. 'You go back down if you want to. Don't let me stop you.'

She pouted, looking forlorn. 'But you are stopping me.'

'I'm really not, Tilly. I've told you to go back to the party a number of times now.'

'But I hate the thought of you sitting up here on your own... working on some stuffy work.'

'I like doing audits.'

She rolled her eyes and sagged dramatically, hanging her head. 'If you don't come to the party, I'll lose my bet.'

His eyes widened. 'You bet on me going to the party?'

She bit her lip, looking up at him from beneath long, dark lashes. 'Only a little.'

'You're kidding me.'

She grimaced. 'So, you either have to come to the party or at least tell me why you won't.' She lifted her chin, challenging him with her gaze. 'And the reason needs to be way more convincing than you having to do an audit.'

It was as though she could see into his soul; as though she knew that he didn't *need* to do the audit tonight. The audit had been his oven-ready excuse if, despite wanting to try to go to the party and feel comfortable about it, he found that he actually couldn't face it.

'I can't believe you did that.'

'It was only with myself.'

'You bet with yourself?'

'I thought I'd be able to persuade you.'

He shook his head, running his fingers through his wet hair, but felt the robe slip and held onto it again.

'That's ridiculous.'

'The bet or me trying to get you to enjoy yourself?'

'Both.'

'And what's wrong with wanting to have a good time, Dexter?' She moved away from the door frame. 'I just wanted to see if there was a different side to you outside of the hospital. A side that wasn't all seriousness and solemnity...perhaps a side that could relax, have fun, be friendly. I'm sure those things are in there...somewhere. You should let them come out to play once in a while. What's life for if you don't?'

She left, closing the door softly behind her.

He let out a breath. She'd done it again. Just as he'd thought he was still in control, she'd confronted him head-on, threatening to breach the barricades that had kept him safe for so long. Tilly Clover had once again ruffled the very fabric of his carefully constructed and controlled world, stopped him in his tracks and made him think.

He'd agreed to come to this wedding because he liked Geetha and didn't really want to let her down but, more than that, he'd liked the prospect of spending time with Tilly. But he'd known there'd be parties involved, and he'd known he absolutely didn't want to go to them, so what the hell was he doing there? It was because he was fascinated by her...drawn to her. So drawn to her that he was rapidly losing his senses. Tilly Clover was testing him like he'd never been tested.

He rubbed his hair and face roughly with the towel. He had to take back control. He needed to stop thinking about her all the time. She didn't have to affect him in this way…or in any way at all. She was just someone he worked with and, for a couple of nights, with whom he was being forced to share a room for a work function. That was all.

But the way she'd met his gaze just then, with that all-seeing, sexy-as-hell glimmer in her eyes, had heated his blood it didn't seem cooling down was likely to happen any time soon.

CHAPTER SIX

TILLY GLANCED AT the now closed bathroom door. Maybe he didn't want to be looked at. Maybe she'd looked at him in the wrong way.

As if she wanted him.

Which she did.

She walked over to the window that looked out over the courtyard below. Part of her wished she was still down there, dancing. But another part of her wanted to stay in the room. With Dexter.

He'd been determined not to stay any longer at the Mehndi party but, as he'd turned to walk away, just before he'd dropped his gaze, he'd faltered... It had only been for a second, but she'd caught his look—that of a child who wasn't sure which way to go.

Why didn't he like socialising? Why was he so closed off?

The bathroom door opened and Dexter came out, a towel secured around his waist. Maybe he didn't mind being looked at after all.

'It's too hot for the bathrobe,' he said, by way of explanation.

He'd towel-dried his hair but it was still damp and tousled. A lock of it fell loosely over one eye. He flicked his head to dislodge it but it stubbornly fell back. He was a tall, strong, bronzed tower of masculinity and her fingers wanted to find out what he felt like.

'Bathroom free now?' she asked.

'All yours.'

Closing the bathroom door behind her, Tilly pulled her dress over her head and draped it on a hook on the door. She squeezed toothpaste onto her toothbrush and stared at her reflection in the mirror as she brushed.

Did the towel around his waist mean he hadn't brought nightwear? Were they both going to be naked in that bed together? She rinsed and glanced back into the mirror, her eyes going to the pale scar on the right side of her chest. The portacath had helped to save her life, and having a scar was a small price to pay, but she was conscious of it nevertheless. Her fingers went to it. The scar had lightened a little in the years since they'd last pumped the chemo into it, but it was still a reminder of a difficult time—lost years, years to be made up.

She put on the too-big bath robe, pulling the tie at the waist and taking a deep breath before opening the door to the bedroom. Was tonight going to be one of those times when lost years could be made up for?

Dexter was at the desk typing, his laptop open. He'd pulled on a white T-shirt and black shorts. He didn't look up.

'The audit?' she asked, walking over to him. 'Anything interesting?'

'Depends if you find the sepsis resus care-pathway interesting or not.'

'Well, of course it's interesting,' she replied, dragging a chair to sit alongside him. 'Anything we can do to help with the early detection of sepsis has got to be interesting. What does the audit show?'

'Compliance with the Sepsis Six protocol is good but I'm setting a goal of one hundred per cent compliance. There's no reason we can't achieve that.'

'Is it all six of the interventions we're not compliant with or just one of them?'

'We're one hundred per cent with monitoring output, giving oxygen and starting fluids, but less with taking blood cultures, measuring lactate and starting antibiotics. It's nearly there but I won't settle for anything less than perfect. Doing those things in that first hour after admission increases survival rate significantly.'

'We'll need to organise some training sessions with the staff to remind them about the importance of completing all six parts of the protocol. I can speak to the comms team to see if we can have a month where the screen saver on all department computers and devices highlights the protocol. Staff will see the messaging every time they log on or even walk past a screen. What do you think?'

'I think that's an excellent idea.'

'Great, I'll get on it as soon as we get back.'

He nodded just a touch, watchful eyes lingering silently, not leaving hers, sending a searing heat blazing through her. Was this a night to make up for lost time?

Did he want her as she wanted him?

He lowered his gaze, returning to his laptop. No; he'd turned away, back to his work.

'Apparently, it's perfectly acceptable to sleep in the same bed with someone you're not married to as long as you both keep one foot on the floor,' she said, standing and dragging her chair back to its original position, hoping her voice sounded lighter and more in control than she felt.

'I'll sleep on the sofa,' replied Dexter, not looking up.

He definitely wasn't interested.

'Don't be silly; you'll have a bad back tomorrow if you do that. Don't worry, I don't bite.' She clamped her mouth shut but it was too late...the words had been said. She was glad he had his back to her.

Where had that come from?

If he was happy to sleep on the sofa, then that was probably the best option. *He* might well have found a T-shirt, but she didn't have anything that would double up as nightwear. Did she want to be naked in the same bed as Dexter Stevens?

Hell, yes.

No way.

Talk about a dilemma...

'I'll be fine—I've slept in worse places.'

'Have you? Where?'

'The doctors' mess is much worse.'

Tilly laughed, relieved he'd ignored her errant comment about not biting.

Dexter turned his head to look at her. 'I'm not joking.'

'It's not that bad. At least there's a bed.'

He didn't react but turned back to his work. She sat down on the end of the bed watching him from behind as he tapped away, dark head bent. His white T-shirt clung to every dip and curve of his muscles. He stopped typing and sat up straighter, stretching his arms high above his head, grasping one elbow and then the other, stretching more deeply, his muscles flexing beautifully. She picked up her phone.

'I'll set an alarm for eight... Breakfast is from seven thirty and the wedding ceremony starts at eleven.'

'Mm-hmm.'

'I think I'll go to bed now, then.'

'Mm-hmm.'

If she was looking for riveting conversation, then Dexter Stevens was definitely the wrong guy. The only time he engaged was when he was talking shop and, what with the emergency tracheotomy in the castle courtyard and the Sepsis Six protocol, she was done with talking shop for this evening.

'Will you be long?' Tilly pulled back the duvet on the bed and undid the tie on the bath robe.

'No idea. Don't wait for me, though.'

She let the bathrobe fall to the floor and slid into bed, pulling up the duvet even though, really, it was too warm for it. Was he going to get into bed? What would she do if he did? Lachlan leaving the scene like a bat out of hell after her telling him about her leukaemia had taught her many things—

one of which was that, if she ever found herself being drawn towards another man, he would either have to be a short-term bit of fun or absolutely be able to handle her medical past.

She was drawn to Dexter Stevens. And he didn't do fun. Neither would he be the kind of solid, understanding, empathic support she wanted from someone. In fact, he was everything she didn't want in a man, so why was her heart banging so hard in her chest that she was sure he'd be able to hear it?

Tilly lifted her head and punched her pillow before resting back on it again. Dexter was still apparently deep in concentration. She peered at him from over the top of the duvet and her heart-rate notched up. His dark silhouette was enhanced by the glow from the angle-poise lamp.

He wanted to sleep on the sofa. *Was she disappointed?* She should be relieved, really. She knew nothing about him. She didn't know if he had family, where he was from, what he enjoyed doing outside of work or if he had any longer-term plans and goals—nothing, *nada*, *niente*. He was a closed book. And that was a good reason to stay well clear of him.

It was also the reason he intrigued her.

Like a beautifully wrapped gift found hidden at the back of a mum's wardrobe just before Christmas, Dexter was a deliciously mysterious, forbidden secret. She knew she shouldn't feel it, but she couldn't help that his very mystery lured her towards him and made her want to peel back the wrapping paper to take a peek at what was inside.

CHAPTER SEVEN

Tilly opened first one eye and then the other. The room was dark and, lifting herself up onto her elbows, she looked around as her eyes adjusted. Chinks of daylight slanted through the edges of the heavy curtains at the windows, lighting the blanket-covered and still-sleeping body of Dexter on the sofa a few feet away. She could just make out his rhythmic breathing.

Sitting up, she reached for the over-sized bath robe she'd dropped onto the floor last night. It would have been a mistake to risk being in the same bed together—Lord knew what would have happened, and where would that have left her? Potentially embroiled in another relationship with a wholly unsuitable, emotionally void man.

Lowering her feet to the floor, she stood, pulling the sash tightly around her waist. She'd have a nice shower, get some breakfast and enjoy the wedding—that was why she was here, after all, not to end up in bed with a man who didn't come anywhere near ticking any of her boxes.

Treading stealthily across the carpet towards the bathroom, Tilly didn't take a breath. She wanted to lock the door and get into the shower before he awoke—she wasn't going to have a repeat of yesterday. But a floorboard creaked as she trod on it, bringing her to a halt. She swung round, looking back towards the sofa. Dexter moved and the blanket he'd covered himself with fell to the floor with a soft thud.

Her errant gaze slid down his body—he was naked apart

from his boxer shorts. Her pulse quickened and she closed her eyes, scolding herself for looking. When she opened them again, he was wide awake and looking at her, the blanket still on the floor. She gasped. Her instinct was to bolt for the bathroom and slam shut the door but her feet seemed to be stuck to the floor.

'Morning,' she managed.

Dexter swung himself upright, yawning and stretching his arms high above his head before leaning to pick up the blanket.

'Morning,' he replied.

'Good job you don't sleep completely naked.' The words were out before she'd even thought them, and her fingers and toes curled.

'Quite.'

She nodded towards the blanket, which now lay beside him on the sofa. 'With the blanket falling off, I mean.'

He glanced at the blanket.

'Don't worry, I haven't taken photos for the notice board at work.'

She smiled, knowing full well it was probably the most awkward smile in the world. What the hell had happened to her mouth? Could she make this any worse?

Stop talking, Tilly.

Dexter's eyes widened. 'Thanks for that.'

'Right, well, I think I'll get a shower.'

'Okay.'

Heart hammering, she managed not to run to the bathroom, but when she got there she locked the door, turned on the shower and stepped under the warm water, her face turned upwards and relief flooding through her that she was no longer standing before an almost naked Dexter, who must be wondering what on earth had got into her. But she knew exactly what had got into her. She'd seen more of his heavenly body in the last twenty-four hours than she could ever have dared to hope…and it had sent common sense running for the hills.

Damn this room mix-up.

At least she only had one more night to get through and she could manage that without being tempted again by him… surely?

Dexter went over to the window to pull back the heavy curtains and flood the room with bright, early-morning summer sunshine. He looked over to the bed she'd slept in—the bed they both could have slept in. It was a crumpled mess and he instinctively reached for the duvet to straighten it. The sheet was still warm and he withdrew his hand, as though it had burned him. Suddenly it seemed too intimate to touch her bed linen.

Watching her to check she'd fallen asleep last night before he'd tried to make himself comfortable on the sofa had also been too intimate. She'd been spread out like a starfish under the duvet, her ebony and amethyst hair fanning out over the pillow, her lips parted slightly, her breaths long, deep and contented.

What if he'd accepted her invitation to share it with her? He'd never shared a bed with a woman platonically. And that was what she'd invited him to do, with the whole 'one foot on the floor' suggestion. But he hadn't trusted himself and he hadn't trusted that erotic fiery gleam in her eyes last night when she'd caught him in the shower either. Tilly wasn't a one-night stand sort of woman. She deserved better than that. She deserved better than him. He wasn't a match for her. He knew what he was—an uptight, hard-boiled, frosty loner and he didn't want her spirit crushed by that.

'All yours,' said Tilly, walking across the bedroom and opening the wardrobe. 'I'm going down to breakfast, so I'll see you down there.' She glanced out of the window as she passed. 'Gorgeous day for it.'

'Sure,' he replied. 'Yes.'

She wasn't waiting for him, then. Just as well. They were

colleagues and he'd do well to start trying to remember that. Anyway, he didn't want to see that gleam in her eyes again. It was way too tempting.

Tilly nudged his arm. He looked down to where she pointed at in the small brochure provided for guests who'd not been to a south Indian wedding before, which explained each step in the ceremony.

'This is the most important bit,' she whispered, her eyes gleaming with excitement, as usual making him not want to look away.

The guests were sitting in the courtyard of the castle. A beautifully ornate mandap had been erected as an altar and was decorated with flowers and mango and banana leaves, under which the bride, groom and wedding party sat on golden, flower-covered chairs, almost like thrones. The scene was one of vibrant, sunny, jewel colours and the guests were all dressed brightly, many of them in traditional Indian robes of beautiful, opulent fabrics.

Dexter glanced back at Tilly, who sat beside him watching the elaborate ceremony, clearly enthralled. She wore a traditional sari of a deep pink and orange and edged with a pattern in golden thread. He looked down at her small hands which she held in her lap. The henna she'd had done last night had darkened into a rich red-brown colour, the design intricate and quite beautiful. The lulling chanting of the priest grew louder, making Dexter look back at the bride and groom who stood from their thrones and began to walk round the dish of sacred fire in the centre of the mandap.

Suddenly, Tilly's hand was on his forearm. 'The seven steps,' she whispered excitedly, not looking at him.

He smiled, dropping his head as he did so. Why did she make him want to smile so much? She had an enchanting, childlike quality about her sometimes that did that to him. He didn't like weddings and usually did everything in his power to avoid them. Why two people, logical in every other aspect of their lives, could make such an illogical decision as tying themselves together for ever, he just couldn't fathom. How could two people ever be so 'right' together that they'd risk their whole future on each other? Why would anyone want to bare their soul to another person, let them know everything about you, be judged, chewed up and spat out by them?

Tilly released his arm and held her hands clasped together at her chest. She drew in a deep breath and watched the scene in front of them. The bride and groom threw rice, herbs and flowers into the sacred fire, making the flames momentarily flare higher.

He glanced down at the order of service—Dhanya Homam, offerings to Agni, the god of fire, to solidify the bond between their two families. He glanced at all the players on the stage—both sets of parents were beaming, looking happy and proud, and he caught a look between the groom and his father that stilled his heart. A smile from son to father, a returning smile and a slight nod from father to son—an acknowledgement, an understanding, passing between them—mutual love, pride, respect and a warm, trusting bond strengthened over the years.

Family. He'd never had a family. He'd imagined what it might have been like if he had, though. His young mind had invented a mother he'd never known. She'd have been warm, kind and smiling; she'd have hugged him when he'd come home from school, cook meals for him and read him bedtime stories. She'd have been there when he lost his first tooth, won races at sports day and graduated from medical school.

She'd have loved him. He'd fallen asleep at night, willing what he could only imagine to come true, wishing he'd known her. But he'd never woken up in the morning to see her in the kitchen making breakfast, slipping a box of sandwiches into his school bag for lunch or kissing him on the top of his head as he left for school. Instead he'd awoken each day wondering which version of his father would be there—the one who had passed out on the sofa surrounded by bottles, cans and cigarette ends or the one who would try to help him with his homework.

He closed his eyes, squeezing them shut, willing away the sights and sounds of those days. His father's red, angry face swam into view, his mouth moving, shouting at him, a shower of beer-smelling spittle splattering into his young face. Instinctively he moved backwards, away from it, his eyes snapping open, his breathing deeper, his fingers gripping the order of service.

Suddenly there was applause. Everyone was clapping and the wedding party stood in a line at the front, all beaming smiles as the photographer clicked away. Tilly nudged him with her elbow and frowned at him, nodding towards his hands. He joined in the applause as the happy couple began to make their way back down the aisle between the rows of clapping guests.

'Wasn't that gorgeous?' said Tilly, looking as though she'd won the lottery. 'They look so fabulous and so happy.'

He knew what he was supposed to say. 'They do; very happy.' She was right. The difference was that she felt it and he didn't. Years of careful programming not to succumb to the danger of allowing feelings into his life had made sure of that.

They filed down the aisle with the other guests, Tilly taking a handful of flower petals from a bowl on a table.

'Take some,' she instructed.

He sighed. Hadn't his duty been done now? He'd turned up to the wedding and they were married now. Wasn't that enough?

'Go on,' said Tilly, nodding towards the bowl. 'Don't be a party pooper.'

He took a handful of petals. 'What are we supposed to do with these?'

'Make tea with them,' she replied, rolling her eyes. 'What do you think we do with them?'

He stared at her. 'I expect we do the entirely illogical thing and toss them at the newlyweds, creating a mess for someone else to clear up later?'

She pursed her lips. 'Not everything has to be logical, Dexter.'

'The world would be a far better place if people were more logical and less governed so much by their emotions.'

She looked at him, puzzled. 'I think you actually mean that.'

Of course he did. Emotions completely messed up logical decision making and turned normal people into defenceless victims.

'Ready, everyone?' the photographer called.

'Come on, party pooper,' said Tilly. 'Come and throw your illogical petals and pretend as if you're happy to be here.'

He wasn't happy to be here. *Was he?* He was happy to be with Tilly.

'On three,' called the photographer, as everyone held their hands aloft and poised, ready for the staged 'spontaneous' throwing of petals. 'One…two…three!'

Brightly coloured flower petals rained down on the newlyweds, who ducked, dodged and laughed as the guests cheered and the photographer captured the moment.

'They look so happy,' said Tilly. 'Shall we go and check on Grandpa again, now the ceremony is done?'

Geetha's grandpa had been discharged from hospital after the emergency tracheostomy yesterday, only on the basis that Dexter would be around. He'd spoken to the ENT consultant on the phone and assured him that he'd monitor him so that the old man could see his granddaughter get married.

'Fancy a walk on the beach before the meal, while the photographer is doing her thing?' said Tilly, taking a sip of champagne.

'I might go back to the room and finish my audit.'

'No! On a day like this? It's a wedding, it's a glorious summer's day and the beach is just down there. You can't go and sit in a hotel room and do a stuffy old audit like a complete Grinch. Come on, drink up. Let's check on Grandpa and go to the beach.'

Geetha was bending down and hugging her grandpa, who was sitting in the wheelchair the hospital had provided so that he could attend the wedding. 'Here he is,' she said, beaming as she stood and saw Dexter approaching. 'Our hero.'

Dexter cringed. He didn't need a whole new round of awkward hugs and slaps on the back. He directed his attention to his patient, squatting on his haunches beside his wheelchair.

'How are you doing?'

Tilly stood beside him.

Geetha's grandpa nodded, smiling, but Dexter noticed a slight ashen pallor to his skin, which concerned him.

'I'm just going to check your pulse,' he said, reaching for Grandpa's wrist. It was a little fast but steady. If they'd been in hospital, he'd have had an array of medical equipment to hand. As it was, he was glad he'd requested that the local hospital send some kit to the castle instead.

'Everything okay?' said Geetha, frowning.

'I'm going to do a proper examination,' said Dexter. 'Inside, with the equipment from the hospital.' He looked at Grandpa. 'Is that okay with you?' The old man nodded in agreement.

'I'll come with you,' said Tilly, taking the handles of the wheelchair and kicking off the break.

'May I come too?' said the patient's wife.

'Of course,' replied Tilly. 'It's just the normal checks we'd run after doing a tracheostomy, don't worry.'

'I'll come too,' said Geetha, but Tilly touched her arm.

'It's your wedding day,' said Tilly. 'We'll be back before you've even missed us, and Dexter will update you straight away.'

Dexter collected the equipment from a storeroom, confirming with the receptionist that they could use one of the adjoining offices as a makeshift examination room. The tracheostomy yesterday had been performed as an emergency, using less than ideal equipment and in less than ideal circumstances. They'd avoided the immediate complications of bleeding, tracheal rupture and laryngeal nerve damage, but there were other issues that could come a little further down the line, and that was what concerned him right now.

Tilly joined him in the store room.

'What's worrying you?' she asked, her voice lowered.

'Infection.'

She grimaced. 'It's a distinct possibility, isn't it, with it being done how it was? It wasn't exactly a sterile procedure.'

'Exactly. I want to check his sats and temperature and have a look at the wound.'

'Sounds like a plan.' Tilly pushed open the door to the makeshift surgery. 'We're back,' she said to the grandparents, who were holding hands as they sat side by side.

Dexter took the oxygen saturation probe out of its box, putting it on one of his fingers to test it before placing it on the patient. Portable probes these days were as accurate and reliable as those in hospitals, and he was confident this one would do the job. Tilly pulled out a tympanic thermometer and explained what she was doing before she inserted it lightly into Grandpa's ear. It beeped a few seconds later.

'Thirty-eight,' she announced, brightly, not giving away that the figure was concerning. She was clearly as aware as Dexter that Geetha's grandparents gaze was on them, watching for any signs that there was a concern. No need to worry them. This was likely an infection due to the lack of sterile equipment when he'd had to perform the procedure. He'd have been lucky not to develop an infection, really.

Dexter glanced at the probe on the man's finger.

'Sats fine at ninety-eight; heart rate ninety. I'm just going to have a quick look at the neck wound, if that's okay?'

Tilly had already opened a sterile pack, laying it on the desk. He donned the gloves. Tilly had already done the same and proceeded to remove the tracheostomy dressing ready for him to inspect it. He could have managed this examination on his own, but having her there with him, knowing how competent she was, added a level of reassurance that was oddly agreeable.

With the stoma site exposed, it was easy to see that he'd been right in thinking that their patient's symptoms added up to there being an infection at the incision site. It was disappointing, but not unexpected. Tilly had poured some saline solution into a small sterile pot and he dipped some sterile gauze into it, swabbing around the tracheostomy site before drying it and applying a fresh dressing.

'I think a short course of antibiotics would be advisable,' he said, pulling off his gloves and dropping them back into the opened pack. 'Perfectly normal after a procedure like this.'

'I'm sure I noticed a pharmacy in the village,' said Tilly. 'We can pop down and pick them up for you.'

'That's very kind,' said Geetha's grandma. 'Thank you… both of you.'

They took the steps down to the village from the castle. They were quite steep and Tilly needed to lift the fabric of her sari with one hand and hold onto Dexter's arm with the other. She didn't ask if she could take his arm; she just held onto it as if it was the most natural thing in the world to do.

Suddenly, out of nowhere, a golden retriever came bounding towards them.

'Hello, girl,' said Dexter, taking hold of the dog's collar and glancing round, looking for an owner.

'Sorry,' said an older man, jogging up to them and panting a little. 'She slipped her lead.'

Dexter crouched beside the dog, ruffling her ears. 'You're all right, aren't you, girl? Just excited to be off your lead and on a run.' He took the lead from the man and reattached it, handing it over to him. 'She's gorgeous.' He smiled at the dog, still stroking her.

'She can be a bit of a rogue,' her owner replied. 'But, yes, she's a good girl…most of the time. Sorry, anyway—I'll leave you two in peace.'

'You've made a friend there,' said Tilly, watching him as he got to his feet.

'Dogs will befriend anyone who's kind to them,' he replied as they continued the walk into the village. 'And they're way less complicated than humans.'

His relationship with dogs was the only relationship he trusted. They were the only ones who'd never let him down; the only ones he could rely on come rain or shine. They were non-judgmental, unprejudiced and completely logical. Dog relationships were simple, safe and predictable. Human relationships were the exact opposite.

'You're probably right there,' said Tilly, laughing. 'Here's the pharmacy.'

Dexter wrote out the prescription for the antibiotics and they took them back to the castle, ensuring that Geetha's grandpa started the course immediately and keeping a close eye on him for the rest of the afternoon. To their relief, a repeat temperature check later on after the meal indicated that his condition was stable.

CHAPTER EIGHT

DEXTER WANTED TO RUN...or hide...but he wasn't really in a position to do either. He had to go to the party; of course he did. He was in a senior position in the hospital and was required to attend the wedding of another very senior member of staff, whom he did actually like and respect. In addition, Tilly clearly wasn't going to let him off the hook, so his hands were tied but, hell, he'd do almost anything not to go. Perhaps he could just leave early.

'Ready?' said Tilly as he came out of the bathroom.

He drew in a breath. She wore a midnight-blue silk dress that cinched in at her waist and flowed to the floor, shimmering like the dark waters of the deep ocean. The colour accentuated beautifully her ebony hair and porcelain skin, which seemed to have an almost ethereal glow. She held a silver chain with the outline of a heart at her neck, which nestled just above her cleavage.

His body reacted instinctively. He swallowed. 'You look lovely.' The words escaped his lips before he'd even realised he'd thought them.

She curtsied, smiling. 'Thank you...and you don't look too bad yourself. Would you fasten this for me?'

He took a step towards her and she turned, still holding onto the ends of the necklace. Moving her hair to one side, he took the ends of the chain from her fingers, trying not to touch her skin but desperately wanting to. If he touched her, even lightly, he wouldn't want to let go.

The evening was warm. Beautifully decorated tables were dotted around the green, and guests were mingling, chinking glasses, finding their place names and sitting down. The hum of amiable chatter fused with music playing softly from the speakers. Dexter took a sparkling water from the tray a waiter offered him and Tilly opted for champagne. They'd been seated at the same table, but apart, and Dexter missed her presence beside him; missed having her smile all to himself. He answered questions put to him by the guests next to him but found his gaze kept wandering back to Tilly, who was chatting as easily as she always did, laughing and making those around her laugh with her.

There was an announcement from the DJ to gather round the dance floor, as the bride and groom were about to have their first dance. Dexter watched from the back of the crowd and spotted Tilly right at the front, beaming with delight as the couple swayed and twirled to the song before beckoning everyone else to join them. Tilly was the first onto the dance floor, arms in the air, laughing with the others who'd also joined in until the floor was crowded.

He glanced around. Everyone was either eating, drinking, dancing, chatting or laughing. The atmosphere was one of happy, good-natured revelry but he still felt a tightness in his gut. He knew only too well how apparently good-natured fun could so quickly and easily change into something quite different. A crack and a hiss behind him made his jaw clench harder—the opening of a can was an all too familiar sound from childhood, one which had usually signalled an evening of unruly, rowdy behaviour, coarse jokes, cursing, arguments and sometimes worse.

A couple of men walked past him to get to the dance floor and one bumped into his shoulder, making his drink slosh and spill slightly.

'Sorry, mate.'

Dexter nodded. He'd learned to put up with worse. He'd learned not to answer back when his father had shouted at him for no good reason; not to ask why there was no dinner money for school or why they couldn't turn on a radiator in the winter. He'd learned to accept in silence whatever had been thrown at him when his father was drunk. Doing otherwise had been futile…and dangerous. He'd mastered the art of lying about the bruises.

There had been a huge, old oak tree in a park that he used to climb—it had been a great place to hide from the world and find some peace and stillness. That old oak tree had not only given him shelter from the raging storm that had been his father, it had also provided him with plausible reasons for the regular bruises and probably prevented him from being taken into care.

Tilly made her way through the crowd and stood on the edge of the dance floor, still dancing and beckoning for him to join her. He shook his head but she continued to beckon him, pretending to look crestfallen. The last thing he wanted to do was to get onto that dance floor; in fact, he didn't even want to be here. He wanted to be up in the safe, secure branches of his oak tree.

Someone reached for Tilly's arm, spinning her round, and she shimmied her way back into the crowd of dancers and was lost. Relief washed over him. He needed to get away. He made his way away from the lights, music and revelry and walked towards the castle walls and coastal path.

'Dexter! Where are you going?'

Tilly. He turned around. The sight of her walking towards him in the twilight, the breeze playing with her hair and the soft fabric of her dress, moulding it against her body, pulled every breath of air from his lungs. She caught up with him and fell into step beside him.

'I haven't seen the coastal path yet.' He hoped his voice

sounded normal because he sure as hell didn't feel normal—the strength of his response to this woman, the deeply unsettling effect she had on his pulse, defied all logical reasoning. He needed time on his own; time to work out how he was going to deal with having to spend another night with her in that room without making a move he'd regret.

'Can I come?'

'Not in those.' He nodded to her feet, upon which were high-heeled, strappy sandals. 'You go and enjoy the party.'

'I'd rather be with you.'

Dexter stopped walking and stared at her.

Rather be with him when she was the life and soul of the party and lived to be around other people and have fun?

'If we go to the beach instead of along the coastal path, I can take my sandals off and go barefoot.'

She wanted to be with him.

And he wanted to be with her…even more than he didn't.

'If you're sure?'

'I'm certain,' said Tilly. 'What could be nicer than an evening stroll along the beach as the sun goes down?'

They descended the stone steps to the beach. She kicked off her sandals, swinging them by the straps as they walked, then she stopped, turning to him and grinning. He knew that grin.

'Race you to the sea,' she said, picking up her dress. She began running, looking behind her and laughing. 'Come on, Dexter.'

He looked down at his feet. He wore black patent dress shoes, completely unsuitable for running in the sand. But he wanted to follow her, to run barefoot with her towards the roar of the ocean on this wild, beautiful, Northumbrian beach. He'd never run barefoot across sand. He'd never been coaxed to do it by a beautiful, clever, funny, warm-hearted woman with sparkling eyes, the brightest smile and amethyst coloured hair.

But he wanted to nonetheless.

What was she doing to him? This went against everything

he knew to be right. What had happened to his mantra of keeping his distance, keeping illogical emotions out of it and staying in control?

'Come on, Dexter!'

She turned round again, her hair blowing in the breeze. She captured some of it, tucking it behind her ear, but it whipped back into her face. He was powerless to resist her.

'Last one in the sea has to sleep on the sofa tonight.' She started skipping backwards, still looking at him, holding up the ocean blue fabric of her evening dress, her warm laughter carried away by the breeze.

Dexter squatted on his haunches, undid his laces, kicked off his shoes and socks and began to jog towards her, not quite believing what he was doing. Tilly squealed, turned on her heel and ran headlong for the sea. He caught up with her easily and she turned to him as they ran alongside each other, his heart responding to the exertion, but singing too. Why had he never done this before? *Because no one like Tilly had ever asked him.*

'Don't let me win,' she called, a little breathlessly.

'You don't mind sleeping on the sofa tonight?'

'I'm not going to be sleeping on the sofa.'

'Unless I let you win, you will be.'

Tilly laughed, hitching her dress up higher, picking up the pace and speeding ahead. He caught up but jogged alongside her, not wanting to race ahead and lose sight of her. The sand beneath his feet began to change from soft, dry and powdery to cooler and damp as they neared the edge of the water; the crash of the waves grew louder and the breeze stronger. Tilly ducked as a squawking seagull swooped in front of them, making her laugh as if she didn't have a care in the world.

The pace of his heart picked up and it was more than obvious it wasn't entirely due to the physical exertion of running headlong into the wind. He could have run flat out on a treadmill on an incline and it wouldn't have felt the same as it did jogging easily alongside Tilly. It wasn't the running that made his heart thump hard in his chest—it was being with her.

Tilly gathered her dress up higher as she reached the sea at the exact same moment he did. 'It's freezing,' she shrieked, hopping from one foot to the other and darting back out again.

She was right, it was. And he'd completely neglected to hitch up his trousers, which were now soaking wet from the knees down.

She pointed at them, laughing. 'You should have taken them off with your socks and shoes, Dexter,' she called over the sound of the waves, doubled over laughing and catching her breath.

He should have. Logic should have warned him. But when Tilly had hitched up her dress in one hand, held her sandals in the other and run laughing, headlong towards the sea, calling to him, logic hadn't been in charge.

'At least I can't go back to the party now,' he said, squeezing some of the water from his trousers.

They began walking back up the beach towards the castle.

'Why do you dislike parties so much?'

He closed his eyes, opened them and studiously avoided looking at her. *Don't, Tilly.*

'It's a huge expanse of beach, isn't it?'

'It is, but that doesn't answer my question.'

Should he open up a little, as she obviously wanted him to? *What would happen if he did?*

He sensed danger.

No, keep it light.

'I guess your assessment of me is correct—I'm just a Grinchy, sourpuss party pooper.' He smiled, hoping it looked genuine and light-hearted, but guessing it wouldn't. 'It's still pretty warm, isn't it?'

'But you're not, Dexter. You're not really at all like the character you'd have everyone believe you are.' She grinned. 'Your trousers are testament to that. And you care about people; you always do your absolute best for patients. And look at how you were with that dog earlier—she adored you. And dogs are very intuitive—they can sense the good in people.'

'Dogs accept people as they are,' he replied. 'They don't have hidden agendas. If you're good to them, they simply accept it. Unfortunately, people aren't like that, which is why I try to hang around with dogs more than I do people.' He smiled, again hoping to keep the conversation light.

'You pretend not to care; why do you do that?'

This was getting way too deep for his liking but she wasn't giving up. She was probing him for answers, pushing his boundaries. He didn't like it.

Then give her something...a little nugget of information to satisfy her curiosity, something she couldn't make anything out of; something innocuous.

'Have I told you I volunteer at Battersea Dogs' and Cats' Home?'

Her eyes widened. 'Do you? Wow.'

He frowned. *Why was that so hard to believe?*

'Why "wow"?'

She blinked. 'Well, I just never...'

'Well, I do...a few times a week, whenever I get chance.' He felt slightly affronted by her surprise.

'Well, that's great; how lovely. You must really enjoy it.'

'I do and I'm not sure why you sound so surprised. I do have a life outside of the hospital, you know.'

'Of course you do.' She gave him a sidelong glance, her lips curving into a smile as she looked at him from beneath lowered lashes, making his stomach clench. 'I just imagined you spending your time at the gym or running, or something like that.'

He didn't reply.

Why did she look at him in that way? She was all sassy challenge one moment and coy seduction the next. His head was spinning.

'I manage both, and one or two other things too.'

'But not parties.'

He stopped walking and turned to face her.

'No.'

'Pity.'

He frowned. 'Why?'

Tilly opened her arms wide. 'Because I think you'd enjoy yourself. You just need to let go a little.'

'I don't like letting go.'

She gave that look again—she looked at him from underneath those luscious, dark lashes and her lips went into that barely there but totally sensuous pout. It was a look that made his stomach clench and all rational thought disappear from his mind.

'Oh, but I think you do, Dexter... You've just run headlong into the sea fully clothed.'

He raised an eyebrow, trying to ignore the fact that his heart was suddenly trying to break out of his chest. He started walking again.

'I have the distinct impression that lurking beneath that cool, buttoned-up mask, there is the possibility of endless fun.' It was almost dark but he could see the gleam in her eyes. 'Come back to the party, Dexter; let yourself go. It doesn't matter if you can't dance; no one will care if you make a fool of yourself.'

But *he* cared. He didn't want to let go. And the burning embarrassment he'd felt as a child when he'd tried to fit in with his father's friends and ended up throwing up in front of them all, making a fool of himself, still stung. He wasn't making a fool of himself again by trying to please.

'Tilly, if you want to go back to the party, please feel free, but I just don't like being in rowdy places with crowds of drunken revellers, that's all; it's just not my thing, okay?' He didn't want this conversation.

'It's not a rowdy, drunken party, Dexter, it's a wedding reception.'

'Same thing.'

'You're such a—'

'Stop it!' said Dexter, turning to face her. 'Stop telling me what a spoilsport I am. If you want to go to the party, please go, but don't try to force me into being in an environment I've tried to avoid all my life.' He hated himself immediately for raising his voice to her. 'I'm sorry.'

'What happened to you, Dexter?' Her voice was soft, luring and beckoning him as if towards a safe harbour in a storm… a harbour he'd been searching for his whole life. He lifted his gaze, met her soft, kind, amethyst eyes and was lost. Gorgeous, lovely, enchanting Tilly had said she wanted to be with him. And she wanted to know about him. Because she cared.

'My father used to like a lot of parties…' The words came out of nowhere, surprising him.

She looked at him, holding his gaze, giving him time and space, allowing him to speak or not.

'They always involved a lot of alcohol.'

She closed her eyes slowly before opening them again and fixing her gaze back on him. She was beginning to understand. And, somehow, he wanted to tell her more. But people didn't want to hear about his pain, not really; that was why he kept quiet about it. That and because he couldn't even begin to find the words to explain he'd ruined his family, caused his father to seek solace in drink and killed his own mother by being born.

How could he tell her that? Tilly was so in tune with other people and their feelings; so full of empathy and compassion. She'd be full of pity for him…and that was the last thing he wanted. Pity wasn't going to erase what had happened. He'd answer her question, in part, but he wasn't going to tell her everything.

'Don't get me wrong—he wasn't all bad. When he was sober, he could be good, kind—fun, even. It's just that didn't happen very often. Most of his wages went on booze, leaving very little for food, clothes, heating… Then, when he lost his job for being drunk at work, there was even less to go around.

He spent most of his time either at the pub, round at his mates' places or at home, drinking.'

She nodded slowly, looking sombre. 'I see.'

But she didn't…not yet. 'Alcohol has different effects on different people, doesn't it? We see it all the time in A&E. Some people are merry and fun, some become morose and others become aggressive and violent. My father was in the latter category.'

'Oh, Dexter…'

He began walking again. He didn't want pity but he did want her to know that about him, for some reason. He wanted shelter from the storm…just for a moment.

'I survived…my father didn't. He died of liver failure a few years ago.' He knew he sounded cold, but it was a fact; a cold, hard fact, simple as that.

'What about your mum?'

'She died.' He couldn't say the words which would explain any more than that. He couldn't tell her that her death had been his fault, neither could he say the words out loud that he'd known were true for so long—that his father's drinking had probably been his fault too. His father had most likely sought solace in alcohol to help him forget that his only son had killed his wife.

'Dexter, I'm so sorry.' Tilly had stopped walking but he carried on, not wanting to see the sympathy he knew would be there in her beautiful eyes. He wasn't one of her patients. When she caught up with him, she touched his arm and he flinched, but she held on to him, making him stop and turn towards her.

'I don't need pity, Tilly. It's a period in my life I'd rather forget. I'm over it. It just means that I don't like alcohol-fuelled parties, that's all.'

'Okay, no sympathy.' She held up her palms in surrender. 'Not for adult Dexter. But allow me to have a little for young Dexter.'

He frowned. 'Bit late for that.'

But Tilly looked up into his eyes and he could do nothing but surrender to her gaze. 'I wish I could have been there to stop what happened to you.'

Dexter swallowed. No one had ever spoken to him like this.

'Thank you.' His voice was thick and he didn't trust himself to say anything else.

'I know you're not a huggy person, but a hug might help.' She smiled at him tentatively, almost shyly, and he nodded. Wrapping her arms around his waist, she drew him in close, squeezing him, resting her head against his chest as he closed his arms around her.

He'd never learned how to be hugged and it had always felt alien, awkward, something other people did—people who'd grown up in loving families. He didn't want to let her go, didn't want to leave the safe, warm harbour, but he broke the embrace, still unable to trust himself to speak.

'Should we head back before the sun sets completely?' asked Tilly. 'We don't need to go to the party.'

Dexter nodded, unable to look at her. They began walking back up the beach side by side, their hands accidentally brushing each other's on occasion. It would have been so easy to reach for her but that would mean admitting things to himself that he wasn't ready to admit.

CHAPTER NINE

'Let's go up to the battery terrace,' said Tilly. 'The sunset over the sea will be stunning from up there. I love being by the sea; it's why Australia is where I want to be.'

'You want to go on holiday there?'

'I want to *live* there,' she replied, looking at him quizzically.

Dexter stopped walking and stared at her incredulously. '*Live* there?'

'Of course.' She laughed. 'How am I going to work there if I don't live there?'

'You're going to *work* there?'

'Yes.'

He didn't know. But he wouldn't, would he? He didn't listen to chatter, didn't care about what was going on in people's lives and wasn't interested in making friends.

'I didn't know.'

'Sorry, I just thought you did. Everyone else does.'

'Well, don't hold your breath,' he replied. 'It can take months.'

'I applied over a year ago.'

'Have you registered with the nursing board?'

'Yes.'

'Passed the exams?'

'The qualifications I have already mean I don't need to sit any. There's just an orientation programme when I get there.'

'Have you applied for a visa?'

'Already got it.'

'Which visa?'

'It's an employer-sponsored one.'

'So you have a job lined up?'

Tilly clasped her hands in front of her excitedly. 'Only in an A&E within a ten-minute walk of Bondi Beach—how amazing is that?'

He stared at her a moment longer then began walking again. 'Excellent…really excellent. I'm pleased for you…if that's what you want.'

But something in his tone told her he didn't mean what he'd said and there was now space between them as they walked that hadn't been there on the way up from the beach, when she'd been able to feel the warmth of his skin as it had brushed her own.

They came to the edge of the battlement with its distinctively shaped merlons where huge, black canons stood in the crenels between them, pointing out to sea, fending off would-be intruders from breaching the walls.

'Wow,' said Tilly, standing beside Dexter and leaning on the cool stone. 'Look at the colours in that sky. It's so dramatic and mystical; a dreamy symphony of colour as the sun prepares to sleep and the day surrenders to the dark night.'

'It's actually because the shorter blue colour-wavelengths of light are scattered off particles in the atmosphere when the sun is lower, letting the red and orange wavelengths become more visible, hence the reds, oranges and pinks you can see.'

Tilly scowled at him.

'What?' said Dexter, looking puzzled.

'You just ruined it.'

'Ruined what?'

'The awe-inspiring romance and magic of a beautiful sunset.'

'By explaining the science behind it?'

'Yes—it's a very Grinchy thing to do.'

'Science can still be awe-inspiring.'

'It can't be romantic and magical, though, can it?'

He looked at her, his cobalt eyes reflecting the golden embers of the sinking sun, a slight frown creasing his brow. Her heart picked up its pace and that now familiar-heat at his proximity flooded through her. He was so near—close enough to touch—but also so far away. This *could* have been romantic. If he wasn't such a cold fish.

'Is that what you want?' he asked.

'What do you mean?'

'Romance?' he replied. 'Magic?'

His face was a composed mask but his eyes held hers with a blazing intensity that jolted her pulse into overdrive.

'Isn't that what everyone wants?'

Where was this going?

'I'm probably not the right person to ask.'

Tilly let out a breath. Of course he wasn't. Dexter saw everything in black and white. Everything was science and logic and things that weren't...well, they weren't worth bothering with.

'Why not?' she asked, watching him, her head tilted to one side. She wanted to know. What made Dexter Stevens tick? But he broke their shared gaze and looked out to sea.

'I don't believe in happy-ever-afters.'

'Oh, don't say that. We're at a wedding—we're right in the middle of a happy-ever-after. I mean, look around...' She held her arms wide. 'This place is stunning; nature has painted a beautiful canvas of colour on the sky, everyone's happy and we're here to celebrate love. Of course there are happy endings.'

'I'm glad you think so. I just don't happen to share your conviction.'

'Why? Have you been hurt in the past?'

It was bold, but why not be bold? Life was too short to prevaricate, and time was running out to uncover what lay behind the cool, handsome mask that Dexter Stevens wore.

'No,' he said, obviously lying and turning away from the sea. 'Neither do I intend to be. I'm going back to the room.'

'To finish the all-important audit? To squirrel yourself away like Scrooge and pore over boring old facts and figures while everyone else is having a good time and there's this beautiful view to behold?' She braced herself, waiting for his response, her heart pounding.

He turned back round to face her and took a step closer, towering above her. The fresh, salty, warm summer evening air was eclipsed by the musky scent of him. Hands in his pockets, he looked into her eyes, studying her, that lock of dark hair falling forwards as he tilted his head.

'You want romance?' His voice was a whisper so soft that the sea breeze carried it away almost before she was sure she'd heard it.

Heart hammering, she looked up into dark blue eyes, glinting in the remaining light from the sleepy crimson-gold sun. He was looking at her as though he *knew* her and she could barely breathe as expectation pulsed between them.

'Who doesn't?'

'I don't,' he replied. 'But that isn't what I asked.'

'Of course I want romance.'

'I can't give you that, Tilly. I don't do relationships.'

She dropped her gaze, her heart slowing its pace, her breathing easing. Of course he didn't. So why was that such a devastating disappointment?

Dexter drew a hand out of his pocket and reached for her chin, lifting it gently between thumb and forefinger. She lifted her gaze, drawing in a breath as their eyes locked and everything around them faded into nothing. The intensity of his gaze drew her in with a power she hadn't known was possible.

'But I can give you this…'

He dipped his head and she held her breath as he brushed his lips against hers, sending a shocking wave of tingling, sparking desire right through her, making her stumble backwards.

His hand went to her waist, steadying her. Instinctively, she reached up, placing her palms on his chest, her fingers spreading wide over his firm, sculpted contours. Holding her head gently with his other hand, he tilted her face upward, deepening the kiss, crushing her lips with his as she groaned beneath them. Sliding her hands up, rising onto tiptoes, she touched his neck and slid her fingers into his hair, pulling him in closer, only wanting more of him.

Then he pulled away. And she couldn't breathe for a long moment.

'I wouldn't call that romance,' she managed, conscious that her lips had cooled the moment he'd stopped kissing her.

'It's all I've got.' But there was still a fire in his eyes.

'I think you've got more than that, Dexter.'

The hint of a smile played at the corners of his mouth and his eyes flared with a golden glow. The atmosphere between them crackled and time stopped until he spoke, breaking the silence of their long gaze. He pointed across the castle courtyard.

'Shall we go back?'

For what? Was he offering his version of non-relationship romance in the bedroom? Was that what she wanted?

'The sun has almost gone now,' he continued. 'I don't want to leave you here on your own in the dark.'

Maybe he wasn't offering bedroom romance. He was being a gentleman. He might not be the archetypal romantic hero of a Hollywood movie, but Dexter Stevens was most definitely polite…and a gentleman. His morals didn't allow him to leave her alone out here in the dark.

'I'm going to watch the sun disappear first,' she replied, looking away and back out at the darkening sea, swallowing her disappointment.

'It's almost dark now. Come on, I can't leave you out here alone.'

It was enough to take her right back to the years she'd spent being protected from the world, when everyone around her had shielded her from what they saw as a danger, when she'd been frightened of everything. And it was enough to cause her well-practised heels to dig in. She'd fought hard to leave all that behind her. That was why Australia meant so much—it was her ticket to freedom. It was the way she was going to prove to herself and others that she was perfectly capable of taking care of herself. And, if she was going to take care of herself ten thousand miles away from home, she could certainly make the five hundred yards back to the castle.

'I'll be fine, thanks; I just want to watch the sunset.'

But only the topmost, orange crescent of the dying sun remained sitting on the horizon, waiting to slip beneath the waves.

'The sun has almost set,' he pointed out again. 'Come on; it's getting chilly.'

He was right. The temperature between them had gone from blazing heat to decided coolness and it was because of him. The sun sank into the sea and was gone.

'I don't need looking after.' She walked towards him, but tripped on an uneven stone, and he caught her, steadying her.

'Of course not,' he replied. His lips were pressed together but the glint in his eyes told her he hadn't missed the irony. Chin tilted upwards, she marched past him as he stood watching her, before following and quickly catching up.

'Unless you're wearing high heels on uneven, thousand-year-old cobbles.'

'Apart from that.'

Damn him.

'Or get caught off-guard by a kiss.'

'That too.' She marched on towards the turret, her face burning, glad the cloak of darkness would hide her silly blushes.

'But not other than that?'

'Nope. So don't try to look out for me again, thank you.'

'Such belligerence. Where does that come from?'

Tilly pushed on the old wooden, studded turret door and it

creaked open, but was so heavy she had to put her back into it and groaned a little with the effort. Dexter reached over her and pushed it open easily.

Damn him again.

She started up the spiral stone staircase.

'I guess it's a throwback to being locked away like Rapunzel when I was…' Her thoughts froze. *Where had that come from?* 'Younger.' She'd almost said 'ill', but she'd learned that lesson, hadn't she? And she didn't want Dexter doing a Lachlan and running a mile—not tonight.

'Rapunzel? What do you mean?'

She carried on up the staircase. 'Oh, nothing—my parents were a little over-protective, that's all. I feel a bit mean saying that, to be honest. They're lovely.'

'So you've wanted to prove your independence to your family.'

She glanced at him as she opened the door to the room. That was insightful, coming from a man who didn't seem to know that human emotion existed.

'Something like that.' She kicked off her sandals and padded over to the bed, picked up her bath robe and headed for the bathroom. 'Still do.'

'Hence Australia.'

'Exactly.'

Closing the door behind her, she stepped out of her dress and looked into the huge gilt-edged mirror. Her fingers went to the portacath scar—her reminder for ever of what she'd been through. Her reminder that its discovery by Lachlan—after months of trying to hide it from him and then trusting him enough to let him see it—had signalled the beginning of the end of their relationship. He'd asked about it, as she'd fully expected him to, and she'd been ready to explain. What she hadn't been prepared for was the horror on his face—the way he'd recoiled from it—or the way he'd distanced himself until, a week later, he'd ended it. He hadn't wanted the responsibility, he'd said—he was too young.

Try actually having leukaemia, Lachlan.

Would she ever be free of her old foe reminding her it might still be there? That it could rear its head any time it liked and rob her of more time…or of life altogether? No, was the answer. The risk would always be there. Each year that had passed, she'd breathed a little more easily, until now, when she didn't think about it anywhere near as much. But she lived every day with the fallout.

Battling with people who wanted to protect her was one of its legacies. Wanting to be seen as normal, strong, capable, and starting over with a clean slate in a new job in a new place where no one knew of her past, was another. Counting her blessings, trying to take joy from every day, looking at the world with wonder and embracing all it had to offer were others.

Moving to London and taking her new job at Trafalgar Hospital was a test run—an attempt to try to start a new page before the much bigger goal that was Australia. She'd persuaded her parents that she'd be fine, that she was still close enough to home should she need them. But that had been more for their reassurance than hers…hadn't it?

She drew in a breath. She'd been fine. Yes, it had been a huge step moving to the city and yes, it was a little scary at times, but she was handling it. The confidence she'd missed out on building growing up was starting to build within her now. Every day, the city and her new role became more familiar and the urge to go running back to the safety of her warm, loving, secure home in the countryside became less. Being able to survive on her own on the other side of the world was slowly morphing from being nothing but a dream into reality.

She stared at her reflection and smiled tentatively—she was proud of herself for getting this far. The next step was the huge one, though, and her stomach flipped at the thought of it, but she tilted up her chin.

You can do it, girl. Go out there and live your life.

She leant in closer to the mirror and put her finger to her lips, running it along them.

Talking of living your life... They still looked the same but felt as though they ought to be swollen.

She'd taken what Dexter had offered. She'd embraced his kiss. Her heart began to pound a little harder and her breathing deepened. He'd said that was all he could offer, though. And he didn't do relationships, whatever that meant.

Pulling on the bath robe, she tied it at the waist.

Should she go out there and see what else he had to offer? Tingles shot down her spine, fizzing through her, heating her very core and thawing her objections to Dexter's gentlemanly protectiveness of her. She glanced back at the mirror. Her cheeks were pinker and she was biting her lower lip.

She wanted adventure, didn't she? Watching her reflection as her eyebrow rose and a slow smile spread across her face, she wrapped her arms around herself, as though she was chilly. But it wasn't a cold chill that slowly spread through her; it was one of tingling anticipation. Life was way to short not to seize every possible opportunity there was and enjoy it.

She had a decision to make.

This was their last night.

He'd kissed her.

He wasn't offering a relationship or romance, but he did have more to offer than just a kiss.

Was that what she wanted?

She loosened the tie around her waist, pulling the fabric at her cleavage a little further apart...just enough to expose the hint of curves. She pushed her fingers up through her hair, licked her lips and opened the door to the bedroom.

If Dexter Stevens thought he had more to offer, she was sure as hell going to find out exactly what that was. Enigmatic, always composed, grumpy-bear Dexter had suddenly gone straight to the top of her adventure to-do list.

CHAPTER TEN

DEXTER SAT AT the desk, the glow from the laptop the only light in the darkened room.

'You're not going to work on that now, are you?'

'Got to be done,' he replied, not looking up.

Leaning against the desk, facing him, she glanced at the screen.

'That's not the audit.'

'I'm checking emails.'

'You're on holiday, for goodness' sake, Dexter; take a break.'

He looked up at her, his eyes flicking quickly from her cleavage to meet her own. But she'd seen him look and her pulse quickened.

'This isn't a holiday; it's a work event.'

'It's a wedding! How can that be work?'

'Because I'm *expected* to be here rather than *wanting* to be.'

'Oh, you complete killjoy!'

Dexter looked back to the laptop. 'Your name-calling vocabulary is far more extensive than I thought.'

Tilly folded her arms and sighed deeply. 'Do you prefer "curmudgeon"?'

'No.'

'"Grinch", then?'

He looked at her incredulously.

'I can see you trying to hide a smile now.' Tilly dipped her head and leant in towards him, as though inspecting his face.

'I can see it; the corners of your mouth are trying to smile and you're fighting it. Let it smile…it won't hurt, I promise.' She grinned at him, taunting him playfully.

'Stop it.'

'Let it go, Dexter. That poor little smile is trying so hard to break through…and you're much more handsome when you smile.'

His eyes met hers and her breathing quickened. The same amber flames were in them that had been there on the battlements…right before he'd kissed her.

'Stop teasing me.' But his eyes weren't telling her to stop.

'I'm not the one doing the teasing tonight.'

'Which implies that I *am*?'

'You're the one who kissed me then pulled away and have acted as though nothing happened. I'd say that was pretty teasy.'

'Because you wanted more?' Dexter pushed back his chair and stretched his long legs out in front of him, folding his arms. A shiver ran down her spine, an awareness of her nakedness beneath the bathrobe rising within her. Having been emboldened by her need to feel alive, she suddenly faltered in the face of the intensity of his eyes and words. Suddenly, *he* was the one teasing *her*—the tables had been turned and he'd turned them.

She nodded slowly, not breaking eye contact.

Yes, she wanted more.

Dexter crossed an ankle over one knee and tilted his head to one side, observing her. 'Is that a yes?'

She held his gaze. What was she agreeing to? Another kiss? Or something more?

'I need to know.'

'You didn't stop to ask out there.' Tilly nodded towards the window through which shafts of silvery moonlight filtered through the old, mullioned glass.

'That was only a kiss,' he replied, sitting up straight and steepling his hands, his chin resting on his fingers.

'And what is it you're asking for my consent to?'

'I think you're looking for more than a kiss.'

'Only if you want more.'

Dexter stood and she drew in a breath as he took a step towards her, his warm, musky scent filling her nostrils, and she tilted her head upwards as he tilted his down. His lips were so near, the heat from them warmed her own, and it was all she could do not to reach a little higher to press her lips to his, to taste him.

'Only if you do, Tilly. I can't offer anything more.'

His breath was hot; it brushed her lips lightly, making them part. He was waiting for her to make the move this time. Was that what she wanted? Could she handle someone like him? Someone so sure of himself and in control? Someone so full of dark mystery? Someone who wasn't offering anything more than this night?

Life was short.

Pulling her phone from her pocket, she selected a playlist and placed the device on the speaker on the desk. The soft, haunting, opening notes of 'Unchained Melody' filled the room.

'We missed the party tonight—you owe me a dance.' She opened her arms, holding them as though ready to waltz, watching him draw in a breath, his eyes not leaving hers. She took a step towards him, taking hold of his hand and placing it on her waist, then took hold of his other hand in hers, pulling him towards her gently until there was the merest breath of air between them.

'I don't know how to dance,' he murmured, his self-assurance disappearing, standing fixed to the spot, as though unable to move.

'Follow me.' She began to sway and after a moment felt him relax a little. Moving her feet, she took some small steps, swaying, turning a little, feeling the song build and Dexter relax more until he took over…and she realised he was leading her instead and had closed the breath of space between their bodies.

She hummed the lyrics about being hungry for touch, her eyes closed, lost in the song and the perfection of the moment. She looked up at him and he smiled down at her, gently…in a way she'd never seen before. His eyes left hers, focussing for a moment on her lips before gazing at her again, luring her in, robbing the breath from her lungs.

Life was short.

She lifted up onto her tiptoes, tilting her head as he dipped his, meeting his lips with her own, bringing her arms up and snaking them around his neck, pulling him towards her. Strong arms circled around her waist and drew her in impossibly closer, crushing her to him as he responded to her kiss, deepening it as they tasted each other, their tongues testing, probing and exploring.

But she wanted more. She found the buttons of his shirt, undoing them and pushing it from his shoulders, letting it fall to the floor. Her fingers were now able to explore the expanse of his broad, smooth chest and the firm contours of his well-defined muscles. But he took hold of her hands, stopping her, and for a moment she thought he was pulling away again, but his eyes told her something else entirely—their amber flames burned with aching desire and promise.

Yes, Dexter Stevens had much more to offer than a kiss. Holding onto her hand, he led her towards the bed in the centre of the room and stood in the shaft of moonlight that filtered in through the window.

'My turn,' he murmured, stroking her jawline with his finger before tracing it along her collarbone, over the curve of her breast and down between her cleavage to the tie that held together the only item of clothing she wore. He undid it, lowering his head to plant a featherlight kiss on the top of one shoulder as he slipped the robe from it, and then on the other shoulder, pushing the fabric until it fell to the floor.

Instinctively her hand went to her portacath scar but the silver moonlight that bathed them in a shimmering, gossamer-fine cloak was nowhere near bright enough to make it visible. Tilly watched him as he took her in. His eyes closed briefly as he took a breath, as if savouring the moment, before opening them again and fixing her with a gaze loaded with hunger.

'You're very beautiful,' he murmured, tracing his finger back along her collarbone, down through the centre of her cleavage to her navel and back up again. Every inch of her skin was on fire; every fibre in her being sparked as his hand trailed lower, cupping her breast. It sent a shockwave of searing heat through her as she arched her head back and he took the other breast in his other hand, brushing fingertips over hardened nipples, making her gasp and deepening her need for him.

Reaching for his belt, she tugged it, finding the buttons to his trousers, opening them and pushing them down until he could step out of them. Sitting down on the bed behind her, she looked up into his eyes. He remained where he was and she allowed her gaze to roam the length of his body, following the tantalising hollow down the centre of his perfect abs until she got to his boxers, just inches from her face, his erection straining against the fabric. She looked back up at him and he smiled slowly.

'I see now that you can offer much more than just a kiss, Dr Stevens.'

She raised an eyebrow and held his gaze as she slid backward onto the middle of the bed and lay on her side, one hand propping her head. She beckoned him, slowly as he placed one knee on the mattress, his eyes not leaving hers. Her pulse quickened, sending heated blood to every cell in her body and flaming her skin as he prowled towards her, his eyes never leaving hers. His body was perfection...and she wanted to feel it against her own; explore its dips and curves. He lay on his side, mirroring her, one hand supporting his head as he looked at her.

'Are you sure about this?' he asked. 'I've told you, I can't offer anything more.'

But, right now, this was all she wanted. This was enough.

She reached out and ran her fingers down his arm, reaching his fingers, lifting them to her lips and kissing them lightly before placing his hand on her breast, drawing in a breath as her skin flamed. His touch sent darts of desire zinging through her. But Dexter released her, moving away, and gut-wrenching frustration flooded through her. But he was smiling as he rolled off the bed.

'One moment,' he said, opening one of the drawers.

Ah... She'd have forgotten about that completely, but thankfully Dexter had retained at least a modicum of logical thinking. Striding back over to the bed and ripping open the packet, he rolled the condom on as she rolled onto her back, and in one swift movement Dexter was on top of her. Her thighs parted instinctively. All she wanted was to have him inside her—to quell the aching deep within her.

His eyes lingered on hers, burning, telling her he wanted the same. And as he closed them he lowered down towards her and pressed his warm lips against her own, brushing her hardened nipples with his perfect chest. Pulses of desire surged through her as his erection nudged at the place between her thighs where she wanted him most. Instinctively, she arched towards him, groaning, breaking the contact between their lips, needing more air to feed her hungry lungs.

She opened her eyes to take him in. The soft moonlight glistened on his smooth skin and she placed her hands on his chest just to make sure he was real.

Was this happening? Was this perfect specimen of a man about to make love to her?

He wasn't the man she needed in her life long term—he wasn't safe, steady or reliable. But he *was* what she needed right now. Right now, she needed to feel alive, needed to take risks, needed to run free. Being given a second chance at life didn't mean simply doing more of the same. It didn't mean living a hum-drum existence. It didn't mean hiding away in corners, too scared to come out.

Dexter kissed his way down her throat as she arched her neck, taking his kisses on her collarbone and down on her breasts, sending darting flames down through her belly and into her core.

This wasn't doing more of the same. It was living, and she didn't have to try to relish every second, because every touch from his lips, his fingers and his palms set every fibre of her being alight. It turned every atom within her into firecrackers that sparked, sending pulse after pulse of increasing, building pleasure coursing through her.

He brought his mouth back to meet hers, sucking at her bottom lip, pulling gently before easing back and looking deep into her eyes, increasing the pressure between her thighs and pushing forward as she parted them further. She gasped as he entered her then paused, closing his eyes, as if savouring the moment. Her fingers grasped his shoulders and he began to move, building the pace slowly. Her hips rose to meet him, his breathing more ragged as every rhythmic stroke built the tension further and further, until he brought her to the very edge of the exquisite precipice she knew he would take her crashing over. She held her breath for one long moment before he thrust into her again and sent her spiralling over the edge and freefalling into blissful, breathless oblivion. He arched, slowing the last few strokes, squeezing his eyes closed and groaning as he reached his own climax.

She wrapped her legs around him.

'Stay there,' she whispered, unable to bear the thought of him withdrawing. He rested above her on his forearms, breathless as she squeezed him with her thighs.

'I have to lie down,' he managed after a moment.

Reluctantly, she released him, and he lay beside her, his forearm on his forehead, eyes closed as his breathing settled.

Tilly looked up at the high stone-buttressed, vaulted ceiling and then across at Dexter, almost jumping when met by his gaze. She smiled, shifting her position to lie on her side. He shifted too, smiling back—a smile rarely seen, which lifted his whole face and warmed her heart. How long they lay like that, she'd never know but, as her eyelids grew heavy and sleep settled over her, his eyes were the last thing she saw before sleep took her.

CHAPTER ELEVEN

LIFE HAD SUDDENLY got complicated.

How the hell had that happened?

Waking up, for a second he had not realised where he was. Then he'd turned to see Tilly sleeping beside him, her head to one side, her dark lashes fanning her cheeks with her ebony and amethyst hair spread over the pillow. He'd wanted nothing more than to watch her sleeping, wait for her to awaken and make love to her all over again.

He'd also wanted to run. Because it had become more than obvious that his feelings for her were much more than physical. It wasn't only the two days they'd spent at the castle, when they'd worked so well together on Geetha's grandpa or when he'd found himself wanting to tell her a little about his past. It wasn't only that her presence had meant that he'd actually enjoyed parts of the wedding or that she'd coaxed him into running barefoot in the sand and dancing to a slushy love song. No, this had been happening for longer than that. Tilly Clover had been affecting him for months.

'Thanks for listening, everyone.' The sales rep's voice broke into his thoughts. 'Any questions?'

Yes. What on earth made me think that sleeping with Tilly would result in anything other than trouble?

He'd been straight with her. He'd told her he didn't do relationships. But it wasn't her he'd needed to explain that to… it was himself. And he'd promptly forgotten his own words.

They'd spent almost every minute together at the wedding. They'd been back for two days.

And he missed her.

It had been his choice to get up the morning after they'd slept together and go for a run along the beach before she'd woken up. When he'd got back to the hotel, she'd been down at breakfast with some of the other guests. He'd told her he didn't do relationships and she'd taken him at his word, clearly treating their night together as a classic one-night stand.

It was his usual MO. Except Tilly wasn't like any other woman he'd ever spent a night with. And he wanted more of her. But the rules of the game had been set and they were both obeying them.

He'd got what he wanted.

No promises.

No commitment.

No emotion.

But he did *feel*. He felt things he'd never felt before and it scared the hell out of him. That was exactly why he'd bottled it that morning.

Dexter got up, walking towards the door and slipping in his wireless earbuds—his way of preventing people from speaking to him. He could get back to the department. Back to Tilly—his one-night stand.

It was what he'd wanted…wasn't it? No strings?

But it didn't feel right. He was unsettled, uneasy, edgy…as if he'd made a mistake but wasn't quite sure what it was he'd done wrong. Maybe he shouldn't have slept with her. Maybe he shouldn't have placed restrictions on it.

Pushing open the doors to the department, Dexter saw Mark.

'Everything okay?' he asked the charge nurse.

'Well, I'm not going to say the "Q word", but it's under control at the moment. The parents have arrived, by the way.'

'Parents?' Not saying the word 'quiet' was one of those

silly unwritten hospital rules designed not to tempt fate, which Dexter thought was ridiculous superstition.

'Of the two lads in from the RTC earlier? They'd like to speak to you.'

'Oh, yes. Where's Sister Clover?'

He needed Tilly. It was his now instinctive reaction. He was only too aware of his own limitations when it came to speaking to relatives. He didn't have any problem explaining the clinical situation, but relatives always wanted much more than that. And he knew that was where he fell short. Tilly had become his go-to person when it came to handling situations like this.

But that had been before they'd slept together…before he'd broken his own rules and allowed himself to feel something for her. Her revelation about Australia had shocked him but it was probably best she was going, so he could take back control and stop spending every minute of every day thinking about her. It was the logical solution to this problem he'd brought on himself.

'Right here,' she said, walking towards them. And inexplicably he relaxed, his heart lighter. Her pretty, floral scent filled his nostrils; her light, musical voice lifted him.

This was the very definition of illogical.

'We need to go and speak to the parents of the two boys from the road-traffic collision.'

'Okay,' she replied. 'No problem. Mark's already had a tray of tea sent in.'

Dexter nodded, staring at her. Staring at the woman who, against his better judgment, had muddied his thoughts, made him question what he wanted and wonder if he'd maybe even begun to have feelings for her. She'd made him smile; she'd made him want to dance and actually feel the music in his soul; she'd made him want to wake up with her in the morning, make love to her all over again and slake his hunger for her.

But, as much as he'd wanted those things then, the realisation that he wanted them again had troubled him ever since.

It meant he wanted her more than he'd ever wanted anyone. Which meant he cared. And he didn't want to care, because caring weakened a person. It left them vulnerable…wide open to whatever the person they cared about wanted to put them through.

Anyway, he'd never be enough for her. Tilly wanted romance—he didn't even believe in it. She lived to have fun—he was so uptight, he hadn't even been able to relax enough to feel comfortable at a wedding party.

'Shall we?' said Tilly, her palm outstretched towards the door.

Dexter hesitated. He needed to clear the air. This was the first shift they'd worked together since the morning after their huge mistake. The morning after the night they'd made love. The morning he'd slid out of bed quietly, like a thief in the night, and had pounded the beach until he could run no more instead of facing her and what she'd made him feel.

He opened the door to a laundry cupboard near the relatives' room.

'We need to talk first,' he said, indicating she go inside. He followed her in, closing the door. They stood opposite each other beside the racks of freshly laundered white linen.

'Something wrong?' she asked.

He took a breath. 'We have to work together, Tilly, in spite of…what happened at the wedding.'

She smiled. 'Don't worry; I won't tell anyone you had a dance.'

He raked his hand through his hair. 'Can you be serious, just for once?'

Her smile disappeared and he instantly regretted the sharpness of his tone.

'What happened shouldn't have happened, Tilly. I wish I could turn the clock back and make it unhappen, but I can't, and we have to work together, so we just need to…' He paused for breath. 'We just need to forget it ever happened.'

Tilly took a step back into the shelving laden with white sheets, her complexion fading almost to match their colour. She blinked, staring at him.

'Wow.'

He frowned.

'Okay, Dexter... I understand. I didn't really need the explanation, given you'd already set the rules with the whole "I don't do romance or relationships" thing, but thanks for making sure I'm fully in the picture. Appreciated. Shall we go and see these parents together—professionally?'

He nodded, opening the door, relieved to have got that conversation over with. At least they'd be able to work together without there being any awkwardness between them now. They both knew where they stood. His position was clear and his life was back in order. But that uncomfortable edginess still niggled at him.

They went into to the relatives' room, in which sat two sets of highly anxious parents waiting to speak to him to find out about the car crash their sons had been involved in and to ask the question he always dreaded: *Are they going to be okay?*

He didn't know the answer. And he never knew how to respond when they shed tears or wanted to hug him. He preferred it when they got angry. Anger, he could deal with. He'd honed that skill many years ago as a small child.

'Get me a kebab from the chippy,' his father would yell, waking him in the early hours, reeking of beer and cigarettes.

'I don't have any money, Dad,' he'd reply quietly, inching to the top corner of the bed against the wall, as far away from his father's reach as he could get.

'I gave you some the other day. What have you done with it?'

'That was last week, Dad... I bought your cigarettes with most of that and a couple of pies for tea the other night.'

'Don't cheek me... Go and get me a kebab or you'll feel my belt on your backside.'

And Dexter had dressed quickly and walked down to the kebab shop with the few pennies he'd tried to save in the hope of buying some food for lunch at school the next day. Emre, the kebab shop owner, had often let him off paying full price, but he'd known he couldn't rely on the man's kindness too often.

Anger was best managed by being numb to it, by avoiding it at all if possible, and if it couldn't be avoided then meeting it with passive acceptance. It was how he'd got through his childhood. Being numb meant not feeling pain.

'You're very welcome to stay here,' said Tilly, leaning forward and lightly touching the hand of one of the mothers opposite, who was tearful. 'Or I can take you up to ITU so you'll be there when they arrive on the unit from Theatre.'

The meeting with the shocked parents went well. Tilly was her usual warm, empathic, supportive self, handing out tissues along with kind, well-chosen words. They didn't weep, didn't need a hug and weren't angry.

He wasn't transported back to a time when fear for his own safety had been paramount in his mind and he'd had to hide his own feelings of terror at what his father did to him. He'd hidden those feelings so well for so long that he no longer knew if he could express them at all... In fact, if he could express any feelings at all any more. His father's violent rages, his unwillingness to care about anyone but himself, his mockery of everything Dexter ever did and, worst of all, the repeated accusations that he'd been responsible for the death of his mother had been the most effective anaesthetic against feeling pain...against *feeling*.

But one question lingered in Dexter's mind. He'd mastered the dark art of denying emotion, of pushing it away and refusing to acknowledge it, but there remained a fear that he'd inherited the traits of his father.

What if a drink turned him into the same man? What if he allowed emotion into his life and let go of the tight self-control he'd wound around himself? What if he cared about someone—what would happen then?

He'd learned to deal with other people's anger but it was the uncontrollable anger that he might have within himself that terrified him the most. The uncontainable fury his father had unleashed time and time again, even when he'd lost his job, had all but destroyed their home and had made a frightened enemy of his only son.

What if he'd inherited that? He didn't want to find out. He didn't want to become his father.

Which was why keeping feelings out of his life, all feelings, was his only option. If only he'd remembered that when he'd allowed Tilly into his life. If he had, maybe his well-ordered world wouldn't be shaking on its foundations right now.

The cardiac-arrest alarm suddenly sounded, shrill and very loud, and Tilly leapt from her seat, walking swiftly towards the red flashing light over cubicle two, wheeling the arrest trolley as she went, then throwing back the curtain.

'Anaphylaxis,' said Dexter. 'Eight years old; came in with severe abdo pain and pyrexia. Penicillin given; no previously known allergies.'

Tilly drew up the required drugs as Dexter took a plastic airway from Anika and inserted it, attaching oxygen and giving two squeezes on the reservoir bag he'd attached to it. He instructed Pearl to take over airway management as he reached for defibrillator pads, ripped the backing off them and applied them to the child's chest. The green waveform showed them what they suspected: a flat line.

'Compressions,' said Dexter, looking at Tilly directly, but she'd already kicked the footstool into position and stood on it, hands poised above the child's chest.

'What are you doing?' shrieked the child's mother who'd got up from her seat and stood next to Dexter.

'IV adrenaline,' said Dexter. 'Please sit down, Mrs Green,

I need space to treat your daughter.' Flipping back the top of the cannula, he pushed the drug into the child's vein.

'What's that?' said the mother. 'What are you giving her? Doctor, you need to save her—she's my only child.'

'I'm doing my best, Mrs Green; please, just give me a little space.'

'Anika, can you take over compressions please?' asked Tilly, moving aside to let her in.

'Let's stand here,' she said to the distressed mum, taking her by the shoulders and moving her gently to the edge of the cubicle to keep her away from Dexter as he tried to save her daughter's life. 'Lottie's had an allergic reaction and the doctor is giving her a medicine that we hope will reverse that. The oxygen is to help her breathing; the other doctor is helping her heart to beat until the medicine begins to work.'

'IV fluids,' said Dexter. 'Crystalloid; ten mil per kilo, stat. Check rhythm.'

They all stopped what they were doing.

'Sinus bradycardia,' he announced. 'Stop compressions; adrenaline.' He administered more of the drug.

'Her heart's beating again but is a little slow,' explained Tilly. 'So we're giving a little more of the medicine to bring it back to a normal rate.'

'Is she…going to be okay?' asked the little girl's mum, clutching Tilly's arm.

'Spontaneous breaths,' called Pearl as the little girl gave a cough.

'Remove the airway,' ordered Dexter. 'Heart rate sixty-five; BP rising. Hello, Lottie, are you waking up?'

The little girl's eyes flickered open; she looked puzzled.

'Lottie!' shrieked her mother, letting go of Tilly's arm. 'Don't ever do that to me again.'

'My throat hurts,' said Lottie.

'You can have a little drink in a moment,' said Tilly, relief flooding through her.

'Thank you, Doctor,' said Mrs Green, flinging her arms around Dexter's shoulders and holding him, vice-like, as he stiffened until she released him.

'You're welcome,' he replied, taking a step backward the moment he was released, straightening his dislodged stethoscope and running his hand through his locks of hair that had fallen forward.

He met Tilly's gaze briefly before looking down and away.

'Good work,' he said, addressing the team. 'Pearl, can you prescribe an antihistamine and a non-penicillin-based antibiotic?'

'Sure,' replied the registrar.

'Anika, can you clear up for me, please?' said Tilly. 'I'll write the notes up. Mrs Green, I'll speak to you again before you go up to the ward.'

'Thank you, Sister.'

'Fairly straightforward,' said Dexter as they made their way to the nurse's station.

'It was very straightforward as far as paediatric cardiac arrests go,' agreed Tilly. 'Right up until the point it was all over.'

'What do you mean?' said Dexter, pulling out a chair and sitting down in front of a computer.

'Until the grateful mum hugged you and you turned into an ironing board.' She looked at him, a dark eyebrow raised.

'I don't do hugs.'

Tilly glanced around but no one was nearby. 'You do sometimes,' she whispered. 'But don't worry; I won't tell anyone about that either.'

Dexter drew in a breath, seemingly engrossed in the screen in front of him.

Tilly glanced around again, her voice still low. 'What happened doesn't need to affect our working relationship. We both knew what we were doing.'

She hadn't expected him to have left by the time she woke up that following morning, but really, he'd been clear about his stance—he didn't do relationships. What should she have expected? And he'd reinforced his feelings on the matter very clearly, earlier in the linen cupboard, leaving her in no doubt at all about how he felt. She wasn't going to allow herself to be hurt just because he'd preferred to go for an early-morning run along the beach than wake up with her, or that he was so desperate to make sure she knew that the offer of his version of romance had been a limited, time-only deal.

He nodded, still staring at the screen, apparently engrossed in a page of blood results. 'Good.'

'Still a man of few words.' Nothing had changed. They'd spent two days together. She'd thought they'd made some sort of connection. He'd opened up a little but he'd closed right back down again. And she only had herself to blame. She'd known months ago that she shouldn't go anywhere near Dexter Stevens. But she'd ignored that huge red flag warning her to keep away from him.

She'd wanted adventure. And she'd got it. And now she had to live with the fallout: stinging rejection; mulling over where she'd gone wrong. Had he felt the portacath scar? Unlike Lachlan, Dexter would have known straight away what it was. But, like Lachlan, perhaps he'd not wanted the responsibility either.

Whatever. He wanted a professional-only relationship and she could do that. She refused to be hurt. She refused to let it show at least.

'Lactate,' he growled.

'Beg your pardon?' said Tilly.

He pointed to the screen. 'Bloody lactate. How many times do I need to tell them? Doing a lactate is part of the sepsis screening.'

Tilly stared at him. She'd never heard him swear before or appear irritated. Cool and standoffish, yes, but not outwardly irritated.

'Well, just ask someone to do it now.'

'It should have already been done.' He sighed and jabbed at

the keyboard, closing it down. 'I've got an exec board meeting and, as the department doesn't need me right now, I have no excuse to get out of it.'

He stood, scraping back his chair, and walked away from her, stopping only to speak briefly to one of the doctors, no doubt to instruct them to do a lactate on the patient he'd mentioned.

'No, now!' were his parting words to a slightly startled Pearl.

Whatever had got into him? He usually kept his feelings on a leash more taut than a tightrope.

'Tilly, I've got a six-year-old asthmatic in Paeds; would you give me a hand with him? Mum's pretty anxious and not really helping…' It was Ally, one of the other junior doctors.

'Of course,' said Tilly, following her, and frowning as the door Dexter had just gone through banged shut.

CHAPTER TWELVE

TILLY GLANCED AT the clock on the wall. *How had it got to four o'clock already?* She'd made sure the other staff took a break, but had yet to take one herself, and was by now desperately in need of a coffee and something to eat.

Sitting at the nurse's station, she sensed Dexter approach. Was it his too-familiar warm scent she'd noticed or his dark shadow approaching and falling on her? Her stomach knotted. A large hand appeared in her line of vision and placed a lidded cardboard cup in front of her on the desk. She looked up… into piercing cobalt eyes…and her stomach knotted further.

'Peace offering,' he said, lips pressed together, watching her.

She frowned, looking from him to the cup and back again. 'For what?'

'For being what you would no doubt call a "sourpuss" earlier.'

'A sourpuss?'

Dexter sighed. 'Or Scrooge, or maybe a killjoy…or, dare I say it, a party pooper?'

A slow smile spread across her face. It was good to have the banter back. Maybe having a professional-only relationship with Dexter would be okay.

'Slightly uptight grumpy bear,' she said, noting the quiver at the corners of his lips. He raised a dark eyebrow and nodded slowly.

'I'll give you that,' he replied, his lips curving very slightly towards what could have turned into a smile had he not looked away. 'Drink that.' He nodded at the cardboard cup. 'We can't have you keeling over.'

'Thanks,' said Tilly, picking it up. 'Is it coffee?'

'Strong and black, just as you like it… It's what you ordered at breakfast…at the wedding.'

He'd remembered how she took her coffee…

'You looked like you needed it,' he added.

She rolled her eyes. 'Extra shifts. The money's great but they do take their toll. My flat looks like I abandoned it months ago and, although I love my job, I'd quite like to see walls that aren't A&E walls some time.'

'Thanks for everything, Sister, Doctor.' A grateful patient was wheeled past the nurse's station on his way to a ward.

'You're welcome,' replied Tilly. 'Don't be in a rush to visit us again.'

The patient smiled. 'I won't.'

'Another happy customer,' said Tilly, smiling at Dexter.

He raised an eyebrow. 'Leaving only forty-three patients in the department still to be seen.' He held up his hands. 'And, before you say it, I'm well aware that's a very *Grinchy* comment to make.'

'It certainly is, Dr Stevens. What astounding self-awareness you have.' She took a sip of coffee.

'Developed possibly because, almost continually for the last four months, you've been pointing out to me that I have a slightly more serious side than some.'

Tilly snorted, suppressing a laugh and bringing her hand to her mouth. 'Don't! You nearly made me choke.' She placed her cup back down on the desk.

'Did I say something amusing?' The trace of a frown appeared between his brows.

She pressed her lips together, trying not to laugh, then shook her head. 'I give up, Dexter. I've tried, but you are who are, and I'm just going to have to accept that.'

His frown deepened. 'What's that supposed to mean?'

Go for it, Tilly. You've nothing to lose.

'I'd always wondered if you had hidden depths lurking beneath your cool demeanour... Maybe a sense of humour; perhaps an ability to open up a little, or possibly to show some emotion, some passion.' She bit her lip. 'And you do... sometimes.' She picked up the cup of coffee and took a drink, watching him from over the rim.

His frown melted as he looked at her and his dark eyebrows rose. Then he smiled...slowly. A devastating smile spreading outwards and lighting up his eyes, giving them a rare sparkle that squeezed all the air from her lungs.

'Careful; someone might see you,' said Tilly, still eyeing him from the rim of the cup.

He leant in closer, his voice low. 'That's your fault.'

'My fault?' She feigned innocence and held onto the cup as though it protected her from his sudden nearness and the intensity of his gaze, which was doing untold damage to her heart rate. A gaze she'd thought she would never see again.

He gave an almost imperceptible nod. His eyes were mesmerising, inches from her own, his soft breath whispering across her face as he spoke. He glanced away for a second as a porter walked past the nurse's station and she immediately missed being held in his gaze. But his eyes locked back on her before her heart rate had time to adjust back to normal.

'You do that to me, Tilly.'

Every nerve ending in her entire body became alert.

He glanced around but there was no one nearby. Their hard work today meant that the department was currently under control.

'I make you smile, you mean?' Her pulse raced.

'Smile, laugh, dance, run headlong into the sea fully clothed...'

'But not want to be romantic?' she challenged.

His eyes held hers, searching them, as if trying to decide

what to say or do next. 'Come with me.' He stood, tucking his chair under the desk.

She looked up at him. 'To where?'

'We have a meeting.'

'We do?'

Ally walked towards the desk. 'Dr Stevens, can I just ask you about taking a day's annual leave next Wednesday?'

'Yes,' he replied. 'It's fine. Send me an email for the leave booking system.'

Ally looked taken aback. 'Oh, wow...great, thanks.'

'Sister, we have a meeting.'

Tilly picked up her coffee, got up and followed him to her office. He held open the door and closed it behind them, turning the lock with a click. Heart hammering, she stared at him. Somehow his eyes had darkened.

'What's the meeting about?' she asked, clutching her cup, a flush of warmth spreading through her.

'Romance,' he replied, walking towards her, taking the cup from her hand and placing it on the desk behind her.

She swallowed. 'Romance?'

'The word keeps cropping up...it must be important to you.'

He was inches away from her; she could feel his warmth, inhale his scent.

'It's important to most people.'

He smiled, his eyes locked on hers, smouldering embers igniting within them. Tingles shivered down her spine.

'I have a sense we've been here before, Tilly.'

'You told me you don't do romance.'

'I don't.'

'Or relationships.'

'No...but I *do* do this.'

Dipping his head, he closed his eyes as his lips brushed hers, their bodies remaining chastely, tantalisingly, apart. But she wanted more than a chaste kiss. Dexter Stevens didn't do romance, but he knew how to kiss, and she knew only too well that he had more than this to offer. She closed the gap between them, reaching up and drawing him towards her, pressing against his warm, hard body and hearing his groan as she raked her fingers into his hair. She gasped as he pulled her closer, deepening the kiss, tasting her and leaving her in no doubt that he wanted her.

She didn't want to pull away but she needed air, and pulled back, breathless, her heart racing. Dexter's pager sounded and he groaned.

'Timing.' He unclipped the pager from the waistband of his scrubs, glancing at it. 'I'll have to get this.'

'Of course,' she managed, pulling her uniform straight.

'Would you like to go to dinner this evening?'

'Okay…'

Dinner? But he regretted them sleeping together, didn't he?

'Seven p.m. at the Italian on Queen's Walk, by Tower Bridge?'

She nodded. 'Sounds good.'

He lifted his mobile phone, tapping to find his contact, unlocked the door and was gone.

She couldn't move.

What had happened?

She sat down on the edge of her desk, unsure if her legs could take her weight any more. The heat that had cooled so quickly between them since the castle, and had been doused further a short time ago in the linen cupboard, had flared into life…out of nowhere.

Unless it hadn't been from nowhere.

Had he changed his mind?

What if he wanted more than a one-night stand?

What if he wanted to break his own rules?

She glanced at the clock. The shift was over. It was just as well, because there was no way she could think straight now, and if she was going to negotiate a new set of rules with Dexter she really needed to be able to think.

CHAPTER THIRTEEN

DEXTER ARRIVED AT the restaurant early, making sure they had the best table, overlooking the River Thames from the south bank. He checked his watch, glancing up when the door opened, then reached for his glass of orange juice and took a long drink. But his mouth was still dry.

Why was he so nervous?

He looked out of the window. A pleasure cruiser sailed by, disappearing under the bridge. People walked past, pushing prams, walking dogs. A grey squirrel ran up a nearby tree. Normal, everyday activities were going on all around him but nothing felt normal or every day.

How long had he managed to keep his distance from Tilly after the castle? Two days off work and then half a day once he'd seen her again. He'd tried not to think about her all the time. He'd tried not to miss her. He'd tried really hard not to want to smile when she walked into the room, and he'd tried even harder not to remember how it had felt to have her in his arms and make love to her.

But he'd failed…epically…and he was very aware that he'd become a little irritable as a result. He'd apologised to Pearl for his outburst earlier.

He hadn't planned to ask Tilly to dinner, just as he hadn't planned to take her into the office on false pretences and kiss her. But he'd seen that playful, sexy flare in her eyes over that coffee cup as she'd caught his look... His resolve had evaporated and the words had tumbled out of his mouth.

But he didn't do relationships. Or feelings.

Leaning back in his seat, he raked his fingers through his hair. He was being tested. Could he hang on to what he believed in—that logic was the best policy and feelings, emotions, were for the weak? Clearly not, because he was sitting here in this restaurant waiting to have dinner with the only woman who'd ever made him question that belief.

He spotted Tilly in the distance and his heart rate immediately quickened. Tilly, with her beautiful amethyst eyes, infectious smile and irrepressible love of life—the woman who'd made him smile and laugh when he'd thought they were things everyone else did. Who'd made him want to tell her about his past and made him question every truth he knew about himself.

Was he really someone who didn't know how to have fun?
Was he the cool-hearted killjoy she'd accused him of being?

She had a point. In fact, she'd probably read him perfectly. Being like that kept people away from him. It stopped him from having to deal with feelings, emotions and everything that came with those uncontrollable human faults: the rejection, pain and fear.

It hadn't kept her away, though, had it? And he'd found himself wanting to be with her, spend time with her and get to know her. Gradually, without him even noticing until it was too late, she'd percolated into his being, making him want to smile, laugh and do things...illogical things...he'd never done before.

Perhaps his logic was flawed.

And, though he'd tried to shake the thought from his mind, he'd even begun to wonder whether the reason his resolve had weakened and he'd kissed her again earlier was because he'd begun to develop feelings for her. He'd looked into her eyes and seen them flame and it had sent a shot of desire through him. But it was more than sexual chemistry that had filled his senses these last few months.

* * *

'So sorry I'm late,' said Tilly, sitting down in the chair he'd pulled out from the table for her. 'I fell asleep when I got home. Thanks.'

'You fell asleep? It was a pretty busy one today but I didn't think it was that bad.'

'It was on top of an evening shift I'd done the night before,' she replied, reaching for the menu. 'Cumulative effect. Have you chosen yet?'

'I'm going to have the *arrabiata*.'

'I think I'll join you. Shall we share a garlic flatbread?'

'Sounds good.'

She picked up the wine list automatically, but then remembered. The waiter took their order and she asked for a sparkling water.

'Don't let me stop you from having a glass of wine,' said Dexter.

She grimaced. 'It'd probably put me to sleep again. I'll stick with water.'

The waiter came over and they put in their order.

'You think my company will be enough to put you asleep? Charmed, I'm sure.'

But he was smiling that rare, warm, genuine smile that made his eyes sparkle and made her want to gaze into them. There was no way Dexter's company would put her to sleep, especially after that kiss earlier. She'd been annoyed she'd fallen asleep when she'd got home after work—she'd wanted more time to get ready. As it was, she'd only had time for a quick shower, a change of clothes, a whisk of mascara and a slick of lip balm. And now, with his eyes on her, she wished she'd had time to do more.

'I've never been bored in your company, Dexter…not even for a second. You're very entertaining.'

He looked at her quizzically.

'Entertaining? Dare I ask how?'

She pressed her lips together, her eyes narrowed thoughtfully, her chin resting in one hand.

'In many ways.' She lifted an eyebrow.

'Name one.'

'Ooh, let me see. You're an excellent teasee.'

'I don't think that's actually a word.'

'Oh, it is—it means someone who's good at being teased.'

'And I'm good at that?'

'Most definitely. You're so straitlaced.'

'Not always.'

He gazed into her eyes across the table, through the flickering flame of the candle, and her breathing quickened. There had been nothing straitlaced about how he'd lured her to a 'meeting' in her office and kissed the breath out of her. Or about how he'd taken the lead from her as they'd danced at the castle and moved her towards the bed. Or about how he'd made love to her. And there was nothing straitlaced about the fire in his eyes right now.

'No, not always.'

The waiter brought the food and she reluctantly dragged her gaze from Dexter's to acknowledge him. She didn't want to break the spell between them. She wanted to reach over and touch his lips; she wanted everyone else to disappear and leave them alone together. And, from the way he was looking at her, it seemed he wanted the exact same thing. The black ink in which he'd written into his rule book his self-imposed rules of the game was fading to grey.

Tilly glanced out of the window and across the river to the Tower of London.

'We seem to be drawn to castles.'

'But we have a river this time, and not the sea, so my trousers might survive the evening.'

Tilly laughed.

'The night is young—anything could happen.'

He looked at her over the flickering candlelight, the glow

from the flame taking her back to the sunset on the battery terrace…right before he'd kissed her. Would he kiss her again tonight? Her pulse quickened. She wasn't going to stop him if he did.

They turned to their meal.

'Any dessert this evening?' asked the waiter shortly afterwards, collecting their plates.

Yes. I'll have the man sitting opposite.

'Not for me, thanks,' replied Tilly, raising a questioning eyebrow at Dexter.

'Me neither…we need to get back. Just the bill, please.'

The waiter nodded and took the dishes away.

'Need to get back?' repeated Tilly, a smile playing on her lips. 'Do we?'

Her heart rate picked up as she saw unmistakeable desire flame in his eyes.

'You're tired.'

'Am I?'

'You fell asleep earlier.'

'I'm not tired now.'

He swallowed, his Adam's apple sliding in his throat. 'We have work tomorrow.'

Tilly checked the time on her phone.

'I'm allowed to stay up after nine p.m.….even if I have work the next day.'

He looked at her as though he was trying to work something out.

Was he deciding if he wanted more than a one-night stand? If he wanted to finish what he'd started in her office?

They paid the bill and stepped outside. Grey clouds had slipped in front of the sun and the air had cooled.

'I'll get a cab,' said Dexter, looking up at the sky. 'Looks like rain.'

'I fancy a walk along the river…come on.'

They walked along the riverside path of Queen's Walk, past

Tower Bridge and a family of ducks, watching a couple in a canoe paddle past.

'It's so peaceful here,' said Tilly. 'A little out of the city centre… Makes a nice change.'

'I bring the dogs out along here sometimes for a walk.'

'I still can't get over how you love your dogs.'

'Why is that so hard to believe?'

'I don't know.' Her lips pressed together in thought. 'I'd always thought of you as…'

'An unemotional, antisocial Grinch?'

She feigned a look of being impressed.

'Again, such self-awareness.'

He rolled his eyes. 'I just thought I'd save you saying it.'

'Actually, that isn't what I was going to say. What you told me at the wedding about your father puts it into context… makes how you are much more understandable. Did you ever have counselling?'

Dexter looked at her quizzically. 'I don't need counselling.'

'You went through a huge trauma growing up…losing your mum, too. If ever you need to talk about any of it, I'm quite a good listener.'

'I don't…thank you.'

A clap of distant thunder sounded.

'Sounds ominous,' she said, looking up at the sky.

'We should have got that cab,' replied Dexter. 'I can feel rain.'

'Oh, we'll be fine…a drop of rain never hurt anyone. Anyway, I like being in the rain. It's refreshing, and a good storm always makes you feel so alive, doesn't it? Come on, let's walk.'

Another clap of thunder.

'It's getting closer,' said Dexter.

'Walk and talk quickly, then. Now we've cleared the air from the awkward morning after, we can relax with each other a bit, can't we?'

Dexter looked doubtful.

'Dexter, look, we had sex—it happens. And, hey, it's the twenty-first century—you don't have to worry, I'm not expecting you to marry me. Chill out.'

He stared at her, his eyes wide, and she laughed.

'I had a boyfriend once who was the exact opposite of you.' She continued walking along the river path.

'So I'm not even your type, then,' he replied, falling into step with her.

'Far from it, Dexter, so you really needn't worry—I'm not looking for a happy-ever-after from you.'

'So who was this person?'

'Lachlan. He was a guitarist in a band I met on a night out from work.'

'And in what way was he the exact opposite of me, dare I ask?'

Tilly smiled. 'He was—probably still is—a very "rock 'n' roll" sort of guy. He liked a good time, loads of fun…always looking for the next adventure.'

'Sounds perfect for you. But it didn't last?'

'No,' she replied. 'And that's where the differences between you end. Lachlan, much the same as yourself, didn't want commitment.'

He didn't want the commitment of being with someone who might need to lean on him a little one day.

'And you were looking for commitment?'

It was a little more complicated than that, but she wasn't going to tell him about her illness. He'd literally run away after spending only one night together. She could imagine how far and how quickly he'd run if she told him she'd had cancer and that it could come back at any time.

'Sort of,' she replied. She looked up at the sky. The clouds were darker. A large rain drop landed on her upturned face and she held out her palms.

'It's definitely raining.'

'We're not too far from the next bridge,' said Dexter, turning up the collar on his jacket. 'We can shelter under there.'

'Your turn, then,' said Tilly. 'What about your romantic past?'

'I don't have one.'

'Oh, no, of course. You don't do romance. Tell me about your last girlfriend, then.'

'Helena.'

'Don't do that to me, Dexter—don't go all mysterious one-word answers on me now. What happened?'

'She taught me that happy-ever-afters don't exist.'

Thunder crashed overhead so loudly, it made Tilly duck. And then the heavens opened.

Dexter drew his jacket more tightly around him but Tilly stood, face upturned, arms spread wide as another clap of thunder crashed and the rain came down heavier, soaking her in seconds.

'Come on,' said Dexter, raising his voice over the noise of the falling rain. 'Don't just stand there; we need to get under cover.'

'No,' called Tilly, laughing. 'This is your chance to prove it.'

'Prove what?' he replied, pulling up his collar further.

'That you're not Grinch.' She twirled round on the spot, face still turned up to the sky, her eyes closed. 'Walk in the rain with me. Let yourself get soaked. Don't run from it... embrace it.' She opened her eyes to look at him. He stood with his shoulders hunched, his dark hair getting darker by the second. 'Come on, Dexter, live a little.'

'I'd hoped to stay dry this evening.'

She grinned at him. 'It's too late for that.'

A puddle had formed on the path in front of them. Tilly stood on the edge of it and jumped in, both feet together, the water splashing up her legs and making her laugh. She turned to face him, her hands on her hips.

'Do it,' she ordered, pointing at the puddle.

Dexter shook his head slowly. 'Not a chance.'

'Don't be a—'

She didn't have chance to complete her sentence. Dexter jumped into the puddle and stood before her, trying to suppress a triumphant grin. Tilly gave him an approving smile then turned, ran over to one of the old black Victorian-style lampposts, hooked her arm and swung around it, belting out the old Gene Kelly track 'Singin' in the Rain'. She stopped and beckoned him.

'Absolutely not,' he shouted back as more thunder crashed overhead. 'That's where I draw the line.'

Tilly laughed and ran over to him, grabbing him by the hand.

'Come on,' she said. 'Run in the rain with me.' She pulled his hand, breaking into a run, and they ran along the river path, through puddles and back towards the city until, breathless and laughing, they reached the sanctuary of Tower Bridge.

Tilly leant against the wall, pushing her soaking hair away from her face and getting her breath back. Dexter had his hands on his knees but recovered quickly. He looked up at her and, although her breathing had been settling, suddenly she was breathless all over again...but for an entirely different reason.

Their eyes locked and he took a step towards her.

'You keep doing this to me,' he said, searching her eyes, as though trying to work out how she'd done it.

'Doing what?'

'Getting me wet, making me run with you...making me want to kiss you.'

Her heart thudded so hard, she feared it might stop.

'Not on purpose.'

He raised an eyebrow.

'I think you know full well what you do to me, Tilly.'

'But you don't do romance.'

He shook his head. 'No.'

'And yet, in the right circumstances, holding hands and running through the rain can be extremely romantic.'

'Can it?'

She nodded. 'As can being kissed under a bridge.'

A slow smile curved his lips. 'Is that what you want?'

She held his gaze. 'I think that might be nice. What about you?'

His eyes flamed. 'I think it would be more than nice, Tilly.'

He closed the space between them, placed one hand either side of her head on the wall of the bridge behind her, enclosing her, and brought his lips to hers. She closed her eyes, inhaled his warm scent and tasted him, running her fingers up into his drenched hair.

This *was* romantic.

He could be romantic.

And she wanted more.

'I think my place is closer,' she managed as he pulled back. 'If you'd like to…' *Come and take your wet clothes off* '…dry off. It sounds as though the rain's easing.'

He swallowed, searching her eyes again before nodding and holding her gaze.

'I think I should…dry off, yes.'

CHAPTER FOURTEEN

LEAVING TILLY IN bed to get home and changed before returning to the hospital for his shift had been monumentally hard. He hadn't gone to dinner expecting it to end with them sleeping together but it had quickly become apparent that that was where the evening was going. The chemistry between them was undeniable, and Tilly inviting him in had left him in no doubt that sex was on the agenda. How they'd kept their hands off each other until they'd got inside the flat, he didn't know. But this time, unlike at the castle, he hadn't sloped out at dawn, regretting what had happened—far from it. It had been a wrench leaving her.

The Saturday evening chaos in the department at Trafalgar began a little earlier than usual with the arrival of a small group of men who'd been to a football match and begun drinking too much, too early and had various injuries as a result of some sort of fracas. There'd been no need for him to intervene other than to brief the Plastics team on the details of the wounds.

'Dr Stevens?' said Tilly. 'Would you have a look at a patient in four? I think she's dislocated her shoulder.'

'Sure,' he replied.

Tilly lowered her voice. 'The poor woman is six months pregnant and says she fell down a step. I'm not sure I believe her but we can investigate that after her shoulder has been dealt with. I've tried to assess her but I think she'll need a muscle relaxant before we can examine her. I've immobilised it in a sling for now.'

'What do you mean, you don't believe her?'

'She's got an old bruise under her right eye that she's tried to cover with make-up and, when I asked her about it, she said she'd stumbled and hit a kitchen cupboard.'

'I suppose she might have,' said Dexter. 'Pregnancy can affect balance due to the hormone relaxin, which increases in order to relax the uterus and pelvic ligaments. It's quite common for women to fall when pregnant.'

'There's something not quite right, though,' said Tilly. 'She's jumpy and nervous, like she doesn't want to be here. We should assess her fully and maintain a high level of suspicion she may be vulnerable.'

'Let's go and see her,' said Dexter. 'And we can take it from there. We'll take a muscle relaxant in with us.'

'Hi, Becky,' said Tilly, entering the cubicle. 'This is Dr Stevens, one of the consultants. Is it okay if we have a look at that shoulder?'

'Of course,' said Becky, clearly in pain and holding her arm very still. 'I could do with getting home, really.'

Tilly glanced at Dexter. Becky wanting to get home quickly was one of the warning signs she'd told him about. People who were being abused were often wary of the authorities.

'I'm just going to remove this sling so the doctor can examine you, Becky. Hold your arm nice and still for me.'

Becky grimaced as Tilly removed the sling and pulled down the gown to expose both shoulders, being careful to minimise the exposure to maintain Becky's privacy and dignity.

Dexter moved to stand at the bottom of the trolley. 'I'm just going to look first, Becky,' he said.

Tilly watched him as he studied Becky's shoulders, looking for any asymmetry. She'd already made a mental note of the faded bruises to their patient's chest.

'Just going to palpate the shoulder now,' said Dexter, moving from the end of the trolley and standing at Becky's shoulder.

'The doctor's going to feel the shoulder, Becky,' explained Tilly, throwing Dexter a look that hopefully reminded him to drop the medical jargon.

'Is it going to hurt?' said Becky, her eyes wide.

'Hard to tell until we try,' said Dexter. 'But, if it does, we'll stop immediately. I want to check your elbow and wrist joints, too.' He palpated the wrist and elbow before placing his hands on the shoulder. Although Becky winced as he moved his fingers over the joint, she wasn't in too much pain. 'The humeral head is palpable anteriorly—no need for an X-ray. There's no evidence of neurovascular compromise. We'll do a closed reduction, but let's get some muscle relaxant in first.'

Tilly raised an eyebrow at him. He narrowed his eyes then seemed to understand.

He addressed Becky. 'I can feel that the top of the humerus… the arm bone here…' he touched Becky's arm '…has popped out of place. That's why it's so painful when you move it. It's very fixable, though. We simply need to pop it back into the socket. With this injury, there's also the possibility of nerve and blood vessel damage, but I've checked, and you don't have that. So, if you're happy, we can do a reduction—'

Tilly coughed.

'We can manipulate…move…the arm bone back into place,' he continued. 'We'll give you something for the pain first, though.'

'Have you got any questions, Becky? Was the doctor's explanation okay?' said Tilly. 'And is there anyone I can call for you, to sit with you and take you home afterwards?'

'No,' said Becky. 'There's my husband, but I don't…' She glanced at Tilly and then at Dexter. 'He's at work.'

'Injection going in,' said Dexter. 'We'll give that a few minutes to work and then come back.'

Tilly made sure Becky had the nurse call-bell to hand, instructing her to call if she needed anything, then she joined Dexter in the clinical room. 'What do you think?' she asked him.

'She has multiple contusions, all at varying stages of healing, on the face, chest and upper back,' said Dexter, rubbing the back of his neck. 'Her wrist was tender when I examined her for neurovascular compromise and there were old, finger-sized bruises on it.'

'And she wants to get home,' added Tilly, her lips pressed together. 'And she didn't want me to call her husband.'

'Looks as though you're right. She needs referring to the safeguarding team. We have a duty of care to her. It would be good to get her consent but, if we can't, we still have to make the call and raise the concern. Do you want to try to talk to her after the procedure?'

She nodded. 'I'll see if she's willing to give me any information but invariably people are reluctant for fear of reprisals. It's so frustrating.'

'In a way, it's quite fortunate she's come in with only a dislocated shoulder,' said Dexter. 'It could have been far worse, and at least now we can help her.'

Tilly looked at him. He wasn't simply a one-dimensional, unfeeling, cool operator all the time, was he?

'What?' he said, stepping back, searching her eyes.

Tilly smiled. 'Nothing. Shall we go and sort Becky's shoulder out?'

Tilly was well aware of the personal safety measures every member of hospital staff needed to keep in mind at all times. The problem was that, when she'd initially entered the cubicle to speak to her after she and Dexter had successfully repositioned her dislocated shoulder and applied a sling, Becky had been the only person in the cubicle.

But that had just changed. And the situation escalated very quickly. They were joined by her more than slightly irate husband, Chris, who had called her when he'd found she wasn't at home. And, rather than having come directly from work, he appeared to have travelled via the pub.

'She says she's fine,' he said through gritted teeth. 'So she's coming home.'

Tilly drew in a breath, her exit from the cubicle now blocked by the man, willing her heart to slow a little and her voice not to rise an octave or two.

'I just need to monitor her a little longer. An injury like this can cause nerve and blood vessel damage. You're very welcome to go and get a cup of tea from the café, or I can call you later if you prefer.'

'I'll stay here,' he growled.

'Go and get a drink,' she replied. 'I'm sure you could do with one after a long day at work.'

It was the typical behaviour of an abuser—they didn't want their partner to interact with the authorities for fear of being outed. And the conversation Tilly had already had with Becky, along with the physical evidence, convinced her that this ruddy-faced brute standing before her now was an abuser.

'Have you called social services?' he demanded, taking a step closer towards her.

She stood her ground, not wanting to appear afraid of him and give him the upper hand, but her pulse was racing, her mouth was dry and every muscle in her body was rigid. She was in full fight or flight mode. Becky had refused to be referred, saying it would only make things worse. She lifted her chin, controlling her breathing.

Challenge him.

'Why would I have done that?'

'Because you lot like interfering.' He took another step closer, jabbing a finger towards her. The smell of alcohol and cigarettes intensified, turning her stomach. The need to step backwards and away from him was overwhelming but there was nowhere to go.

'Leave her, Chris,' said Becky. 'She's just doing her job. I haven't told her anything.'

The man swung round to face her, grabbing the metal sides of the trolley on which she was sitting, putting his face up close against hers and spitting words like venom.

'I haven't told her anything,' he mocked. 'Brilliant, Becky, brilliant; that's just made nosey nurse here think we do have something to hide…nice one.'

'I'm sure nobody meant for any of this to happen,' said Tilly.

He swung back to face Tilly, rounding on her, the stench of his breath cloying and hanging heavily in the air between them. She stepped back, bumping into the bedside locker, knocking a glass of water to the floor with a crash.

'Are you accusing me of hitting her?' He bore down on her, his eyes bloodshot, his voice overly calm but sounding a warning.

She swallowed. 'We all have difficult times in our relationships. There's help available if you're struggling.'

'You *are* accusing me of hitting her.' He bore down towards her again, so close now that his face was slightly out of focus. He clamped his hands, one either side of her on the bedside locker behind her, trapping her and pinning her to it. She bent backwards, instinctively trying to create even a little distance between them, but his body was pressed so hard against her that she couldn't move.

The cubicle curtain parted behind him and Tilly's eyes darted to it.

Dexter!

The man followed Tilly's gaze, turning to face him, releasing her from his grip.

Dexter stood, his expression one of mild interest but his stance firm, legs apart, arms by his sides. He was all carefully controlled restraint, appearing almost disinterested, but his hands were balled into tight fists and his knuckles were deathly white.

'Everything all right in here, Sister? I heard a crash.'

CHAPTER FIFTEEN

THE RAISED VOICES had made Dexter look up from the computer at the nurse's station; the smashing of a glass that followed had caused him to leap from his seat, stride over to the cubicle and drag the curtain aside. Ice gripped him, freezing him, locking the air in his lungs in an instant as he took in the scene.

The instinctive reaction to lunge at the man and rip him away from Tilly shocked him, and forcing himself not to took every atom of self-control he possessed. He'd been in similar situations before in A&E but he'd never, ever, had the overwhelming urge to strike someone before. Every sinew in his body was taut, every muscle rigid; his fingernails dug into his palms. But that would be wrong; it would be counterproductive and could escalate the situation, putting Tilly in danger.

Instead, he did what he always did: wore his mask and appeared calm, controlled and unemotional. The only difference was that this time, in this particular situation, he didn't feel those things. He couldn't take the emotion out of it.

A well-built, brutish-looking man with an unshaven, weather-beaten face turned round and looked at him, swaying slightly. He was drunk. And Dexter was transported straight back to when his father's angry face and swaying body had stood before him as a child.

He clenched his fists more tightly and tried to control his breathing. Aggression, he could deal with—he did it almost every day to one degree or another—but aggression due to drunkenness triggered something deep inside him, especially when there was a child involved. And this child, the one Becky was carrying, was so very vulnerable.

'I'm just checking Becky's shoulder,' said Tilly, clearly trying but not quite managing to keep her voice light.

'There's a coffee shop out by the main entrance,' said Dexter, addressing the man. 'Sister will be half an hour—just long enough for you to have a hot drink before you come back.'

The man curled his lip into a snarl and walked towards him, making him tense further, every muscle straining and ready to act if he had to. If the man did strike out, he would be left with no alternative but to physically restrain him.

'If anyone else tells me to go and get a drink, I swear to God I'll—' There was the stench of cigarettes and beer... It was his father all over again.

'Or I can have you removed from the department,' Dexter cut in. 'Your choice.'

The man narrowed his eyes murderously and the two men watched each other for an extended moment. Dexter's expression remained impassive, belying the shocking, raging turmoil beneath.

Make the right decision. Don't make me have to contain you.

Because I will. Because I'm not letting you go anywhere near Tilly again.

Because...

'Do your checks, but I'll be back in fifteen minutes and *she's* coming home.'

The man walked out of the cubicle, past Dexter, being careful not to brush against him, just as Security turned up.

'Everything all right, Doc?' asked Simon, the guard.

Dexter nodded and turned to Tilly.

'I'll get someone else to take over here.'

'I'm fine,' she replied. 'I just need to speak with Becky a moment longer.'

He didn't want to leave her. He wanted to take her into his arms. But Tilly, typically, was putting her patient first.

He turned to the security guard. 'Stay here—he'll be coming back in ten minutes or so.'

'You'll put me out of a job, Doc,' said Simon, grinning and turning to Tilly. 'And he does it with much more class than I do, doesn't he?'

'He does.' Tilly gave him a smile but not her usual wide, warm smile. She'd clearly been frightened. He desperately wanted to hold her but it wasn't possible right then.

Instead, he walked to the changing room a little further down the corridor, his pulse still racing. There was no one else in there and he stood in front of a long mirror on the wall, leaning towards it and resting his forehead on the cool glass as his breathing slowed.

What had happened out there?

He straightened up and looked at his reflection. *Finish your sentence, Stevens. You're not going to let that brute anywhere near Tilly again because...?*

He looked into cool blue eyes. *Because you want to protect her. Be honest. Because you're in love with her.*

He swallowed. *Was he?* Was that why he'd felt so angry? Was that why he'd wanted to take hold of the man and tear him off her...*because he was in love with her?*

His refection frowned at him. It all sounded so logical. His reaction had been instinctive because he *cared*. It made sense. But what was terrifying was the anger he'd felt because she'd been in danger—an anger he'd never experienced before. Was that because he'd never cared so deeply before?

If he did care for her, it had crept up on him with impunity, without him giving his permission.

How the hell had that happened?

And if he did care for her...love her, even...just look where it had got him. It had unleashed the very thing he'd tried so hard to keep under control all his life: anger. Boiling, raging anger that had made him want to lash out at someone.

So he had inherited his father's propensity for rage.

In the right circumstances, he was capable of letting feelings get the better of him. Years of practice at not caring, putting on the mask and not succumbing to emotions—gone in a flash because he'd allowed himself to care.

And now he had to try even harder to control it. That meant not caring. And definitely not falling in love.

He went to the sink, washed his hands and splashed cold water onto his face, wiping it dry with a paper towel. He strode back towards the department. Becky's husband would be back soon and he had to get to her before the man returned and took her home. He wasn't going to allow another child to grow up with an angry, aggressive, alcoholic father and have no support, and he wasn't going to risk that child growing up without its mother either.

Simon stood outside the cubicle.

'Anyone in there?' said Dexter.

'Just the patient and Tilly,' he replied.

'Can I come in?' he called through the curtain.

Tilly pulled open the curtain. He closed it behind him, glancing at Tilly with a questioning stare. She shook her head.

'Becky doesn't want to be referred.'

Damn it.

He stood beside her, resting his hands on the metal side of the trolley, looking down at them. This was hard. Give him a multiple category-one trauma any day rather than have to deal with this side of the job. But it had to be done. He wasn't going to accept that there was nothing he could do for this mother and her baby.

'I know you're frightened, Becky,' he began, lifting his eyes to look at her. 'And I know you think that one day Chris might change…might become the husband and father you want him to be.'

'He will,' she insisted. 'Once the baby is born, he'll change. He just gets so angry, but it's not him—it's the drink.'

Dexter had heard it all before. The same words had been in his own head as a child every time his father had lashed out at him. Every single time that belt had slammed into the backs of his legs he'd convinced himself it would be the last time, that his father would change…be the father he wanted him to be. It had never happened.

But he and his father had never had what he was able to offer Becky. 'He's not going to change, Becky. Men like him never do, not without help and lots of support. If you want you and your baby to stay with your husband and both be safe, you're all going to need support. There is help out there to get him off the drink and there's support for you and the baby.'

'He won't want social services involved.' She looked up at him with frightened, wide eyes.

'He doesn't need to know. I'm going to refer you to the physiotherapy service,' said Dexter. 'They happen to be in the same building as the safeguarding team here at the hospital. I'll explain to your husband that you're going to need appointments for a long time for that shoulder injury.'

She looked into his eyes and he saw the exact moment that the penny dropped.

'Yes,' she said. 'The appointments will be in the day time, won't they?'

'They will,' replied Dexter. 'When your husband's at work. And there's help available with transport, too, if you need it.'

Becky reached for his hand. 'Thank you, Doctor; thank you so much.'

'I'll make the first appointment and the number for the centre will be on the card…if you need to contact them in the meantime.'

Becky nodded, biting her lip.

'I'll explain about the physio to your husband when he gets back.'

'Thank you.' She released his hand.

'Let's get you ready to go home, Becky,' said Tilly. 'While Dr Stevens sorts out your referral.'

'You okay?' said Tilly, sitting down beside Dexter at the nurse's station later. Becky and her husband had gone home. Dexter had walked down to the café to find Chris and tell him his wife was ready, and they'd walked back together, Chris in a much more agreeable disposition.

'Fine,' he replied, tapping the keyboard, updating Becky's notes.

'Can we have a meeting?'

He glanced across at her.

'When? What for?'

Tilly nodded at his screen. 'When you've finished that. My office.'

'I'm done,' he said, logging off. 'Is there a problem?'

'Come on then,' she replied, standing.

Dexter got up and they walked the short distance to Tilly's office. She closed the door behind them, and he remembered the last time they'd both been in this room together…when he'd locked the door and kissed her.

'Have you brought me in here to seduce me again, Sister?'

She smiled. 'My recollection is that it was you who seduced me, Doctor.'

He stroked his chin thoughtfully. 'So it was. So, why have you called this cosy meeting? Have I done something wrong?'

'I just wanted to check you're okay after what happened with Becky and her husband.'

He folded his arms. 'I'm fine. Is that all?'

Tilly leant against the desk. 'You were thinking of your father.'

'I rarely think of him.' He uncrossed his arms, digging his hands into the pockets of his scrubs.

'You thought of him just then. That man reminded you of

him. That's why you were so angry and why you went out of your way to help Becky.'

How did she know this? He glanced round behind him at the door then looked back at her before dropping his gaze. 'I'd have helped her anyway.'

'Your actions this evening have given that baby a better start in life than you had, Dexter. You were brilliant.'

'I just hope they're okay.' When he'd gone down to the café to find Becky's husband, he gave him a chance to do the right thing. He'd given him the number for a counsellor. He'd not blamed him; he'd told him he understood how hard it was to stop drinking; that he didn't need to be the way he was; and he'd explained that he could have a better, happier life…be a role model for his child.

'They have a much better chance of being okay now than they ever had before.'

He looked up and met her gaze. There was no pity in her eyes…just approval. Like the approval he'd always hoped he'd earn from his father one day; like the approval he'd known he'd have had from his mother…if she'd lived.

How could he stop himself from falling in love with Tilly?

It was already too late for that.

CHAPTER SIXTEEN

'MAJOR INCIDENT DECLARED,' said Tilly. 'Serious fire in an office block in the city; all emergency services in attendance and we're the first receiving hospital for any casualties—let's get beds in Resus and Majors freed up and prepped. Pass this on to colleagues, please. Let's go.'

'You okay?' said Dexter. Tilly updated the electronic board as discharged patients left the department to create space for any of the fire's casualties.

'Could do without this, to be honest,' she replied. 'I've had an extra coffee this morning and still can't wake up.'

'First casualty inbound,' called Ally. 'ETA eight minutes. Adult male with smoke inhalation, currently conscious and responding.'

'Resus, please,' said Dexter. 'Early intubation if warranted.'

Tilly rubbed the back of her neck and opened her eyes wide, trying to wake herself up fully.

What was wrong with her today?

It wasn't just today, though, was it? She'd been increasingly tired for a while now—she'd even fallen asleep the other night instead of getting ready for dinner with Dexter and had had to turn up only half-ready. She closed her eyes, snapping them open again quickly. Was the tiredness due to something more than the extra shifts she'd been doing?

Her haematologist's words rang in her head.

Don't ignore any symptoms, Tilly.

The doors to Resus crashed open and two paramedics wheeled in their first patient.

No time to think about that now.

'Ciaran O'Connor, thirty-five, on the fourth floor of the office block where it appears the fire started; extricated by the fire service; no external burns; conscious and breathing; tachypnoeic and sats of eighty-nine on ten litres of oxygen.'

'Thank you,' said Dexter. 'Can you manage to shuffle over onto the trolley, Ciaran?'

Tilly stood on the other side of the trolley, guiding him over. The poor guy was indeed tachypnoeic—his breathing rate was way beyond normal. 'Well done; we're going to be checking you over and taking a blood test from your wrist to measure your oxygen levels, okay? Any questions?'

Ciaran shook his head, coughing.

'I'm just going to remove this mask to have a look at your airways,' added Dexter, lifting the oxygen mask from the patient's face. 'Soot in the mouth and septum. Just going to listen to your chest.' He slid his stethoscope from around his neck and bent, listening. 'Bilateral wheeze. Salbutamol nebuliser, please, Sister; I'll do the ABG.'

Tilly dealt with the nebuliser as Dexter took some blood for an arterial blood gas.

'I'll run that through the gas analyser,' she said, holding out her hand. He handed it to her and she took it to the small room next to Resus, slotting the syringe into the sampling port in the machine and clicking the 'analyse' button.

As she waited, her hand went to her portacath scar, her fingers running over the raised bump. She should have her bloods checked.

The analyser beeped and whirred as it printed out the results and she tore the paper, glancing at the figures as she walked back to Resus and handed it over to Dexter.

'Respiratory acidosis,' he said, glancing at it. 'I've organised a bronchoscopy before he goes to ITU. Ally, can you take a resus back pack and do the transfer, please?'

Ally and Mark left Resus with Ciaran just as patient number two from the fire came through the doors—a thirty-three-year-old, again with smoke inhalation. Tilly greeted the woman with a reassuring smile and began the process again.

By the time the incident was over, there had been twelve patients from the fire, all with varying degrees of respiratory compromise. The major incident had been stood down but there were still other patients to be seen.

She needed to think. *Should she make an appointment to get her bloods done? Could she ignore this any longer? She really didn't feel great.*

'Are you okay?' said Dexter, approaching her at the patient board as she stood assessing the situation in the department. 'You've not been your usual self today. I haven't heard you singing even once.'

'It's been busy.'

'It's always busy—and you always sing, or hum, or just generally sparkle. Is something wrong?'

'I don't have to be the life and soul all the time.' She hadn't meant to sound so sharp but she felt awful. She just wanted this shift to end and get home to sleep…and wake up, feel fine and not have leukaemia. She couldn't go through all that again.

Please don't let this be happening.

He held up his hands. 'Sorry.'

'Sorry, Dexter, I've… I've just got something on my mind, that's all.' She wasn't going to tell him what. The last time she'd talked about it to a man, he'd disappeared from her life at warp speed. She wasn't making that mistake again.

'Do you want to talk about it?'

'No.' Absolutely not. Dexter was the last person she wanted to tell. The king of no emotion? He wouldn't understand how she felt.

A slight frown flitted across his brow but was gone in a flash, his mask intact again.

'Okay, if you're sure.'

She managed a tight smile, but a wave of nausea hit her like an express train and suddenly her legs wouldn't hold her weight. She remembered reaching out, remembered strong arms catching her and then everything went black.

Distant voices…calm and urgent at the same time.

'Blood pressure?'

'Ninety over forty,' came the reply.

Too low.

'Heart rate?'

'Ninety-seven.'

Too high.

'Pass me a cannulation tray and blood bottles.'

Dexter?

'Sharp scratch, Tilly.'

It *was* Dexter.

Slowly, she opened her eyes, looking round sleepily.

'And she's back in the room,' said Mark. 'Welcome back, Tilly.'

'You fainted,' said Dexter, ripping the backing off the cannula dressing and smoothing it in place. 'Your blood pressure and heart rate are returning to normal but I want you to stay lying down.' He turned to Mark. 'Can you get these to the lab asap, please?'

Mark took the samples from him. 'Don't do that to us again, Tilly—it creates way too much paperwork.' He grinned and left the cubicle.

'Perhaps you should cut back on those overtime shifts after all,' said Dexter, pressing the button on the monitor to check Tilly's blood pressure again. The machine whirred as it inflated the cuff around her arm.

'Maybe,' she replied, glancing at the monitor as the cuff deflated. The reading was better. 'Can I sit up a little now?'

'A little.' Dexter raised the head of the trolley so that she was semi-reclined. 'I'd say you definitely need to cut back your hours. Covering shifts to help out is all very laudable, but not at the expense of your health, Tilly.'

'It's not the shifts.' The extra shifts weren't to blame, were they? She knew the signs to look out for. She'd been warned the leukaemia might come back. She'd been increasingly tired for a few weeks now. And there was no point in trying to hide it any longer. Dexter had taken bloods and the results would be back in the next couple of hours. He'd know instantly what was wrong with her.

'You've been doing too many, and too close together, without enough of a break in between. Just cut down a little.'

'It's not the extra shifts, Dexter.'

She was going to have to tell him. Lachlan's face swam into view in her mind. The horror on it when she'd finally told him about her illness… The way he'd moved just slightly, away from her… The way he'd dropped his gaze, unable to look at her when she'd gone further and said that there was a chance she could relapse…

Not telling Lachlan at first hadn't really been planned. He'd been her first, what she'd thought, serious boyfriend and they'd just been having so much fun—going to gigs and hanging out with his band and other bands on the circuit. It had been a whirl of new experiences, new people. The leukaemia had been forgotten. She'd thought they were in love. She'd thought he cared and that she could trust and rely on him—maybe that he'd stand by her.

She'd been wrong.

She and Dexter weren't in love. He didn't do romance or relationships and didn't believe in happy-ever-afters. And, even if she'd held a secret hope that he might make an exception for her, what she was about to tell him would put a very clear line under that ever happening.

'You haven't been eating and drinking properly, either, I suppose—that won't have helped. You need to look after yourself more, Tilly.' He leaned in towards her over the silver rail of the side of the trolley, his hand moving towards hers. But he stopped, glancing behind him at the cubicle curtain, withdrawing his hand, quickly. 'I'll cook for you this evening... make sure you get a good meal inside you.'

She squeezed her eyes shut and a heaviness fell over her. Dexter was a good man. She didn't want to lose him...didn't want him to run, as Lachlan had. But she had to tell him the truth. She couldn't let him sit in front of a computer to check her blood results and find out about her illness that way. The king of no emotion wasn't emotionless at all, was he?

She took a breath. She'd survived before and she would do again...even if the process was painful.

Be positive, Tilly.

'You can cook?' She smiled at him.

'Don't look so surprised.' He feigned indignance with a dramatically turned-down mouth. 'I do a mean lasagne.'

'Is that what's on the menu tonight, then?'

'If that's what you want.'

'Sounds great,' she replied.

'And cookie-dough ice cream to follow?'

'It's like you've read my mind.'

They held each other's gaze for a long moment. What passed between them, she wasn't sure, but suddenly she knew she not only *had* to tell him about the leukaemia—she *wanted* to.

'Can you clip the "Do Not Enter" sign to the curtain, Dexter, please?'

He did as she instructed, returning to stand beside her.

'What is it?' he asked, his eyes dark, serious.

'I had acute lymphoblastic leukaemia as a teen. You might find that my blood results show a relapse.' She searched his face. He wore his mask. 'I just wanted to warn you before you saw the results.'

She saw his Adam's apple slide in his throat and his lips part, just a little.

React, Dexter. Say something. Show something...even if it's horror. She held her breath. Was he going to run?

'I didn't know.'

'No reason you would. When I started at Trafalgar, I told HR I didn't want anyone to know.'

'Why?'

'Because when people know you've had cancer, they treat you differently...they treat you like you're made of fine china. I didn't want to be a patient any more. I just wanted to be like everyone else, you know? Normal.'

'I see.'

She looked up into concerned blue eyes and found she couldn't hold it back any longer.

'Every time they started the syringe driver and the chemo began to drip... In my head, I went to Bondi beach; I walked along the shore and watched the surfers dipping and cresting; I actually felt the warmth of the sun on my skin and the softness of the sand. I even dreamt up what the hospital I'd work in looked like—I had no clue then, of course, but I could build the picture in my mind and even imagine treating patients... making them better.'

'That's where the Australian dream began?'

She managed a small smile. 'A nurse got me to imagine myself somewhere nice. I chose a beach and she guided me through experiencing the beach with all my senses...you know the sort of thing...touching the sand, hearing the waves, tasting the salty sea air...'

'And it helped?'

'It gave me hope. I went back to that beach so often over the years. After a time, the imagery developed from simply feeling the sand between my fingers to imagining the beach house I'd live in; the beach sports I'd take part in. Then I began the research—looking up where I could go to make it all a reality some day. Dreaming and planning made it seem real, even though I knew it might never actually happen… So real, I began to believe it could happen. I got so close…'

'It could still happen.'

'Maybe my family were right—maybe I over-estimated myself; dreamt too big. Maybe I can't look after myself as well as I thought I could. I've been naive.'

'No. Tilly, you're one of the most capable people I've ever met—of course you can look after yourself. And you definitely didn't dream too big; it's a wonderful dream to have. Come on, don't pre-empt the results; they could be fine. Where's that sparkle I…?'

She glanced up at him. *Why had he faltered?*

'Know so well?' he continued.

'It's taking a break. Normal service will…*may*…be resumed at some point.' *With any luck*. Dexter was right—she wasn't handling this in the right way. What had happened to her? Her usually instinctive positivity had deserted her and turned her into a Grinch. She smiled at her choice of word and the irony of it. There was she, being exactly what she'd accused Dexter of being.

She glanced up again, hoping to reassure him that she was still herself, but his deep blue eyes were still full of earnest concern, which he was usually so good at concealing.

'Oh, I'm fine, really.' But the tears came from nowhere, filling her eyes, stinging as she tried to smile through them. 'Look at me! Ignore me, I'm being silly.' She sniffed and fished in her pocket for a tissue.

'Hey, hey, come on; it could all be fine.'

'It's just such bad timing,' she managed, her breath hitching. 'I need to reply to the agency in Sydney to accept the start date. What am I supposed to say to them? They'll give the job to someone else and...' She blew her nose. 'Sorry, it's just... I wanted this so much.'

'And there's still a good chance you can have it. Wait for the blood results—you can't do anything until you have those. Do you need a hug?'

She looked up into intense, kind blue eyes.

Dexter Stevens was offering a sympathetic hug. He wasn't high-tailing it out of there.

She nodded and he wrapped her in his arms as she sank into his chest.

'You've never said that to me before.'

'I've never said it to anyone before.' He kissed the top of her head, making her smile. She dabbed at her nose again, sniffing and smiling at the same time. 'I'm honoured.'

'I'll cook dinner for six thirty. Is that okay?'

'Six thirty is fine,' she replied.

'Good. I'll pick some cookie dough up from the supermarket on the way home.'

'But what about the blood results?'

'What is it we always say, Tilly? Never jump to conclusions... wait for the results. But, whatever the results show, I'm introducing you to the culinary delight that is my home-made lasagne this evening. If that's okay with you?'

She smiled. It was more than okay. It was exactly what she needed. All she had to do now was wait for the lab to send the results to Dexter. What happened after that entirely depended upon them.

CHAPTER SEVENTEEN

'DR STEVENS?'

Dexter looked up from the X-ray he'd been reviewing. It was Mark.

'Can you cast your eyes over this X-ray?' he asked, handing him a tablet that showed the black-and-white image of a child's skull.

Dexter took the tablet from him. 'What am I looking for?'

'It's of a six-year-old who fell through a broken fence in the garden,' explained Mark. 'He has a laceration to the right occipital area, which I can close with glue, as long as you think there are no fragments of fence in the tissues.'

Dexter scrutinised the image carefully. 'No fragments; you can go ahead with glue. Don't forget an anti-tetanus if he hasn't had one.' He handed the tablet back to the charge nurse.

'Sure, thank you,' said Mark.

Dexter returned his attention to the X-ray on the screen in front of him but became aware of Tilly's voice not far away. He looked up. She was talking to a woman who carried a toddler on her hip, stroking the child's head and smiling.

What the hell was she doing?

He got up and went over to them.

'Anything I can help with, Sister?'

'We're all good,' she replied. 'Dylan here managed to get his hand stuck in his toy truck this afternoon, but we've got it out now, haven't we, Dylan?'

The little boy nodded and his mother shook her head. 'Kids,' she said, rolling her eyes. 'You've gotta love 'em! Thank you, Nurse.'

Tilly laughed. 'You're very welcome. You're good to go now. No harm done. Bye, Dylan.'

Dylan waved behind him as his mum carried him out.

Love. That word kept popping up. He'd almost said it to her, hadn't he, when he'd mentioned her lack of sparkle...the sparkle he *loved* so much? But he'd stopped himself from saying it and changed the words.

'He was cute,' said Tilly, giving a last wave as Dylan and his mum went through the doors.

Dexter stared at her. 'What *do* you think you're doing?'

Tilly stared back. 'My job.'

Dexter lifted his arm, swishing his hand in a circle. 'Back to the cubicle.'

'I'm fine.'

'You're a patient.'

'Not any more. There's someone else in the cubicle.'

'What?'

'I didn't need it; I'm okay. I'm just waiting for results, that's all.'

Dexter put his hands on his hips. 'Unbelievable.'

'Thank you.' She grinned at him.

He shook his head. 'And completely obstinate. I can't have you wandering the department, Tilly, you're officially a patient until I discharge you.'

'Discharge me, then.'

'Not yet. You'll have to go somewhere else, then.'

'Where?'

'Your office? The café? Anywhere but here.'

'But I'd rather be busy.'

Dexter got that. It made sense. It was logical. 'Do me a favour,' he said.

'Does it involve sitting on a hospital trolley worrying for the next hour or so?'

He wished he could take the wait away…wished he could make her results normal.

'I've written up a further report with recommendations on Becky Johnson for the safeguarding team. Would you go through it for me—check it reads okay and see if you think I can add anything else to make it stronger?'

She nodded approvingly. 'I can do that. I'll be in my office.'

He watched her walk away and go into the office before he was satisfied she wasn't going to take a detour and go and see another patient. Her results wouldn't take much longer. What if they did show up a relapse?

He sat back down at the nurse's station and reopened the computer, logging on to the imaging system and staring again at the X-ray. He took a deep, calming breath. Another hour, max, and the blood results would be back. This was killing him. If this was where loving someone got him, it was no wonder he'd avoided it all his life. It terrified him how much he cared. Hell, he'd almost punched a man because he cared so much. The anger that had consumed him when he'd walked into that cubicle and seen that drunken idiot pressed up against her, threatening her, had been overwhelming. His father had needed alcohol to give him the strength to lash out, but Dexter had been completely sober when he'd wanted to throw the man across the room and get him off Tilly.

It was caring about her that had done that. He cared about her, had wanted to protect her and nothing else had mattered… not even that he could have hurt someone or lost his job. Not even that it had turned him into his father—his biggest fear. He couldn't help that he cared—it was too late now not to let that happen—but he didn't have to let it go any further, did he?

Tilly deserved much more than he could offer her. Yes, being with her had changed him…a little. He'd been able to open up a little—relax more, run into the sea and dance and laugh in the rain. But, underneath, he was still Dexter Stevens—still lacking the emotional intelligence that came to her so naturally; still unable to allow himself to feel. Tilly needed more than that. He couldn't offer romance and roses and open discussions about emotions. She'd got the measure of him straight away—he was an antisocial, buttoned-up loner. A Grinch. And she deserved better. He'd only drag her down.

And he really didn't want to be in love.

He finished reviewing the X-ray and called to Mark, who was passing.

'Your patient who fell off the horse?'

'Oh, yes?' replied Mark. 'Any damage?'

'Supracondylar fracture of the right humerus,' said Dexter. 'Can you ask the orthos to see him? He'll probably need to go to Theatre.'

'Will do, boss,' replied Mark. 'Thanks.'

Dexter glanced at the time. It had been an hour. Tilly's results could be back. Resting his elbows on the desk, he dropped his head on his hands.

Dared he hope?

He logged onto the pathology reporting system and selected her name from the patient listing: moment of truth. He clicked on the report and a sea of black figures filled the screen. His eyes scanned them quickly.

Red cells normal.

White cells normal.

Platelets normal.

His head fell back and he screwed shut his eyes.

It wasn't his usual reaction to receiving blood results for patients.

He had to go and tell her.

He knocked on her office door. There was no answer. He knocked again, frowning. She hadn't gone and seen patients again, had she?

'Tilly? Are you in there?'

The door opened and Tilly stood looking at him, her amethyst eyes almost wary and without any of their usual sparkle. His heart broke for the anguish she must be going through. He stepped inside, closing the door behind him, turning to her and smiling. A flare of hope flamed in her eyes as she drew in a breath.

'You're fine, Tilly. Your bloods are perfectly normal.'

No words could have been sweeter to say to her. But then came words that stilled his soaring heart…

'I can go to Australia!'

She leapt at him, throwing her arms around him.

He hugged her and she buried her head into his neck.

'I'm so pleased, Tilly,' he whispered, as his heart sang for her and cracked for himself all in the same moment.

This must be what it felt like. He'd been lying to himself. He did love her.

And it hurt—just as he'd always known it would.

CHAPTER EIGHTEEN

'STAY RIGHT WHERE you are,' said Dexter as Tilly threw back the duvet to get out of bed.

'I was going to pop some croissants into the air fryer—a day-off treat and a celebration of my perfect blood results,' she replied.

'I'll do it.' He was already halfway across the room.

Tilly snuggled back beneath the duvet, smiling, but then noticed her laptop on the chest of drawers. She had to send the email.

Dexter clattered about in his kitchen. 'Tilly?'

'Hello?'

'How many minutes do you put them in for?'

Her smile widened. 'Ten minutes, you domestic god, you.'

She'd never met anyone who melted her heart as he did, or whose eyes she could gaze into for ever. Who, even though he could be a monosyllabic grumpy bear, made her smile more than anyone else did. And he'd been exactly what she'd needed as she'd waited for her blood results. They'd grown so close and shared so much now. Did leaving him to follow her dream make sense any more?

Australia represented freedom. No one there knew of her cancer. No one would wrap her in cotton wool or treat her like precious china, liable to break at any moment. She could have a fresh start, a new beginning, where she would be judged for who she was now and not because she'd had leukaemia in the past. The slate would be wiped clean and the thought of that filled her soul with optimism, energy and hope.

If Dexter loved her and wanted her to stay, what would she do? The thought he might love her was joyful and terrifying in equal measure.

Australia was risk-free...a bright new start. But Dexter could hurt her all over again, as Lachlan had. Lachlan had told her he'd loved her, over and over, and he'd still hurt her in the end. Even people who said they loved you could hurt you, and Dexter had never even hinted that he had any feelings like that for her. He'd been the rock she'd needed him to be when she'd told him about her leukaemia. He'd stayed by her side, supporting her, cajoling her, even cooking for her. He hadn't run a million miles away.

But they were only work colleagues—friends with benefits at a push. He wasn't prepared to be more than that. Dexter had been supportive of a friend in need, but would he have been as supportive if they'd been more to each other? Would he have baulked at the pressure and responsibility of that, as Lachlan had?

The red flag still waved a warning she couldn't ignore. Yes, she'd got to know a little of the Dexter underneath the icy-cool exterior, but she still had doubts. He still kept secrets. He could still close himself down when he wanted to. And he didn't love her. He'd never said the words. Although, she'd never told him either. Maybe she should. Maybe she should tell him exactly how she felt—see where she stood.

'Ta-da!' Dexter stood in the doorway to the bedroom wearing nothing but a kitchen apron and holding aloft a tray of freshly baked croissants. 'Coffee to follow.'

He placed the tray on the bed and turned around, pausing only to look over his shoulder and give her the sexiest wink as she flicked her eyes from his perfect ass back to see it. He disappeared again, returning with two mugs of steaming coffee and placed them on the bedside tables.

'Perfect,' said Tilly, sitting up against her pillows with the duvet pulled up in front of her. She reached for her coffee, taking a sip and placing it back down. This had to be done and it had to be done now. She needed to know how he felt about her.

'You were right—you can cook. Lasagne yesterday, fresh croissants today... I think I'm in love with you.'

He grinned. 'With my cooking, you mean. I told you I wasn't bad.'

Her heart hammered. 'Not with your cooking, Dexter,' she replied, gazing into eyes she wanted to lose herself in. 'With you.'

He stared at her and she was certain he paled.

He swallowed, sitting up straighter. 'I'm not sure I understand.' He spoke slowly, as though carefully choosing his words.

He was going to run, but she had to know. Deep breath...

'I love you, Dexter.'

His lips parted, as though he was going to speak, but he clamped them shut, staring at her blankly, his mug of coffee suspended in mid-air halfway to his mouth.

The air left his lungs.

He couldn't think. Every single thought that had ever been in his head, every single word in his vocabulary, vanished. He carefully placed the mug back down on the bedside table, not trusting himself to perform that simple action without spilling it.

She loved him?

Helena had said that too. But he'd spent his life avoiding sweeping, grand, trouble-making emotions like love. How was he meant to respond?

'But I can see it's not reciprocated, so...'

He could only watch her as she reached for her bath robe and pulled it on.

But it *was* reciprocated.

It had been hell waiting for her blood results—it had been worse that she'd been so full of joy that she could go to Australia. Because it would mean losing her in a different way.

Which meant that he loved her.

So tell her.

But he was paralysed. It was as though someone had slapped him…hard.

'Wait, Tilly, where are you going?'

'To get a shower.'

He ran his fingers through his hair.

'Tilly, wait, please…we need to talk.'

He didn't want this. And he did.

Life was far easier the way he'd been living it since Helena. Doing his job at the hospital and at Battersea Dogs' and Cats' Home and looking after the animals, making a difference to people's lives—saving them, sometimes—was all he'd needed. Since Helena, everyone had been kept carefully at arm's length; his world had been ordered, calm and simple. There'd been no bumps or obstacles…at least, not ones that hadn't been easily sorted out by following the correct protocols or having the right knowledge.

Tilly sat back down on the bed, her bathrobe wrapped tightly around her.

But love had a whole different set of rules. And he had no idea what they were.

It had been one thing to admit to *himself* that he loved Tilly—that had been done covertly, inside his own head, without having to divulge it to anyone else. But there was no way he could admit it out loud—that would make it too real. And making it real scared the living daylights out of him. He didn't trust love—it had always let him down. Love had two sides to it—it could fill a person with hope but they always had to be ready to run from it before the inevitable damage occurred. It sent rational thinking and decision-making hurtling out into oblivion. It made a person run into the North Sea fully clothed, threaten people with violence...risk a livelihood.

But he did love her. And he couldn't hurt her.

'I don't—' he began.

'Do relationships?' cut in Tilly, her chin held high. 'Yes, I remember you saying that. I just wondered if perhaps we'd moved on. Obviously not.'

'Tilly, I can't offer you what you're looking for. I'm not that person.'

She laughed thinly. 'That's such an "it's not you, it's me" comment, Dexter.'

'It's true.'

She held up her hand, not looking at him as she reached for her laptop.

'What are you doing?'

'Sending an email,' she replied.

'To the agency?'

'Yes.'

'To confirm your start date?'

'Yes.'

He closed his eyes tightly, screwing them shut as he spoke the word he knew he had to...for her sake. She deserved better than anything he could offer her.

'Good.'

She stopped tapping the keyboard and swung round to face him, the sparkle he loved so much missing.

'Yes,' she said quietly, before continuing.

'It's your dream.' He wasn't about to take that away from her.

'It is.'

'You can't not go.' He was just being logical. She needed this. She needed to make her dream come true, prove her independence. He wanted that for her...more than he could give her.

But she loved him.

Was this what love was—two people hurting? Two people who cared about each other breaking each other's hearts?

He didn't want that. He didn't want her to be hurt. He wanted her to be happy. But he had hurt her and he hated that.

She was better off without him—look what he'd done to her. It was best she went, best she made that new life for herself she dreamed about. Nothing he could give her could match that.

'That's not true,' she replied, turning to him and looking into his eyes, melting his heart with the intensity of her gaze. 'I don't have to go—if I had a reason to stay.'

Was *he* the reason she'd stay? If he told her he loved her, would that mean she wouldn't go?

The words were on his lips. But he couldn't say them. He'd never been able to say them. Helena had screamed at him to tell her he loved her, but he hadn't been able to, and it had cost him their relationship.

Was that happening all over again? There was a choice laid out in front of him, two paths: loving Tilly or holding on to the life he knew…secure behind the walls he'd built around himself.

So, choose: logical or illogical.

What he said next would determine both their futures. It was huge. And being logical was the only way to deal with making huge, important decisions.

'It's your dream…you have to go. I can't offer you anything more, Tilly.'

Her gaze didn't falter. He didn't want to look away. She was the warm fire he'd come home to in a cold winter; the safe harbour after battling through a storm. But she challenged him, too. He'd lost some of the control he'd had in his life. He'd succumbed to feelings he'd never wanted. He was losing his grip on everything he believed in…because that was what falling in love did to people.

'I know you struggle with expressing your feelings, Dexter. I get that, after what you went through as a child, you want to stay in control…never get hurt again. I'm sorry you went through that but—'

'Don't feel sorry for me.' He didn't want her pity. He didn't want reminding of a past he'd rather forget. He'd told her too much already; given away painful secrets he should have kept hidden.

He dragged on his boxer shorts and jeans. The child he'd once been was forgotten—the memories had been packed away in a box in his head, a box that had been locked shut, never to be opened. The only way it could stay locked was if he never thought about it. If any thoughts showed signs of bubbling to the surface, he pushed them back down before they could be fully formed. But Tilly kept trying to prise those thoughts and feelings out of him. This was why he'd never let anyone get close.

'It clearly still affects you, Dexter.'

He pulled his T-shirt over his head. He wasn't going to think about this—he wasn't going to open that box again. He shouldn't have told her what he'd already told her about his past. Why had he?

Because he'd recklessly allowed himself to feel something for her—to care about her, to love her. And love made people think and do things without logic; without taking a step back, looking at the situation and coming to a rational conclusion.

And that wasn't him. He was taking a step back now, looking at the situation…and saw that it was hurting both of them.

'It doesn't affect me any more, Tilly—it really doesn't—and if you think that you don't know me at all.'

A shaft of morning sunshine lay across her, making her ebony hair shine.

'I know you hide behind that cool, hard-edged exterior to try to prevent anything or anyone reaching you. And I know that's not really who you are, because I've seen what's beneath all that armour you wear, behind the thick stone wall you've built around yourself. I've seen the real Dexter, and he's still cowering in a corner, trying not to get hurt again. You don't need to do that any more.'

He stared at her, his mind racing, struggling to put his thoughts into any kind of order.

Was that what she thought of him? That he was still a terrified young boy?

He'd dealt with all that...moved on. He could handle it all—everything that had happened to him. He wasn't a young child any more, terrified about what would happen to him next—one minute hating his father with every atom of his being, the next desperately finding ways to hide his bruises so he wasn't taken into care. He was an adult now, and fully in control of what happened in his life. And he was going to take control of this.

She didn't move, not an inch. Her eyes held his.

He dragged in a breath. He needed to get this over with... so that they could both move on. Tilly deserved so much more than he could offer. Hell, he was in love with her, and was so screwed up he couldn't even tell her. Tilly needed fun and freedom, and a man who'd give that to her. She needed the romance...the happy-ever-after. He couldn't give her those things. She was right about him: he *was* a Grinch. He'd crush her beautiful spirit.

And there was no way on earth he was ever going to allow that to happen. He'd spent his entire life fighting to protect himself in one way or another, then she'd come along and now his barricade lay broken...in pieces.

She'd got him to open up.

She'd shown him how to let go.

It had been exhilarating. And terrifying.

If this was what love was, he'd been right to steer well clear of it.

'I told you I don't do relationships, Tilly. You should send that email.' He picked up his phone and slipped it into his pocket, but he didn't want to go, and stood looking at her a moment longer. At the woman who'd got under his skin so much that he'd taken his eye of the ball and allowed himself to feel something for her, to care too much about her…to fall in love with her.

'I promised I'd help out at Battersea this morning.'

That was why it was so hard to walk away now. But it was also why the words that told her to leave slipped so easily from his mouth, even though saying them was the hardest thing he'd ever done. Because it was the right thing to do. The logical thing.

'Are you telling me it's over, Dexter?'

The sunlight fell on her hair. He wanted to touch it. He wanted to look into her eyes for the rest of eternity. But her eyes were misted and it killed him to see what he'd done to her. He needed to leave.

'Send the email. I can't love you, Tilly.'

She needed her adventure…she didn't need him. He was everything she didn't need in her life.

And *he* needed to take back control of his feelings.

CHAPTER NINETEEN

'You okay this morning, Tilly?' It was Mark, who'd pulled up a chair beside her at the nurse's station. 'You seem a bit quiet.'

'Just thinking how much I'll miss this place,' she replied, managing a smile. She'd sent the email the day that Dexter had thrown her feelings for him back in her face, some two weeks ago now. They'd kept their distance from each other since, Tilly changing her shifts to avoid him as much as possible. When they'd had to work together on a patient, they'd remained professionally polite, but nothing more. The day she'd told him she loved him, and he'd reacted by telling her he didn't love her back, hadn't been mentioned.

'You must be so excited too, though—you've wanted this for such a long time and now and it's about to happen. I'm sure you won't miss us for long, not when you can finish a shift and be on Bondi beach within minutes. We'll miss you, though.' He touched her arm and smiled a sorrowful smile.

'Thanks, Mark—I'm definitely looking forward to beach life. But right now...' she pointed to the electronic patient board '...I need to sort out Mr Parkes in cubicle five.'

She heard Dexter's voice in one of the cubicles as she passed. After today, she'd never hear it again, and she simply had to accept that. Just as she had to accept that he didn't love her.

'Morning, Mr Parkes; my name's Tilly and I'm one of the nurses. So, what's brought you in today?'

She'd told Dexter she loved him and he hadn't wanted to hear it. The words had made him want to run a thousand miles away…or make him want to tell her to put thousands of miles between them. He was doing much as Lachlan had done, except he hadn't ended it because of her leukaemia—he'd ended it because he didn't love her. She was the one who was leaving, but it was Dexter who'd wanted her to. He'd been honest with her from the start—he didn't do relationships or romance; he didn't believe in happy-ever-afters. He'd told her he couldn't offer her more. But, for some stupid reason, she'd thought that maybe he'd changed.

'So, if you're happy,' she said to the patient, 'I'm going to start the antibiotics intravenously and then you'll be able to carry on with them by mouth. Is that okay?'

The rest of the day continued as the days in Trafalgar A&E always did. The only difference was that now she knew that Dexter didn't want her, and her heart was broken. But she still had her dream and she was going to go out there and live it.

The days and weeks in Trafalgar A&E continued as they always did. The only difference was that Tilly wasn't there. And life just wasn't the same without her. He glanced at a photo someone had printed out and pinned to one of the notice boards—of Tilly with her team on the sea in a dragon boat, in the Australian sunshine. She was laughing. She looked happy. He looked away, his heart swelling with pride for her. She'd made it happen—she was living her dream.

And he'd been an idiot.

'Your results are back, Mr Seabridge,' said Dexter, standing at the bottom of the trolley on which his patient lay.

'What's the verdict, Doc?'

'Well, the sudden onset of flank pain radiating inferiolaterally…' The patient's eyes were narrowed in concentration as he listened. Dexter stopped and thought for a moment. 'You have a kidney stone.'

'I thought you were going all technical on me there for a minute,' said Daniel Seabridge, grinning, 'I haven't been to medical school, you know.'

Tilly. It was Tilly who'd shown him how to be a better doctor. It was Tilly who'd shown him how to be a better human being—how to relax; how to enjoy life more. She'd shown him how to run barefoot in the sand; how to run hand in hand through the rain; how to care and how to fall in love.

'I've spoken to one of the specialist kidney doctors and they're going to come along and see you as soon as they can. Have you any questions?'

'Not at the minute, Doc, thanks.'

'See you later,' said Dexter, pushing the curtain aside and returning to the nurse's station to write up his notes.

Mark sat a couple of seats away; Anika scurried past with a trolley laden with equipment; Pearl pointed, giving directions to the fracture clinic to a mum with a young child who had his arm in a plaster, decorated with cartoon characters. Everything was as it always had been—everything was the same.

Except for him. He wasn't the same. He hadn't been the same since the day Tilly Clover had turned up in his department and rocked his entire world.

And he would never be the same. Because she'd changed him. And, stupidly, he hadn't seen it until it was too late.

She'd said she loved him. And he hadn't known how to respond.

Had losing Helena taught him nothing? He'd spent his entire life avoiding emotion, protecting himself from the pain and humiliation of caring and having it thrown back in his face. He'd been so terrified of discovering he was the same as his angry, violent father that he'd fought against feeling anything deeper than respect for other people.

But he hadn't banked on Tilly dancing into his life and filling it with warmth, joy and the possibility of genuine happiness. He hadn't been able to accept her love for him was real. All he'd seen was the fear that ran underneath loving someone.

He'd loved her for a long time. He knew that now. If he'd stopped to think for a moment instead of fighting against it, he would have realised that, even though he'd fallen in love, nothing bad had happened as a result.

The world hadn't ended. He hadn't turned into his father—in fact, quite the opposite. The world had become a better place—he'd been able to run barefoot in the sand and headlong into the sea fully clothed. And, when pushed to the limit, needing to defend Tilly from a violent man in A&E, he'd controlled his understandable anger and dealt with the situation as a professional.

He'd fallen in love with Tilly and he'd never been happier.

And then, he'd thrown it all away. Because he'd been afraid to say the words he should have said to her a long time ago—that he loved her too. The barricades he'd put up to protect himself from getting hurt had been counterproductive. They hadn't protected him at all. They'd prevented him from being able to accept the only happiness he'd ever had the chance of.

Did he want to regret that for the rest of his life? If he didn't, there was only one thing to do—he had to find her and he had to say the words he'd never said to anyone.

CHAPTER TWENTY

TILLY SAT ON the beach towel watching the surfers ride the waves as the late-afternoon sun warmed her skin and the soft sand trickled through her fingers. Her long-held, far-off dream was now her reality and she closed her eyes behind her sunglasses, lifting her face to the sky and listening to the waves pounding the beach. A cool shadow fell over her and she tentatively opened one eye. There had been no clouds in the sky when she'd last looked.

A dark figure towered over her, standing at her feet and wearing blue swimming shorts.

She froze. She'd know that toned torso anywhere.

Dexter.

Lifting herself to a sitting position, she took off her sunglasses. It *was* him.

'What on earth…?' But even if she *had* known what she was going to say next, she didn't have the chance to say the words. Dexter dropped to his knees in the sand beside her.

'I miss you.'

It would have been so easy to look into those deep blue, earnest eyes and lose herself. She replaced her sunglasses.

'You came halfway across the world to tell me that?'

'And other things.'

'What other things?'

'I…'

She stared at him. *He missed her*—but it had taken him three months to realise?

'Are you here on a conference or something?' He hadn't come all this way just to see her, surely, not after he'd told her to go?

'No, I came to find you.'

Her heart rate picked up. Damn that he still had that effect on her... 'Why?'

'Because I...miss you.'

'You're the one who told me to leave.' Her voice was quiet. It was still hard to acknowledge that he'd rejected her so coldly; hard to say the words. 'You told me you didn't want a relationship.'

'I was stupid.'

'You're still a man of few words, I see.'

A smile played at the corners of his mouth.

'You know me so well.'

'Knew,' she corrected. 'Or thought I did.'

'You know me better than anyone.'

'You kept so much hidden.'

'You should have seen me before you came along.'

'Meaning what?' She knew she sounded a little terse, and didn't mean to, but suddenly seeing him again after all this time was a little overwhelming, to say the least.

'I was a Grinch.' He smiled—a tentative smile, almost shy, as though he wasn't sure whether it was appropriate or not, but it made his dark blue eyes sparkle just the same. And it made her want to gaze into them.

'And now you're not?'

He dropped his gaze for a moment before lifting his eyes and fixing her with them again. 'Less so.'

She raised an eyebrow at him.

'You look well,' he said. 'Happy.'

'I am happy.' She opened her arms wide, looking at the view before them. 'Who wouldn't be, with all of this?'

'I'm not. Not without you.'

Her heart began to thump harder.

He'd flown across the world to tell her this. Dexter—king of no emotion...

But he'd rejected her. She'd told him she loved him, and he'd told her to leave. She'd been hurt and humiliated...she still was.

And she still thought about him. Too much. Even being thousands of miles apart hadn't stopped that.

But it didn't matter. He didn't love her. He said he'd missed her—not that he loved her. She wasn't angry with him. It had been her decision to begin a relationship with the most unsuitable man in the world—she only had herself to blame.

'Tilly, I...' He glanced around the beach. It was late afternoon and busy with people. A volleyball game was in full swing; couples were walking along the water's edge; children were paddling; a family was having a picnic just a few feet away. He fixed his gaze back on her and she realised that she knew him well enough to see that he was struggling.

He sighed and ran his fingers through his dark hair. 'I've never said this before.' He lowered his head and a lock of hair fell forward again, covering his eyes.

'What can be so bad that you can't say the words?' She spoke softly, gently, dipping her head to see his face.

He lifted his eyes but his head remained bent. His fingers played with the sand beneath them. And then his jaw hardened, his chin lifted and he drew in a long breath.

'It's nothing bad; it's just alien to me. But I've flown over ten thousand miles to tell you this, and I'm damn sure I'm going to make sure you hear me.'

Tilly watched him as he rose slowly to his feet. She sat up and he looked down at her, his feet planted solidly, his chin high, shoulders back. His eyes never left hers.

'I've never said this to anyone before, Tilly, and I never expected that I would, but you've changed that. I was stupid to let you walk away without me and I've regretted it every moment since. Life isn't the same without you. If you've moved on and don't want me around, I understand that, but I've come here to tell you one thing…'

Her head was scrambled; a million thoughts ran around and crashed into each other. 'Yes?' Her voice was soft, urging him to speak, to say the words he'd come here to say. Dared she hope?

He drew in a breath.

'I… I believe I may have misled you into thinking that I have no feelings for you.'

She stared at him and he dropped his gaze, stuffing his hands into his pockets before looking back at her sheepishly.

'This is so you, Dexter.'

He nodded. 'You know me.'

And she still loved him. She loved him for how deeply caring he was, as well as for all the awkwardness when it came to showing his feelings.

'I do,' she replied, conceding a smile.

His jaw relaxed and his face softened.

'I love you, Tilly.'

It was little more than a whisper, but she heard him, and all she could do was stare at him as she tried to remember how to breathe.

'I don't think she heard you, mate.' It was the father of the picnicking family a short distance away. 'You might need to tell her again.'

The mum sat looking at them, her hands clasped together at her chest and smiling with delight. She spoke softly to Dexter. 'Go on, tell her again, love—make sure she hears you.'

Dexter looked back at Tilly and smiled…a wide, genuine, suddenly confident smile that lit up his deep blue eyes, making them sparkle. He opened his arms wide.

'I love you, Tilly Clover.'

And this time she heard him say the words loudly, clearly and confidently. There was a small round of applause from the picnicking family but Tilly only had eyes for Dexter. She got to her feet and stood before him, smiling up into his beautiful, genuine blue eyes.

'Let's go for a walk.' She picked up the beach towel, rolling it and slotting it into her bag. They headed for the shoreline, where they walked in silence along the beach on the edge of the cool, clear blue water that lapped at their feet.

This was her dream: living in Australia; having an amazing job; strolling along the beach with the sun warming her skin; listening to the rhythmic crashing of the waves. And she'd been fine. If she could have added anything extra, it would have been to have all that and a wonderful, thoughtful, genuine, kind and maybe incredibly handsome man beside her too.

And here she was, with all she'd dreamed of and the cherry on top: Dexter.

He loved her. He'd travelled all the way to Australia to tell her, to say the words he'd never said before and never thought he'd ever say to anyone.

But he'd said them to *her*.

'Say something,' he said as she dropped her bag on the sand in a quiet little cove further along the beach. 'Please... even if it's to tell me to go back to London and never darken your doorstep again.'

'I'd never tell you that.'

'You have every reason to—I was an idiot. I qualified it in my head by telling myself that I was protecting you.'

'From what?'

'From me.'

She frowned. 'I don't need protecting from you. I don't need protecting at all—that's what coming here is all about. I've been fine.'

Dexter held up his hands. 'No, not in that way. Look at you—you've achieved what you wanted to and I'm so proud of you. What I meant was that I wanted more for you.'

'In what way?'

He shrugged.

'We're two very different people, Tilly. You're full of fun and sparkle and I'm…well…the proverbial Grinch.'

'But yin and yang balance each other. One can't exist without the other.'

'And I can't offer you romance.'

A slow smile shaped her lips. 'You've flown ten thousand miles to find me, and you told me you love me in front of a beach full of Australians…and you say you don't do romance?'

'Is that romantic?'

She grinned.

'It's not a bad attempt, Dexter.'

He reached for her fingers, touching them lightly.

'I'm really rubbish at emotional stuff.'

She pursed her lips thoughtfully. 'You're learning, though.'

'I've been a blundering idiot, so terrified of allowing love to ruin my carefully controlled world that I ruined it myself by denying it. I've never trusted love, Tilly. I've protected my cold heart from ever feeling it because I thought letting it in was too much of a risk. I didn't want my castle walls knocked down. Have I left it too late to hope that what you said to me hasn't long since died away?'

Tilly held onto his fingers, drawing him towards her.

'It's not too late, Dexter. I still love you…that hasn't changed.'

He took hold of her other hand and, grasping them both, pulled her towards him, dipping his head as she smiled up at him, and pressed his lips to hers. A lifetime had passed since he'd last crushed his lips to hers; it seemed for ever since she'd been in the warm embrace of his strong arms.

'If you'll have me, Tilly, I'd love to explore the option of applying for a visa.'

'For Australia?'

'I've already spoken to my old colleague who moved over here, and he's given me some really useful information.'

Her hand few to her mouth.

'Is that good shock or bad shock?' said Dexter, looking concerned.

He did love her. He loved her so much that he was prepared to move to the other side of the world for her and leave the job that meant everything to him.

'Good shock. And you say you're not romantic?'

'Is that romantic too?'

She smiled. 'I think my yin and your yang have a very good chance of being very good together, Dexter. I'd love you to apply for a visa.'

And the smile playing at the corners of his lips blossomed into the widest grin she'd ever seen.

'I love you, Tilly Clover.'

And, suddenly, every wonderful dream about her future that she'd ever had became very, very real.

EPILOGUE

'LADIES AND GENTS,' said the compere in a broad Australian accent. 'Can I have your attention, please? The bride and groom are about to have their first dance.'

A cheer and round of applause went up in the ballroom. The harbourside hotel in Sydney was perfectly placed for amazing views of the city, the Opera House and the famous harbour bridge. Dexter and Tilly had relaxed on the rooftop terrace there many times in the last year, and it had become one of their favourite places in the city. But they were there now for the wedding of two of their colleagues from Bondi A&E.

Tilly smiled and waved at Isla, catching her eye as she was led to the dance floor by Taylor, her new husband.

'They look so happy,' she said, squeezing Dexter's hand as they stood on the edge of the dance floor watching the newlyweds. He didn't hate parties any more. Living in Australia meant they were invited to gatherings all the time—'barbies' in people's back gardens were almost obligatory—and with Tilly's support he'd begun to relax. He now actively enjoyed hosting a get-together and sizzling sausages and burgers in the sunshine for friends.

'They do,' agreed Dexter. 'I suppose you're going to want to join them on that dance floor any second?' He looked down at her, a question arching his brow.

'Of course,' she replied, grinning at him. 'You can show off your waltz moves.'

'Calling my moves "a waltz" is a bit of a stretch… I can sway a little, that's all.'

'Anyone who'd like to join the bride and groom, please make your way onto the dance floor,' called the compere.

Tilly pulled Dexter's hand and he groaned.

'Don't be a party pooper, Dexter Stevens,' she chided. She wanted to be held by him, and feel close to him, one last time before she told him.

'Wouldn't dream of it,' he replied, placing one hand on her waist, the other hand intertwined with her fingers. He moved his feet, swaying gently to the music, as they had many times at their home in Bondi.

Dexter's visa had come through quickly because of his qualifications, experience and the vacancies at the hospital, and he'd joined Tilly at the house she'd been renting near the beach. He'd settled into his role as consultant quickly and, like Tilly, loved the fact they could be at the beach within minutes of finishing work. He and Tilly had been open from the start about their relationship and had been warmly welcomed, very quickly feeling loved and respected enormously by the team.

The song ended and everyone applauded before the DJ began playing a more upbeat song, and Dexter frowned at Tilly as she began to dance.

'I'll sit this one out.'

Tilly smiled at him. She'd coaxed him into dancing but he was really only comfortable doing so when they were alone.

'Shall we go up onto the roof terrace…watch the sunset over the harbour?'

She had something to tell him and telling him in this very special place overlooking the city they'd come to love seemed perfect. She and Dexter had been so happy together over the last year. Australia was everything she'd hoped for and more. They'd learnt to surf; Dexter had joined her dragon-boat racing team; they were picking up 'the lingo' and had even been told by Aussie friends that their barbie skills were almost as good as the locals.

'Sounds like a much better idea,' said Dexter, smiling. 'In fact, I was about to suggest it myself.'

The lights on Sydney Opera House glowed against the darkening sky and the twinkling water of the harbour below. Everyone else was downstairs in the ballroom, partying with the newlyweds. The rooftop garden was beautifully planted with exotically scented, brightly coloured flowers, lit softly with fairy lights and dotted with benches and coloured bean bags.

The timing was perfect. But, even though she knew Dexter now better than she'd known anyone else, there remained the tiny niggle of concern about his reaction to what she was about to tell him. He wasn't Lachlan, but her news was pretty momentous, and the chance that he might want to run most definitely came with it. But he loved her. He'd followed her to the other side of the world, and he told her he loved her every single day.

'I don't think I'll ever tire of this view,' he said, standing behind Tilly, his arms around her waist, his chin resting lightly on the top of her head.

'Me neither.' She turned to face him and he kept hold of her, planting a kiss on her forehead. 'Let me give you a reason to remember this view for ever, Dexter…to remember this night for ever.'

Dexter smiled and her insides melted, as they always did when he smiled at her.

'I was going to say the same thing to you.'

'Really?'

'Really…it's why I wanted to come up here.'

'Not just because of the wedding?'

'Not to get away from the wedding particularly, no, but the wedding is partly the reason.'

'How so?'

'Weddings make people do all sorts of crazy, romantic things, don't they?'

'Like what?'

Dexter let go of her waist but held onto her hands.

'I love this city and I love you, Tilly. And up here, in this special place under the stars, I wanted to ask you…'

He reached into his trouser pocket and pulled out a small white box, opening it to reveal a white-gold ring set with diamonds and amethysts. 'If you would do me the honour of becoming my wife.'

Tilly looked from the ring to his face and his cobalt eyes which were full of love…for her…and her heart swelled to the point she thought it would burst. She nodded, smiling, unable to speak.

He cocked his head to one side, looking at her. 'Is that a yes?'

'It's a yes, Dexter.'

Taking the ring from the box, he pushed it gently onto her finger.

'It's beautiful, Dexter; thank you.'

And, when she looked back up into the eyes she could lose herself in for ever, they were misted with genuine love. And in that moment she knew that the news she'd been about to tell him—that they were expecting a baby—wasn't going to make him want to run… If it was possible, it was going to bring them even closer together than they already were.

* * * * *

*If you enjoyed this story,
check out this other great read from
Colette Cooper*

Nurse's Twin Baby Surprise

Available now!

MILLS & BOON®

Coming next month

FORBIDDEN FLING WITH THE PRINCESS
Amy Andrews

Dios! A man should not look that good in what were essentially blue pajamas.

'*Xio,*' he greeted as his gaze roved over her face and hair and neck and, god help her, lower.

She'd dressed this morning in her favourite form-fitting, v-necked, pink t-shirt with a glittery tiara stamped across the front, teaming it with a flowy, layered skirt of soft tulle that hid a multitude of sins and flirted with her ankles. For comfort, she'd told herself. Nothing stiff or formal for a long day sitting in the hospital keeping Phoebe company.

But in truth, she'd worn it for him, this man who seemed to have such a preoccupation with her clothes. Because she'd wanted him to look at her as he was now, his gaze brushing her neck and the swell of her breasts. She'd wanted to see his amber eyes darkening.

She'd wanted him to look at her like she wasn't some pretty, unattainable, untouchable princess on a pedestal but like she was a woman who knew her own power. A woman who craved his touch.

And in those long beats she totally forgot herself and their surroundings. And that two of the palace security detail were witnessing this mutual display of ogling that violated all kinds of royal protocols. Commoners should never look upon a royal princess with such unbridled lust. And the princess should definitely not be wondering how easy it was to get a man out of a pair of scrubs.

Continue reading

FORBIDDEN FLING WITH THE PRINCESS
Amy Andrews

Available next month
millsandboon.co.uk

Copyright © 2025 Amy Andrews

COMING SOON!

We really hope you enjoyed reading this book.
If you're looking for more romance
be sure to head to the shops when
new books are available on

Thursday 28th August

To see which titles are coming soon, please visit
millsandboon.co.uk/nextmonth

MILLS & BOON

afterglow BOOKS

Afterglow Books is a trend-led, trope-filled list of books with diverse, authentic and relatable characters, a wide array of voices and representations, plus real world trials and tribulations. Featuring all the tropes you could possibly want (think small-town settings, fake relationships, grumpy vs sunshine, enemies to lovers) and all with a generous dose of spice in every story.

♪ @millsandboonuk
◉ @millsandboonuk
afterglowbooks.co.uk
#AfterglowBooks

For all the latest book news, exclusive content and giveaways scan the QR code below to sign up to the Afterglow newsletter:

SCAN ME

afterglow BOOKS

THE CODE FOR LOVE

Her perfect plan has a gorgeous glitch...

NEW YORK TIMES BESTSELLING AUTHOR
ANNE MARSH

✈ International

⛅ Grumpy/sunshine

🚻 Fake dating

OUT NOW

To discover more visit:
Afterglowbooks.co.uk

FOUR BRAND NEW BOOKS FROM
MILLS & BOON MODERN

The same great stories you love, a stylish new look!

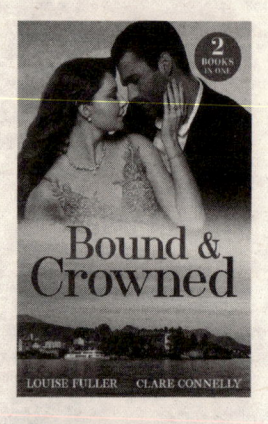

WED IN A HURRY
KIM LAWRENCE · LORRAINE HALL

Bound & Crowned
LOUISE FULLER · CLARE CONNELLY

Love to HATE HIM
JULIA JAMES · MILLIE ADAMS

RECLAIM ME
CATHY WILLIAMS · DANI COLLINS

OUT NOW

Eight Modern stories published every month, find them all at:
millsandboon.co.uk

LET'S TALK
Romance

For exclusive extracts, competitions and special offers, find us online:

- **f** MillsandBoon
- **X** @MillsandBoon
- **◉** @MillsandBoonUK
- **♪** @MillsandBoonUK

Get in touch on 01413 063 232

For all the latest titles coming soon, visit
millsandboon.co.uk/nextmonth

OUT NOW!

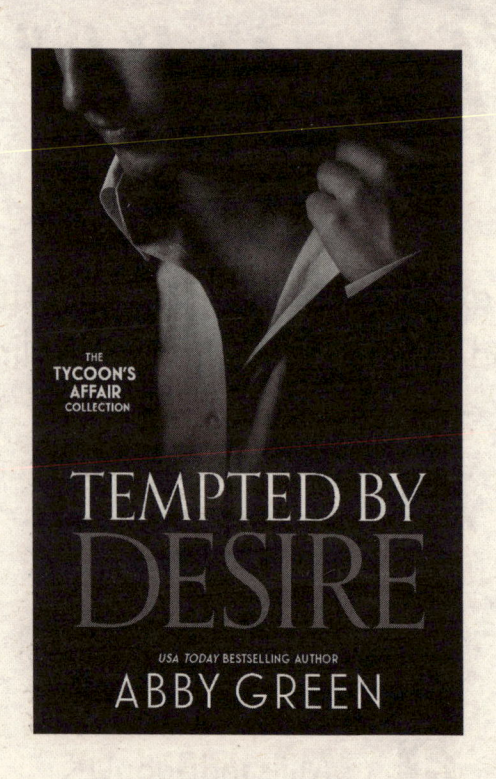

THE TYCOON'S AFFAIR COLLECTION

TEMPTED BY DESIRE

USA TODAY BESTSELLING AUTHOR
ABBY GREEN

Available at
millsandboon.co.uk

MILLS & BOON

OUT NOW!

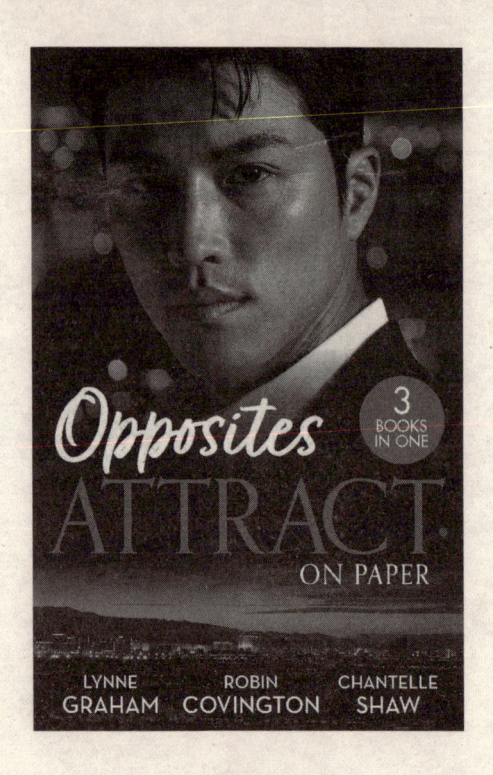

Opposites Attract On Paper

3 BOOKS IN ONE

LYNNE GRAHAM ROBIN COVINGTON CHANTELLE SHAW

Available at
millsandboon.co.uk

MILLS & BOON